FAMILY
FEELING

Novels by Helen Yglesias

HOW SHE DIED
FAMILY FEELING

FAMILY FEELING

HELEN YGLESIAS

The Dial Press New York 1976

Library of Congress Cataloging in Publication Data

Yglesias, Helen.
   Family feeling.

   I. Title.
PZ4.Y49Fam   [PS3575.G48]   813'.5'4   75–33831
ISBN 0–8037–5365–9

The lines on pages 148–149 are from "It's A Sin To Tell A Lie" by Billy Mayhew: Copyright © 1933 & 1936 by Bregman, Vocco And Conn, Inc., 8255 Sunset Boulevard, Los Angeles, Calif. 90046. Copyright Renewed 1960 & 1963 by Bregman, Vocco And Conn, Inc. International Copyright Secured. Used by Permission. All Rights Reserved.
Chapter 1 of this work first appeared in *The New Yorker* and Chapter 6, in *Seventeen*, both in slightly different form.

Manufactured in the United States of America

Second printing 1976

Design by Karin Batten & Elliot Kreloff

FOR
MY DAUGHTER, TAMAR,
AND MY SONS,
LEWIS AND RAFAEL

This is a work of fiction.
None of the characters,
including the narrator as "I" or "she,"
represent persons
real, living or dead.

FAMILY FEELING

B ehind my mother I see the ocean, the only one I knew when I was little, the Coney Island Ocean. Behind that, nothing, as if the world were flat. In front of her I see a kitchen sink, a coal stove, the New York *Jewish Daily Forward* with its oppressive, heavy black letters. The bare board kitchen floor, flooded with sudsy water, is also a sea. She scrubs on her hands and knees, with a wooden-backed brush, while I ride the waves, my boat the unevenly balanced kitchen table. Outside the window, a monster rattles by. I transform the Myrtle Avenue El into the terrifying noise and flash of the famous storm of her crossing to America on her voyage from nowhere to the here where I am born to give her substance.

I am the only one of her children delivered by a doctor in a hospital, St. Anne's, and I am named Anne in gratitude for the skill that saved my four-pound life. She worries that the name Anne is too goyish, and changes it to Anna which becomes Hannah in the sighing speech that sends her vowels airborne, and with the inevitable diminutive endearment, ends as Hannahle. I will laboriously lead it back from Hannahle to Hannah to Anna to Anne, but on the kitchen table I am Hannahle, and though her name has undergone a sea change from Feigele to Fanny to Fay, I know her only as Mama.

I make the effort to unroll her life backward across that flat ocean to the real places she really inhabited—to the London slum where she worked and married and had her first children and beyond that to the village in Poland where she was born and grew up. The spare bits of information make a stilted history which I reconstruct painstakingly into a sampler of my mother's early life.

When she was a little girl, she saw gold shining in the distance beyond her village and pleaded with her father to help her collect the fortune that would make them rich. Her father took her hand and walked with her across a rutted frozen road to show her the late winter setting sun and how the gold was fading from the windows of the houses in the neighboring village. "My father was a saint," she told me. I embroider the grandfather I have never seen in golden thread and give him her heavy-lidded, deep-set, brown eyes flecked with gold.

Make it pretty. Why not? I can invent any background I please —Russian intellectual, rich peasant, colorful poor, *Fiddler-on-the-Roof* musical comedy. There are no hard facts, no place names, no records, no towns, not a clue to pursue.

She claimed to have been a singing teacher in England, a lie so transparent that it was remarkable on my part to have believed it until I was quite grown up. Her repertory of songs, picked up from English working-girl friends, was sung in a small, true, sweet voice, tinged with the rowdy mockery of the music hall. "Jesus loves me, yes I know, 'cause the Bible tells me so." "There was Brown, upside down, knocking all the whiskey on the floor." "Mother, dear, oh did you hear the news that's going 'round? I'm afraid to go home in the dark," followed by gruesome tales of Jack the Ripper. And from another part of her life, a Yiddish song about the red flag, the red flag, drenched with the blood of the working man, set, to my adolescent snobbish astonishment, to a Beethoven theme.

She left her parents when she was sixteen. She ran from a traditional marriage to a local boy, but not because of the boy. She liked her curly brown hair. It was too terrifying, having to shear it off. Bad enough to have seen her sister transformed overnight into an old woman in a black wig with a part made of seamed yellow cloth. She was smuggled across the border in a wagon filled with bales of hay. There were openings to breathe through, but she was sure that she would suffocate. In London she spent long days in a basement workshop and the short evenings crying into a towel so as not to be heard by her aunt and uncle and their two children and the boarder from the old village.

She hinted at a sad love affair with a violinist before she met Papa. Another lie? I see her in the crumpled shirtwaist of the working girl. The long, black skirt outlines her graceful figure and delicate waist. She is on a crowded London street, at an omnibus stop, threatening and pleading with a young man in her shrill peasant voice. He is deserting her for another. He is a small, dark, neat man with a little moustache. He carries a violin case. He answers her in short bursts of passionate self-defense. They are quarreling in Yiddish. She turns on the English people standing about watching the spectacle, scolding in her Yiddish-accented Cockney speech. "Who are you looking at? Monkeys in a zoo? You think my misery is a penny show?"

In their wedding photograph, she is still pert, young, tiny-waisted, though ten years older than my straight-backed, tall, smooth-faced father. She had gone to Paris during the Exposition at the turn of the century to find better-paying work and found my father, a fellow operator on furs.

Of her seven children I was born last, when she was in her forties. She didn't want me and tried to get rid of me, but I stuck, draining the last drops of warmth and calcium. She had no time and place for me. She carried me in a bushel basket from the top floor of the tenement where we lived to my father's grocery store a few blocks away. She relieved him while he napped and ate his meals.

"You don't remember that," my sister Jenny says. "Come on, Anne. You can't possibly remember that."

I see my mother at the kitchen sink scrubbing a pot. She has wedged the pot against the faucet and she is scouring with her left hand because the right arm is broken, immobilized in a splint and a sling. She begins to sob and to smash the pot against the faucets, and when she has completely smashed the pot, she stops crying and laughs.

That must have been just before her two-week nervous break-down. The doctor ordered a rest in the country as a cure. Only my brother Barry and my sister Shana and I shared that first American holiday with her. We went to a Jewish farmer in Connecticut. I had thought of her as so totally ignorant that I didn't know what to make of her expert knowledge of the woods. She wandered about digging, picking, sniffing, rubbing between her fingers, tasting, rejecting. She gathered mushrooms, sour grass, berries, roots,

and leaves, and returned to the room rented with cooking privileges carrying treasures for preparation into dishes I wouldn't
touch. She milked the cow and drank the warm, frothy, disgusting
milk fresh from the udders. She cured the farmer's dog of an
infection and he adopted her and slept outside our room every
night. I could hear him panting his love through the space under
the warped wooden door.

She found a waterfall and brought soap and towels to wash our
hair under the cold, delicious spray, and when we were dry sent
us ahead to the farmhouse to be free to undress and wash herself.
Some teasing from my brother and sister made me run back to
her. I saw silky nakedness and rounded buttocks splashed with the
brilliant water of the falls in a half-lit sprinkled sunshine. It was
mystifying to recognize beauty in my harassed old mother. I ran
off at once, afraid to face her with my blazing new knowledge.

She wasn't my dream parent. I would have given her up for a
mother who could read and write English. I dreaded her coming
to Open School Week, but she looked quite distinguished in a
dark-blue suit, only a tiny edge of her curly gray hair showing from
under a blue felt hat borrowed from my aunt in millinery, and was
introduced, without embarrassment to me, as "Anne's mother,
Mrs. Goddard" in the mannerly charade staged by Miss Ryan for
our social good. I showed off like mad, answering every question
the teacher allowed me to, drunk with relief. Still I despaired of
her understanding how smart I was. What did she know about
fractions or the Boston Tea Party? What did she know about America, about being American, about my struggle to swim in this
dangerous sea without markers or channels? There was no path
from her past to my future. We were caught, she and I, in a
misunderstanding. She was a source of shame to me, and not to be
forgiven. She had come from someplace else. She was a green-
horn. I had to squirm away from her and dig in my toes where I
could stand. Remember, I told myself, remember, you musn't be
like her.

I wasn't pleased that she cried while her daughter answered
questions, zing, zing, zing, one after the other, absolutely correctly. I saw her take a snowy, holiday-white handkerchief out of
her pocket and wipe her eyes. That wasn't what she should have
been doing. She should have been watching me with a slightly
sour look, the way Adele Falkenburg's mother eyed Adele. *Not*

enough. Not good enough. That was the way Jewish mothers who could read and write English responded to their clever daughters.

At least she found my friends not good enough. "I don't give two cents for Mrs. Fancy Stuck-Up Falkenburg," she said, but stayed up nights sewing me a new dress for Adele's birthday party. It was made of white, filmy stuff and had a plain round neck and long, fitted sleeves. All its decoration was in the overskirt of attached lace-edged handkerchiefs and in its soft velvet sash. I earned high honors at the party for my beautifully worked dress and my beautiful hair and my beautiful manners. So my sister was told when she came to pick me up, right on time, the first to arrive to take a child home. The afternoon had been a triumph for my family. I was the only schoolmate invited who came from our side of Fort Greene Park—the slum side.

I came home sick. My mother held my head as I retched into a pail. She blamed my illness on the rich food at the party, but I hadn't eaten anything. I didn't dare. My body had threatened betrayals at every attempted move. I would spill, break, pee in my underdrawers, slip, fall, scream, burst into tears. The dining room was unimaginably grand, with a crystal chandelier from whose brilliance swirls of twisted crepe paper and balloons exploded softly. In the center of the huge table an elaborate cake radiated ribbons to each child's plate which we yanked at a signal to win a ring wrapped in tissue. On my skinny finger, the ring dangled weighty as a handcuff. Adele was an only child. Her parents were young; they seemed hardly older than my oldest brother and sister. But they were very different from us. How smoothly Adele's mother moved, how benignly her father's smile floated above his bow tie, how calmly, between them, they governed the holiday air of the party. The information that in my world there might be Jews to emulate made me sick with excitement.

Getting sick was a way to force all my mother's attention in my direction. Any ministration would do—a long sock filled with salt heated in a frying pan and wrapped around my throat to draw the inflammation, a shockingly cool alcohol rubdown, covers suffocatingly piled on to sweat out the poisons, egg nog with a drop of *shnapps*, beef tea and mint tea, and a wonderfully aromatic brew of steeped dried raspberries—even Papa's cash register receipts to count at midnight when he closed the store.

I thought of myself as her favorite child. We all did. Privately,

we each put the question to her. "I'm your favorite, right?" She
had no hesitation in agreeing. Whichever child was at her side was
her favorite. She was the proverbial Jewish wife who could cut a
herring into enough parts to feed a large family, but it was herself
she pieced for our hungers.

She was dead before I thought to ask her all the things I wanted
to know. Toward the end I hurried.

She was living with my father and a temporarily unmarried
sister in a house in Miami, cushioned in a steady material comfort
at last by my brother Barry, who had cut his own path through the
thicket of bankruptcies, dispossesses, summonses, and creditors
that had been my father's notion of business. When I was young
I thought those terms were Yiddish words for troubles that came
down only on the heads of small grocery-store owners. Barry had
come up with new words—production, profit, capital investment,
merger, spin-off, money.

I set up a bilingual correspondence between me and my mother
from New York to Miami. I explained that I would have a friend
translate her letters for me. Did that information give her a stage
fright that made her foolish? My friend was an expert in Yiddish
literature. Perhaps he was the fool. He was embarrassed by her
sentimentality, by the pages splattered with tears and endear-
ments (my dear child, *meine teire kind*, my sweet daughter Hannahle, *meine zeese tuchter*, soul, *nashuma*). I took the letter from
him when he stopped to explain that my mother wrote an illiter-
ate, mawkish slop without punctuation or structure—very difficult
for him to read and translate.

"No need to go on then," I said.

I folded the letter in my fist, protecting it from exposure. If she
was going to turn out to be the fool of my father's stories, I didn't
want the proof. I would stick with my own image. I put her letters
away unread, answering them in the same general way. *Dearest
Mama, I received your beautiful letter*, and going on to what news
I could find to report. I typed my meaningless letters at my desk
at the office. She had taught herself to read English print.

Soon she is too ill to write, and the problem solves itself.

My father's favorite story is about her arrival at Ellis Island to
join him. He had come three months earlier to find a job and a
place to live before sending for his family. She had met a *chuchum*
on the voyage. The know-it-all's advice was that my mother would

ease her entrance if she told the authorities that her husband had preceded her to the States by two years. They held Mama for hours unraveling snarls in a situation which included her three-year-old and eighteen-month-old children and a pregnancy visibly too far gone to last another month. My father loved to mimic how Mama signaled him from her caged enclosure, holding up two fingers and winking and nodding with a satisfied show of her cleverness in outwitting the officials. Papa swore that the children, born and unborn, were his. And they could see for themselves that the three-year-old, my oldest brother Saul, dressed in his best English serge knickers in a ninety-degree heat, and with his soft brown hair twisted into Lord Fauntleroy curls, knew his father and was calling, "Papa, Papa."

They take their place in the mythology of the Jewish immigration, subjects in a Lewis Hine photograph, except for my mother, who cannot keep a dignified stance in the tableau. She plays the clown, even looks a little like Harpo Marx; she has vomited too much on the stormy crossing and is crazy from dehydration; she thinks my father is abandoning her there in the compound on Ellis Island.

Actually, she looked more like Albert Einstein. In her last years she tends her garden in Miami—one avocado, one grapefruit, one lemon, one lime, one mango tree. The wind blows her white hair into a ridiculous halo. Her eyes are monkey-wise but with the pink-rimmed human vulnerability of the eyes in a Rembrandt portrait. She calls the utility shack my father has had built on the edge of a disliked neighbor's property "the spite room." She mishears the phrase "the new-mown hay," and calls the sweepings of the freshly cut lawn "the Dumont hay." When I was in high school, learning by heart, "Tomorrow, and tomorrow, and tomorrow, creeps in this petty pace," she follows me declaiming nonsense: *"Shulimdrip, shulimdrop, alla gense auf der fence . . ."* Did she lie to me about having seen Sarah Bernhardt play Hamlet with a wooden leg?

She was nobody. She has no importance.

My father liked to complain that it was she who had halted his activity in the cap-makers' union after the failure of a twelve-week strike, dividing the blame for the collapse of his revolutionary hopes between his wife and hungry children and the bad job the Bolsheviks were doing in Soviet Russia. His first job in this country was as an operator in a hat factory. It was our Aunt Sadie Jacoby, already "making good," who set him up in his grocery store.

"I don't blame him for my life," my mother says.

She is dying in a Miami hospital, fading from exhaustion, not responding to the newest drugs to soup up her failing heart.

"I kept him like a spoiled child all his life," she says to me. She is angry with him because he falls asleep in the armchair when he comes to visit her at the hospital. Still she whispers—not to disturb him. "Women nowadays know better what to do. Don't be fools like us." I was in the middle of a divorce. "Don't get married again. But if you do, don't have any more children." She closes her eyes. My father is snoring. With her eyes shut, she says, "Will I see a book from you, please God, before I close my eyes for good?"

She was always old. She was always having trouble with her teeth. Pyorrhea—another Yiddish word. The first one home from school, I am the first to see her false teeth. They are such *false* false teeth. She turns my dismay to comedy, grotesquely working the teeth in and out of her mouth, jabbering ape noises. Fifteen years later, when I am twenty-five and visiting in Miami she is again having trouble with her teeth. The original clumsy upper plate has long been replaced. This is bottom-teeth trouble. She has cataracts; she is deaf; and her feet swell with long sitting, but my father and I insist that a movie will do her good. We enter in the middle of a double feature. She asks a lot of questions about the plot into which we've been plunged. I try to answer them briefly, while my father shushes us and darts fierce, condemning glances at her. She has brought things to eat in a paper bag—nuts and grapes and a couple of oranges and apples. There are more furious glances from my father, but he eats everything she offers us. So do I. The orange she peels yields a marvelous scent. She falls asleep in the middle of one movie and wakes in the middle of the other and on the walk home puts them together into an entertainment better than the one we had seen. My father laughs and calls her a fool, pleasantly.

Now I am fifteen and she has been sick for a long time. She has had a spinal operation and is immobilized in a cast. Though we were all cooperative in the beginning, we're tired of her illness. Nobody wants to be responsible anymore, even if we did drain the calcium. My father has still another failing store, in the South

Bronx. My brother Barry helps him after he comes home from work, between sessions at night school. It's a matter of weeks before the creditors will descend. After the settlement, we'll all make a trip to carry off as much stock as my father thinks we can get away with. For the next few months, we'll eat a lot of canned salmon and so will the families of my sister and two brothers who have married and gotten free of us. Another sister is working. My next eldest sister, a year out of high school, is staying at home to take care of Mama. I am in my senior year at high school. I'm supposed to rush straight home this day. My sister must do something important and Mama will be alone for an hour or so before I'm due to arrive.

I can't get myself to go home. I can't drag myself away from my friends, the charged, silly talk, the electric promise in the air that everything is possible. I'm in love with a dozen people. One is an older married English teacher who takes me for a ride in his car and parks under the trees on the Pelham Bay Road and strokes first my right and then my left eyebrow with a trembling finger as we discuss D.H. Lawrence—he's even *Irish*. One is the school's leading poet, a beautiful girl, younger than I, who has read everything—Robinson Jeffers, Ezra Pound, Gerard Manley Hopkins— and can quote whole poems. There is a real American-looking, square-faced football star who admires me wordlessly and then invites me to the senior prom and whose first name, shockingly, turns out to be Moishe. Most important is Miss Dillon, another English teacher with whom I begin a passionate friendship as puzzling and searing as anything I will ever experience. This after- noon she has brought around a new girl and a new boy—two of her "specials." We are all her "specials"—that's how we meet. Miss Dillon's "specials" call her Beth. Beth thrills me by showing open displeasure that the other English teacher, my Irish one, has spoken possessively of "her Anne." The English department had been discussing graduation awards. It looks as if I will get the gold medal. Beth is jealous of the other teacher's involvement in my fate. It makes me drunk to think of it. The new girl intensely watches the scene Beth and I are playing. She responds, magically, to everything we say—nodding, laughing, opening her eyes wide, just as I would have her do in a daydream. The new boy is on trial. He is dark and romantic-looking in a coarse Italian fashion. But he too turns out to be Jewish. He doesn't make the effort to follow what's happening. It's enough for him to feel cherished and to have been allowed to join us. He rolls an orange up one arm, along his shoulder and the back of his neck, and down the other arm, and catches it neatly with a twist of his wrist. Then he juggles three oranges successfully. "For love of three oranges," I say, and win an admiring nod from Beth. We make fun of the new boy's lowly skill and he joins us to laugh at himself. He has passed the test. Perhaps I'll be in love with him too. He has an empty house. His family is visiting relatives in Philadelphia for the weekend. He knows how to make spaghetti and meat sauce. He'll cook it and we'll all eat it together, in an empty house. We make plans to all meet in an hour.

At last I hurry home. My mother has wet herself. She doesn't look at me or speak as I change her bedding and nightgown. She is encased in the steel support of her cast and in a cold, solid despair. Her feet have become shapely and white from the long year's invalidism. They twist my heart. I don't care. I don't care. I just want to go to my friends. I dump the wet things in the kitchen washtub and run water and add suds and leave the drainboard off so that someone will notice the linens and take care of them. I wash my face and change my blouse and brush my hair and am ready to run off as soon as someone arrives.

My mother calls me. She keeps her face turned aside, but she forces herself to speak. "Help me make Shabbas, Anna," she says. I place tall, white candles in the brass candlesticks brought from England, and I hand her a clean white dish towel. I light the candles and she covers her head with the towel and waves her arms over the flames in the mysterious beckoning motions of the Sabbath ritual prayer. Her now-fine white hands cover her eyes and she sways as she prays. When she finishes I want to joke as my brother would. "Did you put in a good word for me, Mom?" But her face is forbidding.

I have no part in that anyway. Though I have had a little Hebrew education and can say a decent *brucha,* it is her sons who are her prayer insurance. They will say *Kaddish* when she dies.

I leave my children with a baby-sitter and take an hour's trip to attend early-morning services with my father and brothers. My mother's body has been brought to New York for burial in a Brook-lyn cemetery plot. The family gathers daily at my brother's grand, comfortable house in Westchester for the mourning period. We sit *shiva* on fine period furniture and eat food prepared by a Negro cook or ordered in from a delicatessen catering service. The men go to temple in the morning and evening. They are astonished that I join them this morning, but they accept my action as a sign of distraught grief.

My brother is a member of both temples in this suburb, the reform and the conservative. We are in the conservative one—a new, square, simple structure more like a Quaker or Unitarian church—in which the old rituals, tephillin and all, are carefully observed by surprisingly young, vigorous executive types. My father eases his real grief with the considerable consolation of his son's success, which he wears as if it is his own. Is it not? How preposterous of me to have ever worried that Jewish was not American.

I have come to hear poetry. I have come to connect with my mother through a magical and powerful incantation. I have come to hear *Kaddish* said, but the service drones on without it. I turn the pages of the prayer book, looking for the mourner's prayer, but my father thinks I'm lost and he does for me what he always did for my mother. Without interrupting his singsong murmuring, he takes my prayer book, finds the right place, and, keeping his finger firmly on the spot, returns the book to me. He is a dignified, senatorial figure in his prayer shawl and silken skull cap. The service is at the spot where the congregation is blessing God for an assortment of good things. The men bless God because He has not made them women. The women, in smaller print, bless God for having made them according to His will. I am the only woman in the temple. I turn the book away from my father's overseeing gaze to find what I was looking for, the transliteration of the mourners' prayer.

Yisgadal v'yishkadash . . .

I read to myself, not bothering with the English translation, giving myself up to sound alone.

Yisborach. v'yishtabach v'yispo-ar v'yisromam v'yisnaseh v'yis-hador v'yisaley v'yisha-lol . . . When I finish, I am peaceful and comforted and feel free to go outside into the air to cry.

I have other magic. Now I keep my mother's candlesticks in my kitchen on the Franklin fireplace mantel of my New England cape. From my garden I cut a spray of fresh dill and add it to the last cooking minutes of the chicken soup and evoke her in the delicate, sharp scent. I insist on her existence, and on my own.

II

_____

I am rushing to join my family at Pennsylvania Station. I'm late. In a few minutes, The Silver Meteor is due to arrive from Miami with Papa and my sister Jenny, and in the baggage car Mama's body in a coffin. It's a very hot day. (Is the baggage car refrigerated?) I am on the subway, headed for the *old* Penn Station, of course (before it was ripped out and rebuilt), because Mama died the summer of 1950; and because it's the 1950s I'm dressed in the way that mattered then—in ensemble and matching accessories, all black—a knife-pleated silk dress and soft felt hat, off-black silk stockings and high-heeled pumps, even gloves. I strip off my damp gloves and place them in my flat clutch purse. Why must it be so damn hot? Is there a heavenly injunction funerals must obey to be held only during violent weather? The subway jounces me about and my thoughts skitter and bounce, avoiding the fact I'm traveling toward. I worry about the way I look, and about the new hat I bought at a neighborhood store, in a hurry, on my way to the subway. I search for my reflection in the window opposite my subway seat, for reassurance that my family won't find my new hat ridiculous. I notice my hands—blotched, stubby-nailed, uncared-for hands. I take my gloves out of my black bag and force them back on my sticky fingers. Then I strip them again, almost immediately.

What's the matter with me? Apart from the fact that I'm traveling toward my mother's funeral, and apart from the fact that I'm going through a divorce (an ordeal which I have brought on myself but which nevertheless laces each day with its measure of acute, binding pain), apart then from death and divorce, I should be happy (I *am* happy) because I'm in love and the man I love says that he loves me (and here I record my usual difficulty in rejoicing at and believing in any good luck that comes my way), and happy also because I love the work I do and get paid for, and between love and work I am acquiring a sense that my life with my two children is actually moving toward the calm, fruitful place where I want it to go; but of course there is no such thing as "apart from," and even apart from "apart from" the happy parts of my life are harassed by so much hard work, worry, and guilt that not even they conform to my notions of the sunny fields of clover that I imagine happiness to be. Grief for Mama is submerged somewhere in this sea of agitation, the surface of which I allow only trivial concerns like the suitability of my new hat to ruffle.

What am I, anyway, "a false daughter, a child with a heart of stone"—that horror of the letters column of the *Jewish Daily Forward*, reported upon by Mama with disbelief that such monsters can really exist?

I don't think so—I hope not—though I'm aware of a certain hardening of the heart having taken place during my struggle to reach the age of twenty-nine, a struggle to grow up, to become "mature," a state I think of as distinctly different from the state I'm actually embroiled in—another room whose threshold one crosses at a precise moment in development, to the safety of an area where temperatures remain blessedly constant and evenly moderate. The mask of self-possession I am trying to maintain belongs to the cooled-down occupant of that room, but I'm also aware that her covering is thin and that her grasp of the technique of keeping "maturity" in place is weak. I think of her as another person. I think of her as she, Anne. I wish her luck. I put her outside myself, as far away as possible from the center of my being where, try as I may to compose myself, a hot liquid ball of unmanageable grief and loss roils and steams. I see her as "she," Anne, a young woman dressed in black seated on the subway, on the way to her mother's funeral.

She looks very young, too young to be the mother of two children and in the middle of a divorce from their father, because she's adolescent slim and because of the eager way she looks about her, as if seeing everything for the first time. Her eyes study the subway car, its advertisements, its riders, with avid interest. A strange man returns her glance. He has misunderstood the agitation in her eyes and is offering an invitation. She drops her eyes, then raises them again to see in his face, if she can, what he thinks of her new hat. He smiles. She frowns, turns her head sharply in cold discouragement. But his smile has reassured her. If her hat is all right, she must be. Then, in a panic, because she thinks that the strange man is about to approach her, she rises and walks to the end of the subway car to avoid him. The train pulls into her station and she rushes through the door, out through the exit and up the ramp leading to Penn Station—fleeing an unseemly encounter. Unseemly to be picked up while on the way to one's mother's funeral. She shudders. Intense heat may cause chills. Interesting. She stops before a vending machine mirror for a last checkup. The hat. Not too big a brim—not too floppy? Suitably black. Perhaps too black—everything too black? *Nor customary suits of solemn black . . . good mother.* Good mother, good woman, whose example must be shunned for purposes of my own life, forgive my foolish self-concern, forgive my enervating self-consciousness, forgive my selfishness. She hasn't said it aloud, has she?

She runs. A drumming energy drives her, but she is very tired. She has been up and doing for many hours—though it is now only midmorning—fixing breakfast, helping her children dress, tidying her apartment, arranging for a sitter to replace the sitter who neglected to show, deciding what to wear, buying the new hat, and through it all pretending to a forced calm for the sake of her little son and daughter whom she feels an obligation not to damage with a traumatic introduction to death, since she has already damaged them by separating from their father. Through all her rushing about, they had watched her with grave, intent faces. Who knows what in their little heads they were deciding about death and divorce and forced calm? Not she.

When she enters the great vaulted expanse of the station concourse, some of the breathless oppressiveness that is choking her lifts from her chest into the soaring space. She loves this place. Through the soot and smoke, streams of light descend in slow, whirling movement from the domed glass roof high above. Fingers of God light, romanticized and defiled in one breath. Noise too is transmuted, rising from the din of the teeming, marble floor into upper space, intensified and muffled, played out into the steel-ribbed cathedral area like a kind of music. To mourn becomes a possibility in this housing, expansive enough to hold a thousand individual griefs, like a synagogue or a church. Her eyes smart. She's late. Perhaps the train has already arrived. *At least this time Mama is lying down,* she thinks, with an angry click for Papa's stinginess. He would never spend extra money on a sleeper when he and Mama made their infrequent trips to New York. "Who wants to sit locked up alone in a compartment? It's a more interesting trip in the coaches," was his excuse. She brushes that thought aside, determined to meet her family emptied of the useless, dragging baggage of resentment and damaged love she carries with her. She owes that to Mama, she feels, to meet Papa and her brothers and sisters with clean, open love, if she can only manage it. She searches frantically for her family among the bunched, waiting groups of people, and when she spots the Goddards, she rushes forward, lifted on a swell of familiar expectation and excitement. Family gatherings excite her. She's glad to see them there together in a bunch, the Goddards, her family. But what is she expecting? This isn't a party, for God's sake. She draws a deep, sooty breath and plunges in, entering the outstretched arms of the first Goddard to greet her as if breasting the smallest wave of an ocean that threatens to engulf her.

She enters the arms of her oldest sister, Connie. Connie hugs her closely, kissing her on the cheek, then pulls back to look at her and carefully wipes away the lipstick smudge she has marked Anne with. She hugs Anne closely and puts her at arm's length again. Anne sees that Connie's eyes are swimming in tears before Connie hugs her once again and says, "You look stunning, Anna."

Anne's relief brings her to tears herself. The hat must be okay. How good Connie smells. Comfort exudes from her silky skin like a perfume. She's like Mama in this. Anne feels harbored, safe, elated with reassurance.

"The baby," Connie says, not releasing Anne.

Connie's husband, Sam Schwartz, crowds close, patting Anne's shoulder, gazing into her turned face fondly with his large, protruding green eyes. Anne nods and smiles at him, imprisoned by Connie. Why isn't Connie letting go? Anne's ease slides into worry that Connie's hold signifies assurances covering problems—that Connie is conveying a sense of alliance and defense against whatever anybody else in the family may think of Anne, and that as the oldest of the four sisters she is prepared to play Mama to Anne now that Mama's gone, provided Connie can arrange matters without too much inconvenience to her usual routines. Anne stiffens. If she needs all this mothering and protection, then there must be something wrong with her. But if not the hat, if she looks stunning, *what* then?

Anne knows perfectly well what. Her divorce. Her politics. Her goy lover. Her career ambitions. Her lack of money. The entire un-Goddard shape of the life she's working so hard to make for herself.

"Anna's here," Connie hollers to gather the others, but still holding Anne in her arms. "Anna's here, everybody."

Connie's voice is unpleasantly loud. Anne hears in it the cackling of ladies playing Mah-Jongg, kaffeeklatsching, knifing their friends in endless daytime telephone conversations, screaming at their adolescent kids, arguing senseless drivel at shrill women's-club meetings. She mourns Connie as a woman doomed to serve out a dull, middle-class life sentence without reprieve or pardon or the guts to break away. As if remembering a dream, Anne hoards a misty vision of the young, unmarried Connie of Anne's babyhood—a remote, romantic, graceful figure in a heavy brocade pink dancing dress, swirling her thick brown hair into a weighty bun, sitting at a window catching the light to buff her constantly tended long nails with their large, perfect half-moons—a melting, pink Connie who disappeared into marriage with a forbidding-looking stranger and emerged, as if bewitched, both, into conniving Sam Schwartz and his busy, loud-voiced wife. Anne has treasured through the years a single splendid memory of an outing with Connie, before Connie married, to a movie and a vaudeville show at a theater that Anne thought a palace among great castles and forts in downtown Brooklyn, and coming home in the dark, in the rain, with moving colored lights reflected on the wet pavement like magic decorations, her hand secure in Connie's silky fingers and her senses charged with the mystery of Connie's height and age and life soaring beyond Anne's childish reach.

They were all beyond her reach—except for Shana. A whole family of grown-ups. Perhaps her brothers and sisters continue to loom so large on her horizon because they were so big when she was little? She reminds herself to stop endowing them with powers to cure or harm her that they themselves never dream of, and

loosens herself from Connie's arms to greet Shana as the easiest to
contend with. Shana always came in her size, was only a little
older, there should be no problems here. But there are. Near or
far, there are burdens and terrors in sisterhood, and perhaps the
nearer, the more complicated. They kiss with what seems like
lightness, but Anne shivers at the emotions quivering at the tips
of Shana's fleet, nervous touch, tightening at the dry, quick brush
of Shana's thin lips. *My sister,* Anne thinks, *my self, beloved and
detested, make a pact, forget our shared history lying between us
like a bed of snakes, remember only the good times when we
helped one another, when we laughed a lot.*

They are strikingly alike, she and Shana, the two youngest Goddards, even more so than the rest of the Goddards, who all look
alike. At first, acquaintances find it hard to tell one sister from the
other, or to determine which is older or younger or more or less
attractive. Intimacy ends confusion but leads to worse troubles—
friends and lovers insist on choosing between them, rating them,
weighing their comparative values, and once arrived at the conclusion that Shana and Anne are, after all, remarkably different,
end by disliking one sister and championing the other. When they
were little, Mama dressed them as twins for special occasions.
Whatever made her do that? A money-saving notion probably—
one dress pattern, one width of material made to serve for two.
With Anne's conviction that everything shone on Shana and
looked miserable on her, it was the purest misery to be dressed
alike. That kind of misery marks one for life? *Snow-white, rose-red,
black-eyed,* saftige *Shana, my sister, my self, tell me I look stunning.* Shana looks okay in her straw pillbox hat; what's terrific is
the elegant cut of Shana's dark-green silk suit and her new curly,
gamine hairdo.

"Is my hat all right?" Anne is forced to say, since Shana has
offered no comment.

"It's fine," Shana says, holding her voice flat. Anne senses in this
control Shana's desperate shakiness. *Don't cry,* Anne commands
her. *If you cry, I will. If you break down, I'll go down with you.*

"You don't think it's too black?" Anne says.

Shana makes an impatient face, then rouses herself to study the
problem. "Wait a minute," she says, suddenly vigorous. She opens
her large pocketbook and brings out a fistful of tangled beads—a
string of jade, amber, wooden brown beads, another of mother-of-

pearl. With deft, nervous fingers Shana unwinds the mother-of-pearl from the others, thrusts the rejects back in her bag, and turning Anne around, fastens the white beads to Anne's neck.

Josh is on top of Anne, kissing her, laughing at them, protesting, "What are you girls doing? Turning Penn Station into a boudoir?" This brother has been out in the midwest for some years; Anne sees him so seldom that it is a shock to realize again how handsome he is in his flashy show-biz style. He smiles his vivid, disconnected smile and rolls his black eyes heavenward in mock male despair. "Ah, the ladies, the ladies, God bless them!" he says, attempting to put his arms around her, but Shana turns Anne back toward herself, studying with intense seriousness the effect of the white beads on Anne's all-black outfit, arranging their fall with swift, deft touches to Anne's chest. "That's perfect," she announces. "That's just what was needed," and releases Anne with a series of nervous, lingering pats.

"Remind me to give them back," Anne says, turning toward her brother Josh, and hears Shana, behind her, as Josh is embracing her, urging her to "Keep them, Anna, for goodness' sake. Can't I give you a string of beads if I feel like it?"

If you're giving, Anne thinks, *I would have preferred the jade or the amber*, but she pushes that dissatisfaction aside as a blemish on the occasion, and kisses Josh's cologned, manly, stranger's cheek.

His vivid smile is frighteningly fixed on her face. "Look at our baby sister, folks," he calls out. "A regular Greta Garbo." But as if he too has had an inner reminder about the nature of the occasion, the smile clicks off, and his face is instantly desolated. "The baby," he says, his eyes reddening and filling. "Mama's Hannahle," he murmurs, overcome by his own sentiment.

Anne is acutely embarrassed by him. All her memories of him are tinged with embarrassment, vague remembrances of the years he spent trying to make it "on the stage," the hard-learned vaudeville patter and the tap dancing, the gravelly singing voice and plodding ukulele playing. The collection of terrible jokes. All embodied in the vivid, faked, white-toothed smile of those days— more and more desperately set against failure.

In her memories he is mixed up with memories of Saul, standing directly behind him, advancing now to kiss her next. Soft, silent Saul—his kiss wipes itself away as it is being delivered. She thinks

of Saul and Josh as one, though they are very different. They go
together the way she and Shana do. The two oldest Goddard
brothers are "the boys," the two youngest sisters are "the girls."
(In between are Connie and Jennie and Barry, clear-cut in her
mind. Perhaps because they have always been distinct entities?)
Saul should stand out, he is the firstborn; but he melts away in her
memories. Was it Saul or Josh, or both in turn, who tormented her
by walking her to school so late that she had to run all the way,
keeping up with their long, striding walk to the trolley they took
to work, and leaving her to cross the Flatbush Avenue Extension
alone while they watched from the opposite curb—as if that would
have done any good if she were run over. Saul and Josh fade into
a distant relationship—more like uncles than her brothers. If there
is some sharpness in her memories of Josh, poor Saul is filed away
in her mind in a large, empty compartment. He is a flat, one-color
surface to her. Silent Saul. She can't think of anything Saul ever
said to her that was memorable. "That little tramp!" pops into her
head, a judgment against her by him, but what misdemeanor
prompted his description? She can't remember. She remembers
his misdemeanor, but only because it caused her discomfort.
When he was a young man he stole seventeen dollars from the
cash register of a store in which he was clerking, and spent a night
in the Tombs before he was released in Mama's custody. The
Tombs! Terrifying words, even now, yet no romance or compassion attaches to Saul from it. The romance enriches the thick
Oriental colors of her portrait of Barry. An item about Saul's theft
and imprisonment appeared in the *Daily Mirror*, a newspaper
read all over the neighborhood, and the kids on the block followed
her and Shana yelling, "Your brother is a thief, your brother is a
thief!" until Barry, in an avenging rage, descended to the street
and scared the hell out of them. Brother Barry—dark savior.

Now Josh and Saul are prosperously, smoothly absorbed under
the cover of Barry's business, running his midwest operation—
incompetently, according to Shana's husband, Merv, whose opinion carries weight, coming as it does from the higher echelons of
the New York Office and the Board of Directors.

Where is Merv? Anne doesn't see him. She must still greet the
wives of her three brothers, and her brother Barry, but Sam
Schwartz intervenes, Connie's husband, who returns for "a real
kiss, little sister-in-law," and plants one full on her lips, leaving her

unpleasantly wet. She wipes her mouth with the back of her hand, hoping he won't notice, and plunges further into these exhausting waters, pecking at the pancaked cheek of Josh's wife, Brenda, and distractedly soothing Lil, Saul's wife, who is immediately in tears at contact. Beyond them stand Barry and his wife, Pauline, not crowding in like the others, but waiting for Anne to come to them, waiting for their due under the unwritten rules of family protocol. Barry rules the roost and Pauline is his consort.

She has arrived at last at the center from which all Goddard energy radiates. It is time to greet Barry. She pauses, already worn out by the greetings accomplished. How will she ever get through the long day ahead? But her pause is for more than drawing breath. She pulls against a yearning to win a special greeting from Barry—in revulsion against another dive into those swirling waters where her brothers and sisters thrash about him, clutching and gasping, and she approaches Barry coolly, but when he responds in kind and kisses her without warmth, she is pinched with disappointment.

"Anne," he says. He is the only one of her family who uses her real name, the name she uses out in the world. "The train is delayed. If the last posting is correct . . ." He speaks in a slow, rabbinical voice whose affectation of solemnity dismays her, yet she believes him to be in real pain, and underneath the controlled artificiality she hears a rough, worn hoarseness caused by crying. He is correctly and conservatively dressed with just a touch of Seventh Avenue in his white-on-white shirt and fashionably narrow black knit tie. His thick, straight, black hair is carefully barbered, and about him float manly smells—after-shave lotion, hair stuff, cologne, shoe polish. Now she would be glad to have another chance to greet him, to embrace him with warmth, except that his hard black eyes bounce her off. "If the posting is correct"—he often repeats the last phrase before an interruption, like a man accustomed to giving dictation—"we may have forty minutes of waiting, if not more." With no warning to herself, Anne is crying and he is instantly in charge. "Come on now, you're all hot and worn out. Didn't you take a cab? Anyone who rides in a subway on a day like this . . ."

He pulls out of his jacket pocket an amazing collection of coins —quarters, dimes, half-dollars. There are even some silver dollars in the lot. "Get yourself a cool drink."

Something in Anne's attitude deters him from dumping the change on her, and instead he turns to Saul's wife, who puts out both hands to receive it. "Lil," he says, "take Anne to a stand out there and get her a cool drink."

Lil squeals and protests while dropping the load in her bag. As if Saul's silence demands a countervailing effect, his wife Lil is a constant natural source of sound and movement. Busy, busy, busy, the air around her. "Barry, what's the matter, you think I'm so poor I can't afford to buy Anna an orange drink? What kind of a shlep do you think I am anyway?" She pulls at Anne's arm to hurry to carry out Barry's orders. Lil too works for him in the midwest operation. "Your wish is my command," she likes to say to him, and Anne hates to hear. Anne hates it all, his excesses, Lil's obsequiousness, her own false position as the recipient of this piddling largesse. She ignores Lil and greets Pauline, Barry's wife, who is flamboyant in a dress, long coat, and little visored hat ensemble of a dark, wildly printed silk which Anne sees is painted, expensive stuff when she embraces her, and sees also that the huge beads of Pauline's necklace, bracelet, and earring set aren't costume junk but real star sapphires. They kiss by bringing their cheeks parallel but not touching, and turn their lips outward to the empty air.

Then she allows Lil to lead her away. Anne takes a few sips of the soda she doesn't want, while Lil babbles on, running tears for Mama Goddard. Lil's tears are a family joke (out of her husband Saul's hearing)—remarkable for their spontaneity and copiousness and the curious way in which they gather on the lashes of her large, empty blue eyes and splash upward into the air, "just like a park fountain," Mama would say.

"Here comes pish-eyes. Raise your umbrellas, folks," is more Barry's style.

Lil's tears turn off as precipitately as they start, and do now as she switches to delight in the dollars of change in her bag.

"Your brother," she says, wagging her head. "What a guy! What are we going to do with all this, divvy it up?"

"Give it back to him," Anne says. "Give it back to Barry. It's his."

Anne's distaste, her embattled pride, is as excessive as Barry's generosity, but she doesn't understand that then. She sees herself as held up by "values" the others don't comprehend or share. She hurries away from Lil's greediness as if from more infection, but what is she hurrying toward after all but Barry, the center from which all infection radiates? She sees her brothers and sisters ahead, in their look-alike faces. The Goddard face. Is it beautiful or repulsively ordinary? Grotesque, maybe? Their foreheads are good—broad, rounded, *almost* noble—with handsomely defined hairlines; and the eyes are good—large, passionate, commanding. There's something touching about the narrowing, sharp jawline bringing what might have otherwise been too coarse to a delicate finish, though the best-looking Goddards, Josh and Jenny, have rounded jaws. All their noses are too big, except for Jenny's. But Jenny is a beauty. Is that the formula—a small, straight nose and a rounded chin with a faint dimple? Add the clear liquid of Jenny's eyes, the luminosity of her skin, her shining, dark, almost-straight hair, and a provocative smile constant in her eyes and on her curving lips. Jenny could wear any hat without fear—any kind of hairdo. Let a hairdresser loose on the rest of the Goddard sisters and out from under the dryers appear Louis XIVs or their handsome brothers in drag. Connie today, in her stiff hairdo and small, oddly shaped hat, is one of the founding fathers—George Washington. Shana's new haircut would be better for Connie, though Connie's hair is not so curly. What is it with the Goddard face? In her family Anne sees her features played with, reproduced, distorted, turned into pure line, while at any moment she may catch her own face in a mirror wearing Barry's heavy frown, Shana's defensive squint, Jenny's helpless open-mouthed laughter, Saul's slack mouth, Josh's pretty hairline, Connie's dim, tired eyes. She has even seen Mama's feet in her own. It frightens Anne.

Barry begins a conversation with her as she approaches, as he often does, by plunging into the middle and counting on her to follow headlong. Perhaps he does this with everybody, but she hugs it to herself as a compliment.

"I've been remembering the time when Mama got the news that her mother died. She hadn't seen her mother since she was sixteen. It was a terrible, terrible thing for Mama. You probably don't remember anything about it. You weren't old enough."

Anne thinks maybe she does remember it, or family stories about it. Locating the event in one of the many places they had lived would help her memory.

"Was it on Fox Street?" she asks him.

"I think it was that miserable dive on East 174th Street."

"Definitely the Bronx," she says. "Maybe it was that top-floor apartment on Union Street."

"Avenue," Barry says. "And we called an apartment a flat in those days. It could have been Southern Boulevard, under the el, tze de beck." He laughs at his use of Yiddish jargon. "To the back. The rear apartment, top floor, that's where we usually ended up," he says.

The puzzle is where they all slept. She remembers very few rooms and cannot locate in those rooms a corner for herself. Was she still sleeping with Mama and Papa? Too old. It was the apartment she came back to after her tonsils were removed, and where she had started to menstruate. Ignorant, not-yet-twelve-year-old, skinny kid, walking around bleeding into her bloomers, without the words to describe the mystery to anybody. She was paying a penalty for maturing out of the natural family order, ahead of next-older Shana. If Shana had begun first, as she should have, she would have been pleased to be able to pass on such a prestigious piece of secret intelligence. Connie was married and gone. Jenny was too grown-up and prudish to discuss such matters with an eleven-year-old. (It was amazing to Anne to think back on the prudery practiced in their close family quarters. The only totally naked body Anne had ever seen without peeking was Shana's, and as far back as she remembered Anne had known how to dress and undress without revealing a patch of naked skin.) To confide in Mama never occurred to her. Mama *had* to be ignorant of this puzzling, evil flow. She kept the fact of the bleeding hidden, sleeping in her blood-stiffened underpants to keep them out of sight, waking morning after morning with the hope that the plague visited upon her had disappeared. But it went on for four days. Barry took her to an open-air movie that night. It was a wonderful movie. *The Sea Pirate* with Milton Sills. Her trouble was forgotten until she stood up, and unbelievably felt the blood still running down her leg and into her socks and shoes. She wanted to tell Barry then because she counted on him to be rational and helpful, but because the blood was from *there*, she didn't know how to describe her ailment, and anyway she held a dim belief that the flow was God's punishment upon her for her daydreams of hopelessly enamored boys and fantasies of delicious male brutality she could hardly wait to continue from night to night, mute, and on fire, shoved over as far as she could get in the double bed she shared with Shana and Jenny.

Of course, *that's* where she had slept, in a tiny room, overlooking a courtyard, just large enough to hold the bed and a dresser, where she woke to a tableau of Shana and Jenny and Mama studying her underpants against the weak light from the window. She had taken the bloomers off at last. She was dying anyway. Let the whole world find out.

In a bewildering mix of excitement, whispers, giggles, and a strong blast of resentment emanating from Shana, they encircle her.

Mama slaps Anne's face with a light tap. "Stay away from boys," Mama says.

How mystifying! Boys, men, fantasies, punishment—all that was true then? Now Mama kisses her and is crying and blushing and seems proud of her and worried about her, all at the same time and in the same dismissive, embarrassed manner.

"Tell her how to take care of herself," Mama says in the general direction of Shana and Jenny, but Jenny sloughs *her* embarrassment off on Shana, and now Shana gets her own back by explaining the bloody mystery in the most disgusting terms she can invent.

Too funny—stuff for a Freudian comic strip. Anne laughs aloud.

Barry, happy with the thought that she is enjoying his joke, repeats, "Tze de beck."

"I think I remember," Anne says. She sees Mama sitting on the floor with her head on the seat of the pull-out couch. The house is clean and supper is cooked. Jenny needs to practice at the piano in the sitting room and Shana and Anne need the table for their homework, but they whisper and tiptoe around Mama's immobile, silent body. No, she has made all that up. Anne remembers nothing but Mama's bent back and how her legs are twisted under her on the linoleum rug and how Mama's head is face down on the seat of the couch. She remembers an unnatural hush, and her own wonder that Mama can be overpowered by emotions that have nothing to do with Anne and her brothers and sisters, and that keep her from serving the family supper. She remembers Barry, guarding Mama's right to grieve unmolested.

Anne and Barry are left standing somewhat apart from the others. In this court, allowance of a few minutes of privacy with the king is guaranteed to every family member, for the seeking of special favors. But the others hover. They would like to know what's going on. They are irresistibly drawn to the conversation, because it's about the old days, and when they overhear the old Bronx addresses, they rush in.

"Twelve seventy Southern Boulevard," Connie says. "I'll never forget that address. Mark was only four months old but I bundled him up and came all the way from Kingsbridge Road to be with Mama. Cousin Maury from England brought Mama the news. The one who went into antiques and made a fortune."

"I remember him," Anne says very quietly, hoping to lower Connie's voice by example. "I loved the way he spoke."

"You can't remember *him*," Josh says. "You were too little."

Their combined insistence on robbing her of what memories she has is maddening, but worse, undermining. Is she making it all up?

"Cousin Maury thought we were rich and he came to New York planning to stay with us. That Southern Boulevard apartment was quite a shock to him." Barry laughs. "He could have shared a bed with the three girls or the three boys. Or there was always an extra folding bed behind a door, as I recall."

"I remember him," Anne says stubbornly. "He took me and Shana to see *The Jazz Singer*."

Shana shudders. "Don't remind me," backing up Anne's memory and lessening some of Anne's tight anxiety. "He was horrible. Talk about wandering hands! I was practically a baby," and Anne is once again lost in a dark, furtive place she had no hint of then.

Connie says, "Our cousin didn't have much use for us once he saw there wasn't any money."

"Give the man his due," Barry says. "He tried to give Mom a couple of bucks before he left. Mama thwarted his generous impulse. 'Thank you,' she said, 'but you must need it more than I do.' " He pauses, tossing what followed aside. "That branch of Mama's family made a persistent effort to contact me on my last trip to London, but I found I was just too busy to return their calls."

Saul's wife Lil savors that with unpleasantly liquid, gasping laughter. "That's a good one, Barry. You're really something. Too busy. Did you hear that? I bet they got the message. Didn't they? Did they?"

Barry keeps a hard, blank, closed-in expression and continues as if Lil isn't there. "And that other contingent, Papa's side, the Jacoby clan, that whole bunch are suddenly very moved by the loss of Mama. They're coming to pay their respects."

"Aunt Sadie Jacoby's coming? I can't believe it. They're crazy, those Jacobys. She and Papa haven't spoken to each other in I don't know how long," Josh says.

"It's got to be at least thirty-five years," Saul says.

"They're not so crazy," Barry's wife says. "They know who to suck up to."

"I can't stand hypocrisy," Josh's wife Brenda says, hurrying to agree with Pauline. Brenda apes Barry's wife Pauline in every way she can, but since moving to the midwest she is less and less successful at advance guessing Pauline's decor. She's off target today, topped by a beehive hairdo Pauline has abandoned months ago, but the mouths and eyebrows of both are shaped the same, the eyebrows in disdainful surprise, the mouths in sexy discontent.

Barry shifts his hard, filmy gaze in their direction. He blinks. Anne thinks of a lizard. "How unusual! How noble!" he says.

Anne recognizes sarcasm, but she's not sure of its aim. Shana stands behind Anne, her hand resting on Anne's shoulder. Anne feels the apprehension in Shana's restless, tapping fingers. Is Barry going to become difficult and let out his mood on the family?

"Let's not talk this way," Shana pleads. "Not today. Let's be kind today."

"Don't get nervous, Shana," Connie screams, "just because you keep in touch with the Jacoby side."

"They keep in touch with *me*," Shana protests.

"Sure," Barry says. "They really love you. Especially since Merv became a board member."

"For God's sake, Shana," Sam Schwartz says, "they know Merv is one of Barry's top men. It's Baruch Goddard they're trying to reach through you."

"They like *me*," Shana says and looks ready to cry. "Aunt Sadie Jacoby always liked me."

Josh begins a little shuffling dance and sings, "That's friendship, friendship . . ."

"I'll always hate Aunt Sadie for what she did to Mama," Connie says. "She treated Mama like dirt. Just because Mama never cared about money. She always acted as if Mama was a fool. She always tried to make Papa think Mama was a fool."

"Your Aunt Sadie Jacoby can make herself a million bucks," Barry says to Shana, "she'll never touch our mother for real refinement."

"She's not *my* Aunt Sadie," Shana says.

Connie is sorry now that Shana is under attack. "Let's check the board again and cut out this silly talk," she says, and reaches for Shana's hand, but Shana won't leave with Connie. Saul goes with her instead, and Sam Schwartz leaves to take a rest on a bench. Shana stays, scratching at Anne's shoulder in a panic to which Anne responds automatically. What is the danger that she and Shana share? The danger of a family storm—and worse, the terrifying danger of invoking Barry's anger. Of being cut off by him. But Anne doesn't float in his orbit. She has put herself outside that constellation in which he is the source of all light and energy. She is here because her mother died. She has nothing to fear, she reminds herself, nothing to lose or gain from Barry.

She sees herself as a little girl clinging to Barry's leg, wound around his ankle like a monkey, astride his foot, coasting down a long, steep city street on roller skates. She is hanging on in a desperate, joyous, reckless faith that he will carry her backward into unseen risk and danger and bring her home safe. She bursts with love for his bravery and energy and generosity in sharing this exploit with her. He has made her part of his body. She belongs to him, the way his foot does. She is going wherever he goes, in a head-splitting, grinding, bumping moment of glory.

"Hitch up with me, Anne, and you'll go right to the top with me," he had said to her ten years later. But she was no longer with him all the way. He had become corny and embarrassing to her now that she was in her sophisticated teens. She winced at him. Young man on the vulgar make.

They were in a taxi riding through the garment district to the offices of his first business venture on his own. He had asked her to come in with him as his confidential secretary, and she had said yes, because jobs were hard to get even with the degree she had just earned. But she was filled with misgivings.

Anne mocked his style. "Stick with me, baby, and I'll put your name in lights."

Barry had momentarily lost his sense of humor. He threw himself back against the seat and seemed to study, out the window, the confusion of frenetic effort of the garment district streets. "Do you understand that mess out there?" He kept his head turned from her. "You pride yourself on your social views, you pride yourself on having all the answers. You're supposed to understand 'the system.' You're supposed to be a 'socialist.' Do you know what's going on out there?"

She doesn't answer.

He turns to her now to judge her response. "You think I'm a fool," he says. "Delusions of grandeur. But you have a surprise coming. I know how things work. I'm not wandering around with a head full of very pretty theories that will never work. And I'm going all the way. Right to the top."

Even then at her most arrogant and ignorant she didn't think him a fool. She had fallen in love with a boy in the movement, and fallen passionately in love with a theory of social organization that promised safety, growth, plenty for all mankind. *State and Revolution* had answered all problems, and in the seizure of power by the masses and in the withering away of the state, she clearly foresaw a paradise on earth—and soon. Why was Barry potchkying around with capitalism—that dying form? Why wasn't he lining up with the good guys? And why, just because it was the middle of a depression and she couldn't get a job anywhere else, was she yielding to his siren song of money and putting herself on the wrong side of the barricades?

Barry, watching for her response, apparently didn't like what he saw. She felt the heat of that ambition he had been eager to closely wrap them in together receding from him into something as cold as hatred. When they arrived at the office in which everything was new, down to the sharp smell of the freshly printed stationery, he took even decisions about the placement of letterheads out of her hands and she waited like a lump on his orders, his dictation, his requests for her to put through telephone calls. She felt emptied out, humiliated, confused. She thought then of quitting, but was afraid to confront him, and after a few hours he told her that she didn't seem suited to the work, standing behind her where they couldn't face one another, and she swallowed the fact that he had fired her.

Just as I do, Anne thinks to herself on the waiting room bench, Barry forgets or alters or lies about his history to make himself look good. What would be his version of how she had been hired and fired—if he even remembered it.

Next to her on the bench, Barry's head is thrown back, his long eyes decorated with heavy brows and thick black lashes are fixed on the wonderful arching rise of the vaulted space above. In the diffused, blue-tinted light, he has the face of a Persian prince. Since their no-history cuts off behind Mama and Papa like the fakery of a stage backdrop, any invention is possible. Maybe he has indeed come down from Persian princes.

"Beautiful, isn't it?" Anne says of the lighting—and of him.

He seems to come back to her from another place. He blinks. "Terribly inefficient use of a major piece of property." He scans the area, his eyes calculating and busy. She has seen that look before. Once he pinned it on a little boy's denim outfit her son Danny was wearing—an expensive gift from a friend. Barry had asked her to remove the terry-faced jacket and turned it inside out, handling it with quick, capable movement, while Danny stood patiently in his matching shorts waiting for his top to be returned.

"What did you pay for this?" Barry had said.

"I didn't. It was a gift."

"About five dollars, you think?"

His seriousness is appalling to her. "More, I imagine. I really don't know, Barry. It came from Lord & Taylor from a rich friend."

"I'm going to make that suit to sell for two ninety-eight," he said, and slipped it back on Danny's pliant body, "and earn money on it." He had said that as if he were besting her in some way.

She reaches for Shana's hand on her shoulder. "Let's see what Connie and Saul have found out, okay?"

Shana comes with her, passively, but when they are beyond being overheard, bursts out. "I can't stand all that ugliness. Ugliness. Ugliness." She shudders exaggeratedly.

"Oh, it's just family talk," Anne says, and to cool Shana down asks after Shana's husband Merv. But that's a mistake.

"Naturally," Shana says fiercely, "Barry had something for him to do. He'll be here soon." Shana's eyes narrow in a way that makes Anne fear for her, and for herself. Maybe all the Goddards are crazy? "He orders Merv around as if he owned him. You all like to act as if Merv belongs to the whole Goddard family."

Anne puts her arm around Shana. Whatever quarrels have pulled them apart, Anne is tied to Shana in ways she cannot explain even to herself. She never feels entirely separate from Shana.

"Don't," Anne says, "don't be upset."

Shana circles out of her area. "Stop *advising* me so much. I'm sick of it. You have this conception of yourself as Madame Wisdom.

Sickening." Another theatrical shudder. "Ugliness. Ugliness. Why can't you all be a little good-hearted? Why are you all so mean? There's nothing wrong with Mama's family or with the Jacobys. Just because they have a lot of money? Suddenly it's a crime to have money. People with money can be good. Money. Money. All my family ever talks about is money. Barry can't stand the Jacobys because they're as rich as he is. He can't stand them because Papa owes them something. Papa still owes Aunt Sadie a lousy couple of thousand dollars for his first store. It's eating Barry up. Aunt Sadie Jacoby doesn't need that money. She's got as much money as Baruch Goddard any day."

Anne is surprised. "Does she really?"

Shana turns on her violently. "How should I know? I don't go around counting other people's money. She's got the biggest resort in the country, so it stands to reason. But money doesn't matter to me the way it does to you and Connie and Josh and Saul. I won't even refer to Barry. *And* Jenny—for all her artistic sensitivity."

"To *me*?" Anne says.

"Yes, to you, to you. Just because you don't have any, doesn't mean you're not concerned with it."

"If you mean that I'm worried about where my next penny is coming from, I guess you're right."

Shana turns to Anne and shows her almond black eyes wet and gleaming. As if the quarrel has relieved her, she can now put her arm around Anne. "I can't believe she's gone," she whispers. "I keep expecting her to walk off the train with Jenny and Papa. I can't live without Mama. I can't. Nobody else loves me the way Mama does. She *appreciates* me."

Now Anne pulls away. She doesn't want to hear this, or suffer the image of herself, one among the rest of the Goddards, shoving and pushing for a center position to receive Mama's love and appreciation. Poor woman for whom her children were all one in her love, who couldn't reach a single kid's name without sliding down the whole scale—"Saul, Josh, Connie, Jenny, Barry, Shana, Hannah—*Hannahle*, come in the kitchen and have a little something," lying beyond reach at last in a coffin in the baggage car of The Silver Meteor. Time to stop being greedy kids. Anne is almost thirty and the rest are all older, some even *old*. Time to stop grabbing from one another.

The train is suddenly a living image for her, the baggage car at the end of a long string of trains, the compartments and sleeping berths, the dining car and smoky club cars, the disconnected talk, the couple of drunks lurching up and down the aisle, the debris in the coaches, the used paper cups piling up near the spilled water coolers, the crying babies and running kids and the sleeping passengers sprawled in the torturing discomfort of the cramped seats. Mama's body in the middle of that? And Jenny and Papa? Are they spending the long, boring ride up the flat deadly land-scape in silence, or in tears—or bickering? She sees Papa in the dining car. He kneads a pellet of bread into a hard object that he spins on the edge of the table. She sees Jenny sitting at a window. Jenny's soft hair has come loose from the twisted bun. She doesn't care. She is too sad. She gazes out the window with a mournful, unseeing stare. A man walks through the aisle, and without mean-ing to, she turns her exquisitely pretty hazel eyes toward him and smiles, sadly but invitingly.

Connie and Saul are running toward them. The train is finally arriving. The track number has been posted. Barry deploys the troops—Josh and Saul are to go to the lower level, he and Connie to one end of the upper-level gate, Shana and Anne at the other across the broad marble floor. Josh's wife Brenda clings to Barry's wife Pauline and both cling to Barry. Saul's wife Lil lopes around this group like a lost dog. She has already begun to spout tears. Barry strides impatiently ahead, shaking the rest of them off, only allowing Connie at his side. Nobody bothers to get Sam Schwartz from the bench he has found somewhere.

Shana's husband Merv has appeared just in time, and after the briefest consultation with Barry joins Shana and Anne. He offers himself as a rock to anchor themselves to. He gives each one a strong arm in a pin-striped de Pinna suit, but first kisses Anne full on the lips and squeezes her hands hard to show her that she need not feel alone and unattended because she's in the middle of a divorce and without a man; but Shana reacts as if Merv's intent was to irritate her and make her jealous. Is it impossible for Shana to imagine herself anywhere but at the center of any emotional exchange?

Shana says, breathlessly because they're walking very fast, "Just remember that you're not married to all the Goddard sisters, Merv, just to me."

Mervin frowns at what seems to him to be a coarse response to his delicate behavior, which he feels he all the more owes to Anne because Bill Morris, the husband she's divorcing, had been his best friend. It's because of him that Anne met Bill, and even if he doesn't share in the measure of irresponsibility that had brought Bill and Anne's marriage to this bad end, he does feel some pressure to make amends for males in general. He pats Anne's arm reassuringly. And perhaps Shana's, with the other hand?

Anne says, breathlessly, as they hurry to their post, "Among the American Indians, a man married first the oldest sister, then each of the younger, as they matured."

Merv says, "That leaves only you, which is fine with me."

Shana looks bewildered and alarmed.

"Joke. Joke," Anne says and makes a kissing motion with her lips toward Shana.

Shana is outraged. "Stop it, Anna," she says. "Stop it. What a time to act silly!"

First to reach the top of the moving stairs, Anne sees Papa below, leaning on Saul, his first-born, and on the step below that, Jenny with her back toward them, facing Josh, who is gazing upward into Jenny's eyes with pained love. Merv has dashed across the floor to get the others, and by the time Papa has floated to floor level, all are bunched together to receive the blessing of those who kissed Mama last.

Anne yields her front place to Barry. She does this without thinking, deferring to the strict protocol of family heirarchy. She expects her father to turn to her after he greets Barry, if for no better reason than that she's there, though she is also counting on an intensification, at a time of family loss, of his sentiment for his youngest child. He looks splendid in his Florida tan and lightweight dark suit, even if grief has "scribbled up" his face, as Mama would say. He passes Anne by, though much later in the day he will single her out for special comment. "Look, she's gray already," he will say, lifting a strand of Anne's lightly flecked hair. "If my baby is gray already, so where am I?"

In his late sixties, hardly gray at all, and with most of his hair still on his head, Anne's father, after greeting his son Barry in a silent, tearful embrace, turns from Barry to look blindly through Anne and step beyond her down the table of organization to the next most powerful family member. He falls sobbing on Barry's wife's shoulder, where she nestles him, while above his head Pauline

smiles her satisfaction around the group at the proper homage she
is being shown. In turn, Papa greets them all, but Anne considers
her share to be the least crumb of the emotional fare she had been
expecting as her due. By what right does she count on collecting?
By blood right. She is flesh of his flesh and of the flesh about to be
buried, and she knows all about that from the earliest days when
she slept with Mama and Papa and they "shook the bed." Doesn't
she have a right to his love even if she never gave him a penny?
Besides, she *has* given him a penny and would share anything with
him if he needed it, which he doesn't. Does he expect her to
compete with Barry and Pauline, moneywise, for God's sake?
Anne is enraged, before she has lifted her hand from the broad,
moving-stair banister, where stationed to receive Papa Goddard's
blessing, she has been ignored.

But not by Jenny. Jenny empties her grief into Anne's open
arms, the first she reaches. Anne receives her with overriding love,
kissing her, inhaling her sad, stale train smell, stroking her soft,
loose hair. There's something ludicrous about the way Jenny looks,
and not only because her hair is coming down and her lower lip
is trembling excessively. Anne involuntarily looks down to check
if Jenny's silk stockings are unhinged from her girdle and hanging
over her shoes like pirate's boots, because she knows that remov-
ing her girdle and letting her stockings hang is the first thing Jenny
does to get comfortable, but it's not that that's wrong. Jenny's
blouse has been put on inside out. In the ladies' room of the
uptown restaurant (spacious, old-fashioned decor, known for its
kosher cuisine and for its Upper West Side colorful habitués)
where they will lunch before moving on to the funeral parlor a few
blocks away, Anne helps her put the blouse to rights. The three
sisters handle Jenny tenderly. She is a precious object, the vessel
used to contain their mother's death—there must be no breakage
or spillage. They smooth Jenny's clothing, comb her hair, and help
her freshen her makeup. In the disinfectant-scented, cracked-
marble-and-worn-red-velvet ladies room, they wait upon Jenny
and wait for a ritual to be performed. Jenny must relate the last
ordeal before they join the others and order drinks and corned
beef sandwiches. It is the sisters who must hear the story of
Mama's last words first.

Sitting on a chipped gilt stool, her elbow propped on an un-
steady dressing table, Jenny cups her trembling jaw in her hand.

"So alone," she says. "So alone. Why did you all leave me to go through this all alone?" Is she watching herself in the mirror?

Her lids close slowly over her eyes. The most remarkable aspect of her remarkably pretty eyes is the lids. She can do anything with those lids, operating them at will as if they were simple pieces of machinery, like an awning. She can flutter her lashes at different levels and wink each eye independently of the other and even sleep with her lids partly open, the expressionless hazel iris gleaming through the fringes of her long lashes in a frightening simulation of death. Now she is pulling her lids slowly open again, as if by drawstring, somewhat unevenly.

Anne feels the flow of sympathy in the room disrupted. Her awareness of the subtle change in the atmosphere is a burden to her. She wishes she knew less about her sisters. She knows that Connie's reaction is, "Aha, she's starting already. It has to be *somebody's* fault. Even Mama's death she's trying to blame on somebody else. She has to be the only good one," and that Shana's reaction is the whine of raw nerve endings, "Don't tell me. I don't want to know how awful it was." Connie's eyes meet Anne's in judgmental, conspiratorial greeting, but Anne avoids the intelligence. She has already heard, in a long telephone conversation, Connie's story of how Connie went down to Miami to help during the last illness and was driven out by the ceaseless bickering of Papa and Jenny around Mama's sickbed.

She turns her back on Connie's verdict. Who needs it? And anyway, she has her own version of that family story.

Down in Miami to see Mama for what Anne knew would be the last time. Mama unexpectedly rallied enough to come home from the hospital. It was Mama herself who insisted on coming home and insisted also on plans to prepare, a few days later, a real Friday-night supper, gefilte fish and all. Anne chopped the fish, a job she had expected to find loathsome but which turned out to be pleasing because of the pearly iridescence of the raw fish flesh. They had had a good day, she and Mama, though Mama's alternating spurts of strength and frightening exhaustion were unnerving, and it took a bit of maneuvering for Anne to carry the burden of the cooking while leaving Mama with some sense that she was still in there, alive, counting for something, doing what she knew best to do. When Jenny arrived home for supper, she was sullen and mysteriously offended. Nobody knew where she had been. She was going through a bad time, between husbands, and in a dreary clandestine love affair with a married man down the street. She was negotiating for a tenth-rate concert series, but money was never Jenny's real problem. She always had Papa and Mama to take her in, whatever was going on. Shabbas supper wasn't much of a success, with Papa and Jenny mostly silent and Mama too ill to sit at the table at all.

The fight—the inevitable fight—erupted as they were finishing the dishes.

In the spotless, Formica-gleaming kitchen, Jenny, rubbing lotion on her hands, spread her long, strong fingers against the air to dry. "You wouldn't dream that these are the hands of a performing artist. If you didn't know of course. The way I allow myself to be misused with menial labor," and then switches, without warning, to a condemnation. "I must say, Anna, I really can't help saying to you that it was a most cruel and thoughtless thing for you to force Mama to make Friday-night supper."

"Jenny, I didn't *force* her, she wanted to. I was just trying to help her do what she wanted to."

"What she wanted to! What you wanted, you mean. Perfectly ridiculous. In the condition she's in."

"What difference does it make now?" Anne cries out in anguish at the impending, unavoidable death, but Jenny has heard something else.

"What difference does it make? What *difference?* Maybe not to you. Maybe it doesn't matter to you. But Papa and I have feelings you wouldn't understand. You've always been a coldhearted, selfish person saving all your feelings, whatever cold-fish feelings you have for your intellectual friends. At least they think they're intellectuals. God knows *what* they are."

Anne makes a terrible mistake. She responds. "Oh God!" she says. "Here we go. We're off. I knew it. I knew it would happen sooner or later."

"Is that so?" Jenny has begun to breathe deeply. "Is that so? These degrading scenes are easily avoidable. Just don't come here. Why don't you take off right now, take off and go back to the people you think are so fine and leave me and Mama and Papa alone in peace the way we should be? You certainly did force her. You certainly did. God knows why. You don't give a damn about Friday night. I know all about that new fellow you're carrying on with. . . ." It is as though Jenny is running a charged stick along Anne's nerve ends. ". . . He certainly isn't Jewish. For all we know he's Negro or Porto Reecan, not that I give a damn if you take up with a cat or a dog or a monkey's uncle, in the life you lead, that would probably be an improvement—anything would be an improvement. You're not kidding me, sister, not for a minute, I know perfectly well why you flew down to Miami pretending it was to see Mama when all the while the whole thing was an excuse to go to Atlanta with the scum of the earth and I don't need a psychiatrist or a private detective to work it all out either. Who do you think you are anyway? Some kind of superior being who can put over anything she pleases? One isn't quite that stupid, my dear, no, not quite. Holiday Inn! We have our ways of figuring things out and we're seldom wrong, let me tell you. Why don't you just pack up your suitcase and leave the way you came and good riddance to bad rubbish? Stop off in Atlanta again for all I care! If you think I'm breaking my heart over your affairs! With your little box and that disgusting thing lying in it! You think you can act any way at all you please and we'll go on as if nothing's happening and look the other way, but you have another thing coming, my dear. Picking up with the lowest of the low and pretending he's the I-don't-know-what—the savior of the world or something—it's too much for sensitive people to bear, I swear to God. I don't know how we put up with it."

Jenny pauses for breath and Anne hears herself say, "Why don't you try shutting up?"

Refueled, Jenny turns to an invisible judge. "You see? You see? Now you'll see what she's really made of. There's her much-vaunted love and devotion! There it is in a nutshell. I know very well what you think of me, my dear. I wasn't born yesterday. I'm well acquainted with your sentiments. The pity is I can see right inside your mean, cold, intellectual brain that you think is so superior, though where you think it's taking you God alone knows without a penny to your name. What's going to become of your two children, those poor darlings, will be *our* problem, of course, that's what it always comes down to, doesn't it, my dear?"

Anne yells, "What, what? What are you *talking* about, you lunatic!"

"That's right, that's right. Now it's all coming out. Now I'm crazy, of course. Now you'll see." She turns again to the invisible spectator who materializes into Papa in the kitchen doorway with the evening paper in one hand and his horn-rimmed reading glasses in the other, shaking his head sadly, condemningly, and maddeningly evenly, at both daughters.

"Sisters. Sisters." He too calls upon an invisible judge. "Look at them. They call themselves sisters."

"Yes, sisters, sisters." Jenny is clean out of control now. "Ask her. Ask her. Just ask her for a few sound facts. Miss Innocence. Little Miss Innocence. Doesn't know what anybody is talking about. Never heard of Atlanta. Dear, dear. Poor little dear. Misunderstood Betsy. With that thing in its little box all powdered up. Does she think we're so stupid?"

"I can't stand it," Anne yells. "I'm out of my mind for having anything to do with any of you." She is stung by Papa's undiscriminating blame. "Morons," she yells. "I was born into a pack of morons."

"Ah. Ah." Jenny is quieter now, but more deeply excited, and takes tremulous, sucking breaths while her eyes brim with satisfied tears. "Now, now she's beginning to be her real self. She's a born anti-Semite. She was anti-Semitic from the day she was born. God knows where it comes from, though she can pick up any infection from the muck she rolls in and calls by all kinds of high-minded names. Now she's even turning on her mother and father, not enough on her sisters and brothers, though she's quick enough to take, take, take, take whatever we grant her from the kindness of our open hearts, though her heart only knows solace for the scum of the earth, she'd rather worry about some murdering Arabs and Negroes than give a thought to her own kind just because we're not groveling in the dust begging for bread—or drugs and liquor more likely. Why don't you frequent flophouses instead of Holiday Inns? For all I care, my dear, you and your cohorts can all go hang yourselves on that highbrow New York magazine you're preening yourself about that nobody reads or understands or gives a plugged nickel for. Too fine, oh yes, much too fine to earn a good salary and the respect of the world on the kind of publication decent, intelligent, above-average people want to read and not all that muck and homosexuals. Gertrude Stein! For God's sake, there are plenty of good Jewish writers, though I don't expect Miss Big Brain here to know what a lowly person like ignorant me is talking about. We're supposed to be down on our knees, I suppose, giving thanks that you were able to leave your precious work, your precious work and your precious portable behind you to spare a few moments at your mother's bedside. Glory be to God! She didn't bring her work! The way you did the last time. If I hadn't taken those poor darlings to the beach they would have gone home as ' white as they arrived from that slum you think is such a perfect place to raise them."

Jenny suddenly pulls up short, and the rest comes out in a dignified and slow delivery. "Whatever you do, whatever you think of me, and whatever you say to me, my dear, isn't going to make an iota of difference so far as those two innocent children's place in my heart is concerned, though God alone knows what poison you're feeding them about an individual who's never been anything but a loving aunt and will never, never forget them no matter what their mother does, no matter what their mother is, and no matter what she may become. My generosity is beyond reproach."

What has defeated Anne before and will defeat her now is the ritual of the fight. Jenny's words and Anne's responses erupt from the same underground, uncontrollable fount. Anne hears other voices under the scalding splash of Jenny's words, a squeaking, sobbing pleading of little maddened, frightened creatures seeking shelter, but she cannot locate the spring in her nature which will release Jenny into the safety of silence. And in fact since Anne is really guilty of the Atlanta Holiday Inn part of Jenny's accusations, she feels somehow guilty of all of it and is obliged to dance out her part of the frenzied act.

Anne strides from the kitchen with contemptuous glances for Papa and Jenny. "It's ridiculous," she says, and is surprised to hear her voice shake. "There's nobody to talk to here. I'm not stooping to your level. I'm going to bed."

Anne shuts the door of Jenny's bedroom, which she is sharing with Jenny during her visit, but Jenny immediately pushes open the door with a bang. All the little perfume bottles jiggle on the dresser. The room is aseptically clean. The twin beds are made up as if for show in a department-store window, flat and hard as boards. No fooling around in those beds—no body smells, no nightmares, longings, ailments, long sieges of laziness. On the matching night tables are twin tole lamps, and on the open shelf below, tissues in matching tole containers. Does she know too much about

Jenny or not enough to reconcile the bare, polished surfaces and snowy-white curtained virginity of this room with the actual mess of Jenny's life? As if Jenny herself were as pure as her room, the sterile orderliness is a reproach to Anne's sooty New York life. How about that mess Anne lives in, stacked up against her beliefs in the possibility for order, peace, plenty for all mankind—with a program like that for the whole world, shouldn't she be able to keep one apartment orderly? She thinks of the room at the far end of the hall in her apartment which she calls "the work room," a clutter of books and papers, toys, bicycles, clothes to be taken to the laundry or waiting to be ironed or folded and put away, or for the kids to grow into or out of enough to be given away—the stuff to be mended—a broken record player, lamps to be rewired, good smashed pottery to be glued together someday, abandoned knitting, needlepoint, crocheting, all of it sitting there waiting for gestures on her part that would never come. Jenny would have thrown out the whole kit and kaboodle in a minute.

It's Anne she's throwing out. "Get out of my room. Get out. Get out of my room. With your high-and-mighty ways. Get the hell out," and she gathers Anne's few things from the perfectly arranged closet and the one dresser drawer Anne is using and shuts them into Anne's suitcase in a jumble. She shoves Anne and her suitcase and the fur jacket she had given Anne the day before out the door, assuring Anne, "I'm no Indian giver, my dear," while her lower lip trembles absurdly and the tears stream down her now ravaged face.

Anne has had enough. She wants to stop now. She would be glad to take her bag, call a cab, and be driven to the airport to fly out of this enclosed swamp of emotions to her own messy life, free of her family, if it were not for Mama, watching her from her bed in the other bedroom. Mama beckons Anne and motions with a finger to her lips for complicity. Anne puts down the suitcase and the fur jacket she now hates and knows she will abandon to "the work room" and goes to Mama's bedside. Exhaustion has robbed Mama's voice of any timbre—it makes a small, creaking sound.

"Hannahle, don't mind her, don't answer her. She's feeling bad these days. She won't even remember what she said in the morning. Take linens from the closet and make yourself a bed on the living-room couch, and whatever she says to you, don't answer. Papa knows where to find a pillow and blankets. He'll help you."

Is Mama on Jenny's side too? Anne abandons that line immediately. How weary Mama looks. It's peace Mama wants. We'll be running after her straight into her grave, crying, me, me, me.

Papa picks up Anne's suitcase. He is still on his first tack. "Sisters. Sisters. They call themselves sisters." He dramatically shakes his handsome head with its neatly cut and combed hair. He's very fond of his comment and repeats it and repeats it, with subtle variations of intonations.

Anne can't help laughing, and Papa turns on her furiously.

"It's funny by you? What's so funny? So what's so funny?" He turns on Mama too. "She has a very funny sense of humor. Your daughter has a wonderful sense of humor. Wonderful," and is quite abruptly in a suicidal despair which demands another manner, fiercely intimate. "You know what I think, my dear ones. I'll tell you frankly. I don't give two cents for the whole business of living, not two cents for the whole life from beginning to end and from top to bottom—and that's all I have to say."

He walks out with the suitcase, but walks directly back in again without it. "I wash my hands from the whole proposition. Finished. The end." Again he walks out and right back in. "And if a father is allowed to open his mouth in his own family to make a simple request, my request is we should have a little peace and quiet, if not for your father then please have a little respect for your sick mother. And if I have to take the law in my own hands, I'm fully prepared, fully prepared if I hear any more loud words and disrespectful words from one sister to another tonight under my roof, I'm picking up the telephone and calling the police, so help me God, even if it is my own flesh and blood and the whole neighborhood is talking about it," and he walks out.

Nobody takes *that* seriously. Mama's eyes remain closed behind the deeply carved lids. No sound from Jenny, shut into her room. Without opening her eyes, Mama says in her new, creaking voice, "Hannahle, I'm thirsty." In her accent, Mama has said, "I'm Thursday," and Anne is afraid she's going to laugh again. She controls it and says to both parents, because, of course, Papa has walked back in again, "I'm sorry about all this silliness. I'm sorry," but sounding out the childish words has brought on a bout of tears, and it has come out, "so-oo-oo-r-rry" in a comic wail. Papa is placated, and Anne goes off to the kitchen to get Mama something to drink.

The house is closed into an after-the-fight quiet, though Anne feels herself in a state of internal dishevelment which is acutely embarrassing and depressing. Alone in the kitchen, she remembers that Mama has eaten nothing, and she studies the open refrigerator for something suitable among the jars and bowls of gefilte fish and chicken soup and potted chicken and tsimmes, jellied and dead-looking now in antiseptic cold storage. There is a compote of dried fruit which has a strong smell of cinnamon, but it's worth a try. Anne makes a dainty arrangement on a silver tray—cloth napkin, silver spoon, compote in a cut-glass bowl, a mild mixture of orange juice with sugar and water in a goblet. It triggers another time for her.

She is a child, carrying a luncheon tray up the dark caged staircase of the first of the many public schools she attended, near the Brooklyn Navy Yard, in the service of the assistant principal, having been granted this exceptional honor because she is the smartest kid in her 2A class. She is small and skinny and her arms burn to drop the intolerable burden, but the way is apparently endless from the basement kitchen to the third-floor office, where a huge woman with a rat's-nest head of hair greets with icy anger the offering Anne has finally been able to put down on her desk.

"What's your name?" the woman asks.

"Anna Goddard," Anne says. "I mean *Anne* Goddard."

The assistant principal's glaring eyes astonish her. "What have you forgotten, Anne? Is your name Anne?"

"Yes," Anne says. "I forgot my name is Anne in school."

"Not that," the woman shouts in a fury. "What have you forgotten?"

Anne's heart swells as if it will kill her. *What* has she forgotten? The air is charged with possibilities and she plunges in and grabs for something she has been well drilled in.

"My name is Anne Goddard, Class 2A–1 . . ." and adds "Ma'am" as an effective afterthought.

"Not Ma'am. Ma'am is vulgar. Miss Adams. Repeat that."

"Miss Adams," Anne says.

"Repeat the entire sentence, you stupid girl," Miss Adams says in a terrible voice.

Anne's tongue has become an alien in her dry mouth, an enemy to subdue before she can speak. "Anna—I mean—Anne Goddard, Classroom 2A–1—" She garbles it slightly, but gets "Miss Adams" right, and at the frightening woman's nod, Anne turns to flee this inquisition, but Miss Adams says sharply, "Did I dismiss you, Anne?"

Anne stares, unbelieving. What's happening?

"I'm speaking to you, Anne," Miss Adams says. "Did I dismiss you?"

Desperately, Anne decides the correct answer is, "No, Miss Adams," and, inspired, adds, "I'm sorry, Miss Adams."

She senses that some of the acute danger has been dissipated by her clever, blind thrust, but waits, unblinking and unmoving, for whatever will come. She plans no further initiatives. Miss Adams lifts a huge mannish hand and beckons Anne with the curved finger of a witch. Is she going to be beaten and caged by the assistant principal? Miss Adams is wearing a long dress of heavy shiny stuff whose smell is horrible, but it is Miss Adams who pulls away from Anne's approach as though infection is alive on Anne's person.

Miss Adams points downward to the tray on her green-blottered desk. "How would you like to eat a lunch that looked like that?"

The question bristles with difficulties. Anne studies the problem. The setting for the food is neater and prettier than Anne is accustomed to at home, where food is ordinarily served in a slapdash way and the family eats in relays except for holiday meals, but what is on the tray seems disgusting to her—a milky green (green!) soup and a thin slice of dirt-brown meat (she assumes) in a thick, grayish gravy, and other foods she can't even identify. At the moment she is also sick to her stomach with apprehension, with the exhaustion of the physical effort of carrying the tray, and a generalized revulsion brought on daily by school smells. She's terrified that she's about to vomit all over Miss Adams's desk. She holds her quaking will to the problem of the right answer. The right answer, the answer acceptable to Miss Adams, the only kind of right answer there is, evades her, but right answers is what school is all about, they are what Anne excels in, and she is so dismayed and lost in this failure which has sneaked upon her without warning that she turns to God. It seems to her that he responds.

"Oh, yes, Miss Adams, I'd like to," she lies ardently.

God has betrayed her. Miss Adams becomes even angrier, and grasps Anne's skinny arms between fingers like hard rope and shakes Anne until Anne cries. How she has failed is not clear to

Anne, though the assistant principal makes it clear enough that it was wrong to slop the soup around and to forget the butter and to let the coffee get cold. Surely the last, at least, is Miss Adams's fault?

She stops herself from trying to think. The tray is thrust back into her hands. She submits.

"Take this disgusting mess down below and bring me another in proper condition. Five minutes! By my stopwatch! Or you'll take the consequences. March! March!"

In the basement kitchen, once again overwhelmed by *its* nauseating smells, she is nevertheless grateful to hear the Irish cook bear out her own theory. "The old witch will drive us all crazy." When she puts a newly prepared tray in Anne's hands, she advises, "Hold it straight, girl, and run, run."

How strange that the scene cuts off for Anne at that point. She knows she vomited as soon as she got home safe to Mama, and that she stayed away from school for the rest of that week. The beginning of that routine, was it? How blissful to pull out, to lie in bed, to read, gobbling up mysteries and penny candy in sickening gulps, to daydream, to be at hand for any stray shaft of love breaking out of Mama's busy day, or to cut out altogether, without even Mama knowing, to roam the streets and hole up in a library and appear at home at the end of the day, worn out and starving, just as if she had really gone off to school.

She would pull out now if she could, but she cannot find a way to remove herself from the ridiculous, heartbreaking family scene without making things worse. Staring into the refrigerator at the jars and bowls of food that earlier in the day she had felt so good about, she allows herself to be overcome by theatrical Goddard despair and closes the door on her earlier labors at good family feeling as if on a major intellectual failure.

Mama can't eat the compote. She sips a little syrup and a drop of orange juice, while her eyes, brightly curious, search Anne's face. Unprepared for what Mama whispers, Anne thinks she has misheard her.

"Is it a real romance?" Mama asks.

Anne says nothing.

"Your sweetheart in Atlanta? Is he a real lover? Are you happy?"

The old-fashioned words confuse her. How is she to discuss Guy Rossiter with Mama? Yet how simple—and how truthful—to just say yes to Mama's questions. What had happened between Anne and Guy in the plush new Holiday Inn, with its smorgasbord of bathroom gadgets and dimmer-control lights and twenty-five-cent jiggling machine that shook the bed the way Mama and Papa used to, had to be romance, love, happiness. What else could it be? But she is afraid to think so, afraid to say "Yes." That would be committing herself to faith in love, in romance, believing like a fool that happiness could really exist out there, to hand, to *her* hand, to grasp from the unlikely source of New-England-correct, comfortably rich, handsome, distinguished man of letters Guy Rossiter, her boss, on top of the rest, and twenty years older than she—and an ex-alcoholic and notorious womanizer. Try explaining all that to Mama.

"I want you should have it," Mama whispers. "A real romance. Wherever it comes from. Doesn't matter from where. You shouldn't listen to Jenny. Listen to your own heart. If it comes out good, everybody will be free with their compliments, if it comes out no good—nothing but criticism and I told you so. Nothing succeeds like success. Advice is cheap with them. You're the one who'll pay, whether it's good or bad. Take, Hannahle, it's your right. In this life, all we get is a little piece of happiness. Don't make a mistake when it comes. Take. Take. God shines on such selfishness."

Released by Mama's words, hope for herself and Guy rises in Anne's chest—a great bird in throbbing, painful, wonderfully exciting flight—and lodges in her throat like nausea.

Mama's long whispering speech has exhausted her. She makes a grimace and motions away the fruit. "I have a terrible heartburn. Maybe a little plain water, a little pure water to drink? Bring me, Hannahle, please."

And these have been almost her last words to Jenny, too. The sisters listen in silence, in the ladies' room, while Jenny repeats the cherished last words.

"I keep hearing her asking me for water, again and again. I can't get the words out of my mind. 'A drop of pure water, Jenny, please.' I can't close my eyes without seeing her lying in the hospital bed with her mouth open and the water sitting there on the bottom of her mouth, the little drop I gave her, staying there in a little pool on the bottom of her mouth. She didn't have the strength to swallow it. '*Ich kenn nisht mehr oishalten,*' she said— and then she was gone."

The violent trembling of Jenny's jaw overwhelms her and she

sobs, rattling the frail table on which her elbow rests. The three sisters close about her to comfort her and one another, but Anne enters the circle abstracted from the despair she should be feeling. All her energy is flowing to a solution of an exact rendition of the last words. She searches among alternatives as if salvation—hers or Mama's—will be rated against the skill she displays in this last act of communication. *I can't hold out? I cannot endure it any longer? I can't stand any more?*

III

M ama Goddard is sitting in
a wheelchair at the far end of the beach, in the shade of the palm
trees, singing.

Anne has left for New York, following a morning-after recon-
ciliation with Jenny. A happy morning, with Mama feeling well
and sitting up at the dinette table, though she doesn't want to eat
any of the lox and onion and egg that Jenny prepares. Papa too is
in a rare mood of tenderness. He confides a romantic account of
the first time he saw Mama, sitting at her machine in the cramped
furriers' shop in Paris where they had found jobs, laughing mis-
chievously behind her hand, whispering to the other girls, keeping
her bright eyes on him.

"From that moment, I was stuck to her," he says. "Nothing
could drag me away, for a whole lifetime."

The pressure of loss leads him to exaggeration, but Mama enjoys
it.

He launches an expansive plan for a trip to England, to all the
places he and Mama knew when they were young. "We'll look at
Whitechapel, again, Feigele. It's time we should enjoy a little. We
have many years ahead yet. Now you're feeling well again, now's
the time."

Mama's eyes shine like a girl's, but by the afternoon she is back
in bed, Papa is morose, Anne is gone, and Jenny is nervously
cleaning. In the stale air conditioning of her bedroom, Mama feels
that she will choke to death. She is tormented by a longing for the

sea. Jenny and Papa find her crying, and she tells them that she is crying to be by the sea, and they go into a flurry of arrangements to rent a wheelchair (to be delivered to an efficiency apartment at the beach) and a limousine to get them there. They want to give Mama anything she wants now, since she has always wanted so little.

But even now, down on the sand, Mama Goddard is frustrated in her thirst for the sea. She is too far back on the broad beach to see the water, and the noises in her head confuse and drown out the sound of the surf, though she smells the sea in the humid air. Jenny sits nearby in a lounge chair, reading and dozing, and so long as Jenny is occupied with herself, Mama is pleased to have her, though something Jenny is wearing is making Mama very sick. Imprisoned in the plastic heels of Jenny's sandals are two vividly colored birds. Mama can't look at the shoes, and when Jenny rouses herself to fuss over Mama, bringing the poor birds closer, Mama becomes so distraught, she seems mad to Jenny.

Jenny has been trying to tie a kerchief around Mama Goddard's wildly blowing hair, but Mama pushes Jenny away as if Jenny is a stranger to her. For a second, Jenny is frightened by Mama's strange unmanageability. She goes back to her chair and watches Mama, who is singing with extravagant gestures and facial expressions, her loose mouth grotesquely opened wide, and her eyes glowing insanely. The wind instantly eats up the faint sounds she makes, and Jenny hears nothing, like a silent movie.

It is intolerably hot and Jenny tries to persuade Mama to return to the air-conditioned apartment, but Mama becomes very agitated, and Jenny thinks that perhaps it would be good for Mama to be left alone to calm down while Jenny takes a few-minute break. A cool drink in a snack bar away from the heat and the relentless light would be a relief.

Mama Goddard is happy to be left alone. She is sorry that the birds have come between her and Jenny. She loves Jenny and she would love to please her. She has even sung a song especially for her, a song that Jenny used to sing at the piano with the tears streaming down her cheeks just because some foolish young man wouldn't marry her. But "Lover Come Back to Me" is not one of Mama's favorites, and she was glad to finish with it. She likes best songs that groups of people sing together. She sings "La Marseillaise" and "The Internationale" and "James Madison High/With fair vision and confidence wrought/On you we rely . . ." till the words give out and she la-la-las the delightful waltz. She sings "The Star-Spangled Banner" and "God Save Our Gracious Queen" and the Yiddish song for the fallen martyrs. She believes that she is performing wonderfully—that her tones float loud and true into the oppressive air. She feels that her body may easily follow, soaring above the people suntanning on the beach, and above the tall palms bending and swishing in the heavy breeze. She knows that she has the power to be in her chair and everywhere else at once. Her thoughts wing about. Her mind is light and empty but crowded with this lightness, like a sea filled with darting fish and waving sea flowers, amorphous delicate dreams of ideas she cannot quite catch and hold firmly but which are as real to her as the sea she can neither see nor hear.

Soon she must get up and walk down to the water's edge, but first she must carry newborn Hannahle safely home from the hospital. She is running from the hospital as if it were a prison. The spring air is fresh; she hears a trolley car rumbling by, and the shouting of kids playing in the street. She is elated by her escape. She had halfheartedly tried to abort this baby, but it has survived, and she too has survived the hospital and its drugs and needles and its killing coldness, though God alone knows what they have done to her there. She has never felt so weak after a birth. Barry, smelling of spicy sweat and street dirt, rushes upon her from a game. "What'd you buy, Mom? Hey, what've you got that's good?" He's tall and strong for his years, and his fierce energy totters her. She shouts at him but he persists, shoving his hard, black head at her arms carrying the package. She shows him the tiny, round, purplish face. He turns away in disgust. "Yicch, another one? I thought it was apples."

She sees him sitting at the kitchen table in the upstairs apartment of the two-family house they have rented in the upper Bronx. He is a grown young man. He already has a very good job. He earns more money than all the rest put together. Milk drips down his face, coagulating at the tip of his nose and in the cleft of his chin. At the climax of a quarrel Jenny has dashed a glass of milk in his face. What was the quarrel about? He sits perfectly still, in a silence like a drama. She expects him to get up and kill Jenny, but all he does is reach for the kitchen towel Mama is holding and wipe his face. He gives Jenny a terrible look and walks out. It is

Jenny who becomes hysterical. She screams, "Don't look at me, don't look at me. It's your fault. It's your fault."

She sees Barry now. Baruch Goddard. He is a powerful, important man. She sees him in a dark suit and a topcoat and a brimmed hat, and on his face is a slight, composed smile to help him control the same energy he had when he was a boy. He is pretending he is a big important man.

What was her fault?

She sees white-sheeted figures in the night; the night hints of mysterious, evil passions. If she looks the other way, they will go away. On the ocean floor there are black, sharp-toothed, floating shapes. Nothing is evil between her and her smooth-bodied husband. He is a silken sheet against her skin. Even now any woman on the beach, from the youngest to the oldest, wants him. Her lover. However small he likes to make her look in other people's eyes, she knows what they have shared. She feels joyous and strong and knows that she will live forever. They will travel to England. What worries her is the food on the ship. Will she be able to tolerate the food on the ship, with her terrible heartburn? And what about Jenny? Jenny musn't wear those shoes. Poor Jenny has nobody right now. She sees Jenny asleep with her lids slightly parted and the glistening dead iris showing between the lashes. She sees Saul behind the crisscrossed screening of the visitors' room in the jail. Seventeen dollars. He didn't know how to be a thief in this country. She sees him on the patio of his house with his busybody wife. Are those his children? No, they're his grandchildren. No, they're Josh's children. Josh is making a fool of himself entertaining them. No, she's mixed up. She tries to count her children and their children and their children, but she comes to a stop with Jenny. What will happen to Jenny? She has nobody. She was too beautiful. Once again the mysterious, white-sheeted, evil night descends. She sees Jenny smiling a provocative smile at strange men she doesn't want. Why does Jenny do that? She protects Jenny, a young girl still in school, from Papa's punishing hand. She defies Papa, putting her body between him and Joshua, who grins, showing brilliant teeth and desperate eyes. She hides timid, wrongdoing Saul under the bedcovers until Papa's rage has cooled down. She holds Barry's hard black head against her breast to shield him from Papa's leather strap. "But we won, Papa, we won!" Barry screams, bleeding from the gang fight, but triumphant. Barry believes that winning should save him from punishment. "No hooligans in my house," Papa yells. "No tramps in my house," he yells at Connie and Jenny. Papa thought that yelling was the way to be a good father. In the scuffle to protect Barry, she falls and breaks her arm. She laughs. That was a good one on Papa.

She sings, "Hail, hail, the gang's all here, what the hell do we care, what the hell do we care. . . ."

She thinks how she overheard Papa's sister, Sadie Jacoby, talking to Papa, very angry because Mama is pregnant again. "Tell your Feigele it's enough already. Any cat can have kittens." It burns. She says it aloud now. "Any cat can have kittens." It burns again. "Any cat can have kittens." It will never stop burning. That was Baruch who would be born. That was Baruch Sadie Jacoby was dismissing so scornfully. It was her whole life.

Now is the time to get up and walk to the sea. She sings, "Oh how I hate to get up in the morning, oh how I love to remain in bed . . ."

A little creature comes close, touches her with a cool, spidery finger, singsongs, "Old lady, old lady, crazy old lady," and dashes out of reach in front of her. Is he one of her children, her grandchildren, her great-grandchildren? In the shimmering, dazzling sunlight, he is a black stick figure, dancing a mocking, finger-pointing jig, all joints and skinny arms and legs, like a giant black grasshopper. She laughs with delight at his dance. If he's Negro she's sorry for him. They're the next to be exterminated. If she had stayed in Poland she would have been exterminated. She smells the acrid scent of insect spray and sees cockroaches fleeing blindly into the baseboard of an ugly, cracked wall. Why did they move so many times, from one miserable flat to the next? Three months' concession and a painting. She hears the sound of a stick being run against the guard rails of the windows of their basement flat and smells the sickening odor of the Ward Bakery bread-factory ovens a few blocks away. At a railroad siding, women with young bodies, useful bodies, removed their clothing before entering the gas showers. What kind of men drove beautiful bodies to the showers? That was a terrible waste. The same kind of men could go to a dump, a bargain basement, a pushcart, and search for an old spoon, a pot, chicken wire, a brass bell. The gold teeth were saved.

The little whirling devil of a Negro boy has gone away. She

should have asked him to help her walk to the ocean. She doesn't
care whether he's a grandchild or not. She's lost track of them.
Some she knows, but some she could pass on the street and not
recognize—she could walk right by, if she could still walk. She will
float. She is floating. She's a raft, on a pearly ocean. The water is
so pure and still, she can see to the bottom of the sea floor. She
sings, "Sailing, sailing, over the ocean blue . . ." Connie floats
silently alongside, watching her with grave, loving eyes. Her oldest daughter. Her good friend. She embraces Connie and Connie
kisses her with soft, fragrant lips. Saul and Joshua are floundering
in the water. She pulls them safely onto the raft and hugs them
both closely to her, her first three children, and she feels strong,
as she did then when she thought she could contend with anything. She holds Connie in her lap, a round-faced, solemn child,
and Saul and Joshua stand like little men in their good knicker suits
and their long curls—stand straight at her side though the raft
lurches, as the boat did, and she is afraid she will vomit. Saul is
made of silk. Her firstborn. He will grow up to be a prince. Everything about him is fine, hushed, velvety. She turns his soft hair
around her finger into a perfect curl. Papa knocked Saul around
too much. He thought he was being a good father, but she knew
better. Why did she let him?

All her children are swimming in the sea. The calm waters are
gone and she is terrified for them, thrashing about in the enormous, toppling waves. She works to keep the raft intact, to pull her
children aboard. She pulls Jenny in first, with her paper-white face
and with her hair streaming flat back from her round, perfectly
shaped head. She shouts encouragement to Hannahle to keep her
head above the waves and she listens, paddling like a desperate
little dog. She pulls Shana in, who laughs and rolls about as if in
a game until she rolls out again into the strangling waves. She pulls
Baruch in and Barry ties them all together with a heavy rope. He
has gathered them all somehow, but now the raft is losing pieces
and the sea is full of others, struggling like them. Where is Papa?
She must relieve him at the store. She hurries, hurries through the
streets under the el with the little pots and jars of hot food for
Papa's dinner. Her head pulls her exhausted body, leading her as
a horse's head does. She sings, "Heigh-ho, Silver, A-a-wa-a-y," just
the way they do it on television. She will go to heaven like that,
a heaven where she will see again her mother and father and her

sister Dina in her girlhood hair, before the *sheitel.*

She must get up now. She has something wonderful to tell Papa. At last he can stop being nervous and dissatisfied and stop shaking his foot when he sits and talks to strangers, making himself big in their eyes. There is a thrilling idea pressing to burst from her head, a plan about how they will live now that she is so strong and will live forever. She must tell it to Barry too. He's clever and will know how to work it out. It's a plan for everybody, for everybody's happiness, tearing out of her chest in swirling mists of pain and glory. Here, here he comes—her lover, her man, running toward her with his hand holding his chest. But it is her chest that is being torn open for this birth, this burning vision, not his. He must put his hand on her breast quickly, quickly, before the clanging noises of sirens and a roaring sea become too loud for him to hear her.

IV

S ix years after Mama died
Papa Goddard married again. Mama had always said that there
were plenty of women who wanted him. She was right. He let the
most determined one win the prize—Bessie, a woman some years
younger than he, loud and lively, with a good income and the
talent and energy to steer him around the dance floor of the cruise
ship on which they met. The couple won the golden-age waltz and
rhumba contests. Dazzled and breathless, Papa married Bessie
when the ship reached England, where Bessie lived, before any of
the Goddards had viewed the bride or offered up an opinion on
her suitability.

"My God!" Anne reacts to the first sight of Bessie, Papa's new
wife, with disbelief. "She's the second lead in a Yiddish musical
comedy. The relentlessly comic one. Color coordinated!"

Guy, on the other hand, is delighted. He loves colorfulness and
comic ridiculousness in the Jewish family he's married into.

A family party is being held at Shana and Merv's to greet the
happy couple on their arrival from Europe. Anne and Guy's responsibility to the festivities is to pick up Papa and his wife at the
pier, see them through customs, and deliver them to Long Island,
where as many of Papa's children as are gathered on the East
Coast will be present to grudgingly bless the union.

Papa's new wife maneuvers the dangers of the gangplank in
spike heels, teetering skillfully against the constraints of the fuss
and bind of her "outfit"—all gunmetal-colored: shoes, stockings,
suit, blouse, hat, bag, gloves, and scarf, including the costume

jewelry on her throat, wrists, and ears. Everything about her swings, rings—bursts its bounds. Her plentiful flesh puffs out in heroic liberation wherever it can escape its metallic prison. Her voice, in effusive greeting, is also made of brass. She has small, merry eyes in a snoutish face, heavy with makeup.

Papa appears different to Anne. He looks healthy enough and smiles a lot, but it's a new nervous smile and he seems physically smaller at Bessie's side.

In the car on the trip out to Long Island to Shana and Merv's, Bessie establishes an instant intimacy with Anne.

"Too thin, my love," she says, weighing Anne's slender body disapprovingly with her clever little eyes. "I know it's the fashion, but you're getting on now. Time to put a little flesh on your bones. Musn't play the little girl too long."

She embraces her own corseted body, smoothing the steely lines of her solid middle and ending with congratulatory pats for the escaping flesh ballooning at her low-cut blouse. Little cushions also blow up around the thin T-straps cutting into the softness of her instep.

She's pleased with Guy's courtliness and his air of amused and genial interest in her views, and so forgets that Papa has told her that Anne is "married to a goy, but a better person you can't find in this world."

"Every Jewish family should live as well as this," Anne hears her confiding to Guy about Merv and Shana's impressive, modern house.

Guy laughs. "And the rest of the world go hang?"

Bessie listens to his laugh, not his words, and beams. She rushes to unpack, to display the dance trophies she and Papa have won.

Guy can barely contain his delight in Bessie. He alone champions the notion that she is entertaining. Anne knows that he is storing away Bessie's responses to add to his anecdote collection of life among his Jewish relatives.

"You have to admit," Barry says, choosing his words judiciously, as if he were negotiating a sensitive deal, "you have to admit that the woman has a lot of energy."

Bessie and Papa have both gone up the stairs of the split-level ranch, to a guest room, to freshen up.

"Rhumba!" Shana says, astounded. "Whoever knew Papa could even dance!"

She and Anne giggle hysterically. The glasses on the tray Anne is holding are threatened.

"Careful," Barry says, but breaks into laughter himself.

"All I could think about," Shana says, whispering and gasping, "at the first look, was how Mama would have mimicked her."

"He might have waited a bit before he married her," Jenny says, when she stops laughing. "I fail to see the necessity, at their age, to rush into marriage. He could have waited at least until we all met her."

Barry says, "And then thought better of it?" and adds, with an edge of pride, "It wouldn't have made any difference. Papa knows his own mind."

"He's nothing but a stubborn ox," Jenny says, and without transition, in a choked voice, "Thank God Connie couldn't make it east. The sight of that woman would kill Connie. Nobody loved Mama more than Connie."

"Come now," Guy says, teasing these grown-up children. "She's a very amusing stepmother."

"Stepmother!" Jenny is outraged. "Please, don't use any form of the word mother in connection with her."

"Sh," Shana warns, busy arranging little dishes of pickled herring and black olives on a huge coffee table. "This is supposed to be a party. Let's be generous, even if it kills us."

"It very well may," Anne says. "And I may kill Guy long before that."

Guy smiles at her, winks, mouths "stepmother" again, and refuses Merv's offer of a drink.

"You're all taking this much too seriously," Merv says. "An old man is entitled to his childish fancies."

"Who are you calling an old man?" Shana scolds her husband.

"*I* think Bessie's a delightful person," Barry's wife Pauline says, joining Guy in establishing the rights of the in-laws to a charming personality equal to any old Goddard.

Bessie owns a chain of millinery shops in London, but she leaves most of the running of the shops to her son and daughter. The couple plan to live in Bessie's flat in London for six months of the year and divide the other half between a residence hotel on the Upper West Side of Manhattan and one on the south end of Miami Beach. Between them, their combined income allows them to enjoy a pleasantly luxurious life. Barry is giving Papa whatever he asks for these days.

At first all goes splendidly. Bessie enjoys a lively environment. They trot about, crossing oceans often, and Papa's cheerful letters stream in from far away.

June 9, 1956

Dearest Hanna and Gi.

I. am wery sory for not wrighten Sooner, I. am in London for 3 weeks and cant setteld yet.

I. cam to London Sunday mornig 1130 A.M.*, I. Left N. York Saterdey 7 ackloc* P.M.*, I. had a wonderful trip it Took only ower-naet non Stop., and nating was disterbem.*

I. had a wonderful walcome when I. cam to London. Last Week We went to Bar miztve Party we angoert wery match. and 2 weeks Later we gat a weding Party and Tats is way I. am pasing the days.

from me I. feel fine and starting make Plans to cam home. I. wil be Home for Holiday I. am Leaving Sam time in Aug 16 or 25.

Hoping you all in Best of Health and Let me Know if you went for you wacation. with Low and Kises to your Both and the Children, special the Litele Gentelman, my grand Son.

Pap

Best regard from Bessie

Everything about the letter pleases Guy—the hesitant penmanship with its quavering ambiguous connections, turning simplicities into charming puzzles, and the funny phonetic spelling. He passes the letter around for Anne and Guy's friends to read. Anne laughs with them, but she makes a point of misplacing Papa's next letter.

London
August 11, 1956

My dear Hanna,

received your letter of July 19 and was wery glad to hear from you that you on you Holidy Like They Said in England this min on you wacaiton.

This is the first Letter Since I received from you for my stay 3 monats in London.

But is Still Better from nating

I. am Hoping you Head a wonderful time and made the children wery Good

from me I head 1 wonderful Time in London I was thuru the Soomer on the Sea in Brighton and auther plases. Tank God for This. and now, I am Leaving for Home on Aug 23 wit the Queen Elizabeth and I. wil be Home Aug the 28 and to See you all.

it is 2 week more and I. will Be Back Home.

Thats is all for now. my Daer To Let you Know.

Wit Lov and Kises to you all God Bless you all.

Pap

Regards from Bessie.

It is during the winter months in Miami that the bickering begins. Papa is astounded. He has had no preparation in his life with Mama for living with a demanding woman.

Miami Beach
February 12, 1957

Dear Hanna & Gi,

Pardon me for not ansering your letter Sooner it Took me acaple weeks Longer to anser you The Resen first I gat for acaple weeks Sam Schwartz and Connie and then Jenny wit her neu swithart and Saul for acaple days alon

We alwas Had company and The Time went away.

Special neus nat match to wright to you my Dear it is Gattin too match the good thing Spendin the time Sitin on the beach and looking on the Beach. we all know miami Beach. I. dont feel So good abut miami all together. and special when I. am all alon with jest Bessie. wen the children hear is diffrint ewry-day they cam ower and we sitin talkin but cams time thay gat to go Home.

I. would Like to Hear from you a litele.

Wit low and kises to you all, and special the Litele gentel Man.
God bless you all

Pap

The news that Bessie has flown back to London without Papa
comes via the family. Papa's next letter doesn't mention it.

March 6, 1957

My dear Hanna,

*You letter was Receved Promptly and was a Real Trit for me to
hear from you. I. cant tel you how match I. angoet you letter.*

*abut me I. Hewent match to wright. For the Last capele week I.
dont feel So Good the way I. shuld feeling. I. wold Like to be back in
N.Y. but I. Gat to wait Til the Whether wil be more Spring. Another
3 weeks and I. wil be in N.Y. on April 1 and I. wil See you.*

*Hoping you wit Gi and the children feeling in Best of Healt and
To See you all.*

Wit my best Low and Kises to you all.

And God Bless you all

from Pap and Grand Pa.

It seems there's another woman. Anne gets this detail also
via the family. Did Papa take up with her before Bessie left?
Nobody knows. The point is crucial, since it is on this stake that
blame may be impaled, but it is never cleared up, even after
Papa returns to New York. His version is that Bessie returned
alone because a number of "do's" were scheduled in London
which she wouldn't have missed for the world—a graduation, a
bar mitzvah and a wedding—and Papa didn't go along because
he wasn't feeling well. "Enough with the do's already," he says.
"By me it's nothing special. I can do without." He twinkles at
his clever pun.

Jenny has seen the other woman with her own eyes. Jenny and
her new husband have accidentally run into Papa and the new
woman at the Sixth Avenue Delicatessen. Her name is Rachel, she
is a Jewish refugee from Soviet Budapest, she is little, soft-spoken,

as young as Jenny and as pretty—a darling in a chic foreign style
that is impossible to ridicule.

"This is no Bessie," Jenny says. She lowers her lids in her remarkably slow, uneven way, and shudders. "Anna, he's going to make
a fool of himself with this woman."

Papa has decided that he has made a fool of himself by marrying
Bessie. He wants a divorce, but he feels he must first canvass his
children for permission. As if he were a head of state conducting
secret negotiations, his method is all stratagems and intrigue. He
is lying to everyone about everything. Bessie has been told nothing, and his children are being told whatever seems useful to him
at the moment. The general assumption is that he's seeing Rachel
every evening, since his evenings are always occupied. Nobody
presses him for explanations, but there are many consultations out
of his hearing, and by the time Papa comes to Anne with his moral
problem, she has had some preparation.

Only Barry refuses to discuss it. In an interval following cocktails
and chopped liver in the form of a snake with a bright green eye,
and before sitting down to dinner, Barry walks Anne across the
elegantly wide sweep of his lawn, bordered with spring-flowering
shrubs, to the duplex dollhouse he has had built for his four daughters. They both understand that a quarrel has been avoided by his
excluding her from the tour he had given the others of his new
bomb shelter, but his diplomacy has not entirely cleared the politi-
cally charged air that seems to always surround them now, flashing
warnings on the horizon.

"I know you have the good sense to stay out of this thing about
Papa," he says. "Not like the rest of the family magpies. It's the old
man's business, nobody else's."

She should be pleased at being singled out for superior family
performance, but she is not. Have they reached a territory where
it is no longer possible to be pleased with one another about
anything? Social disgust lies like a slug over all their encounters.
They are equally disgusted with one another, she and Barry, but
in her mind the two reactions are unequal. She's right, and he is
wrong. She's sure about that, in general at least, even if the underpinnings of her political positions have been so knocked about by
real events that the shape they now take is no longer the simple
structure she had built with such absolute conviction in her teens.
Not *absolute*, perhaps.

She remembers a demonstration against the showing of an anti-Soviet film years ago. The decision had been to picket the film to the point of mass arrests, if necessary. Anne, in a fever of indecision, hesitates on the sidelines, unwilling to leave, but unable to join the hundred or so others who are being led off the line into paddy wagons. Her young comrades use words like that—quite dazzling—paddy wagon and clink—even if they do make her uncomfortable and want to laugh, when they chant "Cossack! Cossack!" at the mostly Irish cops rounding up the pickets. She tells herself that it's not jail she fears but the shock it would be for Mama, just recovering from her long illness.

Anne's boyfriend, Bill, is in charge of the protest action—his first major party assignment. Anne is there because of him, and though he tries not to single her out, he surprises himself to discover that he wants to protect her, and that he'd be happier if she weren't there at all. His directives were to keep the line filled as quickly as the police empty it, but he doesn't wave her forward. What if the police get rough with her? It would be intolerable for him to see them bearing down on her fragile bones.

In the excitement and confusion of the scene, Anne's awareness of him as a nice guy who interests her enough to date is heightened into amazement and overwhelming admiration. He is a tall, physically powerful young man with black kinky hair growing out of a deep V on a wrinkled forehead. Everything on his huge face is out of line, and the large, irregular features should make him ugly, but tonight the exaltation and vivid intelligence of his commanding eyes attracts irresistibly. His real name is Morris Levy. He is Bill because he has taken the party name of William Morris. Anne doesn't know that Bill is hesitantly shielding her. She believes it's her own cowardice, unworthiness, "lack of discipline" that lets her slip behind each time the mass surges ahead. In the press of signs and flags and banners and bodies and impassioned faces and hoarse cries, she shouts with her comrades, "Defend the workers' state! Defend the workers' state! Join the line! Join the line!" but then shrinks back and withholds her body. Across the wide Bronx avenue are counterdemonstrators, restrained by stanchions and more police. They chant, "Stalinism is state murder! No defense for Stalinism!" and to add to her confusion two of her old high-school crowd are among them, carrying a banner with the same slogans.

"Who are *they?*" Anne asks the air around her.

"Trotskyites." The boy at her side almost spits the word, and starts a new chant, "Police dogs! Police dogs!" but nobody takes it up, and he desists.

She doesn't see Barry until he's upon her, pulling her away. "You crazy kid. What the hell are you doing here?"

She yields, protesting, but in fact grateful.

"Get home! What do you think you're doing in the middle of this mess? Of all the goddamn idiot ideas! It's not even a good movie. Nobody would go to see it if you weren't giving it all this publicity. What are you trying to do—kill Mama and Papa?"

Okay, to think back on it is to see it as absurdity. But it was deadly serious then. She and Bill mulled over the evening and its deeper meanings for them until they talked themselves into marrying, to save her from the pernicious bourgeois influence of Barry and his blossoming factories.

Barry's reputation is that he has made his fortune by a genius for production methods. Even now, years later, she insists that he's rich because he exploits, because he's chosen the way of social evildoing. Isn't that what industrial genius is all about? He has chosen to limit his sights to profits above all other considerations. The figures have to come out right; that's all that counts.

She has no right to judge him, particularly since her own record isn't spotless. She has made a good life for herself with Guy Rossiter in every way, and first of all financially. She loves Guy for himself she thinks, as she didn't love Bill Morris for *himself*—Morris Levy—but for the romantic, revolutionary, dedicated man-of-the-people costume he had put on like coveralls; but how to separate Guy "himself"—or "herself"—from the ambience and the meaning of Guy's money and the power of Guy's position in intellectual circles? Hadn't *her* admission to the rare air of that life fallen into her lap through her marriage to Guy? Is she going too far now? Her work on the magazine is recognized as outstanding, and her own articles are distinguished enough to have been collected in a book. *Shadows and Images: Women in American Fiction.* By Anne Goddard. On the book jacket, the information that "Anne Goddard is the wife of the distinguished writer, editor, and publisher Guy Rossiter. They live in New York City with their two children." Bill Morris's children. Come now, Guy has been a real father to Danny and Katie, everybody knows that.

Her family had responded to the publication of her book as if she had worked a particularly difficult piece of needlepoint. Papa was immensely impressed with the physical object itself, handling and turning the book with much nodding and shaking of his head and long, aspirant outgoing breaths of wonderment and admiration. He was particularly impressed with the reference to Guy.

Connie wrote Anne: "Congratulations. I'm sure it's very clever, dear, and I'm really trying to read every word of it."

Jenny said, "When are you going to turn your hand to something truly readable, like a novel or short stories? Have you ever read Chekhov? Do you like his stories? Aren't they marvelous?"

Shana said, "Did Guy help you get it published? I wish Merv had gotten into the artistic field. Painting or music. A gallery or an artist's bureau. Something like Guy is doing. *It's so satisfying.*"

Barry said, "You did the right thing, Anne, marrying a man like Guy. Creative people need to have money behind them. Art is a service to the community, but there's no money in it. An artist needs a good, solid, independent income."

Admit that their dividends from Anaconda Copper, ITT, and their new mutual funds would easily keep her and Guy if they never earned another penny in their lives. Anaconda! Baruch Goddard might learn something about profits and exploitation from Anaconda, or from Guy's father, for that matter, who built a new fortune in business machines on the fortune *his* father had made in surface transit.

And as for her, admit that she likes being asked, "You and Guy aren't *those* Rossiters, are you? Not the Boston *Rossiter Drive* Rossiters?" and likes answering, "I'm afraid so. But don't hold it against us."

Unfair. Those moneymaking New Englanders should disgust her at least as much as Barry does. Why don't they? Because they're not Jews and don't have to shine and rise above the rest in loftiness of spirit. Because they aren't her brothers—no, not even Guy is mingled in her blood as Barry is with a fierce yearning for him to be good, to do good, to perfect himself and the world around him. She doesn't care what the Rossiters do or what they are. They exist in that outside world to which she reacts with sensible, intellectual coolness, but what Barry does runs through all her nerves. He is herself.

Anyway, Guy *is* good—comparatively. He collects his dividends, but he spends most of it in good causes and finances a splendid magazine and tries not to do harm, while Barry is out there actively making things worse every minute. Merv has just told her that Barry has initiated a whole new operation—in Taiwan, for God's sake.

Perhaps a different worm is eating her? She envies Barry. *She* wants to be top dog of the family, the most noticed, the most loved and feared, the most successful, the most famous; and she not only wants to best him in this way, she wants him to acknowledge her superiority. She wants him to admire her above all the rest.

She forces herself to remember, as they reach the dollhouse, that he's not an obsession with her, that she hardly thinks of him between family occasions, and that her present irrational, binding emotions are atavisms that disappear as she steps beyond the family circle, but when he opens the door for her to enter the cunning little house, she obstinately refuses to do so, because she knows she will be enchanted and she will not gratify him with that response to his latest toy. It is a place of enticing retreat—the child's dream of playtime secrecy. Through its magic, she is back in her childhood in the barn of the Jewish farmer in Connecticut. From the hayloft, Barry swings a rigging of burlap and rope, a flying contraption on which he rides her the length of the big barn, face down, arms wide, belly held taut by the coarse cloth. She screams her joy in flight. A mysterious light filters through the cracks of the barn boards, and the smell of the hay and manure is sweet and pungent. She is wildly happy. This new, dangerous, country game is safe—like all the others he dreams up.

Why has she remembered that? She would like to believe that Barry will never harm her, that he would always help her. But if that's so, then what is their fight all about?

They walk back to the house silently, and when they reach the terrace, he halts and waves an arm in a wide arc that takes in his circular driveway and the splendid, spreading tree that dominates the lush green of the circle.

"If you and the people who think like you had your way"—his words are disconnected from anything they have said, but she understands him perfectly—"Russian Communist troops would be marching up that driveway to take over what I've worked so hard to gain."

She angers him by her burst of laughter. "You're crazy, you poor thing. You've swallowed all that guff about the menace of Communism." She knows how to wound further. "Besides, even if it were so, you'd never be molested. You're small fry."

"Let me tell you something," he says. "If you and I lived in Russia right now, I'd be on the planning boards and you'd be in trouble. You know why? Because I'm a builder and you're a dissenter. That's the way it is. I'd be making things go and you'd be whining and complaining and lucky if you weren't rotting in jail."

She laughs again. "You're right," she says. "Absolutely."

His eyes are filmed with anger, turning the pupils a hard, glistening black. "Are you still a member of the Communist Party?"

"Are you thinking of turning me in?" She keeps her tone and her laughter light. "Sorry. I haven't been for years."

"That must be Guy's influence," he says, and turns aside for the last cut. "He's the only one with sense in *your* family."

He gathers the kids, who have been racing a collie and a spaniel around the terraces, and leads them inside where, leaning against the grand piano Jenny will play for them after dinner, he gives each child a silver dollar to keep forever—"so that you'll never, never be absolutely broke."

Anne's daughter Katie is sentimental. She shows her shining coin to Anne and repeats the promise to cherish, but Danny's eyes brim with expansive plans for spending. "Do I really have to keep it forever and ever, Mom?" He has asked in a hoarse whisper, but Anne answers clearly enough for Barry to hear. "It's your dollar, Danny, my son, do whatever you like with it. We're for economic freedom for all!"

Shana, quick to fear family quarrels, whisks Anne away to the powder room, where Anne forgets her anger in amused admiration of gilt-swan sanitary wonders that vomit hot and cold water. When they come out, Papa is waiting for Anne to ask if he can drop by her office at the magazine and have lunch with her the following day.

"Of course, Papa," she says, and then makes the big mistake of suggesting the apartment for dinner, instead.

He hesitates, pulling at the tips of the fingers of one hand with the other. The grizzled hairs on the back of his brown-spotted hands grow all the way down the fingers to the first joint.

"Guy is back?" His tone is wary.

"Not for a few more days," she says. Guy is away on a lecture tour. She had explained his absence to everybody. What's bothering Papa? He sighs deeply, tugs at his fingers, wrinkles up his face in perplexed concentration. What insoluble difficulty has Anne put in the way of Papa's desires?

"Would you rather wait until Guy gets back?"

"No, no," he says, and sighs again.

"The office is fine, Papa. Whatever you prefer."

"I think it's better like that, Hannahle. Better I should talk with you private, with no interruptions. Maybe Guy will come home unexpected. Or the children could be listening."

His eyes are pleading and ashamed, but the next day at lunch, he is gay and confident. He likes the restaurant she has chosen with its solid English-style food and large, walled-off booths. He plunges right in, which for him involves a circuitous route.

"So tell me," he says. "This is all there is to life?"

"What? A good lunch?" she teases.

"A good lunch is all right," he says. "But man doesn't live by bread alone, am I right, Hannahle?"

He twinkles and dimples at his philosophical bent and piles the filet of flounder and mashed potatoes on the back of his fork with his knife which he holds in his hands without interchanging, European fashion. He eats with gusto, yet delicately, though he doesn't wait for the waiter to clear but scrapes and piles and pushes away his plates to make a clean space about him, and while they chat, he kneads the dough he has torn from the soft inside of a roll into a tiny spinning top which he sends on short careening journeys across the carefully brushed tablecloth.

Anne is immensely pleased with him. He's a dear little pet. She is living in a fairy tale in which the angry, punishing stranger of her childhood has been transformed into a charming, affectionate, tail-wagging dog. He has also been a small, bobbing, sinking boat when she needed a solid rock. Through all his guises, she has been searching him out and not finding him. Maybe she was only looking for him to love her, as she believed he loved Mama and Barry, best of all, and Connie and Jenny, and all the others better than he loved her. Perhaps all his children feel the same lack. Does he love only himself fiercely, and then jump and beg and lick and wag for others when it suits his needs? He never noticed her when she was a child. Now he turns to her often, but she believes that's because of Guy, because Guy has made her financially sound, and because Guy himself is so amusedly fond of Papa and good to him and enjoys time spent with him, feeding Papa's greedy pleasure in good restaurants and musical comedies and sight-seeing trips. Guy finds Papa's responses charmingly comical and winning. Anne remains outside this love affair. There is more to Papa than meets Guy's eye, but she has no desire to darken the sunny portrait of Papa he and Guy have contrived between them.

It is Guy whom Papa calls on to soothe and help him through his comic disasters. Example: Early on a Sunday morning, when Papa and Bessie are in their New York hotel apartment, Papa, unable to sleep, is reading the paper. In a gesture which he later cannot account for, he knocks his glasses off his nose to the carpeted floor, and in further unaccountable gestures, gets up to retrieve them, stoops to pick them up, loses his balance and steps down, fatally breaking them. To search out one of Mama's old pairs, carefully stored in a small carton with other precious objects, carted about with him wherever he goes—to England, to Miami, to New York, and back around again—he precariously perches a chair on the rounded doorsill of a small, dark closet on whose upper shelf he had placed the carton. The chair slips and pitches him forward against the edge of the shelf. The knock brings on a copious nosebleed and raises a hard, round, amazingly large welt. His yells waken Bessie, who becomes hysterical. At Papa's insistence she calls Guy, and Guy and Anne leave the Sunday *Times* and rush crosstown to their aid. While Bessie makes pot coffee with hot milk to wash down the eggs and onions and bialys, and Anne scolds Papa on the subject of wearing glasses not prescribed for him, and Papa goes into a fit of irritation at the two women, Guy applies ice to the bump and to the bridge of Papa's narrow nose and joshes Papa into a state of peace and good humor.

Later they take Papa and Bessie to a nearby 3-D movie. It is Papa's idea that since the movie house supplies glasses, he won't need his own. A mistake. He's deeply disappointed in the cardboard spectacles, and finds the entire 3-D process alarming. With loud cries and much ducking under his seat, he avoids the cowboys and Indians hurtling at him from the screen, but he doesn't feel entirely safe until they're outside on their way to Stark's for a snack. The adventures of that day are embellished into one of Guy's best anecdotes.

Laugh, laugh. The generation of comics. What would your life be now, old man, if your son had never made it rich, if all your children had remained poor?

"*Imp*-possible." He leans heavily on his version of the first syllable. "*Imp*-possible. My children are too smart to remain poor. Special in such a country. I'm proud of my children and of my country."

So why have you left instructions with your oldest son Saul to place in your coffin, when you die, a bag of Israeli earth, brought back by you from your last trip?

"Because a Jew is a Jew. In the final analysis, that's what it is. The Jew must always remember that in this world he has only one homeland, a Jewish homeland, and thank God, thank God that it exists. You too, Hannahle, you should remember to thank God for Israel, no matter how good it is right now among the goys."

"And Guy? What about Guy?"

"Don't be foolish, Hannah. I'm not talking from Guy, just in general."

She cannot catch hold of him. He eludes her. Suddenly he is all Russian soul, pacing, pacing, pacing all through a sleepless night, asking himself if life has any meaning, if *his* life is to pass away unmarked by accomplishment. The year before Mama died, he had been recording his memoirs in the pages of a tall, blue-and-red-lined ledger, in a fine Yiddish script which makes a beautiful, decorative pattern on the long sheets. In Miami, on her last visit to see Mama, Anne studies the pages, open on the dining room table where he writes. She has forgotten the Yiddish she was taught as a child in the shul. The pretty scratchings in their delicate design remain impenetrable to her. They are both embarrassed when Papa returns, and he shuts the ledger and puts it away in the drawer where he keeps his shirts, which he likes to iron himself, with great care and skill, wetting the cloth generously to make the steam rise with a pleasant hiss. He wets his finger with his tongue and touches it lightly to the hot iron to test it. That too makes a slight, hissing noise. Laundry is a big thing in his life. He runs the washing machine at least once a day in "the spite room," but mostly to annoy a hated neighbor whose activities he spies upon from behind the azalea bushes separating their house lots. Papa says the neighbor is an anti-Semite. Mama says Papa is going crazy in his old age.

"Stop your foolishness," she says. "Occupy yourself."

He takes that for permission to go to the track.

When Anne was seventeen, he convinced her that playing the horses according to his surefire system would make their fortune. Barry, in trouble with his new business and married to a woman from a family with money who must be convinced from the style in which he is supporting her that he has his eye on the right kind of future, finds it difficult to give Papa and Mama more than just enough money to barely manage on. The help sticks in Papa's throat. It was always easier for Papa to swallow his pride on a handsome allowance than on a small one. Saul, Connie, and Josh are married and scrounging on depression job salaries. They throw in a couple of dollars of parent support when they can. Jenny, Anne, and Shana are still at home with Mama and Papa.

Home is a second-floor walk-up apartment of three tiny rooms —Tremont Avenue, in the Bronx—where Anne and Shana sleep in a pullout couch in the living room, Jenny on a pullout chair, and where Anne wakes to Mama's and Papa's early-morning sounds and to an unbearable sense of life having closed down on her and locked her in. She and Shana and Papa go out to look for work every day. Jenny has a job that pays very little. After a while Papa gets a night job as cashier in a cafeteria and Shana ends up in a wholesale fur cooperative where she will be taught to run the switchboard at nine dollars a week. Anne dresses up smartly every morning in her one good summer dress, works up a patter of lies and inventions to dazzle the personnel managers of the offices where she applies as a clerk or typist, and doesn't understand that she's overplaying her hand. She's turned away, every day. She stands outside the large humming cages where the blessed have been allowed to enter to type and keep books, and agonizes over what it is the girls inside have that she doesn't.

After a couple of weeks, she gives up. She moons around the apartment, plays Beethoven and Mozart sonatas on the old upright piano until it's late enough in the day to meet her friends. Mama calls her piano-playing style "grimpling," because it lacks the professional energy and bravura of Jenny's, and Anne has taken over the word for the state of her whole being. She is "grimpling" away the summer, losing her interest in going on with school in the fall, where her courses at the huge city college she attends are all boredom and fakery. She feels like the shlep of the world—everybody's unwanted burden.

Papa's surefire system starts up a blazing interest in Anne. He has made her a proposition. If she can get her hands on three hundred fifty dollars, he will build it to a thousand before she goes back to school. Guaranteed! A minimum of one thousand! Side by side, on a bench in Crotona Park, out of sight of Mama, they pore over the racing sheets together, preceded by his extensive night work, at his cashier's stool, on the same forms. How can he be so fresh? He hardly sleeps, waking early for their morning conferences. He teaches her the system, a scientific consideration of each entry. Age, weight, performance, odds, jockey, owner, track—

"It's not just luck?"

"A system, Hannahle. A surefire system. First, you study very careful and you choose the best in every race. The best means good, steady, no killings. Then, the bet. Every race. Across the board. You don't miss a one. You have to win. No question about it. You can't lose. You have to make money in the long run. Worst comes to worst, one day you break even. The law of averages. *Impossible* you should lose by this system."

The names of the horses have no special significance in the system, but Anne likes to savor them. One A Penny. Prancer Dancer. On Your Toes. Blue Warrior. Heaven In A Mist.

Papa works out three days of play on paper and they follow the results with as much anguish as if their money were riding. Theoretically, they make two hundred dollars the first day, break even the next, make twenty-two fifty on the third. The system is checking out.

Of course, it is he who wins her connivance, not his system. This is the first time he has turned to her in conspiratorial love and need. At last, at long last, he looks at her with longing and pleading, and talks to her. He waits impatiently for her to dress to walk with him to the park. In the just-washed city streets, the hot summer mornings become exquisite. Happiness shakes her like the breeze that lifts and tosses the lush branches of the trees along the park pathway where they settle on a bench. Papa is clean and sweet-smelling in his carefully laundered slacks and shirt; he is freshly shaved and talcumed, his hair combed and water-sprinkled. He carries the racing form folded into the Yiddish newspaper.

They are really about to begin, as soon as she borrows the money. He explains that it's not even necessary he should go to the track. He has his local bookie. Aren't they all gangsters? She shouldn't worry. He knows very good how to handle. The only problem is the money. She should only worry from the money. She has his personal guarantee the investment will be returned in thirty days.

"Abso*lute.* Guaranteed. Abso*lute.*" He puts the emphasis on the last syllable here.

She screws herself up to ask Beth, her former high-school English teacher who has become a close friend. Beth always has some money in the bank. Though they are often together as part of their crowd, Anne calls Beth's home and makes a special appointment.

Beth turns the occasion into a party. She arrives dressed up in a bright yellow cotton dress and her face beams anticipation for a special talk with "her Anne." They meet at the library and take a short trolley ride, sitting side by side on the rattling wooden seat, happy to be together. Then they walk a little, linking their slim, bare arms. Beth clings more to Anne than the other way around, since Anne is tall and Beth is diminutive and seems even smaller because of the severe way she arranges her straight hair, pulled back into a heavy bun at the nape of her neck. They turn into the entranceway of an ice-cream parlor. Inside, there are tall wooden booths and marble tables and big fans circling on the ceiling. The evening is pleasurably warm. The ice-cream parlor is rich with the smells of freshly made candy and syrups.

Beth is working on a sonnet that she promises to bring with her Saturday night when the gang will gather—where? Where are they meeting? Neither one is sure. If there's no free house, perhaps they'll take a ferry ride, the long one from Clason's Point.

The conversation falters. Beth leaves a space for Anne to fill with her special request. It's not the right moment, Anne decides, and she reports instead on how she is wasting the summer.

"Look at *you*," Anne says. "You're writing a sonnet, and you're teaching summer school."

In the habitual postures they adopt with one another, Anne praises Beth, though Anne is outgrowing her intense admiration for her former teacher and she scorns the notion for herself of becoming a mere teacher or of still being unknown and unpublished at Beth's age of twenty-four.

"The thing to do is to always keep working," Beth says. "That's the only way. Write a little every day."

"Listen," Anne says. Her despair chokes her. She cannot describe how she can't even read in the little apartment with Mama
and Papa, Jenny and Shana, how guilty she feels about not earning
money, how diminished she has become through the long job-
hunting time. "I'm reading *Sons and Lovers.* I can't write after
reading D.H. Lawrence. I have to get to be better, a better
writer."

Beth urges her on, but Beth's words make no contact with the
despair lying like a swamp at the center of Anne's being. She sees
their conversation, her own words and Beth's, as if in a printed
balloon attached by a little string to their mouths—comic strip
conversation. Real life is happening somewhere else.

"I want a lover," Anne blurts out. She hadn't meant to say that.
She bends over her strawberry ice-cream soda in embarrassment.
She had meant to say, "I need three hundred and fifty dollars."

When she looks up she understands from Beth's moist, bright
eyes that Beth has heard her words as a plea. Beth is shaking her
head. "No, no, Anne." She speaks in a new, sticky voice. "That's
not *our* way," and her eyes gleam with the gratification of their
tragic, romantic renunciation.

Anne wants to howl like a baby. How will she ever lead the
conversation around to the money now? Now that it's all become
so *sexy,* for Christ's sake? The new, accidentally born concept
squirms and writhes between them. Anne is revolted, not because
she doesn't love Beth, but because that love is so ringed with
restrictions and fears and ludicrous unmanageable facts like Beth's
advanced age, and her exalted, yet despised, position as a teacher,
and the way she can quote Chaucer and Sir Thomas Browne and
Walter Pater at the drop of a hat, and her tiny body of secret,
rigidly controlled sexuality. "To burn always with this hard, gem-
like flame, to maintain this ecstacy, is success in life." Is that what
that was all about? Sex. This then is real life, that always seems to
be happening to someone else.

She plunges from what she has uncovered into a different conversation, but as she does, she has the sense not of fleeing from
Beth but of denying unspeakable longings and hungers that belong to Papa.

She asks Beth if Beth knows that some of the group are fooling
around with politics. "They've all started going to YCL and YPSL
meetings."

"Yipsel?" Beth asks, and the air is cooled down between them by shared laughter, though Beth makes it ring suggestively by dismissing politics with the same phrase she used before. "That's not our way, either, Anne dear," she says, and closes it out.

Anne hangs in the cold void of Beth's "way," bewildered and defeated, and then falls into a nasty adolescent silence, tearing her paper napkin into a shredded pile. She leaves her ice cream half eaten—defiantly. Beth always pays—to bind Anne more closely, Anne thinks, and then rejects her reaction as disgusting, and herself as unworthy of Beth's "way." But if she's all that bad, she may as well go totally downhill and risk everything. In a rush, she asks Beth for the money.

Badly put, Papa's shining proposition falls apart in Anne's presentation. What had glowed with such promise on the park bench becomes transformed into idiocy as it is received in Beth's placid, brown eyes. They grow round with amazement in her round face in the tightly bound hair, and her skin pales and seems to stretch to withdraw from such vulgarity. She brings her narrow lips together into tight disapproval.

"I can't understand your father," she says. "He must be a very strange man. Of course, you're not serious. About this ridiculous plan."

There is no question of the finality of Beth's refusal. Her glimpse into Anne's family life has shocked her into a proposal of her own. Perhaps Anne would like to live with Beth and her family in Mount Vernon until she finishes her schooling? Anne has visited at the rambling old house. She tries to imagine herself in one of the musty beds, her clothes, the little she has, knocking around in one of the big, complicated Victorian wardrobes. She feels the silence of that house and remembers its smell—a smell of repression, like old cheese. Beth's dim, thin-voiced father is in his attic study, fussing with his butterfly collection—really, just like in an English novel. She has never seen Beth's mother, closed into a downstairs sickroom, attended by a series of cheery nurses passing through the parlor on errands that Beth and her father, with equal cheer, ignore. There's a cook, too, serving tasteless meals at the dining-room table, set with linen and real silver. If one of her childish daydreams, to be magically whisked out of her family into another life, is to come true, why must it come in such a dreary package?

"I'm worried about you," Beth says.

"Don't worry about *me*," Anne says.

"Promise me," Beth says, "please promise me not to listen to any of your father's schemes."

"It's okay," Anne says. "You don't understand. Forget about it. Don't worry, I'll be okay." She is angry to feel tears come to her eyes.

They aren't for Beth's words, but for Papa's turning away from her. He will be disappointed in her. His love and need for her, for Anne, will fade from his face. He will pace the living room, pulling on his fingers until the joints crack. He will say, "Eleven o'clock already. Soon it's lunch time and another day is over." He'll say, "So this is all there is to life? Nothing more from this to look forward?"

Of course Beth was right. They would have lost the borrowed money. They would have lost. Papa had lost before and he would lose again. When she was eleven years old, he lost everything they had. He had actually sold a store at a profit; and quickly, before it was all sunk in another store, the older children rented a big one-family house in the prosperous Kings Highway section of Brooklyn with a porch and enough bedrooms for everybody still at home. There was even a lawn, and overarching trees on the block. More money was used for a down payment on a spare houseful of Ludwig Baumann furniture.

"It's time we started living like people should," Jenny says, overconfident, because she has just landed a good job.

There wasn't enough money left to buy a new store, and there was talk of negotiating the grocery concession in a big market. Barry argued that big markets were the coming thing. Saul argued that there was nothing like one's own store. Saul was unemployed, on the loose. Josh was too, but he called it "breaking into the entertainment racket," or "trying to make it in show business." What Papa and his firstborn Saul negotiated was a place in a high-stakes three-day poker game. The idea had been that they would double the money, but they lost it.

Anne was too confused by this disaster to comprehend it. The new affluence—the big house with its unfriendly, formal suites of matching furniture—followed by the sudden poverty of very little food and no heat or light, was a bewildering development.

Nobody explains why the house is dark and cold. The gas has not yet been turned off, and the furniture will be reclaimed in a few days, but while they are there, Mama sits on a new rocker close to the gas cooking stove in the kitchen, and by the light of a candle she grimly works away at an intricate round of ecru string crochet. She doesn't speak to anybody, not even to Anne. Anne is afraid to ask what's happening. Shana whispers to her, "Papa gambled away all our money." Anne would like to comfort him, but where is he? Perhaps behind one of the closed doors of one of the upstairs bedrooms. It must be very cold up there. Anne tags behind Barry down to the basement where Barry is trying to start a fire in the furnace with papers and the scrapings of the empty coal bin. In a fit, Barry grabs a hatchet and attacks the wooden storage closets and shelves, and chops enough wood to get a blaze going. He works for an hour, chopping and feeding the fire. He has rubbed soot into the skin around his eyes, and out of this blackened, maddened face, he gives Anne orders.

"See if any heat's coming up now."

The running up and down to check keeps her warm, but the radiators remain cold. Barry hacks at what is left of the ruined basement shelves, and sobs, and mutters, "Damn it. God damn it," and turns on Anne and yells at her to get back to the kitchen next to Mama where she can keep her hands warm at least, and drops the hatchet and rubs Anne's fingers which have turned a waxy white and ache terribly with the rubbing, and with Barry's fury and the agony of his frustration.

Did Barry too want a rock for a father and suffer the same bewilderment in that helpless, bobbing boat of a man? At least Barry wasn't looking for a lover in Papa.

First Papa was harsh and aloof, then he was inept, now he is charming, and throughout he was a joke. Are these true pictures of her father? On the wall of the study in her Fifth Avenue apartment she keeps a photograph of Papa in the uniform of the Czar's Kremlin guard for which young men of good looks and height were specially chosen. In the photograph the dashing, severe uniform is a little long in the sleeves. Papa's face is so smooth and pearly it seems that he must not yet have started to shave, but he wears a fine, small moustache. He has told her that he was nineteen when that picture was taken, and that underneath the uniform his shins were permanently scarred from the kicks of the officers, who kicked because he was the only Jew.

His history will not compress into the dapper man in his English tweed jacket dimpling at her across the luncheon table.

In another photograph on her wall he lies cross-legged in the foreground of a group of Jewish Russian revolutionaries. The camera reports their daring, their pledged lives, their romantic hopes fully exposed on their open faces. Behind him is his sister Sadie Jacoby, the one Mama hated, who built a run-down Catskill farm into one of the great moneymaking resorts of the country, the sister who staked him in the grocery business and to whom he still owes the borrowed money. Where does that clue take her?

The little spinning top whirls toward her across the tablecloth. She returns it, with a smile.

He sighs. His conversation has been remarkably without substance—a vapor of dissatisfaction with Bessie, a breath of hope for future happiness—not a solid word about the new woman. But when he asks, "So what do you think, Hannahle?" she knows very well what he wants to hear.

"Papa, do whatever you want to. Whatever makes you happy." She had been about to add, "Life is too short," but she stops herself. He's almost eighty.

He says it. "Life is too short," and sighs again.

He has abandoned the pellet of dough, and is twisting a ring on his little finger, Mama's old wedding ring, a thick, plain, rounded band that he had taken from Mama's finger when she died and that he has been wearing since. With his head down and a little twisted smile he says, "This whole business, this woman nonsense I'm involved. . . . It's nothing, Hannahle, you shouldn't take it too serious. . . . By me, it's only a game, a side-show."

Now he pulls himself up straight and looks at her seriously. "When I put my head down for good, my children will know where to put me, where I belong. And God will forgive me . . . ?"

He may have meant to make a statement, but what has come out is a question, accompanied by what he perhaps intended as a disarming smile, but that too has gotten away from him and looks more like an anguished plea for pardon, not only from God but from Anne—if she can manage it somehow, given the facts.

V

Papa died in England during a heat wave that was knocking people over like flies. Aunt Sadie Jacoby died the following night in a Monticello hospital, and the morning after that Herb Rosenberg, Papa's nephew, keeled over in a cab on Ninth Avenue in New York, on his way from his uptown to his downtown nightclub. Heart. Services were all being held on the same day. That morning, Anne received a letter from Papa three days after she knew that he was dead. Her heart slid down her side as if it was trying to escape. She stared at the envelope addressed to her in Papa's quavering script. Something supernatural at work? Signs and portents. Messages from beyond. Now, at last, everything that puzzled her about Papa will be explained?

"May I?" Guy asks, and stands at her side to read the letter with her. She would like to say, "No," but she knows that he means it as a gesture of support. They read, together.

London
August 27, 1959

My dear Hanna,

Received your letter and was wery Glad to hear from you that all feeling fine and Special the news and this is Importint wery match that your desidet to by a House and you bart the House wat you like. I. cant tel you So match my Dear Hanna and Gi that I.

77

Wish you and the Childran the best Look in the World and used
in the best of health and wit Hapines.

and my Promis to myseluf wil be far fult to Help you farnised
out the House wit evry luxury But you Gat to Wait alitele wail
acaple weeks til I. cam back and stratenen out alitele mine afairs.
I expect to be Back in October. and you wil Gat from me 1,000
dolla for you Present.

Nating match from me. I am in London now with Bessie in the
flat. ewery night it is a ful House and the Party Beginig til Late
in The Ewing.

Now the Life goes Jest normal. and then I. wil See.

Now pleace Hanna one thing you gat to doing for me. I. Lost the
masher wat Gi given to me I. cant fint it. Send to me, pleace. I am
wery disterb I shuld be so carles.

I. feeld fine Til Last Week. I Gat Dr. now I feel match better.

natig more for now Hoping to hear mor Good news from you.

and remember you Promist me a letter Ewry week.

God Bless you all

Yurs Pa

Best regard from Bessie
The adress from hear is the same like last year

"What's the 'masher'?" Anne says, and cannot help laughing.

"I know what that is," Guy says, and mounts the stairs quickly
to his study and returns with a small, cunning, heavy brass measuring tape in the palm of the hand he extends. "He coveted it when
he saw it on my desk. I gave it to him, but he forgot it, forgot to
take it."

"We could give it to him now. Something to take along." Anne
surprises herself with that thought.

"I was thinking that," Guy says, and slips the little object into
his jacket pocket. "What is this house we're supposed to have
bought that needs furnishing?" Now Guy is laughing.

"I told him we had bought a larger duplex in the same building,
but he seems to have gotten mixed up." Then she laughs. "Never
pay today what you can put off paying until tomorrow. Papa's

motto." How typical that the gift-giving should not be consummated. He probably wanted the "1,000 dolla" to stay put in his
account until after the bank's interest-payment period—a strategy
called "stratenen out alitele mine afairs."

The letter has irritated her. She feels let down. Some last words.
Where are the explanations? Why had he gone back to Bessie after
all the drama and mysterious conferences and deliberations about
the darling little woman from Budapest—why had he put aside joy
to return to Bessie, to feel ill in a heat wave and lie down for a
minute on the couch to rest, and close his eyes and with no more
warning than a funny little noise in his throat, according to Bessie
on the transatlantic telephone, die—in an instant, quietly, without
pain, without a scene, without a single last word?

"Now the Life goes Jest normal. and then I. wil See." *What,
Papa?*

Bessie has remained in England. (Nobody objects to that.) The
body is arriving alone. Guy offers to accompany Saul and Barry to
the airport, a suggestion that surprises everyone so much, it is
accepted.

"No viewing," Barry says.

The three men are in Barry's limousine, being driven out to pick
up the body, or at least meet it and send it on its way in a hearse.

"I don't care about that," Saul says, and makes what may be the
longest speech in his life. "No viewing, no viewing. But the coffin
has to be opened. I promised Papa to put that bag of earth in with
him. He left it with me when he came back from Israel his last trip,
and I gave Papa my solemn word."

"Your solemn word," Barry says. His voice is flat, deadly. "The
coffin is staying closed," he says, and leans forward to ask his
chauffeur to turn up the air conditioning. He looks faintly green.
Barry wants no sight of his father, almost four days dead. Who can
blame him?

Guy is on Saul's side of the dispute (he wants to slip the "masher"
into the coffin), but he thinks it best to let the battle subside into
a temporary truce. He is aware of Saul suffocating under the pressure of Barry's power—the trappings of the limousine—air condi-
tioned, chauffeur-driven, window-and-door automated, and mu-
sic-and-bar outfitted ("Help yourself to a drink, Guy, there's ice,
glasses, whatever you'd like right in there"), smooth and sinuous
as lust in its weaving passage along the highway, and positively

magical in the authority it and Barry wield together to open-sesame official doors at the airport and to evaporate all obstacles. The loudest sound in the car is the sound of Saul, heaving deep sighs of capitulation and reverence for the way Barry manages.

Everything secure, Barry breathes easier, turns to Guy with a smile. "Pop would have really enjoyed every minute of this fuss over him."

Back at the funeral parlor, supported by Guy and by some of the rest of the family, Saul returns to the campaign to open the coffin, and, in a soft, stubborn erosion of nagging, wears Barry down to an agreement with carefully set terms. Only Saul and Guy (the Shabbas goy?) will be permitted to be present at the opening, when the bag of earth from the Holy Land will be placed inside and the casket instantly resealed.

"I don't want any hysterical women on my hands," Barry says. "Let them remember their father as he was in life," and quickly leaves.

"Everything all right?" Anne asks Guy when he returns to the room where the family is receiving condolence greetings. It makes her faint to approach the question of how Papa looked in the casket, but she feels an obligation to inquire after Guy's sensibilities, and though she puts it vaguely, implicitly requesting, *Don't tell me if it's bad*, when he brushes the question aside she is uncomfortably left with her own imaginings.

"I gave him the measuring tape," Guy says. His dark, vivid face is strangely elated, and the pressure of his hand on her arm is dry and hot, slightly trembling. In his yarmulke, in his excessive, dark excitement, he is so *Jewish*, she feels betrayed. If she had written a script for this scene, she would have cast Guy as a pillar of WASP marble, the cooling agent in a feverish family scene, but as if Papa had been *his* father, Guy is busy with his own feelings, and worse, with self-conscious abstract feelings of the moral obligation to *feel*, to *show* feeling, for God's sake, as if he owed it to history, to the terrible history of the Jews, to feel Papa's death and to be a good performer, to play his part well in the Hebrew rituals of mourning.

The air of the chapel is subtly charged and torn with complications. Three funerals in the same family, on the same day. The Goddard-Rosenberg-Jacoby interlocked groups are faced with an agonizing practical choice of which funeral to attend. The Rosenberg services are only a few blocks from the Goddard services.

Mourners could conceivably rush from the Rosenberg to the God-dard services, or the other way around, and make appearances at both, but Aunt Sadie Jacoby is being buried near her Catskills resort, miles away upstate. From a practical power angle, Herb Rosenberg's funeral is the most expendable among the three choices, but Herb is also the best-loved, and because of his night-clubs, there's the added lure of big-name show-biz mourners at his services, though Aunt Sadie's following, of course, includes the celebrities who stayed at Jacoby's. Connie is making no bones about her annoyance that Aunt Sadie's obituary began on the front page of the *Times* and continued for columns and columns on the back obit page, where Herb Rosenberg got three paragraphs and Papa's loss was mourned by dozens and dozens of organizations Papa had never set foot in but that Barry contributed to gener-ously.

The hard information is that Papa is nobody, except by way of his son, and that the crowded service is not a gathering of private mourners, but a public occasion for Barry's community to pay tribute. The chapel is stirred by an inappropriate wind of whis-pered arrangements, of comings and goings, of respects paid breathlessly, in a hurry, with darting glances and long, insincerely sincere faces presenting an astonishing variety of regrets at having to leave before the service has properly begun. On this uneasy, heaving wave, Anne's emotions are suspended, as if waiting for a curtain to rise and the action to begin so that she may feel what-ever it is she must feel about Papa's death.

If it's a show, it's Barry's show, and she is aware of his narrowed eyes sweeping the congregation. Is he counting the house? It's SRO, even with those missing who chose the Jacoby side, and those leaving for the Rosenberg performance, and those arriving late, and the hopeless gyrations of those trying to play all sides of this game at once.

Later, at the graveside, among a much-reduced congregation of true mourners, a different drama plays itself out.

Anne is ready to feel now, but she still isn't feeling. The unctu-ous voice of the rabbi is enough in itself to stop any flow. The heat, out in the open, is unbearable. At her side, Guy wipes the sweat from a face whose eyes are glazed with physical suffering. Not so easy, after all, being Jewish. She scans the semicircle of mourners and is startled to see Bill Morris on its outskirts, looking wonderfully young and fit, if hot and sweaty. He too wipes his face and stares with glazed eyes. She watches him for a bit, hoping to catch his eye in greeting, but Bill isn't looking her way. She must remember to greet him later, though she knows it will annoy Guy. Bill has some place here, she supposes. Papa is the grandfather of Bill's children—of Bill and her children. That connects Bill to Papa forever, doesn't it? If family connections exist, that is.

Now the final prayer is being said, before the casket is covered with a handful of symbolic earth, while the mound of real, raw soil waits, concealed under a fake grass carpet of nylon, and a mass of real flowers. Barry stands at the rabbi's side—Barry, Papa's third son, usurping the traditional place of the firstborn, Saul. Is nobody but she aware of this nightmare legend taking place in front of their eyes? The birthright! It belongs to Saul. The rabbi must set it all straight. What's the matter with him? For one thing he doesn't care, and for another, perhaps first of all, he's Barry's rabbi, isn't he, isn't Barry paying him? Out front, facing Barry and the rabbi, Saul stands in the semicircle with his wife and three solemn-faced, pale, grown children. A spasm of recognition that he is being betrayed, his sacred right stolen out from under him, twists his soft, secretive face. He looks about the circle, a series of quick, darting glances. Shall I accept this? Shall I accept this too? Without any display of outward commotion, he glides to the rabbi's other flank and joins Barry in the ritual recitation. His deep, musical, yet oddly toneless voice adds richness to the Hebrew prayer, and he recites with more assurance and expertise than Barry, who is only mouthing and muttering along with the rabbi. Josh steps forward from his family group (Brenda in a ridiculous wide-brimmed hat, and the poor kids drooping in the heat). He hesitates, steps back, then forward again. If all the sons are lining up for the prayer, shouldn't Josh be among them? He settles for a halfway mark, but raises his voice, which he knows how to project from the old stage days. The congregation draws breath. Will there be a graveside scene? The rabbi conveys his alarm by a swift, inquiring glance at Barry. Barry is impassive, his eyes cast down. The smooth passage of the rabbi's leading, lubricating voice is imperceptibly jarred. The still, hot air is thick, is suffocating. Has the Rabbi subtly speeded up his deliberate cadence? In any case, it's over, the ritual has come to an end.

They sit shiva where they sat for Mama, in the luxury and comfort of Barry's Westchester estate—if what they're doing can be called "sitting shiva." No sackcloth and ashes, rent garments, and hard wooden boxes. She takes Papa's letter with her when she and Guy and the two children (home from camp) join the family the following Sunday. Something's wrong with the atmosphere. Things don't feel right. The glue, what was left of it, that held the family together is coming unstuck, drying up, now that both parents are gone. Jenny and Connie work hard to feed a blaze of family warmth, but just beyond the circle there is darkness, cold, night beasts. Which of them are in danger? What is Barry thinking? If they sound Barry's wife as the key to his mood, and the family does, then there's the added worry that Pauline's behavior is not what it should be. Brenda (who has never been critical of Pauline) is spreading the word that she overheard Pauline apologizing to the colored couple who run the house—apologizing for *them*, for the family, for the annoyance and the extra work.

"It isn't as if any of us are staying over," Brenda whispers. "Josh and I and the kids, and Saul and Lil and their gang, go back to the motel every night. It's just extras for meals, and we never have breakfast here—and God knows they've got plenty of food around."

Jenny is whispering that she has overheard Pauline complaining to Barry that "everybody ought to sit shiva in their own houses. Is that against the law? Why do we have to bear the brunt?"

"You can't sit as a family scattered to the four corners of the country," Jenny says, outraged. "She cares more for those Negro cooks, stealing her blind, than she does for Barry's family."

Everybody's question is: Why didn't Barry slap her down? Jenny reports that he didn't even answer her, just walked away. Is he sick of them—or too despondent to care about anything? He has been silent, aloof, mostly retiring to his bedroom or to the upstairs library. What's happening? Where do they stand with him?

In this atmosphere, a family reading of Papa's letter is attempted by Anne. However badly his last words fit the convention, they *are* Papa's last words. Impossible, however, to read them aloud. She passes the letter to her sisters, to read for themselves.

"I suppose you're going to ask Barry to make good the thousand," Shana says, with a hot, condemning sweep of her black almond eyes. She flips the letter to Jenny. "I get the whole picture, Anna."

Anne is too astounded to defend herself. Pull the letter out of circulation before her action is further misinterpreted? It's too late. Connie has joined Jenny and they read together. Connie doesn't read to the end. With no hesitation, she advises Anne to show the letter to Barry, in a whisper loud enough for all to hear. "He'll give you the thousand, Anna. I know he will. Anyway, it can't hurt to ask. Papa promised it." She takes Anne's arm, comes close, exuding the comfort and fragrance of her desire to do good for Anne.

Anne says, "This is crazy. I just thought you'd all want to read Papa's last letter. I don't care about the money."

Jenny has finished reading now. She pulls Anne aside, and in a low, urgently dramatic voice offers different advice. "Darling, don't listen to Connie. Don't speak to Barry right now. He's upset. Listen to me, darling. Wait a bit. If you need the money for something special you don't want to tell Guy about, I have a little to help you out. Whatever was Papa's belongs to Barry anyway, isn't that so? So wait a bit. Later on, you'll have better luck with him. Listen to me, darling."

"I don't care about the money," Anne says and meets Shana's bright, skeptical eyes.

"Oh sure," Shana says.

Does Shana know her better than she knows herself? She does care about the money. She wants every penny of the "1,000 dolla" Papa has promised her. It doesn't matter that she doesn't need it. She wants it as a proof of love. Whose? Papa's? Barry's?

New arrivals are entering the huge room in which they've gathered—Barry's employees, the executives who run his businesses, have arrived with their wives—and Barry himself has come down the stairs to greet them, chatting in a deep, hoarse voice of trivialities which his employees listen to with underling attentiveness. Sam Schwartz and Merv materialize from nowhere to join the group and to listen most attentively. There is a sameness about all these men which goes beyond the good clothing and careful barbering; they share a smiling control that covers nervous depths of manipulative calculation, while their runaway eyes chase around the room, asking where they stand, and make contact with Barry's hard, excluding glance without reassurance. The wives cluster about Pauline, who becomes happier and more animated in their company. Brenda and Lil barge in, talking too loud, laughing too much. Their hold is insecure and defensive. They belong here among Barry's men and their wives as much as anybody, they insist. The women are look-alikes too. Their towering, puffed-out hairdos are stiffly lacquered. They are overdressed, overjeweled, tightly girdled front and back, with their bosoms trussed outward and upward. They strike poses in the one-leg-forward thrust recommended in training classes for the wives of executives. They smile. They smile.

This room is Anne's favorite in the house—the informal living room, so large that Anne can't see from end to end. She puts on her glasses and brings the corners into sharp focus. The whole is beautiful, in spite of the coarse blunders of the showy bar and the *Saturday Evening Post* portraits of Barry and Pauline. The room's airy proportions are anchored softly in the immense, creamy India rug on the French-tiled floor; and in the rise of the full-length leaded glass windows and doors that open out onto the broad, tiled terraces any other errors are dominated and subdued. The room breathes plenty and comfort; it is a triumph of "big is better." The many grouped armchairs and couches, and the drapes at the windows, are covered with a printed linen picturing an idyllic English countryside, a scene straight out of her childhood daydreams of kidnap and grievous loss, torn from the arms of her doting mother and father, an English lord and lady. Did Barry dream up that one too? One of the long-gowned maidens in the scene picks her dainty way across a footbridge, but she is permanently cursed with crossed eyes. Anne searches her out again and again in the repeat, hoping for a cure, but in the maiden's serene journeys across the back of the couch, along the arm rests, and up and down the windows, she remains afflicted.

Guy enters with Saul through the wide French doors at the far end of the room. Saul has taken to clinging to Guy since the funeral, and she senses an unspoken plea on Guy's part to be rescued. She crosses the room where Guy is settling into a wing chair, and sits on the rug at his feet. Guy remains courteously attentive to Saul, who is remarkably talkative for him on the subject of buying a car and getting stuck with a lemon, and though Guy hardly acknowledges Anne, he puts out a hand and places his palm against her back in a gesture that she receives like a benediction. How lucky she is to be touched by him with love. She presses against the pressure of Guy's palm. The laying on of hands. Miraculous cures of touch.

Barry has the touch, too. He sits on the bed Anne shared with

Shana, stroking her forehead. Mama has asked him to check out
Hannahle's mysterious illness. Is she really ill, or smitten with a
weeping disease out of despair at being thirteen, skinny and pim-
ply? Her throat and nose are on fire, she can't breathe, her eyes
stream tears. Mama and her ministrations are the only comfort in
life at the moment.

"It's some kind of hay fever," Barry says to Mama. He strokes
Anne's forehead in long, strong movements from front to back.
"She isn't hot. I don't think she has any fever."

"Should we get a doctor, Baruch? She doesn't get better and she
doesn't get worse."

He strokes, studying Anne's miserable, weeping face. His palms
emanate strength, rationality, soundness.

She thought of him as another parent, but he couldn't have been
twenty yet.

"You think you could get up and get dressed? I'll take you to a
movie. You'll feel better in the air conditioning."

Miraculous cure. On the way home they stop for a soda at
Shlombohm's, and Barry corrects her manner of eating ice cream.
"Ladies don't leave part of the ice cream on the spoon after they
lick. Put a little less on and take it all off at once." He demonstrates.
She's only half resentful. "One of these days a really fine man is
going to want to marry you and you'll need some manners." He
laughs. "Make it a rich fellow, will you? I need some help with our
family."

She has fulfilled that expectation, at least, by marrying Guy.

Danny is playing chess with Shana's son Steven. Danny's pained
concentration alarms her. Is he losing the game? He has wound his
skinny legs around one of the legs of the handsomely carved game
table, as if he will ride the damn game to a victorious finish. She
adds her will to his. Win, Danny, win. Come out best among the
Goddard kids.

Here among the Goddards, she sees how much her son looks
like one, and how little Katie does, dashing past at the head of
a group of Goddard girls. What are they anyway, her children,
in a family sense? Daniel and Katie Morris, brought into existence by William Morris (Morris Levy) and Anne Goddard
(Yagoda when Papa left Russia) Morris Rossiter, the two eight
years divorced and no longer real to one another in the flesh.
Hang that mess on a family tree.

"Are you tired?" Guy says, released at last from Saul's interminable tale of his car the lemon. "You look tired. Shall we leave?"

"I'm exhausted," she says.

It's true that being with her family wears her out. Break it off, forget it, the ties that bind are no more, if they ever were. "Yes, let's go," she says.

As if in response, she hears Barry saying, "You'll see. We're all finished as a family. We'll meet at funerals." It's Jenny he's talking to. "That's what happens when the parents go."

Barry is crossing toward their end of the room, the whole nervous flock following him, quivering to settle wherever Barry does. Barry's executives have gone, and Pauline and Brenda aren't around either, but Jenny, Shana, Connie, Merv, Josh, Lil, Sam Schwartz are all moving forward at once, keeping close to Barry. Oddly, though what Barry is saying should sound bitter, his voice is light, and rings with a tone of relief.

She calls out, laughing, "Don't look now, Barry, but you're being followed."

He is blankly lost, but draws up a formal, cordial smile. "Can I get you something, Anne?"

"We're going," Anne says. "Have to leave now."

"We ought to form a family club. A cousins' club. We could do things together on a regular basis," Jenny says.

"Like what?" Connie hollers.

"Meet once a year in Boise, Idaho," Barry says, "and eat chicken soup, if you can find any in Boise."

"No, New York," Jenny says. "We can all afford to come into New York once a year. We do it when we have to. We'll do it for the unveiling."

"That's what I said," Barry says. "We'll meet at funerals."

"Let's go to Fort Greene next time we're together. Let's go see Myrtle Avenue and the old house," Jenny says.

"I never want to see that hole again," Connie shrieks.

"Why do you insist on portraying our former life in such an unattractive light?" Jenny says, "And in front of Guy, too. All the finest business people lived around Myrtle Avenue, Connie."

"Sure," Josh says. "They were very attached to those toilets in the hall."

"Fort Greene was a fine, residential area in its day," Jenny insists.

"In my day it was Murder, Incorporated," Barry says. "I left a lot of blood on those streets."

"Oh, Barry," Jenny says, "don't exaggerate."

"He's not exaggerating," Saul says. "He saved my life more than once in those gang fights."

"Do you remember Crazy Mary?" Shana says. "I was so terrified of meeting her on those dark stairways."

"She was just a poor old demented woman," Barry says.

"The drunks under the el were what scared me," Anne says. "One fell on me."

"That never happened," Shana says. "That was one of your lies."

"You've all forgotten what it was really like. We had wonderful times. Remember the picnics in Fort Greene Park? And how we'd drag a mattress out to the fire escape on hot nights?" Jenny says.

"Yeah," Josh says, "and the time the Willoughby Street Gang headed us off at the monument and Saul rolled down the steps and split his head open."

"It looked worse than it was," Connie says. "I poured peroxide on the cut and turned Saul into a blond for a couple of weeks."

"Was that nice, sleeping out under the el?" Anne asks.

"You loved it," Jenny says. "You remember."

She remembers being cold, only cold. She remembers the turning reflection of light from a kerosene stove. She puts the cat on her chest to warm her. It jumps away to the top of the upright piano in two marvelous lifts.

"Didn't we have a huge, fluffy black cat that slept on the piano?" Anne asks.

"You can't remember Blackie," Josh says. "It's impossible."

"I don't think we even had that piano then," Saul says.

"They're off," Lil says and brings her face very close to Guy's. "Now we're in for it. We can just pack up and shut up when the family starts reminiscing. Right, Guy? Outsiders don't have a chance with them then. Right, Guy? Am I right, Guy?"

Guy smiles and nods.

Sam Schwartz stirs in the sleep he has fallen into sprawled out in a club chair. He can fall asleep anywhere, instantly.

"It had to be in the Myrtle Avenue place," Connie says. "I stopped taking piano lessons when I started to work, so the piano had to be there. Remember that lunatic who was giving me lessons? He'd hit me on the knuckles to make me arch my fingers."

"We always tried to raise ourselves above the level of the common herd," Jenny says. "Even Connie had music lessons. . . ."

"Even!" Connie shrieks. "How do you like that!"

"I mean that we had aspirations. You know what I mean. My musical education was started on that old upright. It may not have been the costliest instrument in the world but it had a beautiful tone. I believe it was a Bausch and Lomb," Jenny turns to Guy for that aside.

Barry bursts into laughter—genuine laughter that collapses the control of his face into helplessness and shakes his entire body. Watching him laugh that real laugh Anne trusts him absolutely and joins him. He wipes his eyes, sighs, leans across the couch, and strokes Jenny's nose. "Strayed into the wrong category there, shvester. How about an Abercrombie and Fitch?"

"A Baumeister and Loeb. Something like that. Biedermeyer, maybe." Jenny pushes away Barry's hand. Her beautiful eyes look hot. She turns on Merv, who is doubled up with laughter. "Stop laughing, Merv."

Josh tries to get into the act. "How about Leopold and Loeb?" He perches on the armrest next to Barry, throws an arm over Barry's shoulder.

Jenny's jaw quivers. "That's right. Have your fun at my expense. Try to make me out to be a big dope. In front of Guy, too."

Barry shrugs off Josh's arm. "Never mind their laughing. You're a real thoroughbred. Look at that nose. Only an aristocrat could have that nose." He strokes it again, downward, as if he were stroking an animal.

"I'm not a horse!" Jenny explodes, but there is pride mixed in her resentment. She rises and places herself in a wing chair at a little distance, striking a turn-of-the-century straight-backed pose, her feet crossed at the ankles, one hand cupping her forehead and screening her lovely eyes in a gesture to remind them that this is a time of mourning and that mirth is unseemly. "Anyway," she says with dignity, "everybody knows that there are only two great instruments, the Steinway and the Baldwin," reminding them as well that she is the artist performer.

Connie says, "Remember when Aunt Sadie Jacoby bought her pianola and Cousin Dora insisted she could play the piano better than Jenny? She was jumping all over the place trying to keep her fingers on the moving keys and working away with her feet like a maniac, telling us she was doing it herself. It was a joke, it really was a joke."

"That player piano couldn't bang out the music one bit better than Jenny could," Saul says.

Jenny is not pleased. She frowns, sighs, gazes outward. "Poor Aunt Sadie," she sighs. "Ah, poor soul!"

"Poor soul!" Connie shrieks. "She must have left a multimillion-dollar estate."

Sam Schwartz stirs, opens his eyes, goes back to sleep.

"Sam!" Connie says. "Sam!"

"Let him alone," Barry says. "He's tired."

"I bet she left more," Josh says.

"Papa's sister," Jenny murmurs. "On the same day . . . the irony . . . the sad irony. . . . On the same day . . . brother and sister. And no Goddard to mourn her and no Jacoby to mourn Papa. The irony."

"I dropped the Jacobys a condolence note," Shana says defiantly. She glances at Anne, then away.

"Condolence note!" Josh stages a fit of jigging, confronting Shana. "What the hell did you do that for? You never slaved for her, that's why."

"Like galley slaves," Saul says in his quiet, tonelessly rich voice. "The Siberian salt mines, we used to call it."

"And on top of that, listening to her tearing Mama down every chance she got to talk to us. Papa could do no wrong. Everything was Mama's fault," Connie says.

"Papa did his best," Barry says. "He worked like a horse."

"Mama worked like a horse," Connie says. "Nobody saw to it that she took an afternoon nap."

Jenny will not be deflected. "Let bygones be bygones, forget and forgive. Aunt Sadie was a very remarkable woman, one in a million." She holds up a long-fingered, manicured hand against the wave of protest, and lifts her voice. "No, no, no, my dears. Let's not allow envy and malice to blind us to the truth. She was a remarkable woman—intelligent, independent, elegant, forceful and beautiful. She made her way in the world. She deserves every bit of credit for her success, never mind what she had to do to get there, that's the law of the jungle—run with the beasts, fight like a beast, that's the law of the jungle, every businessman knows that."

Barry begins to laugh helplessly again. Again Anne laughs with him.

"What are you laughing about?" Jenny asks furiously.

"What are *you* laughing at?" Shana asks Anne specifically. "You, of all people. Don't you believe that? Don't you believe women should make their own way? What about her art collection? Are you laughing that off?"

"I don't know anything about it, except what's been written about it," Anne says defensively.

"Tell them, Shana," Jenny says, "tell them. Shana and I saw the whole collection. Beautiful. Exquisite."

"That modern stuff," Connie says. "It's nothing but potchkying."

"She didn't only collect modern art," Jenny says. "She collected beauty, wherever it was. Beauty is in the eye of the beholder, you know. Shana knows all about it. Art is Shana's field." She turns to Guy with this information. "Did you know that, Guy? Shana's quite an expert in the field of art appreciation."

Shana looks away from Guy, half turning her back.

"Wonderful evening courses at The New School," Jenny pursues it. "Shana is really devoting herself to the world of art."

"Investing?" Josh asks Merv.

"We've bought a few pieces," Merv says. "Shana chooses. Sculpture mostly."

"You can't go wrong," Lil says. "Isn't that right, Barry, that art is a very good investment? Saul, we ought to buy some art. Why don't we buy some art, Saul?"

"You'd better get some good advice first," Barry says, and smiles. "When in doubt, stick with Xerox."

"Her collection is worth millions," Jenny says.

"What's so terriffic about that?" Connie shrieks. "She had the money to buy what people said she should buy, and she bought. But don't ask what she did to get that money together."

"It was Cock-Eyed who knew how to make money," Josh says, and crosses his eyes to clown up the illustration. "Her brother-in-law, Harry Jacoby, Hymie's brother."

Anne offers an automatic apology to the lady in the drapery landscape. Don't feel bad. Not your fault, dear.

"He can't help his affliction," Shana says.

"Didn't he have them uncrossed? An operation?" Saul says.

"Long ago," Josh says, "but they went back." Again he illustrates.

"Stop that," Shana says. "You're worse than a kid."

"Why are we talking about him as if he's still around? He passed away at least a year ago."

"That could have been a terrible scandal, Aunt Sadie and Harry Jacoby. She knew how to handle everything; she had impeccable taste," Jenny persists.

"It was a terrible scandal," Saul says quietly. "Everybody knew they were a three-way thing, Sadie and Hymie and his brother Harry."

"Sure," Connie says, "as long as you have money, everything is hush-hush. That woman was nothing but a high-class yenta."

"How crude," Jenny says.

"Okay, I'm crude," Connie says, "but am I saying the truth or not?"

"The truth is," Barry says, "that crew would have sold their grandmother for a buck. She had no use for her brother when she saw he wasn't going to make it rich. The only thing that woman understood was money. The only thing she loved was money."

Shana makes a small, scornful sound. Barry picks it right up.

"What's the matter, Shana, don't agree?"

"Well, couldn't people say that about you?"

"What people?"

"Jealous people. Jealous of your success. Successful people are always being torn down by jealousy." She's frightened, defiant, but retreating.

Barry blinks his lizard blink. "I'm a lot more successful, if by successful you mean richer, than any Jacoby ever will be. Maybe you need to be reminded of that, Shana." He turns to Guy. "Did I ever tell you about the hilarious story of the paying off of Papa's lousy two-thousand-dollar debt to her?" His face is still angry, but there is a faint, proud smile working through. "I dreamed about paying back that debt since I was a kid, then it turned into a Lou Holtz stubbornest-man-in-the-world joke. They were two of a kind, Pop and Sadie. They didn't speak to each other for thirty years out of sheer stubbornness. She staked Pop to his first grocery store. I think what she had in mind was his evolving into the equivalent of the great Atlantic and Pacific Tea Company, but he never made it. He worked like a stevedore. My Pop was quite a man, quite a man. He knew what life was all about—"

"I know it," Guy said.

"—but he never got the hang of being a good businessman. He

kept his family fed and clothed. He worked day and night—"

"I know," Guy said.

"—but he never got enough put aside to pay back that debt. We were sent to Aunt Sadie's boardinghouse every summer, us kids, to work for nothing. It was called 'spending the hot summer in the country,' God help us. We must have given the Jacobys thousands of dollars worth of labor between us. Jenny has these trick rose-colored glasses she looks through, and particularly when she's looking backward. I'm a more rational being than she is, with a clearer view of reality. When I look back, lo and behold, I see Jenny on her hands and knees scrubbing. If you come down with housemaid's knee, Jenny, you'll know why. Talk about child labor. How old was Josh, fifteen? And me—nine? Aunt Sadie had me skating around with rags tied to my feet, waxing the dance floor. She got Josh to play the drums she picked up somewhere for a song. Jenny at the piano, Josh on the drums, some shlemiel with a violin—and at Jacoby's Red Barn Casino, there's dancing every night to a three-piece orchestra."

"And we were pretty good, too," Josh says, and mimes a drum roll.

"Wild horses couldn't have dragged me to work at the Jacoby boardinghouse," Connie says.

"If Papa had decreed you were to go, you would have gone, and you very well know it. It was your good fortune and Saul's that you and Saul were already out working. That was your salvation," Jenny says, switching her point of view without warning. Nobody comments. Jenny's flights are not unexpected. "That was what saved you."

Connie eyes her coldly. "You certainly have your own way of putting things. I don't know where in the world you get your mannerisms from. Decreed . . . salvation. Some salvation. Stuck in a bookkeeping job and continuation school before I knew which end was up."

Saul leans forward to speak, but his wife Lil rushes in. "What about my Saul? He didn't even finish elementary school. That was a crime."

"Well, I certainly didn't have any privileges," Jenny says. "My young life was destroyed, my young heart was broken, summers slaving at Aunt Sadie's, crying my heart out night after night, sleeping in the same room with her smelly little boys, and then as

soon as I was old enough to get working papers, condemned to one
terrible job after another, to those prisons without windows, without the light of day. I suffered all that silently, silently. I held my
grief silently in my heart. . . ."

"Not silently, shvester, never silently." Barry laughs, and turns
to Guy in exasperation. "Did you ever hear anything like this? It's
impossible to have a conversation in the middle of these magpies.
Are you women going to let me tell this story to Guy?"

The tale of the repayment of the debt gets told. The great day
has arrived. The meeting place is to be Aunt Sadie Jacoby's suite
at the Ritz Towers. Barry orders a splendid lunch from room
service. Estranged brother and sister see one another for the first
time in many years. Heartbreaking, heartwarming scene. Papa is
aglow, expansive, at his absolute winning best. Aunt Sadie is a
beautiful woman—slim, her hair still dark (and if dyed, then colored with skill and taste) and done up into an elegant French twist.
Her face is skillfully made up, and her dress and long string of
pearls are quietly expensive. The only showy things about her are
many rings on her short, slightly trembling fingers. She looks like
Papa and Jenny, and like them she knows how to play-act, at the
moment as the simple-hearted, great lady, full of sentiment for her
brother and gracious charm for her distinguished and successful
nephew. Cock-Eyed is present, her attentive second, his role to
slant the talk of times gone by so that Aunt Sadie emerges as the
good angel of the family. Cock-Eyed buzzes like a horsefly at the
feast, an extreme irritation to Papa and Barry. Lunch, toasts, extravagant sentimentalizing over, comes the supreme moment—
the exchange of the check for the notes Papa had signed a half
century earlier.

"This is a wonderful occasion for me," Papa says. He has a
surprise waiting in the wings. He's going to knock his sister Sadie
over with unprecedented generosity: Interest on the loan is included in the check. His son knows how to be a gentleman. "Sadie,
my dear," he says, "with great pleasure, I'll take my notes and then
I'll give you back the money you so kindly . . ."

Cock-Eyed, holding the notes in their worn self-tied envelope,
is extending his hand, but Aunt Sadie intercepts his gesture and
grasps the package.

"How about the other way around?" she asks playfully, but her
heavily ringed hands are trembling. "First you give me the check,
and then I'll give you the notes."

"Why should I give you the check before you give me the notes?"

"Barry," Aunt Sadie appeals to a wiser head, "explain to your father that it's a very simple transaction. First he gives me the check . . ."

"No explanations necessary. I don't need to be explained by my son what every baby knows. I was a businessman all my life."

"Ridiculous!" Aunt Sadie says.

"Here's my last word on the subject," Papa says. "I'll give you the check after you give me the notes, and that's final."

"Would you believe it?" Aunt Sadie appeals to the ceiling in a mannerism so like Papa's that Barry has to laugh. "Did I disturb you all these years? Did I come after you with a debt you neglected for more than fifty years?" Her face is dangerously flushed. Outraged feeling chokes her. "Did I come knocking at your door in the middle of the night, waking up the neighbors? I had better things to do, believe me. I thought we were coming together in trust. . . ."

"Your idea of trust and my conception of trust are not the same. If it's trust, then it's not notes and a signature. You kept my notes very careful for fifty years—not 'more than fifty years' like you say, but fifty years exactly, maybe a little less even. I don't call that trust. . . ."

"If I never did you any harm with these notes, am I going to start now? What do I need from you anyway? I'm a wealthy woman—"

"So good! Don't need and don't take and good-bye. I'm leaving."

And they are carried away into further passionate outbursts taking them so far back in time that they lapse into Yiddish and snatches of Russian before Papa storms out, but is led back in again, of course, by Barry to loose a few more bolts at Sadie and receive a few.

Barry is enjoying his story as much as anybody else, laughing hard as he tells it.

Guy is puzzled. "What happened? Wasn't it paid, then?"

"Sure. Reason prevails in the end. Do you know Jacoby's?"

"Of course," Guy says. "If you've been to a convention, you've been to Jacoby's. It's Anne who's never been."

"You should take her sometime. It's quite a place, isn't it? I always got the royal treatment after that. Aunt Sadie in the lobby, with a big kiss and a bouquet of flowers. It's true she also kissed

Nelson and gave *him* a bunch of flowers. . . ."

"Nelson *Rockefeller*," Lil explains in the gloating, liquid voice that power excites her to use.

"And after that scene in the informal living room," Anne says in the car on the drive home, "I was out on the lawn looking for Danny to tell him we were leaving, and I overheard Jenny with Barry on the terrace begging and crying and pleading with him to please keep giving her what Papa was giving her every month or she wouldn't be able to keep up her place on the Coast, and then he started about her boyfriend, was he going to marry her . . . ?" She hears the strain and near hysteria in her voice and stops.

"Why do they upset you so?" Guy says. "They're really very ordinary people, ordinary Jewish people, that is."

"What does that mean?"

"It means you have to put a little distance between you and their extravagant—"

"You think Barry is an ordinary Jewish person?" she interrupts.

"He's an ordinary, charming, vigorous, Jewish genius of a moneymaking bastard," Guy says and laughs.

"I like Uncle Barry," Danny says from the back seat. "He took me upstairs to his library and showed me his books. He has some terrific books. He has this book about the discovery of the world, and it has these maps . . ."

"I hate families," Katie says. She sounds sleepy, pleasant, almost loving. "I hope we never have to go to another one of your family things, Mom."

"There probably won't be any more," Anne says.

VI

I was a liar as a child. I didn't lie to any purpose, but for the joy of it, to light up the moment. Lying was a form of madness or an addiction, perhaps. I never planned a lie in advance. The lie would come upon me in a rush of vivid heat. When I lied everybody listened to me—even my family listened. I didn't expect anybody to believe my lies. It was a shock when they did.

My sister Shana would scoff at these explanations. "You were a born liar. You were always a liar." *Then* she was more dramatic. "Anna's ruining my life with her stupid lies. I can't keep my head up on the block."

I was pretending to be asleep, but I was really listening in on the family council going on in the kitchen.

"She told a big lie about going to Salt Lake City and eating lunch on a tray that stayed on top of the water."

"What water?" Mama asks.

"The lake. The salt lake," Shana wails.

"Like the Dead Sea?" Mama asks.

"That doesn't matter," Shana screams. "It's the *lying.*"

"Sh," Mama says, "You'll wake her up."

We were too close in age, Shana and I. Our friends overlapped. Away from the convincing spell of my stories, they had second thoughts about believing me and checked out my lies with my sister.

Our friends had no special loyalty to either one of us. They were inevitably new friends, because we moved so much. The old new friends were left behind with the old new neighborhood, sometimes with sensationally exhibited regret—tears, promises to visit, to write, to phone—quickly forgotten in the new struggle to make new friends on a new block, in a new classroom, on the broad, dangerous space of a new schoolyard.

I had told that stupid lie about Salt Lake City to win a new friend. She was a girl on the block, midway in age between me and Shana, and finding it hard to choose between us. (She feels that she *must* choose, which makes for my need to compete.) She cannot decide which one will become "her best friend": the glamorous Shana, already in high school, affecting a Clara Bow look—a heart-shaped face, milky skin, a pineapple head of soft-cropped curls, a cupid's-bow red, red mouth—or school-smart, skinny, ugly, twelve-year-old me. I feel no special attraction to this friend—she is short and square with a squint in one eye—but something soft and stupid and graspingly receptive in her makes her a marvelous listener. I invent some of my best lies for her.

I met her the very first day after we moved, a move that turned out to be a disaster. We liked to feel that we were generally moving up into better apartments, and this new location had seemed fine on a Saturday evening when it was rented by Mama and a couple of the older kids. The rooms were too small, and the windows of some rooms opened out only on other rooms, but the block was a plus, an unusually wide boulevard for this section of the South Bronx. The trouble was that our boulevard turned out to be an open-air market. We woke at dawn to the rattling arrival of the pushcarts, and returned in the afternoon to bonfires and the smell of roasting sweet potatoes and chestnuts, of pickles and salted herrings and fresh fish and manure and horses and live poultry among the carts of tablecloths, ribbons, laces, vegetables, pins, dishes, pots, housedresses, fruit, socks, pants, aprons, and the din of trade and the cries of the vendors yelling to attract the women shoppers. "*Veibele, veibele, veibele!*" There was a terrible family fight about who was responsible for the bad move, and in the midst of it I went out and found this squarish, dullish girl and told her that I was only temporarily living here with a Jewish family; through some mix-up I had been accidentally separated from my real parents, an English lord and lady of considerable wealth and fancy manners, who were coming to get me any day now by ocean liner.

The next day I told her that my sister Jenny was studying to be an opera singer and that she was scheduled to begin a concert tour of the world, and might be taking me along.

My masterpiece was the invention of a sister who had become a Catholic nun after a tragic love affair and then died of a broken heart in a convent. My friend cried at the part where Mama and Papa visited the nunnery and forgave their daughter on her narrow deathbed in a stone-cold cell.

After I told a lie I was finished with it. I never meant for it to come back to confront me. I was wildly irritated with my friend when she inquired what I would do if I had to leave with Jenny on the world tour before my real mother and father arrived from England. And what was the name of the sister who became a nun? I was astonished that she believed my lies. There was danger here I had never meant to court.

My heart pounds, I feel the start of a sick headache. It would be simpler to die, but I go on, I compound the lie, I swear my friend to secrecy about my sister, the departed nun, whose name I cannot help inventing on the spot: Celeste. My father has forbidden our tongues to ever form the name, Celeste, and she too, my friend, must swear to never mention that name, Celeste.

The lie she cannot swallow is the Salt Lake City story.

When Shana faced me with that lie, as if I had committed a murder and buried the body in our shared dresser drawer, I told my first real lie. "I never said that. *She's* the liar. I never told any stupid story like that."

My friend quickly became my worst enemy. I would cross the street when I saw her, but she would run alongside, chanting above the noise and confusion, "Liar, liar, liar." She spread the word, and the schoolyard became a circle of torment. I cut school and went to the public library, where I told the librarian a fantasy of private schooling on an entirely different schedule, and told my school teacher a fantasy about terminal illness of a younger brother to explain my absence, and at home I made up stories about what went on in the classroom I wasn't attending.

At supper with Jenny and Barry I found myself launched on a story about the Mayor of New York visiting my school for a school performance.

I tell them that he liked me the best, and that he lifted me to his knee to congratulate me on my fine performance. The story takes shape spontaneously. I demonstrate how well I recited

"Abou Ben Adam (may his tribe increase!) Awoke one night from a deep dream of peace . . ." They are very much impressed, and I am as happy, almost, as if some triumph had really been mine.

But in the middle of the night, as if shouted awake to a warning of disaster, I am startled into realization. The disaster is my lies, my lying. There is an intolerably painful pressure in my head. I'm going to be sick. I shuffle to Mama's bedside through rooms containing the sleeping bodies of my brothers and sisters. I wake Mama with the lightest touch on her bare arm. The unexpected silkiness of her warm, normal skin is amazing. I'll just tell her everything and the nightmare will be over. Instead I vomit and she holds my head.

The long days out on the street, away from school, have wonderful moments, and some dreadful ones, and they're always exhausting. I begin to come back to the house earlier and earlier—even before the time when school is out. I catch Mama studying me with pained wonder. There is no reproach in her look, but her pain reproaches me. It threatens me, too, because I can no longer consider telling the truth. If I collapse my elaborate structure, I myself will go down with it. I have the sense of dangers closing in from all sides, but I keep my face stony and pretend that I don't know why Mama is looking at me with fear and wonder.

"Don't sit and think so much," she says. "Go out and play a little. Take your skates."

I go three or four blocks from home, from the block where I am known as a liar, before I put on my skates. At the end of the block there is a strong, upright metal scale. I speed up as I approach it, jump on it, then off, as I round the corner, in a feat that is gloriously noisy. In a little while a string of kids has joined in. It's become a game, and I'm the leader. We stream down the long block in single file, crash on the scale, off again, arc around the corner, then the straightaway, then the wide curve to return, then crash on the scale from the opposite direction. Excellently choreographed, without preparation or plan, we pace ourselves carefully, not to jam up at the scale, and scream and touch fingertips as we pass one another on the straightaway. We have become ten to twelve in the train before the cop stops us making all that racket.

The ecstasy of the game fades off slowly, as does the light of the late autumn afternoon. Out of breath, burned up, exalted from the exertion of the game, I put my head back and see the sky above me as a black-blue space. Beyond the space I see, I see further space, and further space beyond that, and beyond that more endless space, endless, endless space. Everything is stilled and held. There is a revelation in the endless space. Now that I know it is there, and that *it* knows I am here, and that we have accidentally acknowledged one another, I feel changed. I feel that I have averted some unspeakable danger.

I try to hold that sense while I lie in bed listening to the family council taking place in the kitchen.

"Her life is nothing but a tissue of lies," Shana says, borrowing from that week's movie. She's right. Even this lying about being asleep, while I listen. They have all come together to confer, even my sister Connie has come, all the way from Jackson Heights. She's in a hurry to go home to her husband and children and she makes sharp, dismissive comments. "What a fuss over nothing. Give her a good smack. Tell Papa to give her a good smack. That will stop her." Papa isn't present. He's still at the store, a few blocks away. Barry has come in late from an evening class, and while Mama serves him his meal, he asks for a detailed report. Shana drags in the stiff corpses of my stories. The story of the sister who became a nun has reached the ears of the rabbi of the congregation where Mama and Papa have bought tickets for the High Holiday services. He has questioned Mama about it.

"The little tramp!" Saul says. "She's blackening our name in the whole neighborhood."

Barry makes a sound of disgust. "Can we hear all the facts before we get dramatic?"

Josh laughs so hard at the story of Jenny's world tour, he and Jenny get into a fight. "You may laugh as you will," Jenny says. "True to form, one's own family is oblivious to one's talents. I happen to have a naturally beautiful singing voice."

It's then that Shana cries out, "She's ruining my life. I can't hold my head up on the block," and tells the Salt Lake City story.

Barry is appreciative. "Where'd she get that one from?"

The English lord and lady true parents are dragged in. The librarian has been in touch, and most horrible of all, the school. Miraculously, the story about the Mayor has not been exposed. I listen and feel nothing. I think that dying must be like this— distant, muted no-feeling. Now they whisper and I hear only phrases. Mama is "afraid," she doesn't like how I sit "and stare and think too much." My teacher has come to see Mama. My teacher has actually been in this messy flat where we lead our messy lives and talked to Mama about becoming my "guardian." I lose my bearings. Is this story one of my forgotten inventions? Often I can't remember exactly how I told a story. Is Mama repeating a lie I told her and have forgotten? Mama has a whole set of new words: "falsehoods," "truancy," "exceptional abilities," "opportunity to develop." My dumb compositions are dragged in. "A Visit to Grant's Tomb." What for? Mama's story ends in anguish. "Can they take a child away from a parent because she's smart?" I hear Barry soothing, explaining. "This teacher wants to give her a chance, that's all. What was she like?"

"Like a broomstick," Mama says. "No, not even so strong. Like a straw, like a dried grass. I wouldn't give her a kitten to take care of."

I have stopped pretending to be asleep. I lie on my back, my eyes wide open, fixed on the dimly lit cracked-plaster ceiling. Miss Evanston's faded blue eyes looked at our ceilings. The information confounds me. In the classroom, when Miss Evanston stands at her desk and bends to check the attendance sheet, I am nudged by the girl who shares my seat to note Miss Evanston's long, flabby breasts, a pair of deflating water wings, exposed by the falling away of her printed dress and the loose drawstring of her under-shirt. Mary Kelleher is the girl who shares my seat, big-bosomed, laughing Mary Kelleher, who knows how to turn Miss Evanston's reading of *Julius Caesar* into a riot. " 'These many then shall die; their names are prick'd,' " genteel Miss Evanston reads aloud, and is dimly bewildered at the gasps, giggles, and convulsive jerkings that ensue among her thirty-seven eighth-grade girls.

" 'Your brother too must die; consent you, Lepidus?' 'I do consent—' 'Prick him down, Antony.' "

Miss Evanston's cultivated pronunciation is the cream of the jest. The laughter has become uncontrollable, explosive. Again, she checks the room for causes. Mary's arm shoots up.

"Miss Evanston! Miss Evanston! What does prick mean?"

The class is in an uproar. Miss Evanston raps the desk with her long ruler. "Girls, girls, quiet down." And she answers Mary's question. "The word prick here means to mark the name down for . . ." Pandemonium. Sylvia Saperstein falls off the bench she shares with May Hanson, dragging little May with her to the floor of the aisle, where they writhe in a fit of laughter. Miss Evanston puts them outside the classroom in the hall and threatens to detain the entire class after school. Is it stupidity or heroism that keeps her reading through to the end of the pricks and asses that dot that scene?

The fact is that I feel more for Miss Evanston than I'm prepared to admit to my seat partner Mary. I too never knew that a prick was a man's thing until Mary told me, and who in the world would ever tell Miss Evanston? She has been nice to me, and she's praised me a lot and given me wonderful books to read—*David Copperfield* and *Lord Jim*—and kept me after class to talk to me about them, gazing out over my head with her pale blue eyes to an emotional landscape dotted with phrases about "nobility" and "truth" and "the poetry of feeling" and "the feeling of poetry." But she's so old and ridiculous, and the least she could do is clap her hand over her broken-down chest when she leans over, and keep her tits, as Mary would say, to herself.

The kitchen council is coming to a close. Blessed Barry is defending me. "It's just Anne's imagination. Those lies don't hurt anybody. You should back her up, Shana. Where's your family loyalty? Don't worry about it, Mama, I'll talk to Anne. I'll take her to the movies and talk to her. She'll be all right. She's a good kid. We ought to let that old maid take over and give her a good education."

"No," Shana shrieks. "No, no. I can't live without Anna. You can't send Anna away."

"Oh please, Massa Barry," Josh clowns, "don't take my baby sister and sell her on the slave block, my poor little baby sister."

The council dissolves in laughter. Connie makes a final judgment before she leaves for Jackson Heights. "Anna will never amount to anything, but she won't do any harm either. She's just a dreamer."

Saul says, "It wouldn't hurt for Papa to give her a good smack on the behind."

Shana says, "I bet she's been awake listening to this whole thing."

I don't pretend to be asleep when Shana comes to the bedroom. More than anything, at that moment I want to be close to her, to all of them. She is my own Shana, my pal. She doesn't give me away and call out that I'm awake. She comes close, and hugs me and whispers and giggles.

"Did you hear everything? Did you hear the part about Miss

Evanston? Did you ever hear anything so—superfluous?" Superfluous and insidious are her latest words.

I hug her and cry a little. "I'm sorry, Shana. I'm sorry I ruined
your life on the block."

She forgives me. She does her bust exercises before she comes
to bed. She swings her arms in wide arcs to the count of one
hundred. She considers her breasts to be too small, and she's mor-
tified that a circle of hairs has formed on the outer edges of the
flat, inverted nipples. I assure her that she has the best figure in
her whole crowd. "But look! Look!" she moans tragically, display-
ing the miserable failures.

In large families, today's scandal is forgotten tomorrow. There's
too much going on for one member to hold stage center long. Saul
met Lil and the commotion of that courtship took over. Mama
didn't much like her, Saul was reluctant, Lil shoveled Saul along
pushing hard, Papa was scornful, Barry was furious that just when
Saul had landed a steady job managing a midtown delicatessen, he
would be leaving us. Saul and Lil were married in the spring. The
miseries of my life on the block and in the schoolyard disappeared
into family matters. Josh brought home a stray dog, but it got sick
and died. Things like that. Then one of my fantasies came true. I
was to be awarded a medal at an official ceremony. I had won
second prize in the Fire Prevention Essay Contest and the Mayor
himself would hand it to me.

I feel fraudulent when I make the announcement at home, but
I'm not lying (I think), and I do have an official invitation to show.
The Mayor is a new one, not the one I was supposed to be intimate
with, so there's no difficulty there, but I can't overcome the sense
that I have invented another story—and even on the spot, at the
scene, I can't taste the reality of triumph. Hundreds and hundreds
of public-school kids are receiving awards, dozens of first-prize
winners, hundreds of second-prize winners, hundreds and hundreds of third-prize winners. On the steps of City Hall, after the
marching and the bands and the singing and the speeches and the
brief instant with the Mayor, the ceremonies end, and I must
descend the smooth steps to meet Mama and Papa, watching from
among an immense mass of parents like themselves. They have
gone to great trouble to get away from the store to come here. We
have all been standing in the warm spring sun for hours. Below the
steps, the streets are thick with milling people, and around me the

kids have broken up into yelping knots of dizzying movement. I stand still, enclosed in a veil of disappointment so palpable it has immobilized me in a shimmering bubble. My shame is unbearable. I see Mama and Papa coming up the steps to get me, and that Barry is with them, that he too has witnessed the humiliation I have suffered at my dream come true. They tell me we're going to a Child's for lunch, Barry's treat, on his lunch hour from his job nearby. They all look pleased as they lead me away.

I begin to sob, "I'm sorry. I'm sorry."

"For what?" Papa says.

"It's too long standing in the sun," Mama says.

I know for what, but I can't explain.

VII

Barry would have under-
stood. He knew about wanting to be first. At twenty, he knew that
he wanted to get to the top. It was a question of how, where. To
choose a sphere, move in, and rise—that was it; but which sphere?
He had seen enough failure in his own family to be glutted for life.
He musn't make a mistake. That's how I see him now, at twenty.

He is working in the accounting office of a big corporation in the
Wall Street area. He is surrounded by successful men in their
offices, at lunch, on the streets. He knows that success exists, a
common prize, won by ordinary men, even dumb men. There's
nothing to it. You have to get the hang of production, and of
money and banks. He tries to explain this to Papa on their way
home from the store after closing very late one night. They are
passing a bank where a man is slipping in a night deposit.

"See that money going in? The trick is to get it out." He laughs
at Papa's alarm. "Not rob it. Get it invested in yourself. It's not
doing any good to anybody sitting around doing nothing. In the
hands of the right man with the right ideas, it's good for everybody."

"You're talking like a child, Baruch," Papa says. "Banks don't
make loans without collateral, without security. . . . And especially
now, in these times."

He knew that he was right and that Papa was wrong. There was
a trick here that Papa didn't understand, and that Barry was working on.

Papa wanted him to stick with the law. Clarence Darrow. Paul Muni. A brilliant, eccentric trial lawyer, fighting the good fight in the courtroom. Earn a lot of money, too. Meanwhile how did he stay awake at lectures, sandwiching night school between a regular job and helping Papa out in the store? And there were quicker minds than his in the class. He didn't enjoy being bested.

He could write song lyrics, but he wouldn't even mention that to Papa. He had a real talent for moon, June, soon, tune. That was a way to the top if you hit it. He might even put his mind to the grocery-store business and straighten Papa out. There was money to be made in food. Everybody had to eat.

He brought a beggar home with him one evening. He marched him right into the bathroom to clean up, then he dressed him in his own clothes, from underwear out. They were the same size, but Larry Bateson was fair, with blond hair and small reddened eyes that shifted when you tried to meet them directly. He had a wonderfully American way of pronouncing his vowels. Fifteen-year-old Shana was smitten. I was a little scared of him. Mama fed him well. He ate, and spilled a heartrending tale. Runaway from a brutal drunk of a father and a whore of a stepmother and a hard life on an Ohio farm. He couldn't get any work, though he had tried; that's why Barry had found him begging. "The country's full of decent men living on handouts," Larry Bateson says.

Barry is going to do what he can for him, as if he were a brother. All men are brothers. And that kind of talk. Was he missing his real brothers? Saul was married and out, Josh was on the road, breaking into show business, breaking his balls, he'd never make it. No, he wasn't missing his brothers.

What then?

He was inventing a new brother, an ideal, romantic brother out of the goy who had come after him on the streets of Brooklyn—the enemy he had stood up to and bloodied and subdued, he would now raise up and admit to brotherhood. His gesture exalted him. Too excited to sleep, he planned Larry's future. He'd get Larry a job in the sample stock room of the company. He knew that there was an opening. He'd take care of Larry, teach him everything he'd need to know. They would be buddies, two musketeers, blood brothers. Scratch one, the other would bleed. Legendary sidekicks. He would make a man of this downtrodden wreck, and earn his undying gratitude, his pledged life, his loyalty, and his love.

The wreck slept, taking more than his share of the three-quarter bed, and snored, and startled, and made crazy talking noises, and snored again. A sickening fear surprised Barry. How did he know that he hadn't laid himself wide open to a murdering stranger? The fellow's ridiculous sob story. What if a knife or a gun was hidden in the pile of revolting, stale clothing the tramp had dumped in a corner on the scrubbed surface of Barry's linoleum rug? In the half-light of the outside street lights, Barry forced himself to approach the stench and to touch the rotten mess, feeling for a hidden weapon. Behind him the snoring abruptly stopped, and he heard the sound of the bedsprings being released. Larry was backing himself into the opposite corner, his hands up over his head, palms outward in a coward's gesture.

"Hey. Hey," Larry says. Or is he trying to laugh? "You looking for something?" His pale eyes show wildly dilated.

Terror locks the two young men in an extraordinary embrace, without touch or speech, and then Barry is free. He is on top.

"I'm looking for a goddamn handkerchief, Buddy," Barry says. "Your snoring's driving me crazy. Don't you ever blow your nose? You're making more noise than a boiler factory."

He threw Larry a couple of his own perfectly laundered hand-kerchiefs. "You keep those. And use them, for Christ's sake."

When the fellow fell asleep and started to snore again, Barry woke him up roughly and stood over him and made him blow again and again. When Barry decided the nose was all clear, he told the fellow he could go back to bed. He woke him that way the next night, too, and the next. By that time Barry was sick of him. Poor ignorant bastard tramp. He'd never amount to anything. He was making hash of the work in sample stock. He just didn't have very much in the brain department. He could tell a good story, all lies probably, and he had a talent for hitting Papa's bottle of shnapps every chance he got, and that seemed to be it. There was nobody to talk to there, nothing to work with.

On the morning of the fourth day the tramp was gone. Barry gave him credit for a remarkably stealthy operation for such a clutz. Mama and Papa slept in a pullout couch in the dining room, a room Larry had to cross to leave the apartment, and though Mama could hear a cat change its position, she hadn't heard Larry. He left sometime in the middle of the night, before Papa got up to go to the produce market.

"Dumb luck that he got out without being seen," Barry says. He didn't mention that the clutz had taken the only good piece of jewelry in the flat—Barry's watch—and a bunch of change Barry had been saving in a box in a dresser drawer next to the beautifully laundered handkerchiefs. There were two snotty handkerchiefs on the dresser top, and a note in wobbly printed letters. A premeditated getaway?

Blow your own nose. You stink. Mister you snor yurself. So no thanks. Yur buddy, Larry Bateson.

He tore up the note, hid his losses. He wanted no sympathy, no clucking over him and his foolish generosity. He had to listen to Papa's "I told you so," of course. But the fact was he had learned something. He had to watch himself. He was too soft, too impulsive.

He had to watch himself with Papa or he'd go in over the edge with him. If he could, he would carry Papa on his back to a victory over a quarter pound of cream cheese, two seeded rolls, and a half pound of the *best* coffee, but it was hopeless. Papa was doing something fatally wrong. His stores ate money. All Connie's savings, before she was married, were shoved in to stop the leaks. But nothing stopped the creditors. Papa's prescriptions were laughable. A little more milk in the heavy-sweet-cream cans, a little more water in the milk cans. Now there was some kind of cockamamy strike against the store. It was enough to drive an old socialist like Pop out of his mind. The store was losing money and the union was demanding a full-time union clerk at union wages. There was nothing to do but laugh, Barry said, but Papa stood at the door of the shop and shook his fist at the pickets. That was the end of Papa's working-class solidarity. He went over to Tammany, heart and soul, and asked the local club captain for help. He got some crocodile tears and vague promises. With those boys, Barry told Papa, you have to have something to trade. Papa had nothing.

Somebody had to lead Papa out of the wilderness. Get him out of the small grocery store business for good, for his own good. Barry started talking up the advantages of bankruptcy proceedings. And stopped putting money in. Let Papa see that he was kidding himself. It would be cheaper for Barry to let Papa stay home and give him the money, and a lot less aggravating. Barry had been given three raises in a row that had all gone into keeping the store going. Enough already.

Now something was going wrong with Mama. She couldn't get out of bed, couldn't stand on her left leg, and even lying down couldn't find a position that wasn't agonizing.

"Tell her not to be a martyr," Connie scolds over the telephone. "Mama doesn't like to be a bother. Mama doesn't like to complain."

Barry thought it was more ignorance than martyrdom. Mama believed in natural cures—rest, pure water, and faith in one's strength to heal. Good enough, if they worked. But she got worse.

He was so used to not worrying about Mama that he could forget her completely at the office, but Anne called to remind him. The call was a problem to Barry. He wasn't supposed to receive personal calls, but the switchboard operator put the call through because Anne had pleaded emergency, and because the operator had Barry pegged as the man in the general office who would go far, and it would be just as well if he owed her a few favors. In the wide-open office with the entire staff listening, Barry was embarrassed to be talking with his little sister about his mother's ailments. His tone was short.

"I'm sorry I had to call, Barry . . ." Anne starts, but he cuts her off.

"Just get to the point," he says. "What's the emergency?"

She paused, and he felt a gush of hatred for her sensitivity to his tone, and the reluctance with which she began again.

"It's Mama. She's in terrible pain. I think she must have something bad. . . ."

"Get a doctor."

"She doesn't want one. She says they do more damage . . ."

"Just call one in, don't have any big discussion with her. She must have a doctor. We're not living in the Dark Ages, you know. Just do it. I'll see you at home. I won't go to my class tonight. Hold the fort until I get there."

He walked over to the boxed-in area enclosing the switchboard, to thank Nancy for putting the call through, moving stiffly, in a controlled manner copied from the office manager, an older man whom he admired and had never seen ruffled in any way. Barry was alarmed, but he was determined to show no emotion in that room full of competing people, watching and listening for him to slip up.

It mattered to him not to be humiliated, but humiliation was built into the circumstances of Mama's illness. She was taken to a city hospital by a city ambulance—strapped to a board, a maneuverable object carted by two strange men, only her eyes desperately denying the indignity of this tilting journey down four flights of narrow stairs past twisting landings, curious neighbors, and the kids on the block. The hospital sat on a height two long uphill blocks from the subway station, then up a flight of concrete steps imbedded in the slope of a neglected lawn. Though the building should have dominated the area, it was overshadowed by the elevated tracks and the density of the tenements around it. The enormous ward in which Mama lay was filled with beds—even the center aisle was filled. He had no experience of hospitals, but he couldn't imagine that this was a proper one. It seemed more like his idea of an emergency disaster shelter. He had expected a hospital to be hushed with the restorative quiet of medicine's dignity, but all was confusion, disorder, noise, senseless moving about. In the midst of this, Mama, his Mama. Her face changed from vacancy to brightness when she saw him, but it stayed gray and pinched with torment, and her eyes were yellowed and bloodshot, a face that embodied his own sense of humiliation and helplessness. He couldn't kiss her in the state he was in, but he forced a smile and patted her hand, gripping the edge of the coarse sheet in a child's fist.

"Baruch," she says, "you look worse than I feel, if that's possible," and pulled his head down to kiss him.

"Are you feeling better?"

"If anything, worse. On top of the pain, I can't swallow the pills —only a horse could swallow such pills—and I can't eat the food. Everything they serve here is swimming in a white paste. Whatever they cook they cover with the same white paste. You ever heard of that?"

"Aren't you eating anything?"

"Connie brought me chicken soup and chicken. And the girls brought me Jell-O and orange juice. They saved my life."

"Barry." A cunning look of pleading in her eyes. "Maybe it's better for everybody if I go home. All I need is a little rest. I'll try not to complain about the pain."

"What are they doing for you?"

"The same I was doing home. I lay in the bed. Only I liked it better at home."

He saw that she reacted to his rage as if he had meant to direct it at her. He became violently upset at that and saw her mark that too before she closed her eyes against the whole overwhelming vulnerability of her position. When she opened them, she had determined to lighten his burden. She amused him with ward gossip and did imitations of the variety of groans to be heard through the long night from all sides of the room.

He was laughing when he left her, and then spent almost an hour knocking around the corridors, first waiting for a promised talk with a doctor, or a head nurse, neither one of which actually turned up. He wanted to know what was wrong with her, what the treatment would be, what could be done to alleviate her pain. He was shunted from place to place, told drivel, treated like dirt until he began to shout, then they treated him like a madman and put him out. Defeat made him wild. He walked the long way home ready to smash, burn, kick, knock down the whole damn run-down Bronx. That was his mother being allowed to lie there like a hunk of waste matter. *His* mother—Baruch Goddard's.

He couldn't sleep. They had moved again, in the middle of all this, and he was bitterly uncomfortable in his strange, tiny bed-room in a dark, street-level apartment, the windows barred against the terrors of the street, lit up by the outside street lamps and by passing cars, the shades drawn against people passing but not against the sound of their feet on the sidewalk. It was like living in an open cage. He tried to blot out his awareness of Papa pacing the long narrow hallway outside his door. He sat on the edge of his bed and looked through his song lyrics, still in a carton, unpacked. They weren't any good. He'd end up like Josh, selling candy in a live-show movie palace, and happy about his stinking job as long as he could get in free to see the new show. Josh was nowhere. Lots of people ended up nowhere. Not him. When he became Papa's age, he would not be pacing the floor, cracking his knuckles. In his store Papa acted the commander, tossing cartons of canned goods and barrels of produce as if they were light as balls. He was a big, powerful man, but he was sunk. He saw Papa swimming—his broad back rising and falling in the breast stroke he had brought with him from a violent Russian sea to the tepid, unresistant waves of the Brooklyn shore. Out past the muck of the Coney Island beach, he had carried each child in turn on his powerful back, and one by one taught them how to swim. Now he was sunk. It was too late. He'd never make it anymore. If Barry didn't stop him he'd go on forever tying on an apron, chaining his strength to the counter of a little grocery store, with Mama running with the pots of hot food for his dinner, running forever, if her legs could be made to work again. Women couldn't help themselves. It was men who set the pace, made the difference. His brothers were hopeless. Saul was an incompetent, Josh was an entertainer, a fool. Only he and Papa were real men, but Papa was strangling.

It was up to him to do something about Mama in that charity ward where her leg would fall off before they got around to curing her. Could life really narrow itself to a shaft of demolition, narrow itself to no more space and give than a coffin? Life, chance, luck, whatever it was couldn't do that to him. He wouldn't allow it.

For him history was a man stepping forward out of a crowd. Socrates. Moses. John D. Rockefeller scattering dimes. Lindbergh stepping into his little plane, alone. Benny Leonard, a Jew, fighting his way to the boxing championship.

In his cage of a room, Barry paced, pursuing a punishing circle which threw him back, over and over, on himself. Papa outside, he in this hole. There were rooms a man might step into like a king, where the rugs sopped up sound and spread a comfort of warmth like wine. The once-a-year office party, the big boss himself greeting, making little jokes, noticing with his sharp, attentive eyes, in a room as big as this whole apartment. Barry had hung around with Jim Jeffries, the boss's nephew who was learning the business from the bottom up, temporarily poised at a desk alongside Barry's. They left the party together for a beer and office gossip. Why not? Jim Jeffries was a good fellow. Should Barry hold it against him that he was the boss's nephew? Jim was less interested in Barry than he was in the new file clerk, a girl with an amazing bosom. Barry had had a couple of dates with her. It wouldn't hurt him a bit to hand her on to Jim. It was legs that Barry went for anyway. Jim flattered him, said he was "smart as a whip," "very engaging," that he had a "charming personality," that he was "a winner."

If he was a winner, why wasn't he winning?

Straddling his legs, bending at the knees to see his face in the narrow mirror propped up on the dresser, he looks for signs of charm in his dark, intense, big-nosed face. The heavy eyebrows are more forbidding than engaging. Can he be a loser?

There had to be a way. He had been toying with a plan for reorganizing the general accounting office. Should he do it? Work it out, put it down on paper, take it right on in to the big man himself, set it down before his shrewd eyes? "Mr. Harmon, I'd like to speak to you about a plan to save you money." It hit him that he had really found it, the way. The possibility stopped his pulses and then sent them racing in a flood of energy. He'd do it. He put the song lyrics on the floor, took a fresh sheet of paper, sat down on the bed, and began a sketch of his plan. Give the big man something, ask him for something. He'd get Mama's situation in there somehow.

Nancy, the switchboard operator, smoothed the way with Harmon's secretary. He was ushered right in, before noon the next day. It stunned him that it was as easy as that—all it took was the trying. He had counted on time to concoct a good opening while he sat and waited to get in, but in the speed with which he *was* in, really inside the large, solid office face to face with the old man, not now the gracious host of the evening at his house but a busy, impatient power able to cut him off at any moment, he had no choice but to barge in. He surprised himself by beginning with Mama.

"I need your help, Mr. Harmon. I need your advice. My mother is very, very sick. I don't know where to turn. I don't have the right to, but I feel I *can* turn to you." He can't read Harmon's large, bland face—a territory unknown to him, entirely different from the men he knows, from his father and his brothers. The face of an impassive, smooth American, giving in to a mild show of shock and impatience as Barry continues. Hesitation could be fatal. *He's just a man. He's just another man,* he tells himself, and unleashes a flood of words. "She's in a city hospital, not getting any proper care or attention. . . ." His account brings tears to his own eyes. He is almost in a panic. He controls himself, lets the tears show, but maintains a steady, manly posture, gives his voice a deep, slow, thoughtful tinge to keep it from breaking. Mr. Harmon moves one arm in a quick, angry gesture. Has Barry wrecked his chances?

"Sit down, young man, sit down."

"I don't want to take your time, sir."

"Well, you are taking it, aren't you?"

He looks at Harmon steadily, and nods.

"We'll do what we can for you," Harmon says. "We have to do what we can for you people."

He didn't dare show anger. He could lose everything, make this man contemptuous enough of him to fire him. This was the way men on the power side of the desk behaved. They kept their heads. They were rude.

He didn't sit down. He moved forward and placed on Harmon's desk the folder of papers he had worked on all night. In his beautifully even, forward-marching handwriting, he had written on the cover: "A Plan for the Reorganization of the General Accounting Office of J.P. Harmon & Co. Submitted by Baruch Goddard."

"I've been working on a plan to save you some money, Mr. Harmon. I'm asking for help, but I like to try to pay my way."

Shock again on Harmon's face. Something like amusement. Harmon reads, leafs pages, then he fixes his attention on the carefully drawn chart and finally looks up. "Well, well," he says, his eyes smiling, cool, measuring. "Sit *down*, young man."

There were three chairs at the massive, dark desk: Harmon in one, another directly opposite but set somewhat back from the wide desk, and a third in a chummy arrangement at the side. It was to that chair closest to Harmon that he was being waved. Some preliminary decision had gone his way. His tension eased off slightly.

"Let's hear about this plan to save me money," Harmon said, and nudged his desk clock with a perfectly manicured hand.

Barry had to be quick. He kept going against Harmon's amused smile until it faded and changed to alert concentration on the diagram.

"Are you an accountant?"

"I've studied it. I'm not a CPA. I'm studying law."

"What makes you think this will work?"

"Common sense."

He went over the changes again, without impatience, with quiet deference. There was no reason for Harmon to put his faith in Barry Goddard. It was the plan that must win Harmon over, and the plan was good. It could speak for itself, but there was no harm in helping it along.

"It's logical, sir. All these clerical operations are waste steps. All these bookkeeping steps. And these." He drew circles with his finger around those groups on the first diagram. "Eliminate those and you're down to this setup." He flipped to the next diagram. "Cheaper, more efficient."

Harmon relaxed against the back of his chair.

"Baroosh," he said.

"Everybody calls me Barry," Baruch said.

"How old are you?"

"Twenty, sir."

"I'd like to think about this," Harmon said. He placed his hand on the folder, claiming it.

Was he being dismissed? "Thank you, sir," Barry said and stood up.

"You're a very impatient young man," Harmon said. "Sit down." He sat down.

"Why do you suppose my accountants never saw the logic and the common sense of what you see?"

He sensed danger in that question. Not to be too headstrong, too cocksure. "I couldn't say, sir."

"Mr. Davis, my office manager for twenty years?"

"I couldn't say, sir." What was this? What kind of test? "I have the greatest respect for Mr. Davis, sir."

"What do you think, Barry, do you think old man Davis could make this new plan work?"

"Absolutely. Anybody could make it work."

There was a pause. Barry's leg thumped against the side of the desk in a convulsive jump. He held his thigh with his hand to steady the leg.

"Let's put our minds to your mother's situation, now," Harmon said. "I have an appointment in twenty minutes, so I'd like the facts as quickly as you can give them."

Barry talked fast, but not so fast that he'd sound like a slob.

Early in the afternoon, he received the astonishing news from Jim Jeffries that he had been invited to join the Harmons in their box at the opera. They were in the men's room when Jim told him.

"Very funny," Barry said, and squirted water from the tips of his fingers into Jim's face.

"No kidding," Jim said. "You can bring a date. Here's two tickets. I'm going too, but I have to take my sister. She's one of the old man's favorites."

Jim Jeffries wants Barry to bring Busty Beauty, but that's an unthinkable suggestion. She would disgrace Barry. Absolutely no style. There's a redhead in the typing section with gorgeous legs, but they both agree that she has a mouth on her worse than a truck driver. Back at his desk, Barry examines the tickets as if hints to a correct course of action are coded into the information printed on the face. He's at sea. What to wear? Someone to take. Copy Jim? Bring a sister? Jenny was the logical choice. She knew about music, but she was so goddamn unpredictable and skittish. No judgment. She might rig herself out like a gypsy in her Spanish shawl, with a comb stuck in her piled-up hair—and all of it coming unloose before she even entered the box. She was perfectly capable, in her flamboyant way, of singing along with the performers, and insisting that "all opera lovers sing along, my dear, everybody knows that if they know anything at all." Shana? Shana's current getup was a clown face. She had plucked most of her eyebrows out and penciled in a thin, thin, arched line that made her look permanently and stupidly surprised. And a red, red painted Kewpie doll mouth.

Anne. She was so young anything would be forgiven her, any error in style or speech. Perfect. It made him look good, too—sacrificing, thoughtful older brother. Good son, good brother. Was he supposed to wear a tuxedo? Check with Jim. He was. These opera tickets were turning into a case of good fortune beyond his means.

Just before closing time, he was called to the old man's office, but he was stopped at the outer office by Harmon's secretary. Her manner had changed. She called him Mr. Goddard. A medical consultation on Mrs. Goddard's condition and her removal to a private hospital had been arranged. The details were in an envelope she was handing him, a plain white envelope with Harmon's magic signature scrawled in the left corner and Barry's name scrawled on the center face. She had something for him to sign. He signed the form without reading it and accepted the envelope without opening it. He had to trust himself to these powers. He walked away with the envelope in his inner jacket pocket as though envelopes from Mr. Harmon were routine stuff in his life. An appointment with Mr. Harmon had been set up for nine thirty Monday morning. He was to be at Harmon's secretary's desk ten minutes before that. Personnel needed some additional information on him. Was that good? He thought so.

There was a thousand-dollar cashier's check in the envelope. He had signed a note for it. Good enough. He spent a part of the money given him for Mama's illness on a tuxedo for himself. He could have rented, but buying one with Jim's aid was a promise to himself to live the kind of life where he would need his own.

Tuxedo in its large, unwieldy box, he lugged it into a subway that landed him on the wrong side of Morningside Park. He had to cross the park to reach the hospital Mama had been moved to. In the misty dusk, the limbs of the trees, stripped of foliage, were the only hard lines in a landscape all soft dreaminess and promise. A woman was climbing the steps above him, too far ahead in that vague light for him to know if she was young or old, pretty or ugly, though she was slim with shapely legs. She heard his steps, looked back, and quickened her walk. Suppose he raped her—would he be making her dreams come true? He would change into his tuxedo first. He began to laugh and scared her into a run. He fell back, allowed her to get far ahead and his own heart to quiet itself. What was he so excited about? Nothing had happened yet. He had accepted an invitation to the opera—and a thousand-dollar loan. He must keep his head.

Mama had her own room. There was even a balcony outside. He stepped out onto it into the violet dusk to clear his lungs of the medicinal smell of the room and to reorganize his hopes against the disappointing thud of finding Mama strung up in a medieval torture rigging of weights and ropes, her black-ringed eyes evasive and dull with reproach.

"They're going to make you better here, Mom."

Her eyes slid away and closed against his treachery. She wanted to go home. She had no faith in these medicine men. But he was in charge now, and she wasn't going home to die a cripple like an ignorant European peasant woman. Not his mother.

Jenny dressed up Anne in a dark dress with a white collar and a huge soft bow, but Shana messed up Anne's face with blacking on her eyebrows and enough lipstick to paint the side of a barn.

He yelled, "I'm not taking you anywhere looking like that. I wouldn't take you to a dog show looking like that," and with the flat of his hand rubbed the black down the side of her face.

Hysterics. From her and from Shana. "You promised. You said you would take me." Anne's screams expiring on a long, wheezing breath. "I told my whole crowd I was going. They'll think I'm a liar. I wasn't lying. You have to keep your promise."

Jenny led her to the bathroom to wash her face.

"She's fourteen, for God's sake," he yelled at them.

He hovered at the open door of the bathroom, where Jenny and Shana were bunched up fussing over Anne. He didn't understand his sisters. One minute they'd be at one another's throats and the next all lovey-dovey, forces joined against him, whispering and encouraging one another. Anne would do a hell of a lot better to listen to him. And he would have done a hell of a lot better if he had kept his family out of his affairs.

"If you're not ready in two minutes, I leave without you," he roared, and went to his room to check himself out in the small mirror hung too high now for him to see anything but the upper half of his face. Jenny had assured him he looked wonderful in his tux, but what did she know?

Ready once again, Anne called him, but he saw that Jenny had thrown a ratty fur cape over the child's shoulders. He cursed "these goddamn idiot females" and threw it on the floor.

"Get your regular coat and come on."

It was true that their coats were wrong, but he plotted to make the coats invisible by slipping them off and carrying both casually over his arm as he and Anne entered the lobby.

He had time now, in the cab he had grandly hailed on Southern Boulevard, to glance kindly at Anne, but he was put off by the miserable creature staring out the window, her face scrubbed to an unattractive mix of green pallor and red blotchings, her eyes suffused with tragic visions all out of proportion to what had actually happened. So he had yelled a little. So what? Why did she have to look the way she did? The first thing to learn was to compose the face. Unless you were blessed with the blank, good-fellow brightness of a Jim Jeffries face, you had to study composure, smooth away all that dark Jewish intensity, be wary, smile, move carefully—like old man Davis, the office manager, like the old man himself, Harmon. He practiced the face he would present to Harmon, in greeting.

"You know what to say when I introduce you?" He had almost forgotten that. "You say, 'I'm very pleased to meet you.'"

She nodded.

"Smile," he said. "We're stepping out. We're going to the opera. Not many kids get to go to the opera."

Her response was excessive. Her smile was dazzling, her eyes lit up like candles. She began to spout chatter all the way downtown.

"Mama told me so many things about the opera house. She was so excited that we were going. Did you know that she went to see Sarah Bernhardt at the opera house? A long time ago. Did you know that Sarah Bernhardt was Jewish? And Belmont too. And Otto Kahn. They're the money men behind the Opera. And Caruso's Jewish too, Mama said, and was famous for performing in *La Juive*, the Jew. Mama went to the opera house twice, way up in the balcony in nigger heaven. She said it was a miracle that we were going to sit in a box, in the diamond horseshoe, she called it. She said ordinary people up there in the balcony even have to use a separate entrance. Mama said she could see the diamond horseshoe from up there. It looked like another stage, she said, and the Jewish paper pictured the billionaires with such poison that she expected to see diamonds dripping from their fingers and the blood of the workers—"

"If you talk like that in front of the people we're going to meet tonight . . ." He was going to say he would kill her, but she had already pulled back in terror of his rage. Damned, ignorant women. They never knew what they were talking about, but that didn't stop them.

"I wouldn't talk that way in front of *them*." She was crying again. "I'm not that dumb."

"Listen," he said. "Can you keep two things in your head?"

She nodded.

"Keep your mouth shut. And smile."

If it surprised him that Jim's sister was plainer than Eleanor Roosevelt, and that her coat was shabbier than Anne's, it also relieved some of his anxieties and allowed him to release Anne to Caroline Jeffries's fussing care, to go ahead on Caroline Jeffries's arm to be introduced to Mr. Harmon and led to the ladies' room and the drinking fountain and to a seat at the very front of the box while he remained aloof, listening deferentially to Mr. Harmon's genial talk, masking, with the correctly impassive face he was teaching himself to assume, any show of excited response to this incredible scene in which he found himself. In the general blur of his confusion, he barely defined but clearly sensed the landscape of money surrounding him—women in furs and long gowns, men in tails and tuxedos, top hats and capes, their rich booming voices and rich silvery laughter mixed with the tune-up music of the

orchestra, and the rich smells of perfumes and whiskeys floating
in the brilliant air of the hall, glittering with the lights of crystal
chandeliers and the sparkle of real diamonds. It took a while, as
he was busy settling down in a chair behind Mr. Harmon, for him
to acknowledge that the scene was a disappointment to him, that
there was something familiar and ordinary about this experience,
as if he had been here before, under more glamorous conditions.
Too many movies? Where were the beautiful women? He could
see only middle-aged, plain women in ridiculous getups, like the
woman settling down in the very next box, smiling and nodding
at him, rigged out in a shiny red evening gown that was faded and
discolored under her arms that hung like meat on a butcher's
hook. The dress was popping its side hooks under the pressure of
the woman's solid, washerwoman chest. She had diamonds dan-
gling from all over, even from her hair. The old lady was laughable. Dressed up, Mama would have looked a million times better
than she did.

He heard Anne's gasp when the curtain rose, and the ripple of
laughter from the box that followed, and sweated the thought that
she had disgraced them, but he saw at intermission that Harmon
and Jim's sister were delighted with her. On the walk to Sherry's,
where they grouped around Harmon's reserved table, Harmon
told Barry that his little sister was "enchanting," and he seated
Anne near him to talk to her about the story of *Traviata* while she
sipped her lemonade, while Caroline Jeffries told Barry that Anne
was "so responsive," "so vibrant," it was "such a joy" to "introduce
her to the pleasures of listening to opera." Anne knew how to
listen, Barry noticed. She kept her big, avid eyes fixed on Harmon's face, drinking in Harmon's information through all the dis-
tractions of the crowded bar. Good for her. She wasn't doing him
any harm after all.

Back at his seat, he finally saw a beautiful woman—a golden
redhead all in white walking down the aisle of the orchestra,
followed by a fat, old, dumpy escort. A man like that had won that
gorgeous woman because he had money.

He had trouble staying awake during the next act. He marveled
at Jim's close attention to the opera. Jim really seemed to like the
stuff, something Barry never could have imagined about Jim. He
went to the men's room at the next intermission and, bent over
the marble basin splashing cold water on his face, he had the

extraordinary experience of overhearing two men discussing what they had bought and sold in that day's stock market with no more flourish than he and Papa would discuss the price of pot cheese. When he returned to the box, there had been a reshuffling of the seating arrangements and he was now seated next to Jim's sister. He was uncomfortable with this strange, horse-faced, all-American girl, so awkward and gushing in her manner that Barry felt she must be kidding him, putting on some kind of *shiksa* act that he couldn't understand, swinging her long legs and tossing her head and pulling back her lips to bare long front teeth in an ugly smile. Yet, when the house darkened, bored into a half sleep by the interminable singing, he let himself daydream about bending the creature, whinnying with desire, to her bony knees before his chair.

He had learned one thing that evening. Opera wasn't his idea of entertainment. Only a kid like Anne could cry at the heroine's preposterous death scene. The whole thing was nothing but ridiculous exaggeration and simpleton ideas. A little common sense would have settled the mess in two shakes. Anne thought the show was on stage, but she didn't know what it was all about. The real show was in the boxes, where the money sat. The real story was in the history of how that money was made. That was the story he wanted to hear.

VIII

There is no reason to put any faith in what I say, particularly since I'm a confessed liar, but one of my earliest memories of my brother Saul and my sister Shana is Shana suggesting that we peek at Saul's thing through the keyhole separating the two broken-down locker rooms where we were changing into our bathing suits. That's the thanks he got for taking his kid sisters to the beach on a hot summer day. First Shana looked and then I did. What I saw was Saul's naked backside. It looked okay so I stood up.

"Did you see his thing?" Shana whispered.

She saw by my face that I hadn't, and after taking another quick look for herself, she shoved my head at the keyhole. "Now, now!" she whispered.

I saw it. I thought it was pretty ugly. I especially didn't like its purplish color and that it was settled in a bush of hair. It was a big surprise to find out that hair grew there. The entire incident was very depressing.

What bothered me? Old Testament injunctions? Thou shalt not uncover thy brother's nakedness? He is thy brother. None of you shall approach to any that is near of kin . . . to uncover their nakedness. . . . The nakedness of thy father, or the nakedness of thy mother, shalt thou not uncover. . . . The nakedness of thy sister . . . The nakedness of thy son's daughter . . . The nakedness of thy father's wife's daughter . . . Thou shalt not uncover. . . . Thou shalt not uncover the nakedness of thy father's sister . . . of thy father's

123

brother. . . . Thou shalt not uncover the nakedness of thy brother's wife; it is thy brother's nakedness." And lots more.

No nakedness at home. Locked bathroom doors. Ingenious contortions for undressing and dressing without uncovering nakedness. But nakedness will out—it speaks with most miraculous organ.

I knew all about Jenny and her abortions and the soft-goods salesman who was never going to marry her now that she had given in and gone all the way. I was thirteen then. What frightened me about sex was how *sad* it was. Secret and sad. She kept going back to him, too. She said he was her only hope, her only salvation. Then she'd have another abortion. I wanted to kill Lou Silverman, the soft-goods salesman. I brought cups of hot tea with honey and lemon to Jenny's bedside, where she was resting from one of the abortions that Mama had been told was a flu. Who knew if Mama believed that? She knew how to pretend she knew a lot less than she knew. The dreary "affair" went on for two years. Then Lou Silverman, the soft-goods salesman, married some other girl.

"She's a fool," Shana said. She was seventeen, full of theories. "We're living in a new age. She thinks her life is ruined because she gave that dope her virginity."

They had terrible fights, Jenny and Shana, about Shana's "running around," and a scene that is a revelation to me. Jenny is screaming and showing Shana proof of Shana's sins—white stains spread over Shana's black slip. (White stains? I'm amazingly ignorant—even for a fifteen-year-old virgin.) The quarrel between them ends with tears and hugs.

"I just don't want you to ruin your life the way I ruined mine," Jenny says.

"Forget that old-fashioned morality," Shana says, and strips down to her compact, dancer's naked body, right in front of both of us, before she slips into her pajamas.

Jenny must have forgotten that old-fashioned morality. Because after all the undying love for her one and only soft-goods salesman, after the abortions and the weeping and the tears welling in her beautiful hazel eyes and rolling down her cheeks one by one, just like an actress, and her heartbreaking singing and playing "Lover Come Back to Me" at the upright piano, Jenny married her boss, the owner of a small coat-manufacturing business, a sour-faced, older man who stood half a head shorter than Jenny at the altar.

They had a big wedding—sit-down dinner, band, over a hundred guests—under revolving colored lights, and then Jenny left us to live in a newly built modern apartment house near Kingsbridge Road with a sunken living room, casement windows, a Duncan Phyfe table, Queen Anne chairs (copies, of course) and a real Steinway baby grand. Her husband had paid for it all.

Happy ending to a sad, secret, sex life? Not exactly.

The only other thing I remember about that husband was that he wore a reefer coat and snapbrim hat, gangster style. Though I spent a lot of time with Jenny, it would be during the day when her husband wasn't there. She seemed to want me to be with her. Jenny was "seriously taking up her music," studying with a teacher named Bebe Santos, a light-skinned Cuban Negro with fine Caucasian features and a beautifully barbered head of thick, prematurely white curls. Jenny encouraged me to hang around with them. Bebe Santos liked me anyway. He called me Hedy Lamarr. "Good morning, Hedy Lamarr," kissing my hand, kidding around. It was pleasant, lounging away the days in the sunken living room.

Then it was all over, even before the summer came to an end. The marriage was annulled on the grounds that the marriage hadn't been consummated. Bebe Santos disappeared, though Jenny and I ran into him in the Cloisters of all places one Sunday afternoon years later, and when I saw Jenny smiling her invitational smile at Bebe I took her firmly by the arm of her Persian-lamb-trimmed winter suit and walked her away before anything started up again. By that time, Jenny had been through still another marriage to a department-store manager from Memphis, Tennessee, a Jew who looked and talked just like a Southerner. Maybe Jenny thought she could do anything she liked with Chuck Katz because he had such a soft voice and gentle manner. Maybe they quarreled so bitterly because there really wasn't "any love in the marriage" as Jenny kept insisting, and because Chuck Katz had indeed married Jenny to work himself into a good spot with Goddard Industries by becoming part of the family. If that had been his plan, it didn't work. Barry cast a cold eye on him when Chuck visited him at his New York office. The fellow would have to prove himself a good husband to Jenny before Barry would open any doors for him. Maybe it was all sex troubles again. Whatever caused their grief, it all ended with Chuck Katz packing up and walking out.

Jenny went to the roof of Harkness Pavilion to kill herself, after seeing a nerve doctor because her sleek, shining black hair had fallen out in two perfectly round circles the size of silver dollars from the shock of Chuck Katz leaving her, but she failed in the attempt. Maybe she never meant to really do it. The circles of white scalp, where the hair had come out, broke my heart, and I couldn't help crying with her as I massaged the bald spots with a salve the doctor had prescribed.

I didn't comprehend anything of what was going on. The tip of the iceberg. Yes, yes. And no clearer to me today just because Jenny's hair is all grown back sleek and black (still black) and she's wrapped in a smooth life in a Sarasota condominium with her present husband, Maxie Levine, who thinks everything she says and does is great.

IX

When she was nineteen, Anne Goddard graduated from Hunter College with some useless honors and a useless BA degree (English major, American History minor). There weren't any jobs, so when Sam Schwartz offered her one, she jumped at it. Connie's husband Sam was definitely not to be trusted ("Green eyes," Mama warned. "Only Hungarians have such eyes.") but a job wasn't her real life anyway. Her life was elsewhere, running around with Bill Morris to meetings and demonstrations and study circles and cheap cafeterias and little Italian restaurants and Russian movies or to somebody's house to dance to Sidney Bechet recordings and drink wine and take off all one's clothes. They were free spirits. They burned at capitalism's cruelties and laughed at its absurdities. Sam Schwartz was designated an absurdity. He was Connie's husband, and because she loved Connie she felt compelled to like Sam. Why not? He liked her, Anne, gazing at her in absentminded fondness from slightly protruding, very large, gray-green eyes.

Sam's place of business was a one-room loft on Eighth Avenue in the fifties, a vaguely disreputable neighborhood whose eating places, one Bickford's, one Automat, and two sleazy luncheonettes, were filled with what Bill called the effenjays, "the flotsam and jetsam of humanity, about to be swept into the dustbin of history by the coming revolution"—fading whores and their decrepit pimps, bookies, con men too old and seedy to work their charm games, crazy old ladies muttering into their too-heavy-to-hold cafeteria crockery cups of gray coffee.

Anne was mostly alone in the office. Sam Schwartz came in to sign checks and to tell her what to bill. He telephoned in two or three times a day, and dashed in now and then to pack a couple of huge cartons of stuff to be delivered to plants in little towns she had never heard of in Pennsylvania, North Carolina, and upstate New York, but what the business bought and instantly resold was mainly shipped directly to the customer from the place it was produced. Sam Schwartz didn't make anything.

Sam did business with one customer—the firm in which Barry was now a top executive. It was clear enough to Anne that Sam's business was a neat arrangement between Sam and Barry for kickbacks. Did they count on her to be discreet, or too stupid to figure it out? They never discussed it with her, and she never discussed it with them. She didn't care. The job suited her. She liked being alone in the office with almost no tasks to do. The business ran itself. She read. She wrote reviews and articles and used the office postage to send her pieces out. She used the telephone to discuss the endlessly interesting and painful details of the crowd's messy, intertwined relationships and to arrange their complicated social evenings.

Her friends dropped in to the office at any time. They knew nobody but she would be there. It was almost like her own place, the only one she had ever had. At closing time she would lock up, and walk straight out of that stupid office world to meet Bill. They went to Central Park, sat on a bench till dark, talking of Martin Anderson Nexö and of Eisenstein and of the sad life of Eleanor Marx. They argued theories of literature and life. Was Proust decadent? In a just world where all would be content, would life be colorless? Almost every night, there was a meeting to attend— against war and fascism, for solidarity with striking workers, hundreds of fund-raising events. There was a new world on the horizon—already building—where everything would be different, where work would be meaningful. Meanwhile it didn't matter what kind of work one did for money.

Then something went wrong with Sam and Barry's neat little arrangement. The office was precipitately moved to a drearier loft downtown, and the firm name was changed. For some weeks they did no business at all, and she had to contend with Sam Schwartz on hand, fretting, despondent. Then gradually the ordering and shipping and billing and payments began again, and increased, and again increased, until she was becoming almost busy, and then it all slacked off again, back to the old routine quiet.

Whatever went on at the office didn't matter. What mattered was being in love with Bill and being in love with changing the world. The two came wrapped in a single package. There were no social problems that could not be changed by trying; there were no human difficulties immune to solution in the glowing promise of a happy future. What if, in fact, love (which when you came right down to admitting what it really came right down to was sex) —what if love and sex weren't the glories she had been counting on with all her heart, but had turned out to be a struggle and a disappointment, tinged after all with Jenny's sad dreary colors that she had hoped would never touch her? She and Bill could work their way through any problem. They had to keep trying, that was the thing. But what puzzled and depressed her was just that—the trying, the effort. Shouldn't love just *be*?

There was a huge billboard she passed to and from work daily that advertised Unguentine in a display of a bathing beauty so badly sunburned that she was enveloped in fiery flames and her vapid face was contorted by a suffering so excruciating it looked like pleasure. Me and the Unguentine girl, she thought, on fire and suffering. She ran to Bill's arms burning all around her edges, and ended locked into icy fear and disappointment. Was she frigid? Terrible, terrible possibility. *Lady Chatterley's Lover*, in the unexpurgated edition, had passed around their crowd. Never to be graced with the ringing of Laurentian bells? Terrible, terrible fate.

They tried harder. Under the trees in Riverside Park, in her apartment hallway in the Bronx, and when her family moved to Brooklyn to be nearer Barry after his marriage, they tried in Prospect Park, and when the weather turned cold in the extra beds of friends who were marrying and setting up their own one-room apartments—tried over and over with growing desperation and a smothering effort to silence private anxiety which, under the circumstances, took on the aspect of public, social failure.

Shana wasn't having any trouble. She had stopped running around and had nestled down with Merv, Bill's best friend from their Bronx block, East 176th Street. Shana's only concern was that she didn't have an orgasm every time (Every Time!) and kept asking Anne if Anne thought that would get straightened out when she and Merv were married, in the spring. Anne didn't confide her own troubles to Shana. She was ashamed. A hard growth of loneliness and despair, deeply familiar, was digging into her center. Was she never to get out of herself then? Wasn't love supposed to open one out and let everything rush in?

"Throw yourself into the movement," was Bill's response to any problem. He liked to kid the movement's clichés, but he meant them too. He led her into the Young Communist League. Merv and Shana followed, because everybody in the crowd was going that way. There was no other way. The world had to be changed, and if the only way to do it was by the slow, boring methods of the Party, then that's the way it would have to be. Only through organization, only through endless meetings, endless study groups, endless discussions, endless manifestations, programs, draft programs, revised programs, final programs, and revised final programs, apparently, would the people take power. She had sucked in her breath and become a Communist as if she were leaping from dimness into a hall blazing with exits to revolution, but the drafty halls in which she and her comrades met, full of excitement and genuine hope, apparently only led to other rooms and similar halls.

Papa was outraged that they had joined "the Bolsheviks." "Criminals, a bunch of gangsters," he fumed. Mama didn't mind, as long as they were still willing to pick up the socialist *Forwards* at the corner paper stand for her. Jenny, miserable and alone that winter, toyed with the idea of joining. Wasn't everybody?

Not Barry. Barry was helping to break strikes. Helping? Single-handed, according to Papa.

"Baruch Goddard doesn't know what fear is," Papa says. "He doesn't know the meaning of the word fear. He's a giant."

Papa is going on in this way to Bill and Anne and Merv and Shana and Jenny and Mama at Sunday dinner, around a pullout drop-leaf table in the living room. Does Papa expect this band of ardent radicals to applaud? Obviously, he's making a bid for a fight. She throws a warning glance at Bill—not to allow himself to be provoked by Papa—but she's too late.

"He's got a powerful corporation behind him," Bill says. "Why should he be afraid? It's a company town, he's a company man, with the company behind him what has he got to lose?"

"He has his life to lose," Papa yells and hits the table a terrific whack.

Jenny and Mama leave the room, using the dishwashing as their excuse.

Papa closes in on Bill. "The trouble with you, young man, is that you think you know something and you don't know anything. You think you know about unions. What do you know about unions? Nothing. Ignorance and more ignorance. You know what the books say, but what actually happens is something else. I was raised up in the unions, so you can't teach me about unions. I can teach you about unions. Picket lines! I spit on their picket lines. My son walked straight into the picket line, and I give him all the credit in the world. And not a New York picket line. A mob. And good and anti-Semitic. For two cents they would have killed him."

Papa stands up. He pulls himself erect, preens, and spreads himself out. He is becoming his son, Baruch Goddard.

"My son was dressed like a prince, like a gentleman in a coat and a hat and a white shirt and a necktie. He walked right into the middle of that mob, straight into the mob, and that bunch of cowards melted away from in front of him and he walked through like a king." He pauses, looking around their faces in triumph. "And right away they started negotiating. And before you know it the strike is over. And not only in that plant but in the whole twenty-two other plants all over the country."

"Amazing," Bill says. He is pale and angry, and though for Anne's sake he will not fight with Papa, he looks at her accusingly, and then at Shana and Merv.

Nobody takes up the good fight. They have no hope of winning Papa from his wrong position, they explain lamely to Bill as the girls walk the fellows to the subway station. Bill will not be appeased. They are all bourgeois sentimentalists, closing their eyes to the class enemy in their midst. Shana refuses to be "clarified." She throws away seriousness altogether and dances ahead, luring Merv after her with a siren song.

"Come a-wa-a-ay, come a-wa-a-ay," she calls.

"You're not a serious person," Bill shouts.

Merv laughs and follows her.

Alone with Bill at the subway steps, Anne attempts an explanation. "Papa can't help it. He's proud of his son. He'd be proud of Barry if Barry were part of Murder, Incorporated."

"He *is* Murder, Incorporated," Bill shouts. "Those workers are being starved, locked out. That's killing. That's just the same as murder."

"Oh, Bill," she says.

"Yes, yes," Bill yells. "That's the reality. Not that fairy tale your father told us. The big hero against the anti-Semitic mob."

"Sam Schwartz told me a completely different version," Anne says. "Barry was in his shirt sleeves out in the cold and the snow. He pushed right through the center of the line to reach a spot where he could talk to the men. Barry was wearing a red necktie and one of the workers jostled him and pulled on his tie and acted as if Barry was a pansy. Barry stood still and took the tie off and handed it to the guy with a gracious bow. That got everybody startled and laughing. Then Barry got up on the concrete wall and talked to them and they agreed to negotiate."

"And you believe *that!*"

"I just thought you'd be interested in Sam Schwartz's version," she says, near tears.

They mesh into a bitter, dreary quarrel. The late afternoon is turning cold and windy. In the semiprotection of the subway stairs, they tear at one another; neither one will yield to the other. She hates him at that moment. He's all rigidity and stubbornness, an ignorant boy who doesn't even know how to give pleasure, and thinks he knows everything. She loves him when he's foolish, when he's kidding around, when he dances with her and plays handball with his friends. She's the only one of the girls who goes to the handball courts under the bridge to watch the fellows play. She sits on a bench alone enjoying the power and grace of Bill's body intent on a struggle against unyielding concrete and a little ball. He's fierce to win, and usually does, lifting her from the bench and swinging her around in sweaty triumph.

If she were to generously submit to him in every way, would that be the charm to bring them together simply—to come to rest in one another?

Passing people climbing up and down the subway steps flick their eyes at them. She is exhausted and cold. Exposed. She wants to go home to a warm room. She lets the tears roll.

"You don't really love me," she says. "Maybe we'd better break off. . . ."

He seizes her in a rough grab. "Don't say that." He is kissing her. His face is frozen. The smell of his hot breath is unpleasant. She's sick of him, but very glad that he still wants her.

"You're like a hunk of ice," he says. "I ought to be shot, keeping you arguing in the cold."

He smothers her face against his chest. Still he can't yield.

"I'm just trying to make you admit the truth. You must understand that your loyalty to your family . . ."

"Okay," she says. She looks up. So close to her, his large nose and loose lips and unevenly placed, worried eyes are tossed on the wide area of his face like the debris of an accident. She is terribly sorry for him and for herself. She sees in his tormented eyes that he *cannot* relinquish her to her own opinions, that he *must* have her agreement—more than anything else about her he lusts for her total submission. "I do understand, I understand that he's the class enemy. I hate him for breaking the strike. I hate Papa for defending him. Okay? Does that satisfy you?" She is abashed to hear her own sobs, but she feels safer, she feels that she has locked Bill to her.

X
_____

On a morning when Sam Schwartz was in the office, Barry arrived as well, unexpected and unannounced. Sam Schwartz went popeyed with apprehension. Barry barely nodded to Anne. He kept his hat and coat on and stood in the middle of the loft. That he was in one of his rages was clear from his fixed stare, the whites of his eyes showing beneath the hard black pupils.

"Hi, Barry, how's Pauline?" she said, automatically trying to please. He liked the family to show interest in Pauline, but she felt like a fawning fool when he totally ignored her. Was he mad at _her_?

"What's going on, Sam?" was what he said. "What the hell's going on here?"

Sam suggested that Anne go for a walk and a cup of coffee, for forty minutes or so. She took _The Wings of the Dove_ with her. (She had decided to attempt a major literary essay. None of her little reviews and essays had gotten published. Perhaps a more ambitious project would be luckier—an essay on money in the novels of Henry James, the "Marxist" angle a way of sneaking in an appreciative essay on aristocratic HJ in a left publication.) In the sudden freedom, sitting alone at a little table, drinking coffee, eating a toasted English muffin with marmalade, reading her book, and jotting down quotes, she was surprised by happiness. How simple it was, when it came.

She came back a little later than forty minutes. The office door was locked, and she could hear shouting from inside. Though she had a key, it seemed best not to use it. She sat on the dirty ledge of a dirty, alcoved window and waited.

Barry emerged and went directly to the elevator without seeing her, and she didn't call out. He was forbidding—a presence bristling with rage and authority, impatiently summoning the elevator. She wouldn't have known what to say. *I'm innocent* was all she could think of.

She was out of a job. She didn't know what had happened and nobody explained, not even Sam Schwartz, whose face seemed to have turned permanently gray from Barry's visit.

"Too smart for your own damn good," she had heard Barry shouting while she waited in the hallway. "When you think of another plan to outsmart Baruch Goddard, try again and see where that gets you."

It was all over. Sam Schwartz was no longer a businessman and she was no longer his girl Friday. It seemed Sam also owed a lot of money to some shady characters who came around to the apartment one night looking for him. Mama told them she didn't know where he was.

"A crook," Papa said. "He gives *our* address, not his own. It was a miracle those gangsters didn't come in and beat me up."

"He's protecting his wife and children," Mama said. "He's a child, a son-in-law, don't call him a crook."

Sam Schwartz's financial "affairs" were in an incredible mess. Connie was the last to know of the extent of her husband's involvement in petty, crooked deals, and of the wild scrabbling going on to cover his unlucky guesses with worse mistakes. Connie was on the phone to Papa every morning (until her service was disconnected for nonpayment) with reports of fresh disasters. Their car and their new pieces of furniture were being repossessed. Did that mean her belongings were irretrievably lost? Sam had borrowed heavily on his life-insurance policy and failed to pay the last premium. Did that mean all the money paid in over the years was lost?

"Certainly, that fool, that *ganef*, lost you every penny, every stick you own," Papa bellowed righteously, as if he had never bet and lost in his life. "Thrown out!" he said. "It's thrown-out money. You would have done better to take it straight from your pocketbook and throw it straight in the garbage pail, what that fool has done to you."

As if his misfortunes were translated into physical impurities coursing through his heated bloodstream, Sam Schwartz broke out into boils. A particularly large, angry outbreak on his leg infected into the bone, and Connie's husband came to desperate rest at last in a hospital bed, with Connie standing at his side in stunned, dry-eyed grief that left her loyalty untouched. According to the gospel of the popular songs of her day, Connie believed in the "whatever my man is, I am his forevermore" approach. Connie and her kids moved in with the family.

She knew no more about the causes of the bust-up between Barry and Sam than anybody else, but naturally Connie blamed Barry.

"Take my advice, Anna," she advised bitterly, "don't depend on your brother Barry. You never know where you're at with our brother. One week you're up, the next you're down. One minute he loves you, the next he never wants to look at you again," and away from Sam's hospital bed, burst into tears.

"Take my advice, Anne," Barry said, "Stay away from Sam Schwartz. He's no friend of yours. He's bad news for everybody." Barry was on a flying visit to announce his new policy to his father and mother. He was through paying the rent and the utility bills. He had a wife, a baby coming, his own responsibilities. "Let the rest of your kids take over for a change. The *uhrumas*. Mama's poor kids. Mama's *uhrumas*."

"He's crazy," Jenny said when Barry returned the following night with the rent money and two big bags of groceries. She hugged and kissed him. "In our hearts, we know we can always depend on you."

"Boy," Barry said, "I'm sunk."

But he called a family council. No wives. Sam Schwartz was still in the hospital. Just the family. He was absolutely serious. The subject was mutual responsibility, equal share of the burdens, everybody paying his own way and a part of Mama and Papa's. All Barry would pay was five dollars a week. Immediate agreement, in principle, but in practice, Shana fought to pay only five dollars a week for room and board and to save the rest of her salary toward her wedding to Merv in the spring. For the rest, Jenny was earning very little, Saul had been demoted and given a pay cut on his job, Connie wasn't working and her children were additional burdens, Josh didn't have an extra penny, Papa hadn't had any work since he had lost his nighttime cashier's job, and Anne was out of work.

Under his breath, to Mama, Papa blamed their situation on Barry. Why had Barry insisted that he give up his grocery store? At least the store brought in enough to keep a roof over their heads and a bite to eat in the house. Inactivity was making Papa sick. He complained of chest pains, dizziness, blurred vision. He often sat and stared at nothing, or paced and pulled on his fingers, then jumped up to become aggressively vigorous, washing clothes and ironing shirts, fetching a huge block of ice from an icehouse three blocks from the apartment, carrying the burden on his shoulder to save ten cents, walking to save the nickels in fare when he looked for work every day. He was busy concocting a variety of moneymaking schemes. The whole family ought to start a mail-order business right from the apartment. But what should they sell? Maybe he should open a home laundry. He was looking into buying a chicken farm.

"With what?" Mama asked.

The family managed, under the new regime of "sharing the responsibilities," to keep going for a couple of months, then they were dispossessed and the utilities were turned off. They packed by candlelight, moving in the morning to an apartment a few blocks away, smaller, newly painted, and with three month's concession. On his way to work, Barry dropped in to give Mama the money for the movers.

"It's hopeless," he said.

"Baruch," Mama said, "what do you want from me, what can I do?"

"Not you," he said. "I don't expect you to do anything. You can't help yourself. It's your kids who should be kicked in the ass."

He spoke as if Anne wasn't right there, carefully unpacking the Passover dishes.

"God shines on everything you do," Mama said. "It's not so easy for others."

"God hasn't got a goddamn thing to do with it. I work. I think about my work every minute. I wake up in the middle of the night and think about it. It isn't just happening to me. I do it. I work. God helps those who help themselves."

"You're right," Mama said. "Only he forgets some. I don't know why."

"Because they don't move their asses, that's why. Look at her."

He gestured at Anne. "She's supposed to be smart. If that crook Sam Schwartz doesn't get her a job, she's permanently out of work."

It was true that she hadn't looked very hard. She had had a temporary job at a publisher's printer as a typist. She had earned twenty dollars a week, a good salary, because she was supposed to use her brains. She was in the errata department. She typed scraps —a page, part of a page, part of a paragraph. Page 479, paragraph 2, line 14, change "with reference to the dairy industry" to "with reference to the cheese-producing sector of the dairy industry." At the end of the day her head felt like a sack of rolling marbles. She was happy to be let go.

Again out of work. The evenings filled themselves—meetings, actions, discussions, parties, movies, the business of active youthful hope, organized and socialized, and beneath, the subterranean life of being in love with Bill, a voyage on a dark river, silverlit, but sad with difficulties. The daytime belonged to her. Squander it on useless job hunting? She had better things to do. She worked on her study of Henry James in the reading room of the Forty-Second Street Public Library. To enter that place was to her surprise happiness, again and again. She always chose the Fifth Avenue entrance, guarded by the splendid lions, mounting the broad outside steps between them into the marble lobby. Inside, again she chose the long route, preferring the marble stairs to the elevator, to reach the spacious reading room bathed in quiet, and in the light from its upper windows far above and from the green-shaded lamps on the long tables below, and in the room's thick, nourishing air of knowledge compressed and documented, pinned down for human use. For her use. She sat at one end of a long table, in her separate pool of light, in the company of other workers at their individual labors, surrounded by the props of the life of the mind —a hissing silence, paper, pen, open books—supported and sustained by the buoyant pressure of the right to think, recognized and validated. The life of the mind, a strong and vigorous place, existed. It did.

It was to Papa that she confided her project on the spur of the moment late one night. Everybody else is asleep. At the kitchen table she tells him that she's working on an essay that she hopes to sell to a magazine. Papa is so deeply excited that he falls into using Mama's pet name for her.

"Try, try, Hannahle. Keep trying. One day you'll get recognition, you'll see."

He pulls up his chair very close to hers, to seal the conspiracy.

"To be an artist is the finest accomplishment in the world. What is there to compare with a writer, an artist, a composer? Nothing. Nothing can compare. I don't care what—all the riches, the highest positions—nothing, in comparison. The composer Mendelssohn was already a genius when he was seventeen. When he was a boy of seventeen he wrote *A Midsummernight's Dream*, he wrote the "Wedding March." A genius! You're young. Don't give up. Who knows where genius shows itself? I had high aspirations when I was your age. One day you'll catch on fire with inspiration. A spark can land on you without notice. Mendelssohn walks into a cave. How many people were already in and out of that cave? Hundreds, maybe thousands. A spark falls on Mendelssohn and he writes *Fingal's Cave*. Soon the whole world knows this music. That's what it is to be a genius. A Jew, too, descended from another great Jew, his grandfather Moses Mendelssohn."

She is overcome by instant depression. If she mentions the assimilationist theories of Moses Mendelssohn and the disturbing fact that Felix's father converted to Christianity, they will be launched on a fight. But what is really depressing is all this genius talk. She feels a sickly worry for her modest essay. Failure, disappointment for her Papa, even before she's quite started.

The satisfying days at the library are abruptly ended by Sam Schwartz. Out of the hospital, not entirely cured, limping on a suppurating leg, he is busy, busy, busy—working up new ventures, getting himself "established."

"My family must be brought back under my roof," he says.

At the moment he has no roof. Not even Connie is sure of his whereabouts from night to night. There's no room for him at the apartment, where Connie and her children are still camping on folding beds that are hidden behind the doors during the day. He visits every few days. Mama feeds him, tells him he doesn't look well, that he should rest more. Connie cries when he leaves to run around "looking for the right proposition." His large, green eyes are fevered with tormented determination. He drives on, he dashes from one appointment to the next.

He comes up with a job for Anne. Just the kind of job she likes. One-girl office, alone most of the day, good pay, twenty-two dollars a week. Sounds good, but on her arrival at the new job, it looks fishy.

Sam Schwartz meets her for coffee, nervously intimate and rushed, and escorts her, limping, to the office of his friend. His friend is a fat, despondent man with the broadest backside she's ever seen. He hires her without trial or a single question. Though the small, one-room office is bright with sun, and all the equipment is spanking new, the place has a time-stopped, fly-by-night feel. Except for empty cartons there's no sign of a business, and her new boss's manner is suspect—shooting side glances expressing a worried unease about her that she can sense Sam Schwartz calming and smoothing. In a hesitant, deferential, almost courtly manner, her boss outlines her curious duties. First, he gives her a key. She is to lock up when she goes out for her lunch hour and at five thirty when she leaves for the day. Between those duties, she is to type all the names and addresses from the S section of the Manhattan telephone book.

"In how many copies?" Anne asks.

"No carbons," he says and throws Sam Schwartz a distraught glance.

Sam Schwartz shenanigans—but what does it mean? What's the purpose of this curious setup?

She doesn't care. Not her life, these stupid activities. For two weeks she revels in a clean, bright, quiet, private workspace. Her boss lumbers in and out once a day, and telephones once in the late afternoon. He has no true interest in how quickly she is typing up the S names from the directory. She spends one hour a day doing that, and the rest working up her notes on *The Spoils of Poynton*. The study of Henry James is taking on real substance. She thinks it might even become a book to open a door to a real job on a magazine or in a publishing house.

Suddenly her job is over. Her boss, melancholy, pale, and uncomfortable, tells her that her services are no longer required. A few days later there's a terrible family explosion. In a bewildering development that she cannot comprehend, her paychecks emerge at the center of this blowup—two twenty-two-dollar checks made out to and endorsed by Anne Goddard, cleared through a bank, and now held in Barry's fist, mysteriously metamorphosed into a vile weapon used against him in that world where men deal, and money is made and lost, and accounts settled.

Connie weeps. Too much to bear, not to weep.

"The only reason your husband isn't going to jail is that he's your husband," Barry yells. "That other bastard's going to jail. I didn't study law for nothing. I *know* what I'm doing. They don't. Sam Schwartz thought he had me. Like hell he had me. Keep him out of my sight, you hear, just keep him out of my sight."

Connie weeps.

"I don't know anything about this," Anne says. She feels the blood draining out of her face. Mama comes to her side, takes her hand, but Anne pulls it away. "I don't know what any of this is all about."

"I believe it," Barry says. "You're too damn dumb to know what's going on right under your own nose. You don't even know when you're being used. Ask your sister. Ask your sister what a fool Sam Schwartz made of you."

Connie weeps. Anne is too outraged to cry.

"For two cents," Barry says, and he crumples the checks and pounds them with his fist, "I'd send the pack of you to jail. Pack of crooks."

"Leave us alone," Connie sobs. "We don't know anything about it. We don't even know what you're talking about."

Connie's children hover in the doorway, angry and defensive. They are old enough, nine and eleven, to know they are under attack, but not why. Connie wants them safely out of this scene.

"Go in the other room," she says.

Connie is working to pull her ruined self together. Anne wants to help her.

"Go into the other room, kids," Anne says.

"What's the matter?" her niece asks.

"Everything will be okay," Anne says. "Go inside."

"It won't," her niece says. In the little girl's face there is a stunned wisdom, as if she had known all along that something basic was wrong but that it is the open confirmation that stuns. "Everything is never okay," she says, but she takes her little brother with her and leaves the room.

"I'm not going to stand here and let Sam take all the blame," Connie says, desperately defensive. "You're not lily-pure. I'm not that dumb. You got along very well together when things were going right. Now suddenly my husband is a crook. He isn't doing anything you didn't do."

"Listen to me," Barry says. "Maybe you'll learn something. He thought he could outsmart me. He can't. Do him a favor. Tell him I said not to tangle with me, he'll lose every time. Tell him to stay away from me. And tell him to stay away from Anne. If she's too dumb to figure it out for herself, somebody has to do it for her."

"Barry," Mama says, "what's the good of such talk?"

He gives her a terrible look and leaves the house.

Papa is beside himself. "What did you do, you fool?" he hollers at Mama. "He's the only one who pays the bills and you insult him. What will Sam Schwartz's family eat if Baruch Goddard doesn't give us money? And Sam Schwartz bites the hand that feeds his children!"

Connie weeps again.

Yet when Barry, soon after, strikes out on his own and goes into business for himself and asks Anne to work for him as his confidential secretary, in spite of misgivings and of her view of the business world—she tells Bill—as one big bore of stupidity and more stupidity, she says yes to Barry. In the taxi, riding to his new office, Barry tells her that he's going "all the way to the top," and that he's going to take her with him, and she laughs at him and makes him angry. And then he fires her.

"You just don't seem to have what it takes, Anne," he says, carefully positioned so as not to look her in the eye.

Was his offer genuine—an effort on his part to heal the breach of the Sam Schwartz fiasco? Or has she been an idiot again and left herself open to being used, this time for Barry's gratification—to get his own back, to pay her back for what he thought she had done to him? Walking fast on her high heels through the noise and confusion of the garment center, pushing through a harassed mass of humanity on the sidewalks, dodging the hand trucks and the cars and big trucks in the streets, rushing to Bill, and to put as much distance as possible between herself and the man, her brother, who had just raveled her confidence to shreds, she swears to herself that she was innocent. She never meant him any harm. And what of him? Does he mean to do the harm he does—this brother who swung her through the air, whose foot she rode as if she were part of him? Maybe he can't help himself, she thinks, but I hate him anyway.

WHAT'S NEW
WITH THE FAMILY?

What are your brothers and sisters doing these days?" Barry to Anne. They are having a morning coffee break, during the one day she worked for him.

"Pretty much the same."

"Your sister Connie and her family still in your apartment?"

"Connie and the kids are. Sam's back in the hospital. He's really having trouble with that leg."

"Some fun. Where are you all sleeping?"

"You know, folding beds behind the doors."

"How's Jenny?"

"She's better. I can tell by what she's singing."

He laughs. "What do you mean?"

"She's moved on from "Lover Come Back to Me' to 'None But the Lonely Heart.' "

"Is that a good sign?"

"Definitely. And to 'Who is Sylvia? What is she-hee,' "—she sings it, mimicking Jenny's operatic breathiness—" 'that all our swains comme-end her?' "

"Does she still sing 'Nita, Jua-ha-ha-nita, ask thy heart if we should part . . .'?" Barry sings.

"I don't know that one. It seems to be out of the repertory."

"Do you know I used to write song lyrics?"

Anne laughs.

"Don't laugh. I was pretty good. We have a lot of musical talent in our family. Jenny had the chance to be trained to play the organ

at the Brooklyn Albee or the Paramount, I forget which. Papa
wouldn't let her. He thought she'd be entering a white-slave traffic
den. She would have knocked them dead."

He finishes his coffee.

"And maybe made a little money," he adds.

"What about Shana?" he asks.

"She's fine."

"What about her gay Lothario?"

"Merv? He's a swell guy."

"Is he really going to marry her? That's number one. And question number one A: Can he make a living?"

"Merv's all right. He's a very hard worker."

"Papa was a hard worker too. What does this fellow Merv work
at?"

"He's a salesman, fabric salesman."

"You mean he's a normal, regular guy with a normal, regular
job? How come one of my sisters took up with a normal, regular
guy?"

Anne is wary. The conversation is coming uncomfortably close
to her real life.

"Are they really getting married?"

"Oh, yes, in the spring."

"What about your genius? I hear your boyfriend is some kind of
a genius."

"Bill? Who told you that?"

"Papa. Papa said he's an honor student at Columbia Law."

"Papa said that about Bill?"

"I don't know what his name is. Papa said he's your boyfriend.
Have you got more than one? Isn't one enough?"

She puts up her hands, palms outward.

"No trespassing," she says.

XI

Out of work again. She couldn't slough her care off on others and go back to the library. Too humiliating to beg for carfare. She decided to look into a Sunday *Times* regularly repeated ad. *Refined, college educated, young. Good ballroom dancer. Neat. No experience necessary. Good earnings.* What the hell.

She borrowed Shana's plum velvet suit and Jenny's full-sleeved satin blouse, but didn't make up too heavily. Neat, refined. The studio was one flight up in a building under the Ninth Avenue El, where the tracks curved sharply eastward, and she hesitated at the darkened, canopied doorway under the slanted light of the elevated, afraid to follow the arrow pointing up a wide flight of carpeted stairs to Miss Vilma's Internationally Famous Dance Salon, until a short, dyed blonde with the breezy air of a waitress or a practical nurse passed her and went up and in, and then Anne did too.

The reception room was dim, heavily draped against the daylight and the outside elevated train.

"Siddown," the redhead at the reception desk said. "Manny'll be wid you in a minute."

The man noiselessly gliding over the carpeted floor of the reception room in pointed patent-leather shoes was so typically The Latin Lover that Anne thought she must have fallen into a practical joke. When she stood up at his sign to follow him, she was taller than he by just enough to feel awkward. She was afraid, again, when he shut the door of the studio he had led her into. The room was reassuring—a bare floor, a record player, a stack of records, a mirrored wall—not even a chair. He started a record, led her around in a waltz. He danced superbly, but with such a total absence of joy it became a shockingly melancholy physical experience, unlike anything she had ever experienced. Then he turned the music off and to a kind of military one-two count led her into a few steps each of a foxtrot, rhumba, open tango, and a kind of quick march that he told her was the Peabody. Then he released her.

"No lindy hop," he said. "We don't teach it. We don't need no broken bones. Only classic ballroom techniques. What's your name?" He had a slight, indefinable accent.

"Anne Goddard," she said.

"No good." His melancholy deepened. "What's your middle name?"

She shook her head.

"Awright. Your name is Miss Alma. We already got a Miss Anne. So, okay, you're Miss Alma."

He was on his way out the door, starting down the passage. She was supposed to follow? From the studios lining the hallway came sounds of recorded music, giggling, and a commanding, cheerful female voice. "The other foot, the other foot." There were slits cut into the doors at the man's eye level, and without stooping he peered into each as they walked.

"I'm Manny," he said, and pushed open a similar door at the far end. "Get acquainted with the other girls. See you later."

Two girls in the room, Miss Barbara, Miss Patricia.

"Call me Barbie." Miss Barbara is a kitten, soft all over—body, cheeks, dewy brown eyes, and infant's fluff of short hair.

Miss Patricia is dazzling, a long-stemmed, carved American beauty, breasts rising out of her low-cut blouse like burning suns —impossible to look directly at them, impossible not to—a classic profile on a strong, columnar neck, glowing blond hair, deep blue eyes in sculptured sockets.

"Call me Pat." Her smile commands an extraordinary response —a salute of guns or the singing of "The Star-Spangled Banner."

"Welcome to the Zoo."

"Am I hired? If I'm hired my name is Miss Alma, but call me Anne."

"If Manny brought you to this room, you're hired. Sit down," Pat says. "Take a load off your feet. You'll be dead by the time you go home. Thursday's a tough day."

Pat slides two folding chairs face to face, moving in awkward athletic movements that make her more human and appealing. "Kick off your shoes and up with your feet. I'll hang your jacket on a hanger. The girls' room is down the hall. That's where we change. It's the only room in this jail that doesn't have a peep-hole."

"Change what?"

"Clothes. Thursday night. Party night. Tonight's the night. Do you have an evening gown?"

Anne shakes her head.

"Sunday night dress? You have to have something long. I'd lend you one of mine but it wouldn't fit. And Barbie's are too short for you. What you're wearing's pretty. That'll be okay for the first time."

"What's party night?" White-slave traffic.

" 'Ten cents a dance,' "—Pat sings it—" 'that's what they pay me . . .' " in a light, girlish soprano that doesn't match her phenomenal chest.

Her beauty almost immediately begins to recede, fading into a sister's good looks in the quick intimacy they establish, but for Anne there will always be the first stunning impact whenever Pat enters the room. The three girls in that room are Manny's specials, "refined, college educated, neat," for Manny's high-class clients who want to learn dancing from high-class girls. There are enough of these to keep three girls busy. Pat is busiest, then Barbara. (Barbara is quiet in Pat's presence, talkative when Pat is gone.) Anne (Miss Alma) is at the bottom of the heap, assigned to an appointment chart abandoned by a refined-type girl who had quit the day before. Turnover among the specials is high—even higher than among the regulars. Not much contact between the regulars and the specials, except on party nights when all the students and the teachers are thrown in together.

"The regulars can be real helpful if they want to be," Pat says. "They'll lend you a needle and thread and an extra pair of shoes if you break a heel, or they can be just as bitchy as dogs over a bone. They're moody. Try to keep away from them."

Pat is fixing Barbie's hair for Barbie's first appointment. Then she fixes her own face in the mirror of a round makeup box.

"Dollar an hour," Pat explains. "But only for time spent teaching, not a dime for all the time waiting around in this room. Trial lessons are thirty minutes, but you have to work an hour's worth so they'll sign up. Commissions. That's where the money is. Ten per cent."

Manny opens the door, calls Anne out, leads her to an empty studio, and gives her a quick lesson in the foolproof dance instruction technique.

"Does it work?" Anne asks, back in the specials' room.

"You can teach anybody how to dance badly," Pat says. "It really is foolproof. As long as they dance with *you*, they can dance."

"Is he always like that? Or is something the matter with him?"

"Manny? Manny's either sad or he's mad. That's all there is to Manny. He's okay. He's fair. He won't bother you. Just don't get him mad."

And then, before she has time to digest any of this, here she is, on her own, alone in a studio with her first student, Lt. Raymond Dennis of the United States Navy, a diffident, middle-aged adolescent, stiffly formal in his white dress uniform, braid, medals, ribbons, and all. She faces this stranger with a smile to cover her nervousness, her ignorance. What is she supposed to do? Dance. Teach him the waltz. A tiny, deep-orange bug is venturing out of the immaculate officer's fly. She is transfixed, watching its voyage onto a field of white duck thigh. A ladybug? A bedbug. She shudders. Lt. Dennis is watching her out of his private agony of shyness. He doesn't know that the bedbug has retreated between two straining buttons. He doesn't know that he's wearing a bedbug.

"Be sure it's true when you say I love you," the record sings. "It's a sin to tell a lie."

The bug makes another little foray, ducks back under cover. Anne has forgotten everything Manny taught her. She wants only to stay out of Lt. Dennis's arms. She stands, frozen. Lt. Dennis is beginning to sweat. Something is expected of him that he's not doing. He steps forward.

"Well, little lady, I guess you're waiting for me to show you what a bad dancer I am." He takes her in his arms in a convulsive grab, and blunders around the floor.

She tries to steer him into some sort of dance shape, lugging his squared-away, musically senseless body around the studio floor as if he were a corpse she doesn't know how to dispose of.

"Millions of hearts have been broken," the record sings, "just because these words were spoken."

She arches her body away from his. The dark-orange bug has emerged again, creeping across the carefully pressed crease of the lieutenant's pants. She is aware of Manny's presence at the peephole, darkening, lightening, passing off, then almost immediately reappearing. She has totally forgotten how to teach the waltz. Manny's shadow stays put at the peephole. He is sending a poisonous mist of rage at her through the slit.

"I love you, yes I do, I love you."

What's happened to time? It's standing still, stretching into an interminable, sickening yawn.

"If you break my heart, I'll die."

Lt. Dennis stumbles, stops, excuses himself, and takes out a snowy handkerchief to wipe off his sweating palms. With a piteous sigh he returns to his stumbling labor.

"So be sure it's true, when you say I love you. It's a sin to tell a lie."

Mercifully, the record ends. But not the session. Change the record. Check the bug. Nowhere in sight. Manny has abandoned his station at the peephole. Perhaps the bug is on her now? She shakes herself in a strange, shuddering movement, sees the lieutenant's eyes widen with surprise, fear, a hint of lust. The door slit darkens with Manny's presence.

"The moon and you," the record begins.

Lt. Dennis grabs her and they go round again in a struggling, fighting dance of agony. She is beginning to feel as deeply for Lt. Dennis's suffering as for her own. He groans as he lumbers about, believing that he's singing.

He catches her eye and smiles a desperate leer.

Enough. No more. Let it come to an end. She prays, and the record drags on, and they stumble about and Lt. Dennis groans, thinking that he's singing.

Somehow her head clears. She remembers the first step of the foolproof technique. She may still save herself from being fired. Forget the bedbug. Pull yourself together, she orders, and she takes the hand of Lt. Dennis and explains that what they had been doing was a warm-up and now she's going to teach him his first real dance step.

"Here we go," she calls out cheerfully, determined to ignore the bug, now walking a vertical, bumpy road on the lieutenant's fly. "Put your left foot forward, just as I do. No. Left. Left. Good. Good. That's it. Now right foot to the side, just the way I do it. Good. Now glide, don't step, glide, don't march. Loosen up, now, bend your knees, now close, bring your feet together, slide, slide, don't march, no, no, other way, left to right, good, wonderful! Now let's do that again, Lieutenant."

They have completed one waltz step when the buzzer sounds the end of the trial lesson. He's ecstatic at his progress.

"Miss Alma, you're a whiz," he says. "I didn't know I could learn how to dance so fast. I never would have believed it." He is in a triumphant flush as she flees from him back to the specials' room. The room is empty. She is in a kind of fit, shuddering and shaking out her dress, whirling, flinging her arms and making sounds like smothered screaming sobs. She had submitted her body to an abomination. Wasn't dancing one of the sacred rites? But did she have to make such a mess of it?

Manny bursts in.

"What are you, some kind of a moron? You know better than me how to instruct in the art of ballroom techniques? I've been teaching for twenty years on three continents? Just do like I say, you dumbbell, if you want to work here. Try not to be so goddamn smart." He is very angry, but remains very melancholy. "You got a two-fifty commission coming to you. We shouldn't even give it to you, how you acted. You're supposed to escort the student to the office for the sales pitch. He could of gone right down the steps. Right out on the street. Then we would of lost him. You understand?

"And another thing," Manny says, before he leaves. "How do you always know when I'm at the peephole? I don't like you turning around whenever I come to the peephole. You keep your head the other way, you understand? Don't keep turning around every time I look in the peephole. You understand?"

She understands, more or less.

By the end of the first week Miss Alma has acquired three records of her own, two S. Klein evening gowns, a pair of dramatically arched eyebrows, and a mouth with a full lower lip (courtesy of Barbie, studying makeup along with her other stage techniques). Miss Alma is prettier than Anne. Forget Anne. Anne would not be entering this enormous, ten-cent-a-dance ballroom, praying that the men eyeing the girls will not rate her "a dog," her fears masked by green eye shadow and heavy black mascara and a big smile.

"It's not really that kind of a place," Bill says. (He likes her working there. She can't believe it.) "You're getting ten cents, but the men have to pay more, and they have to be students. It's not as if the men are from off the streets, they're not walking in off the streets."

"Don't let the bastards screw you," Pat says, but she means "cheat." She's dazzling in a pale-blue chiffon gown. "They'll cheat if you let them. No tickee, no go. If Manny catches anybody cheating, they're as good as dead. And if he thinks you're letting them cheat, you're as good as dead. Get a ticket for every dance."

Anne did, jamming them into the beaded purse Pat had lent her. Some of her partners tipped—a dollar slipped into her palm. She was doing something right? Something wrong.

Manny hollered her out in his sad way. "Don't let them grab you so close. They're trying to rub off on you. You call me anyone tries that," and wouldn't let the men who had tipped her get to her again. He saw to it that a man was steered into her arms the second they were emptied. The band shortened up on the length of the dances as the evening progressed. The men grumbled, but not to excess. Excessive grumblers were handled by two large, melancholy men constantly circling the periphery of the floor. She lost all sense of the men as differentiated human beings, except when a real dancer turned up accidentally. That was a sweet relief, but Manny kept these circulating. One wanted to stay with her, and she wanted him to stay, it was so easy to dance with him, but that wasn't allowed. There were two rest periods during the long night. She peed, retouched her face, indestructibly painted in Barbie's theatrical makeup, combed her hair, sat on one chair and kicked off her high-heeled pumps and put her feet up on another chair. A mistake to remove the shoes—painful to put them back on.

There was a steady stream of men down the stairs and back up, to and from a bar across the street, forbidden territory for the girls. Anybody who got too drunk was bounced. Redheaded Miss Vilma, her eyes painted in vivid blue eye shadow and mascara, was an electric beam sweeping the floor for trouble, from a cashier's perch where she sold tickets. Twenty-five cents a piece. Twenty-five tickets for five dollars. The girl's cut was ten cents. Manny circled, circled, a trainer watchful of his cats. Admission was by invitation to students and their friends. To her amazement, there were some women students and two male instructors—pale, melancholy Latin-Lover Manny types—but younger.

She couldn't describe to Bill what that first day had been like—a strangling wave she struggled to survive, leaving in its wake the sweet, strong comradeship of Barbie and Pat and an inexplicable sensation of freedom. Bill came to see for himself. Called out to the reception room by Manny, expecting to find a trial-lesson student, she found Bill, self-consciously perched at the edge of an armchair, leafing through a movie magazine, uncertain and diminished in this strange environment, whispering his greeting hoarsely, turned away from Miss Vilma's watching electric blue eyes. He had come to take her to lunch. But she had a lesson to give in twenty minutes and he had a class in an hour and a half. They walked out into the street and he kissed her in a doorway. Furtive, hot, and bulging—in an empty store doorway, in the plain light of day. She felt she had had an encounter with a stranger. She had become a different girl for him. Desirable. Other men paid money to put their arms around her.

"It takes guts to work at this kind of job," Bill said. "You put aside your middle-class prejudices and entered the working class. I ought to do something like that. Quit Columbia. Work in a factory."

She laughed at him, but it was delightful to have him so ardent. He even rearranged meetings, political meetings, to be able to spend his free time with her. Now it was she whose schedule had to be accommodated, she who was working every day and some evenings, and making a lot of money, too—thirteen dollars on the first day. A fortune.

He opened up when they made love now. He swooshed his lips around in her hair and sucked on her ear lobes. When they got into bed and their naked bodies touched all over, he said "Ah!" in a long-drawn-out, marveling sound. He had always been so tight, so silent. Now he didn't care if there were friends in the next room, he gasped and cried out and when it was over for him he said "I love you," and remembered to think about her. He asked "Do you love me?" and "Are you satisfied?," inviting her to lie.

It was money she was in love with. She wanted to earn more,

more. She worked every day in the week, in order to build up her schedule of lessons. Manny liked that.

"Mostly you girls just sit around, so sit around here. What's the dif? Hang around here, you never know when a trial lesson turns up."

Most of her students were ordinary men who really wanted to learn to dance. Some had their strange kinks and were looking for something else. She had a young guy mad for bones who took every chance to feel her shoulder blades, her hip bones, the little knobs at her wrists and ankles, between Manny's trips to the peephole. That student tipped her five dollars extra every lesson. She told Barbie and Pat about her bone man in one of their breathless interrupted conversations between appointments. She got their histories, or some part of their histories, in these gulps of confidences. Barbie wanted to be an actress. She had a year to prove herself before going back to Binghamton, to Mama and Papa and the high-school sweetheart who wanted to marry her. Pat was working to accumulate enough money to go to medical school. She wanted to be a gynecologist. Pat's boyfriend situation was too complicated for Anne to unravel. She seemed to have a couple of regulars, including one of her students, an old man, over seventy, white-haired, frail, with the manners of a movie aristocrat. Anne had seen him at the Thursday-night party. Dating students was against the rule, subject to immediate dismissal.

"Don't be ridiculous," Pat said when Anne worried about her dating the old man. "All the girls have something on the side."

"What do you two do?" Anne wasn't sure that she wanted to know, given the old fellow's frailty.

"*I* don't do anything," Pat said. "I just sit there. At twenty dollars an evening." She laughed her boyish guffaw.

Pat and Barbie shared an apartment, a one-room cluttered mess not far from the studio. Barbie gave two private dance lessons a week at the apartment. Ten dollars per lesson.

"Dance lessons, here?" Anne said, when she saw their place, and realized at once how stupid she was being.

They advised her, they helped her buy clothes, they gave her a sensational hairdo.

Pat advised her about the bone man: "Give him a hard time if he isn't tipping enough. He'll get the point."

"Keep your eye on the extracurricular activities," Barbie said. "That's where the money is."

Barbie studied acting at the Neighborhood Playhouse. Between appointments and trial lessons she practiced her "technique"— down on the floor with her legs crossed, touching the top of her head to her crossed knees, then rolled up into a soft ball, then stretching out and arching her back like a kitten, then up on her feet, shaking herself, loosening up all over, then rigid again, practicing breathing from the diaphragm, tucking her buttocks in and seating her torso firmly on her soft, round pelvis ("Think of the pelvis as a bowl, tip it until it's flat"), projecting the repetitive, sonorous tones of one syllable over and over, "mah, mah, mah, mah, mah," struggling with sense memory exercises ("If they keep pushing me back into childhood traumas I'm going to end up in the loony bin instead of the Broadway theater"). Communism was the work of the devil, but Stanislavsky was a saint. She was a religious girl, she hardly ever missed church on Sunday.

Miss Alma didn't talk politics or religion with her fellow workers at Miss Vilma's Internationally Famous Dance Salon.

She stayed at Pat and Barbie's apartment on party nights, sleeping on a daybed in what was called the living room of the one-room space that divided up into an alcove for Pat and Barbie's double bed, a stove and refrigerator in a hall, and a sink, bath, and toilet closed behind accordion closet doors. Anne was tense about staying—the quarters were so close, there was the embarrassment at being overheard in the toilet; she had a sense of heat, of darkness, of something being subtly offered, then withheld, that drew her and made her want to run. But she was afraid to go home to Brooklyn alone at that late hour. On the surface nothing happened. They jabbered about the evening's happenings, they counted their money, drank Scotch (which Anne was ashamed to admit she disliked) and went to sleep, waking at the very last moment before a fast walk back to the studio and another day's work. Each time she felt she had avoided something by the skin of her teeth, but she didn't know what.

The life she had led before receded into a mist. She imagined that men who went into the army must lose their former lives in the way she was losing hers. Yet she wanted to hold fast to Anne, not to lose her in Miss Alma.

"You're like an onion," Bill says, startled into a metaphor by his new ardor. "You'll grow in any old ground."

Has he complimented her? There is resentment, wonder at her absorption in her new work, admiration in his words. In the BMT subway, he looks at her with heat, importunately. She is on her way to the studio, and in order to see her at all he has come all the way out to Brooklyn on a Saturday to ride in with her. He reaches out to take her hand, but both her hands are firmly around a book. To mark a trail out of the spot she's in she carries a book by James with her (today it's *The Golden Bowl*) and when she gets a moment she jots down an idea or copies out a passage for her study of Henry James. In the back section of the lined school notebook she is using, she notes passages of anti-Semitism in his works, but she has no plans for these quotes. They simply strike her and she notes them. Is a connection escaping her? Enlarge her theme? Anti-Semitism and money in the novels of the master. Some thesis. She means to laud James, not lynch him. She could hang him as an anti-Semite if she used *The American Scene*.

Bill is annoyed by Henry James in the hands he wants to hold.

"Nobody's interested in Henry James," he says, not at all for the first time. "Why don't you write about Romain Rolland? Or Jack London? Especially now, with the kind of people you're getting to really know."

"Ring Lardner would be more like it," she says, "or Damon Runyon. Some of the things that happen are hilarious," and tells him about the bedbug on the fly of the officer's white dress uniform.

He laughs, is slightly alarmed. "You couldn't catch a disease from them, just dancing with them, could you?"

He kisses her right in the doorway of Miss Vilma's Internationally Famous Dance Salon—a hungry, pressing kiss, sweetened with his greedy tongue.

She hasn't told him about the young man who loves bones, and she hasn't told Shana either. She's glad she hardly sees Shana these days. She wants to keep her new life secret. They know she's working, teaching dancing, earning good money. The good money they know about is her basic salary, between twenty and thirty dollars a week. The rest she keeps for herself. She opens a secret bank account, the first she has ever had, entering through the revolving doors of the bank near the studio and stepping out onto the marble floor with more excitement and fear than when she entered the dance salon for the first time. She deposits all her extras—tips, commissions, party nights. She already has three hundred dollars in the bank. She could go to Europe on a boat, leave everything behind, live a glamorous, starving, reckless, sexy, literary exile life. How did one do that?

One of her students who obviously likes her a lot asked her if she was engaged. "Nobody gets *engaged* anymore," she answers, and then realizes that what he was asking was whether she was a virgin.

It was Tom McMullen who asked—one of her favorite students. He's so American, she's surprised to learn that he's Canadian, an executive with Canada Dry.

"You're kidding," she says. "Canada Dry is Canadian?"

He's a good dancer. He has come to Miss Vilma's Salon for tango and bolero lessons and for company. He's fun—a big, hearty, laughing, open-faced, white-haired billboard character. When he's in New York on his frequent business trips, he takes a dance lesson every day, sometimes double ones. She stays one lesson ahead of him, in the morning picking up new steps from Manny to pass on to McMullen later in the day. He tips well—so far for nothing but a lot of laughing. He shows her pictures of his family—more billboard people, except for his wife. In the center of four blond, smiling daughters and two square-faced, smiling sons is an obese, sad-faced woman.

"Would you believe that my wife was a beautiful girl when I married her? As slim as you?"

"Yes," Miss Alma says. "I can see she has a beautiful face."

"Under all that blubber," he says, "I'm surprised you can tell." His voice is mournful, angry, but he kisses the picture before he returns it to his wallet. "Never mind," he says, "she's a darn good woman, a darn good mother."

He asks Miss Alma if she can fit another lesson in later in the day. Not until six thirty. Too late? Never too late. What is she doing afterward? Here it is, she thinks.

"Against the rules," she says, automatically, pleasantly.

"Of course," he says. "How about breaking the rule?"

She smiles.

"We'll have a barrel of fun together," he says. "I'd like to take you to dinner. I get pretty lonely eating all by my lonesome."

She met him at the Claremont Inn on Riverside Drive. He had

told her to wear an evening gown and that he would wear a tux. "Let's be real spiffy," he had said, and given her three dollars for a taxi. She was in a black Sunday-night gown, little ruffled tiers down to the floor and a ruffled portrait collar that traveled around her upper arms, leaving her shoulders bare. Barbie had made her up and Pat had put a crystal pendant on her throat.

She knew that she looked good. She followed the headwaiter to a table overlooking the river, where Tom McMullen was already seated with a drink in his hand, and as she approached he stood up, a convention never observed in the crowd Anne ran with, but a courtesy obviously extended to Miss Alma. Sunset over New Jersey bathed the place in a spectacularly romantic light, and the band music to which she set her gliding pace across the floor to her admirer, the martini that instantly intoxicated her, the pressure of Tom McMullen's large, sure hands, the sexual excitement in yielding to his insistence that of course she could swallow clams on the half shell (there was nothing to it), the wine, the green after-dinner liqueur and black coffee, his gleaming face, admiring and pleading, inevitably brought Miss Alma to Tom McMullen's hotel, led by him through a lobby as busy and impersonal as a railroad station to a room that turned out to be disappointingly small and shabby.

He undressed her. She had never been undressed by a man. Dress, chemise, garter belt, and stockings. He is tickled by the fact that these are all the clothes she's wearing.

"Hot damn," he says, "don't you get cold?"

He savors uncovering her. He kisses her flat stomach, smooths his hands across her jutting hips to her mound and encloses it in warmth. "The sweetest meat is next to the bone," he says. Another bone enthusiast.

Naked, stripped of props, Miss Alma threatens to become Anne —tight and wary of disappointment. He kisses her nipples.

"You could use a little more in this department," he says, but kisses her breasts again, without any grudge. He pours her a drink before he leaves her to go to the bathroom. "I'll take care of the protection," he says. He returns, ready, and moves in, swiftly and competently.

She thinks, *this is going to be one rotten time,* but the drink has loosened her, his large thighs hold her, his authoritative stomach settles securely into her narrow pelvis, he strokes and moves and licks with honest pleasure, and she finds that she wants him closer and winds her legs around his big thighs and laces her arms across his broad back. What has happened to the bewildering starts and stops of a gallop under Bill? This is a ride into new country. She rises and falls, she soars, she is soaring and singing, she can hear herself singing, she flies, she is incredibly surprised, shuddering with wonder and ecstatic surprise—and then she descends in a long, lovely, grateful loop. Tom McMullen, a middle-aged, heavy man with messed-up white hair, rolls off her stomach and smiles at her in the lighted room. He had kept the light on—another first.

"I knew we'd have a barrel of fun," he says.

She doesn't know what to do with her overwhelming gratitude, but it must be a sin to keep it to herself.

"I'm glad I decided to come with you," she says. "I'm glad I came to your room. I'm glad."

He's puzzled by her state. "Hey," he says, "you wouldn't fool me, would you? It's not the first time, is it? I don't want to take anybody's cherry. The only cherry I ever took was the one I married."

Miss Alma tries to look upon his comment kindly, but Anne is appalled. *Don't talk*, she tells herself, but does. "No, no," she says. "It's not that. It's that I thought maybe I was frigid."

His burst of laughter is a most reassuring sound. "You having problems with some squirt who doesn't know how to keep his end up?" He turns on his side, propped on his elbow, amusement in his seemingly candid eyes which really reveal nothing but bland good humor. "You know what they say, girlie, always get right back on the horse that throws you. Maybe I can get it up again for you so you'll know that it wasn't an accident." He is immensely proud of himself.

"I love you," she bursts out after the second success. "I love you."

She has frightened him. "Now, now. Now, now." He speaks as if to an overexcited dog, and pats her soothingly. "Now, now. Now, now. Now, now."

She laughs, and he joins her and they are past a bad moment.

XII

Nobody at Miss Vilma's knows that Anne is Jewish, not even Pat and Barbie. Pat and Barbie think she's Italian, Manny thinks she's Greek, Tom McMullen guessed that she was French. Descent, of course. They know that she's American.

The word "Jew" is a working part of these people's vocabulary. Prices are "Jewed down," a cigarette lit from another is a "Jew light," Pat has a "Jewboy" student, Tom McMullen talks of "Jew money," "Jew banks," "Jew department stores," Barbie's stingy escorts are "regular Jews," to Manny curly hair is "Jew hair," to all of them Jews are oversexed, smart, tricky, dirty. Miss Alma is into deception too deeply to stop. What could she say? She's ashamed of having kept silent. Why had she not immediately come out with it and avoided the inevitable anti-Semitism? Is she ashamed of being Jewish?

It takes a Jew to spot her, David Kent, a trial-lesson student. He signs up for a full course.

"What's a nice Jewish girl like you doing in a place like this?"

"What about you? Nice Jewish boy."

"What's wrong with coming here to learn how to dance?" His belligerence is familiar, like other tones he rings. He could be one of the fellows in her crowd.

"What's wrong with learning from me?"

"It doesn't seem right," he says.

They move into quick intimacy. He tells her he has just changed his name from Kantorowicz, that he's working in a big firm where he's one of three Jews in the whole place.

"Miss Alma was once Hannahle," she tells him, laughing, but is promptly sorry. She would rather keep the two entirely separate.

He has come to learn how to dance, and he does learn with great ease.

"Natural rhythm," Anne says. "We all have it." He doesn't smile at that comment.

She looks forward to her lessons with him, but he spoils the time by needling her with the nice-Jewish-girl routine. Her presence in that place is really a shocking bother to him. It doesn't fit his preconceptions. It's a *shanda*, a disgrace. Party night. Ten cents a dance.

"I came here tonight only to protect you," he says. He has bought one ticket. He calls her "Hannahle" in a conspiratorial whisper when he hands her the ticket.

"One?" She laughs at him. "Nobody buys *one* ticket."

He is dazzled by Pat, leading her old man about in a tottering waltz.

"That's one gorgeous *shiksa*," he says. "Can you fix me up with her?"

"She's my best friend, and I wouldn't dream of it. Buy a string of tickets. She dances with everybody. We all do."

In their banter, while they dance, he learns that she's a Hunter graduate. It brings him to a total stop, during which the music ends and the band quickly begins a new number. He puts his arms around her to dance again, but she shakes her head, smiles, mimics Barbie's routine: "No tickee, no dancee."

"Cut it out," he says. "I have to talk to you. I knew you were an educated girl. I could tell. You shouldn't be here, doing this kind of thing. What's the matter with your family? Don't they watch out for you?"

He is holding her and forcing her to dance while he talks to her with a worried-uncle expression on his long, dark face, and her struggling against him is meant to be a joke. She has momentarily forgotten Manny, Miss Vilma in her cage, the bouncers. Then she sees Manny circling, Miss Vilma signaling with one finger, the men approaching. They are on her partner in a second, dragging him backward across the floor away from her. She holds fast, but Manny pulls her loose and puts another man in her arms.

"Don't hurt him," she begs Manny.

"Who's gonna hurt him?" Manny shoves her back on the floor. The terror on David Kent's face is her own. He struggles to overcome it, and against the indignity of the way he is being pulled. He fights to regain his feet, slipping and sliding backward across the waxed floor, a skinny fellow with a big nose, eyeglasses, thick wavy lips, and even now in the hands of the goons making a fool of him, maintaining the look of a hunched, thoughtful, in-ward-turning scholar. Save him, damn you, she commands herself.

"He's a regular, Manny. We were just kidding around. He has four more lessons to go on his course. You want him to come back, don't you? He'll sign up for another course, I know he will."

"Nobody dances without a ticket." Manny is dancing with her behind her inept partner. Her partner is a passive filling between them. "He only bought one ticket. We know he only bought one ticket. He danced one dance. Tricky Jew. You gotta watch those people." More in sorrow than in anger, and with a reassuring pat on the back for the alarmed look on her partner's face.

"They're hurting him, Manny," she argues over her partner's bald head.

"You better keep quiet now. You know what's good for you, you keep quiet now."

Manny's tone makes her partner stumble, but Manny keeps shoving and patting, moving them along in their senseless, awkward march, and between the stiff turns and slides, over her partner's head, she sees David Kent in interrupted broken images, dragged to the top of the stairs and then dropped to the floor where he scrabbles helplessly (to the amusement of some of the watchers) to gain his feet and run down the stairs.

"What was happening with that fellow?" Pat asks at the end of the evening.

"I'm too tired to explain," she says.

"Are you too tired to do me a really big favor?"

"Now?"

"You know my old man? I didn't know he'd need me tonight. I've gotten myself into a mess. A real mix-up. But he said you'd be okay. Will you do it?"

"Me?"

Pat nods.

"Do what?"

"Nothing. You'll see."

"He doesn't even know me."

"Well, he saw you. He said it would be fine."

"How does he know?"

"Well, he looked at you."

"Is that what he does? Look?"

"It's nothing," Pat says. "Do me a favor. Otherwise I might lose him. You'll get twenty dollars, and then I keep him."

"But what do I do? I can't do it."

"Nothing, Alma. Not what you're thinking. I've got another date, but I'll show you where you go to his car. You better put these on, because I know you wear a chemise. Sometimes he asks for panties."

"I can't do anything like that, Pat."

"You don't do anything, Alma. He does it all himself. Do it for a friend, will you? There's nothing to it. He's a gentleman. You know I wouldn't. I'm your friend, we're friends, you don't think I'd . . ." bunching up a pair of sleazy panties into Anne's hands. "I get these in the five and dime, in case he asks. Sometimes he asks for a stocking. You want an extra stocking? If you're wearing good ones, don't break up a good pair. Sometimes he asks for both. You have to put them on," Pat says, stopping her from stuffing the panties into her purse.

"He's nuts," Anne says. "What if he does something crazy?"

"His chauffeur watches over him like a baby. Everything will be okay. I swear on a stack of Bibles."

"Why didn't you ask Barbie?"

"We're in a mess. Got our signals crossed. Anyway he doesn't like short girls. Will you *do* it?" She is desperate. "It's nothing. You've done a lot worse, and you *know* it. That poor old soul wouldn't hurt a flea. Don't be so stubborn, Alma."

Barbie, not Pat, walks her to the limousine. The night is wonderfully crisp, a drug to their exhaustion. They walk the two long blocks in silence. The sky is in dramatic movement—piled clouds and a high-sailing moon, startling against the hushed, dark, quiet mass of buildings. On the deserted streets, only cats are out among the garbage cans.

"That's it," Barbie says. She waves at a long black car across the street.

"How do you know?"

Barbie kisses Anne, pats her hair.

"The chauffeur will take you to our place afterward. Here's a key, just in case we're not back by then."

A uniformed chauffeur opens the back door of the car, shuts it behind her, and reseats himself up front, without speaking to her. There is a glass partition separating front and back. It is an enormous automobile. There are drawn drapes at the windows and little vases of flowers at either side, and a dim concealed light that glows from under the seat. It is like coming into a movie house, with the movie already begun.

"Good evening," the old man says. His voice is grave, courteous, thin, tremulous—the voice of an aged school dean.

Her own voice in response is unrecognizably low and husky. She sits back, clears her throat. There is a longish silence while he looks at her. Then she feels his spidery hand at her neck.

"Won't you slip off your coat?" He assists her with the spidery hand. She shudders. Now he leans very close and whispers, as if they are fellow conspirators on an urgent assignment. "You like sweets, my dear? Sour balls? Lollipops? A nice, large, sweet lollipop?" He is overcome by gasping, senile laughter, choked by emphysema. "Tee, hee, hee," between racking, liquid convulsions. The chauffeur raps out a disciplinary signal on the glass partition with his knuckles, but doesn't turn around. The old man pulls back into his corner. He spends some seconds in a strangling recuperation. There is a loud clock ticking in the car, or her heart has fled her body and is knocking against a window. Her fear is so intense she doesn't feel it as fear but as a scolding rigidity. Stupid, stupid, stupid. Idiot Anne. Miss Alma has fled. It's Anne who is in this unimaginable danger. If you get out of this alive—never, never, never, never again, never again, never, never, she scolds, holding herself together and fixing her eyes on the back of the chauffeur's cap ahead, away from what is going on next to her where the old man has thrown back a lap robe to show himself naked, below his formal clothes above.

"Won't you look at me, my dear?" Again, coughing, sputtering —"Tee, hee, hee"—and the chauffeur rapping him to order.

Mind him, guard, *mind* him.

She turns herself slightly toward him, but fixes her eyes off focus on the plush upholstery of this handsome car on a dead street in a sleeping city where by some horrible mistake she has become an

actor in a movie about a maniac and his keeper. His exertions are
strenuous, pitiful, and take forever. He asks her to lift her skirt. He
asks her to give him her panties. He asks for a stocking. She does
whatever he says and remains tilted in his direction, if that will
help. When he collapses in a whimpering heap, the chauffeur
instantly starts the car. The noise is so startling it hits Anne like a
blow. "What? What?" she shouts out, and the tears pour. The
chauffeur raps *her* to order this time around.

Tom McMullen calls her from Montreal. Miss Vilma is furious,
and Manny stands by at the office phone. He pretends that he's
calling to set up his lesson appointments. (He'll be in New York for
the weekend. He has booked a room at the Essex House. Is she
free?) Has he had second thoughts about her outburst of love?
   A new student signs up, so exactly like Tom McMullen that she
mistakes him for Tom the first time she greets him in the reception
room. Ted Browning, with the same billboard good looks, white
hair, hearty laughter, a snapshot of his family in his wallet, one
daughter, two sons, a slim, smiling wife on the lawn of a brick
house in North Carolina. He's an executive with American Mills,
head of sales. He's a heavy tipper. He takes her to dinner at Tavern
on the Green, but she resists the hotel-room routine. He kisses her
in a horse-drawn carriage, riding through Central Park, and puts
his hand up her dress. He too is charmed by the fact that under
her dress is nothing but a chemise and a garter belt and stockings.
She pleads no free time on his next trip to New York, but he tips
her ten dollars in advance, if she'll agree to meet him for a drink.
They meet late, about nine thirty, at the Taft bar, but he becomes
nasty. "Listen, girlie," louder and uglier with each drink, "You
don't think you can get away with this, do you?" When he goes to
the men's room, she runs out into the neon-lighted, crowded
street and ducks into the nearest subway. No more of that. No
more "I love you, I love you" just because a man knows how to
make her come. She was a little mixed up there, with Tom McMullen.
   She and Pat take a day off one Friday on the spur of the moment, following an exhausting party night. They have no appointments until the late afternoon anyway. Barbie has earlier
appointments and a voice class, and she parts from them at the

bus stop. The day is balmy, sunny—more like spring than autumn. They take an open-top double-decker bus. Pat is on a
wild talking jag. Anne is only half listening, drunk with the
pleasure of the street sights below the lurching bus. The outing
feels like hooky playing, a prison break from studio life. Pat
doesn't look like herself without makeup, her incredible shape
shapeless in wide slacks and a pullover, her hair down her
back, pulled into a thick mane tied with a black frayed ribbon.
She's beautiful this way too.

"What if that old man konked out and died on you while you
were sitting there?" Anne brings this worry up without warning,
interrupting Pat. "What if he went totally off his nut? It's too scary.
You have to stop doing that with him, Pat."

"That's nice," Pat says. "Nobody ever worries about me. Everybody says I'm so cheerful, so capable. It's my big hands. See how
big they are? I really love your worrying about me.

"The way my mother worries about me," Pat says, "is to make
up something. She gets on the telephone and talks to her friends
about me. I wonder what she's telling them these days. 'Patsy's so
gal-*lant*, my Patricia's so gal-*lant* about misfortune.' That's her
style. I was half dead from the worst abortion ever done in the
state of Iowa, and I hear her on the telephone to 'the girls.' I was
supposed to be being gal-*lant* about la grippe. I never had a cold
in my life. La grippe. She was just pretending that she didn't know.
She had to know."

She learns in the course of Pat's rambling raving against her
mother that Pat is a year younger than she is.

"Everybody thinks I'm older. It's because I'm bigger. People
like to lean on me. That's okay. Lean on me. I like it."

She pulls Anne toward her on the small, rickety wooden seat,
playfully holds Anne's head down against her shoulder with a
strong, large hand, delivers a straight, bold message with her level,
masculine eyes. They *are* masculine without makeup, Anne realizes. She feels no shock and no displeasure, and no need to pull
away. At 125th Street, where they clatter down the bus's circular
stair on the sudden decision to ride the ferry across the Hudson,
they stop first to buy hot dogs with sauerkraut from a street ven-
dor. They eat them standing on the slip. The air is moist with a
sweet, faintly rotten river smell. There is a bright excitement
coming to life between them. The river brings out the poet in Pat,

but all she can remember are snatches of poems, memorized for school.

> The breaking waves dashed high on a stern and
> rock-bound coast

she shouts into the wind, when they're on the moving boat.

> Oh Captain! my Captain! the fearful trip is done,
> The ship has weathered every rack, the prize we sought
> is won . . .

> Sunset and evening star,
> And one clear call for me!
> And may there be no moaning of the bar,
> When I put out to sea . . .

That one breaks her up into guffawing laughter.
"Come on," Pat says. "Say a poem."
Anne says,

> That's my last Duchess painted on the wall,
> Looking as if she were alive. I call
> That piece a wonder now . . .

"That's not a poem," Pat says.

> Now more than ever seems it rich to die,

Anne tries again,

> To cease upon the midnight with no pain.

"No," Pat hollers. "Sea poems. 'Home is the sailor, home from sea.' You know."
"I'm sorry," Anne says. "I can't think of any."
On the ride back on another open bus, Pat is still wildly talkative, but the breeze has turned brisk and cool and the sun is weak and Anne is tired and dispirited. " 'Let me love entire and whole,' " she quotes to herself. Love Bill—entire and whole? That seems best thing to do.

"I'd like to ride around all over the world on an open-top bus," Pat is saying. "With a good companion. Someone who has the brains to be faithful."

"You think it takes brains to be faithful?"

"I think it does," Pat says. "You'll see. Barbie'll go back to Bing-hamton to that nitwit. She'll give up. Because she's softheaded."

"Maybe she loves him," Anne says.

"She loves me," Pat says. "But she doesn't have the brains to stick with me.

"Do you love your nitwit?" Pat asks.

Pat has met Bill briefly, called him a swell guy then, but now she's being honest, admitting her contempt—or rivalry. Anne doesn't answer that. Instead she tells Pat that Tom McMullen has made her a proposition she's supposed to decide upon by his next visit to New York.

"It's hard for me to say it," Anne says. "I don't know why. I began to think about it the other night while I was having supper. My mother was standing at my side, serving me, and I began to cry uncontrollably. She took me in her arms and I cried the way I never did, even as a kid. Just thinking about it near her."

"What is it?" Pat says. "What does he want?"

"He has to take a six-week business trip to the Midwest. He wants me to go with him. Like a secretary. Fifty dollars a week. He pays all expenses. At the end, good-bye and good luck. He says we'll have a barrel of fun."

"What's the matter?" Pat says. "Not enough money?"

"No, it's not that," Anne says. "I'm afraid. I'm afraid of my feelings."

"Of getting hurt?"

"I'm afraid I would feel I have to love him."

Dressed for work, once again Miss Alma and Miss Patricia, Pat stands before Anne and holds out her hands.

"Aren't they big? Tell the truth."

Miss Patricia is in a low-cut dress from which her breasts rise in a blaze of glory. Every shining, golden hair of her head is carefully entwined into the intricate bun at the nape of her marble, colum-nar neck. Her face is a glowing theater mask, made up to perfec-tion. She circles Anne's waist with the big hands she boasts of, straining to make her thumbs and middle fingers meet.

"See how big!" she says, triumphantly. Her beautiful eyes look directly into Anne's in a bold plea, and then she releases her.

Anne comes back to the specials' room after an appointment
and finds Barbie and Pat quarreling. Barbie is crying. Pat is arguing in whispers in the far corner, beyond the sight of the peephole.
    "Sh-sh," Barbie says. "Don't talk about it anymore."
    "It doesn't matter," Pat says. "She knows about us."
    Barbie puts her head down.
    "Fifty dollars!" Pat says. "Apiece! A hundred dollars for what we
do anyway. Make believe he isn't there."
    "I can't. I'll just freeze up. I won't be able to, I can't. It won't
be any good."
    "Fake it," Pat says. "It doesn't matter. You know me. I come if
you poke a finger at me, so he's bound to get his money's worth.
Barbie, a hundred dollars! You can get drunk first. It's just *me*,
Barbie. Forget him. He'll just be sitting there. Make believe you're
doing it on stage."
    "Patsy, I'd never do it on stage."
    "Oh, Christ, you know what I mean," Pat says.
    The buzzer rings once, summoning Pat.
    She strides about on her long American-beauty legs, smoothing
her shining hair, picking up her records, checking off her calendar
chart, automatically arching her neck and lifting her breasts into
full, floating, leading position. Her distressed, willful animation is
dazzlingly beautiful—irresistible.
    "Say yes, Barbie, before I go, will you? We'll be throwing away
a hundred dollars, baby, don't you understand? Say yes."
    "Okay," Barbie says. "Yes." She buries her face in her soft arms.
Her soft hair fans out and floats above her soft crying, like a benediction.
    Pat is almost out the door when Anne decides she must say
good-bye. "I'm through for the day, Pat. I'll be going."
    Pat turns back. She smiles the smile there is no adequate re-
sponse to. "Listen, can I borrow a couple of your records? 'It's a
Sin to Tell a Lie' and a tango? I'm sick of 'Adios, Muchachos.' "
    "That's the only one I have," Anne says. "I'm sorry."
    "Thanks anyway, Alma," Pat says, and she's gone.
    Anne packs the cheap, round carrying case she uses to cart her
props back and forth from work. She packs everything—her
makeup, her two evening gowns, her extra pumps, her Henry
James notebooks. She kisses Barbie on her lowered head.
    "I'm going," she says to no response.

She stops at Miss Vilma's desk. "Could I possibly be paid tonight instead of tomorrow? I have to pay a bill first thing in the morning. I'd really appreciate it."

"I'd really appreciate some notice," Miss Vilma says, and rings a buzzer.

Manny appears immediately.

"She's quitting. Check her bag, maybe she took some records."

"You're foolish," Manny says, while he pays her in full. "You're making a big mistake. Jobs don't grow on trees, y'know."

"I'll be in tomorrow, probably," she says.

"Yeah, yeah," Miss Vilma says. "I heard that one before."

Manny lifts one shoulder in a melancholy, angry shrug.

Believe me, this time he means what he says. 'I'm washing my hands of this family.' He's going. He's moving away altogether, near his factory. He means it, this time. He says he doesn't have an extra penny, that we should have his money worries, then we'd know what worries are. The unions made his life miserable, that's what it is."

Anne and Papa are sitting on a bench on a narrow island surrounded by the noise and stench of Broadway traffic.

"Why I'm punished with such a life, God alone knows. What did I do so wrong I should deserve such punishment?

"Your mother? She's a bad woman? She deserves this? A woman who gave her whole life for her children?"

The silences between his litany fill with the din of the street.

"What's taking her so long, I'd only like to know."

Mama is across the street and one flight up, having a corn removed by a foot doctor.

"Everybody's a doctor these days. I should hang a sign out, get a new razor and a white coat, and I'm in business for myself. Dr. Goddard."

He pulls on his fingers. He sighs an elaborate sigh. "For such a life, who needed to be born in the first place?"

He turns to Anne with new energy. "Tell me the honest truth. You believe that Baruch Goddard doesn't have a penny to spare?"

"Anything's possible," Anne says.

"Not a penny?"

"It's all relative," she says. "He means it's all tied up. In his new business."

"He means he's plain sick and tired of us. What's a mother and father? Nothing. We're dispossessed. Out on the streets."

She covers an enormous yawn.

"What fool is going to hire an old man like me?"

She rouses herself to reassure. "Everything's going to be all right, Papa, you'll see. We're not going to let you and Mama starve or be thrown out on the streets. We're all pitching in."

"A fine thing. Young married couples. Instead of putting burdens on your backs I should be helping out. Topsy-turvy world. I didn't expect to be an old man so early in my life.

"I'm ashamed for my whole failure of a life," Papa says.

"C'mon, Pop," Anne says. "It's not the end of the world. Things will change. Things will get better. You know how Barry is. He's unpredictable, changeable."

"How about your husband, your Bill, he doesn't mind, he doesn't object to giving your parents a few dollars a week?"

"Of course not," Anne says. "And I'm working again."

"He's a fine boy," Papa says. "He gives a thought to the other fellow.

"It's too bad you lost that good job as a teacher," Papa says.

"This is a pretty good job, this new one," she says. "It's not bad for a secretary's job."

She sees Mama emerge from the building across the street and step out, a lost, limping, bewildered little old lady. She jumps up to help Mama cross against the traffic.

"Why should things get better?" Papa calls out.

"Maybe because they can't possibly get any worse?" answering his question with a question, Yiddish style.

XIII

When my daughter Katie went to Mississippi to join in the voter registration drive (the famous summer of 1964 that the three young men were murdered) she came home a pothead. She also came home, if not disillusioned, then decidedly pessimistic about chances for true equality in the land. Twenty year-olds can get very low about the state of the world. She sat around, glassy-eyed and dejected, with a bunch of similarly dejected types in an apartment in the East Village, and let the days dribble away between her slack fingers.

An obvious irony, here, but of what nature? Out of good intentions, evil? Simplistic and clichéd.

I became Miss Alma the dance instructor directly because of a Young Communist League assignment. Three YCL girls and I were sent to hang around an armory in the upper Bronx to politicize the National Guard. No kidding. We romanticized the assignment—saw ourselves as heroines in a Russian movie, mounting the barricades, arousing the soldiers to turn their guns the other way.

Leaflets and pamphlets in hand, on a dark, deserted street, at a late hour, we waited for the young men to leave their weekly training session. Would a heroine be so nervous? We were watched over by four male YCLers in a car down the block, but the young Guardsmen didn't try anything funny. The few who listened to us listened politely. We spoke rapidly and passionately, explaining. The state—an instrument of monopoly capitalism. The National Guard—police arm of a repressive state. The future—

revolution, and peace and plenty for all mankind. The present—worker solidarity, class consciousness. No shooting down fellow workers in strikes, insurrections, and revolutions. Then they asked us if we'd like to go to a juke joint a few blocks away to talk some more, have a few beers, and do a little dancing.

My best contact among the Guardsmen was Vinny, a short, slim, fair Italian, lit up from the inside out with a wonderfully bright, receptive eagerness. He quickly admitted to an anarchist grandfather.

"He's got that same line of lingo you have," Vinny said. He seemed delighted.

He confided that he really wasn't a worker. In business for himself with his father. "I'm embarrassed to tell you what. Right away you'll laugh or get scared. Brass plates for coffins. It's a good business. And if I say so myself we do beautiful work. My old man used to be a stone cutter, but this is better. Listen, if you ever happen to need a plate for someone in your family (God forbid but it happens to everybody) I'll donate it—no charge. The old man doesn't even have to know."

It was Vinny who told me that I was one marvelous dancer, like a professional teacher at a studio, and because of him I took my courage in my hands and walked up the stairs to Miss Vilma's.

"Your morality stinks," Shana yelled at Mama, addressing herself to the chasm separating the generations. "Nothing but hypocrisy," she yelled. Mama had objected to Shana's declaration that she and Merv were going to bed together on the pullout living-room couch, three weeks before their scheduled marriage. It was plain that Mama's heart wasn't in her objection. All she meant was for Merv to wait until the house was quiet and then he and I could silently change places at Shana's side. Shana's outburst disheartened Mama. "Do what you like," she said and walked out of the room.

Merv and Shana's wedding took place at a third-rate hall. No colored lights—and only a sweet table and wine following the ceremony. They were saving all available money for furniture, including the small promised gifts of money.

Given Merv and Shana's happy history of successful orgasms, who would have anticipated any trouble? Yet, here's Shana, two days after her wedding, meeting me for lunch at a vegetarian bar on Sixteenth Street, crying, and shaking all over between sips of carrot-and-parsley juice, telling me that she's made a terrible mistake and that she doesn't want to be married at all.

Of course that blew right over.

I had already walked down the carpeted stairs and out of Miss Vilma's. Bill had walked out of Columbia Law, just when he was almost at the end, because he had been offered a job as a full-time, paid Party organizer. We were married at City Hall, Merv and Shana in attendance (and one of my old school friends, Edith). Then a quick religious ceremony a couple of days later, a bow to the archaic sentiments of the old folks. Then to the gynecologist to be fitted for a diaphragm.

With my legs in the stirrups I solicit the doctor's advice. Could our sexual difficulties be my husband's fault? (I have my secret memories of Tom McMullen.) Perhaps something very small to adjust surgically? Psychologically? The doctor is an elderly man, kind and bored. He tries out the flat wisdom of the times: Many women achieve satisfaction in giving pleasure. I politely decline. He tries again. "It's best to stick with one mate. Don't change horses in the middle of the stream."

Thus encouraged, we stick with it, and riding, riding, riding, we make it, Bill and I, across a flashing stream to the promised shore—

So far, so good. But I have the tired sense that our true love, if that's what it is, demands as much energy and will to win as a workout on a handball court.

Nothing is what it seems. Or everything is just as bad as my paranoid intuition suspects. Sink or swim between the two markings, feeling with one's toes for the solid earth of reality.

Bill's job includes an impressive title: New York State Communist Party Educational Director. He commands respect and wields influence. He maneuvers me a job as secretary to the National Anti-Fascist Coalition. What I do mostly is send out mailings. We're in good shape, with a two-room apartment in the Bronx, dozens of friends, and a life of ceaseless activity. We are activists, changing the world. I have the illusion that the world is standing still like an obedient child while I mother it, but the world goes about its own business.

Take the question of Spain and Franco. At a mass rally on Fifth Avenue, charging horses are upon us—terrifying, rearing, beautiful beasts driven down upon us by the mounted cops. We are chased right down the steps of the subway entrances. Foot cops are on the platform, ready to knock us about if we don't instantly enter the empty trains and leave the scene. Shana and I run one way, Bill and Merv another. We will resist and regroup with others who are running with us. We run up elegant Fifth Avenue, the charging horses galloping behind. How can this be happening? We have a permit to demonstrate. We are driven against the buildings, banged up against window fronts. There is the sound of broken glass, the sight of blood. Shana is crying and blaming herself aloud. "What am I *doing* here?" she scolds herself as I will scold myself in the enclosed limousine. "Never again, never again," she swears as we flee. She never bargained for bloodshed. She thought it was an acceptable activity—demonstrating in favor of the Loyalist Government of Spain. So did I. But the fact is that Spain's fate has been settled elsewhere. Spain has been traded off to General Franco and to fascism.

I react with excessive pain and disappointment. "That's defeatist," Bill says. "Spain is part of the larger struggle. The fight continues. Spain will rise again."

I'm embarrassed. By him or by my childish will to win *now*? I don't want to write Spain off for now. I don't want to go on struggling. I want Spain, the people of Spain, to win, to be happy and at peace. The people of Spain are the "good guys," the fascists are the "bad guys." They're not supposed to win.

We picket the *Bremen*, a German luxury liner at rest in the waters of the Hudson. Hitler's beautiful *Bremen*. I expect thousands of New Yorkers to show up, but we are only some hundreds. The leaders of the anti-Nazi action have come to an agreement with the police. We may picket but not shout. No signs, no slogans. The *Bremen*'s passengers are on board, ready to sail at midnight, among them important U.S. citizens, people of money and influence, not to be disturbed. We walk in silence, first up the long avenue under the West Side Highway, then down the long avenue. One of the demonstrators has made a makeshift poster. He raises it high above his head as he pickets.

FELLOW AMERICANS
BOYCOTT THE NAZI MURDERERS
OF INNOCENT PEOPLE.

On the dark street, there is nobody but other demonstrators to read his words, but the police order him to roll up the cardboard sign. He does and we continue our silent march. There is no stir from the great, quiet vessel across the broad street. It is rumored that two demonstrators have chained themselves to something, to create a stir, but we don't hear or see any stir.

I'm upset again, railing against the organizers of the action. "What was the use of it?" I ask Bill. "It was like a farewell gathering. Fare thee well. Have a good trip."

He straightens me out. He explains.

I remember that when I was a little girl I felt remarkably lucky to have been born an American child, living in a great, secure, and powerfully free country, safe from the outrages of ancient historical atrocities. Who fed me that line—Papa? And school. Has there been a worse time than our time? The heart halts to contemplate it. Atrocities are the commonplace happenings of the day. Hard to believe. For a long time I didn't believe that there were labor camps in the Soviet Union. The idea of the crematorium was unimaginable. Dresden was unimaginable. And Hiroshima. Ignorance of the world is no excuse. I won't plead it, or go on with the list.

Life disappoints. Everybody knows that. But must it horrify?

I disappointed Bill, though I tried my best not to. He disappointed me. He betrayed me by shrugging his shoulders when I spoke out in a roomful of his Party friends, and raised his eyebrows to indicate how foolish I was. He thought I was turned aside and couldn't see him, but I had turned back to catch the shrug and the raised eyebrow.

He went to a meeting during a quarrel, before anything was settled. First things first. I ran to catch him, to make up, ran down the stairs of our apartment house and up the long, long flight of stairs to the elevated subway station, but he had already boarded the train that was pulling out of the station and disappearing around the curve. Easy come, easy go—without a thought for the polluting effect on love of a five-hour distance and coldness.

And then? Why then the Second World War took place—off-screen. Not for the world, naturally, but for me, on the home front. Bill and Merv were among the first to rush to volunteer to serve in the war to defeat fascism. Shana and I joined up in wartime waiting, after hurrying to conceive babies (one each) in the heat of the need to repopulate a world being efficiently depopulated.

At one point Bill came back to the United States on his destroyer and I and our baby and Bill's mother trekked to Roanoke, Virginia, to a barracks kind of life to sweeten a depressed time for Bill, though we weren't too successful in combatting Bill's deep chagrin that he was serving in the fight against fascism in Pacific waters as a ship's storekeeper. But I cannot tell about that, or about Bill's good, tall, straight-backed mother with a voice like a man's and a level glance, totally without duplicity, because there are limits on how much story can be told. Everything has its limits— not only love. Even mother love, as Shana and I frequently reminded one another in the park, sunning our kids, while our men dangered in secret locations in the Mediterranean and the Pacific (one each).

Shana and I were the only ones in the family living in New York City during the war years. Barry had moved close to his factory in the South and had gathered Saul and Josh (and their families) around him to work for him, and incredibly, a year or so after the others, took Sam Schwartz in, too, in spite of everything that had happened between them, whatever it was that *had* happened between them. Barry wasn't drafted. He was considered "necessary to the war effort." All the other Goddard males were beyond draft age, but as part of Barry's operation they would have earned deferments anyway. Barry's business was growing rapidly—diversifying, expanding into a variety of, to me, unreal interests and locations. Mama and Papa were settled comfortably in Miami Beach, enjoying an even peacefulness at last, free to marvel at their great good luck in producing their successful and generous son. But he was still *their* son, and they insisted on keeping after him—at the moment about Jenny, who was between husbands, and about me and Shana, living through the hard times of the war on dependent-family checks. Barry called one Sunday afternoon when I was out to tell Shana that he wanted to do what he could for us and that he would send twenty-five dollars a week apiece, to help us out. Shana, without asking me, said, "Thank you, Barry, thank you, dear. We appreciate your concern." We had a fight about it, pretty much the only fight Shana and I had during the war years, but I yielded, quickly. Shana wanted that money very much. The deed was already done. It would have been making a terrible fuss to undo it, and the fact was we did need the money, we could use it.

Shana and I did our wartime waiting in a five-room apartment in Washington Heights to which Merv and Bill returned different men, and Bill especially different in the way he had slid from cleaving to the American working class, his buddies on the ship, found seriously wanting by him in their Marxist-Leninist outlook, if not their rock-bottom humanity.

"Anti-Semitism!" His buddies had nicknamed Bill "Angel" after a hideous physical specimen well known for his ugly face and his fakery as a wrestler. Unhappiness and age *had* made Bill a grotesque, with his deep widow's peak and the three deep horizontal furrows in the exposed forehead added to the disarray he had gone away with. "I never came up against so much fucking anti-Semitism in my whole life."

Merv and Bill brought back a mouthful of words like that to the five-room shared apartment. Shana and I tried to protect the ears of the little children, now that there were four of them, (two apiece).

"*Pas devant*," we said, hoping that being cute about it would keep our reminder out of the class of criticism. Those two men were in a highly sensitive condition.

"Fuck that shit!" Merv said.

"I don't want my kids overprotected," Bill said. "I want them to grow up in the real world—not crippled like me by illusions."

It was a disappointing time, the postwar, promised as a new era for all mankind. There was the matter of no apartments. Shana and I had enjoyed cleaving to one another in the wind of war loneliness and child care, hoarding bananas because bananas might give out at any moment and the babies would starve, coexisting in the quiet of the living room after the babies were asleep, writing letters to our hero servicemen husbands. Now they had returned to us, to our shared narrow quarters, in a bitching nervous state of unraveled ends with themselves and with us and with their stranger children who stared at them out of round serious eyes from beyond the strangling entanglements of baby carriages, strollers, bikes, roller skates, galoshes and a shopping cart.

There was the question of fighting, now that there were four kids in the inadequate quarters.

Example: Shana and Merv's two-year-old Jerry is demonstrating the correct pronunciation of banana to one-and-a-half-year-old Katie.

"Blama!" Jerry yells. He is a natural leader, an authoritative voice.

"Nama," says Katie—our angel, our delicate breath of new May flowers. She is trying hard. She lives in violet-eyed awe of dark, strong-arm, older-man Jerry.

"Blama," Jerry repeats, a lead toy truck at the corrective ready in his fist. He has a running nose most of the winter, and breathing difficulties make him testy.

"Ama," Katie tries anew, and raises her voice, hoping that the secret is in the volume.

"Don't yell," Jerry hollers. The truck in his hand descends on the silky blond curls and eggshell skull. Katie screams. Jerry howls with surprise at the blood pouring down Katie's head and face, permanently staining the new pink corduroy overall-and-jacket set sent (late) by my sister Jenny for Katie's first birthday. Shana rushes in from kitchen duties. Her information is incomplete if not downright faulty.

"How dare you strike my child?" Her eyes blaze a terrible, dark accusation. "Merv and I are the only ones who may discipline our child."

Bill slams out of the house. He has been interrupted in a nap, necessary to his postwar nerve adjustment.

"Will there ever be any peace for me?" Merv implores the cracked plaster ceiling.

I steel myself to stanch Katie's life-losing blood with a washcloth and a Band-Aid. The delicate head proves remarkably sturdy.

I happened to be on hand when Katie and Jerry, all grown up, met on the playing fields of Greenwich Village. Katie and I are crossing the wide plaza ending at the arch of Washington Square, an area livened that afternoon by a West Indian steel drum band in addition to the usual show of mixed humanity. Katie's hair is darker, but it still curls at the edges and she is still violet eyed and delicate—a Nefertiti head on a long, arched neck. The baby strapped to her front is a creamy chocolate child with tight black curls covering a solid, unduly large head. We are chatting aimlessly when Katie comes to a halt in a stance of smiling love.

"It's Jerry. Cousin Jerry." She throws her arms wide open to receive him.

I see that the young man who rushes up must indeed be Jerry under a spreading awning of stiff curling hair. We haven't met since the last family get-together, some years ago. Jerry clamps an art portfolio between the knees of his patched dungarees and frees his hands to hold Katie's head and kiss her on the lips.

"Hi, Aunt Anne," he says, without looking at me because he cannot drag his eyes from Katie's. In their eyes, their childhood is lit by love and becomes a liquid, shining lake of remembrance.

I musn't let the impression linger that my Katie has a black illegitimate baby, however natural it may be in these times to assume so on the evidence given. In fact, Katie is married to a fourth-generation midwestern white American descended from mixed Swedish and German ancestry, and Katie and Chris's three children are quite remarkably fair. The afternoon we ran into Jerry was before she had met Chris. She was taking care of her friend Rabbit's baby. I don't know if the true relationship of Katie to that baby ever got properly straightened out in Jerry's mind, however. I don't think he asked. He touched the top of the baby's head with tentative fingertips and just said, "Fantastic!"

It was Stevie, Shana's oldest child, whom I loved as if he were my own. He was the first—born to Shana, after three days of hard labor, with a weight of nine and a half pounds and a length of twenty-two and a half inches, arriving just after I became pregnant with Danny, and pushing his strong, stubborn way past all obstacles to his happiness, such as his father's leaving for the service before his infant navy-blue eyes had time to turn their true dark-brown color, and his mother's consuming devotion to the wall at the side of her half-empty bed which she studied with passive, tragic intensity as if there were some riveting interest in it beyond the cracks and bulges of the last bad plastering job, rousing her by his good, loud yells to diaper him and feed him and bathe his wise, bald head even though she could hardly control the tears or the shaking of her outraged, violated body.

"Postpartum depression," the doctor said.

Both our men gone off to war, our family all far away, alone in the wartime apartment with Shana and her little baby, naturally I felt the urge to be nurse and sister, and mother and father, and aunt and uncle, not to mention grandmother and grandfather, though one must conclude from the state of our present relationship that I failed on all counts.

Ah, Stevie! I can still recite every word of Margaret Wise Brown's *The Noisy Book*, your favorite reading matter at that stage. Stevie was our first genius baby. We didn't know then that they would all be. Stevie could read record labels when he was only two and a half. Honest. Out of the whole collection, he'd pull out *Peter and the Wolf* and the *Trout Quintet*, his favorites. We marveled.

"He can tell from the appearance of the label, the color and design." My friend Edith is unmarried and childless and aloof to kiddy wonders. "Any child could do it."

Could any kid put the inside of a coffee percolator together as quickly as Stevie did at seven months of age, propped up in his high chair while I sat nearby and doted on the sight and felt the stirrings of my own Danny in my body? I mean, everything else being equal in a fair, controlled test situation?

"Hi, Aunt Anne," Stevie greets me coolly on the rare occasions when we now meet, not considering how I crocheted a whole infant blanket in one afternoon and night, steamed up by the adrenalin of worry about his concussion and rooting for the healing power of a brand-new drug, penicillin, and a hospital crib to his yellowed, frighteningly still little self after he tumbled backward from the top of the slide to the concrete below, a material much objected to by the Park Mothers' Association as a dangerous cushion for the heads of foolish, wild-playing children.

That was another civic fight we lost.

Stevie's head is okay. He's chairman of the Department of Sociology at his university, and he travels to São Paulo and Stockholm and Tel Aviv for conferences, where he delivers papers and takes part in seminars.

He probably doesn't remember the time I surprised him practicing how to say "Fuck!" in front of the big mirror that doubled all the bikes and junk stacked in the foyer. As he says the word, he crouches in a menacing posture coordinated to a motion of his right hand cutting the air in a vicious downstroke. A scratch too late, he adds a scowl, for the terror effect. He studies the results carefully in the mirror, then straightens and relaxes his face into its more customary softness before he tries again, with devoted seriousness. He notices that I'm noticing.

"Am I doing it right?" he asks.

I make myself as serious as he. "Well, what is it you're trying to do?"

"You have to do it like that," he says, "if you want to keep the big kids from bothering you."

"How come?" I ask.

"Come on, Aunt Anne." He is sadly disgusted with me. "That's the way you say, 'You rat, leave our game alone.' "

I grab him and kiss the top of his sweaty head. Now Shana has come into the foyer and is noticing us. She sends Stevie into the living room to help Danny build the George Washington Bridge, and leads me behind the closed swinging door of the kitchen.

"I've been meaning to discuss this with you," she says. "Studies have shown that it's very bad for children to be presented with more than one mother image. Confusing. I've been doing a lot of reading and it's made me very aware. Now that Merv and Bill are back I think we have to be careful about keeping our families separate. There's a lot of sibling rivalry between us. Unconsciously you're trying to replace me with my own children."

Like that. Magazines were filled with that kind of talk then. The whispered kitchen conversation depressed me because it made my future with Stevie appear very murky. I must have hardened my heart to him, otherwise I wouldn't have been sitting in Barry's informal living room cheering on my son Danny to triumph over Stevie in a lousy chess game, would I?

"Hardening of the heart is fast becoming the country's number one killer," my friend Edith said.

She was right. Hearts hardened at an accelerated pace in the late forties and the fifties. It became commonplace to pass an entire day without directly meeting another person's eyes. We were like that in our own apartment, the four of us, having a bit of trouble with our eyes meeting. I'm dying, I'm choking, I said to myself with some surprise at the unexaggerated truth of the statement. We four were sitting in the small hostile space of the living room in the early evening after the children had been put to bed.

I said, "Remember when we were conducting an anti-Nazi street meeting on 163rd Street and Broadway and Bill was going great at the mike and a gang of Father Coughlinites started throwing tomatoes and . . ."

I don't know what I had in mind. Building a bridge to a shared past?

Bill frowned at me. Merv looked up, startled. Shana widened and narrowed her eyes in signals communicating the intelligence that an FBI agent might easily be concealed behind the scaling, silver-painted radiators.

Merv said, "I can't believe I did any of those things. It's like a dream. I must have been crazy."

Shana said, "You weren't crazy. You were influenced. We never would have gotten there by ourselves. Bill pushed and pushed. I thought Bill knew what he was talking about. He didn't know any more about anything than I did. I don't know why I ever listened to any of those people. I used to listen to Bill as if he were some sort of oracle. He didn't know anything. He was just saying what he was told to say. And that was all lies. I'm going to do a laundry," she said, and left for the basement.

I'm innocent, I wanted to call out, but she was already gone and Merv and Bill were instantly into a fierce quarrel in which passionate, ungrammatical sentences were hurled about in a space already too crowded with ill will to accommodate any more. A powerful chemical was dissolving the years of Merv and Bill's friendship on the East 174th Street block, the shared immies and bubble-gum baseball cards and stoop ball and handball and trying out girls and the cabin at Lake Hopatcong and the later years when we loved one another all around—Shana and Merv and Anne and Bill. Shana kept coming in and out from the trips to the basement. She kept her wits about her and left in time to move the laundry from the washer to the dryer no matter what.

It was a sad, disappointing time—the postwar that was going to be a new, bright day for all mankind.

WHAT'S NEW
WITH THE FAMILY?

Barry's coming," Shana said. "Help me straighten up the mess in the living room. Tell Danny to help Stevie put the blocks away."

"My bridge," Danny moaned. He rushed to hit Stevie. Anne held him back.

"It's terrific," Shana said. "He has a proposition for the boys. He spoke to Merv on the phone. He's ready to take them into the business."

"What about Bill?"

Anne peeled Danny's coat from his arms, quieting him. "You'll build it again tomorrow. That'll be fun."

"Bill too," Shana said. Radiant. Tidying like a demon.

"Where is he?" Anne said.

"He's not here *yet.*"

"I mean Bill," Anne said.

"Taking a shower. Merv's downstairs buying a cake."

"Is he coming for dinner? With Pauline?"

"No, strictly business, alone, after dinner."

"What's the big rush then?"

"We have a lot to do," Shana said. "We don't want the place looking like a pigpen."

"I mean what about Bill, is he interested? He'll talk to him?"

"Of course he'll talk to him," Shana said. "You don't think Bill's totally nuts, do you?"

"What kind of proposition?" Anne said.

"Brush the couch with a whisk broom, will you, Anna, it's all covered with graham crackers."

"Where's Jerry and Katie?" Anne said.

Bill came into the room, spruced up in a bright plaid shirt. Anne's and Bill's eyes failed to connect.

"Merv took them with him to Broadway."

"You think he can manage?" Anne said.

"I hope he buys the Black Forest Cherry Cake," Bill said.

"Spaghetti with butter sauce for supper. The kids love that, and we have to get the kitchen cleaned up in time," Shana said.

"How come Barry's coming?" Anne said. "From out of nowhere."

Merv rang the bell. Bill let him in. The children flung themselves at Bill's legs.

"Take it easy," Bill said.

"He knows the boys have been having trouble finding decent jobs. Papa's been telling him. Barry *cares* about us," Shana said.

"Everybody's in the business now. The whole family," Merv said. "Aren't we in the family?" Excited.

"They're in, they're out," Anne said. "With Barry, you never know."

"Anna, will you *do* something!" Shana said.

"Voice of doom," Merv said. "Don't throw cold water around, until you hear."

"There's a catch," Anne said.

"There is *not*," Merv said. "Would he be coming here himself? That's family feeling on his part. There's an opening in the Dallas office and an opening in New York, now that he has a New York office. He's moving back to New York, to live here. From the bottom up, these jobs he's talking about, but how can you lose with his backing? We have to prove ourselves. That doesn't worry me."

"I'll bathe the children," Anne said. "Two at a time, okay? No heads though."

"That's where Connie is. She loves Dallas," Shana said.

"Watch out for Sam Schwartz," Anne said.

"Goddard Products has made a fortune out of defense contracts, war contracts," Bill said. "Barry must be a millionaire."

"Did you get the Black Forest Cherry Cake?" Shana said.

"Yeah," Merv said. "Better put it in the icebox."

"I wonder what the hell he's getting into next," Bill said.

"Listen Bill," Merv said, "if you'd rather not be here . . ."
"Don't push, don't push," Bill said. "I can listen to him."

"None for me," Barry said. "I get a lot of heartburn these days.
That whipped cream looks good but I'm afraid of it."
Changed only a little from the earlier Barry. A slower, weigh-
tier, more measured manner of talking. Rabbinical. Full, helpless
laughter still present. Laughed till the tears came at Bill's war
fuck-up stories. Bill was the puzzle. Rapid changes of color, loud
talk, banter, hail-fellow approach, arm around Barry's shoulder,
hollow booming laugh, war stories. Then, retreat into silence and
a close study of the toe of his shoe. Then on again with another
story, laughter, repeat of the above.
Shana served cups of cocoa.
"I haven't had cocoa with marshmallow since Boys' High,"
Barry said. "Is it good for heartburn?"
Danny pattered out in his chlorine-spotted blue Doctor Dentons, his toes sticking through the torn feet of the sleeping suit.
Anne was ashamed of her son's exposed toes. She gathered him in
her lap. Danny cuddled, looked at his stranger uncle with sleepy,
shy eyes, shot up at sight of the cocoa, sipped, tipped back his head
and smiled radiantly into Anne's eyes. Now Anne was ashamed
that her excessive love was showing. Katie pattered in. Her Doctor
Dentons were a pristine yellow—intact and spotless. Wide-awake
violet eyes, alert, busy. She climbed into Anne's lap, crowding
Danny.
"Can I have my very own cup of cocoa?" she said.
"Hello, little princess," Barry said.
Katie looked seriously at her stranger Uncle Barry.
"I'm Katie," she said.
"Can I have my very own cup of cocoa, too?" Danny said. "Move
over, Katie," he said.
Bill brought two cups. The adults poured some of their cocoa
into the children's cups.
"How about a kiss and a handshake to thank me for my share?"
Barry said.
Katie kissed him. Danny shook his hand. Shyness assailed them.
They pulled back and knocked their heads hard against Anne's
chest. They squirmed on her lap. Their wriggling, swinging heels
battered her shins. Anne sat, smothered in baby hair and sticky
fingers and, yes, in prideful love.

"They're the ones we have to think about now—the children," Barry said with a solemn nod.

Barry eyed Bill. Merv's deal had been arranged. It was Bill who hadn't yet spoken up. Anne saw anger under Barry's protecting eyelids. He disliked having his generosity flicked aside.

"This is no way to live," Barry said, gesturing inclusively.

His arm spread contempt on the shabby place, discrediting their attempt to get along without harm.

"God, I can't wait to get out of this dump," Shana said. She snatched a faded green corduroy pillow from the couch, threw it up at the harsh ugliness of the exposed center ceiling light. "Yowie," she shouted, "yippee!"

Barry made a face. "I'd better pass up the cocoa." He took a pill from his jacket pocket, unwrapped its silver foil, flipped it into his mouth.

The children watched with solemn interest.

What was Bill doing? He seemed to be staring fixedly at his wife and children, but Anne saw that his gaze traveled just beyond their rim, as if to a nimbus surrounding them, terrible and tragic to contemplate. His face was contorted with suffering and revulsion.

Katie's delicate backbone stiffened under Anne's hand. "Look at my Daddy!" she said. "Look at my Daddy's face," and burst into pitying sobs.

"I'll get them settled back in bed," Anne said. "Sh, sh," she said to Katie.

"I'll be leaving right away," Barry said.

"I'll be right back," Anne said.

"He left," Bill said. "He said to tell you good night."

Anne and Bill were in the small bathroom. For the privacy.

"I walked him out to his car." Bill was whispering. "I wasn't going to let those two witness my capitulation." He seemed to be grinding his teeth. "I made the deal. I'm seeing his New York man tomorrow." Definite grinding of teeth. "That's what you want, isn't it?"

Anne said, "*I* want? We haven't even . . ."

Bill said, "If I'm going to cave in, it's going to be on my terms. Free and clear. No bullshitting. I told him. Barry, I said, you've talked about my sacrifices as a serviceman, about my responsibilities to my family, about how I deserve a chance to prove myself.

Okay. Now I want to tell you something about me. I gave up law to become a full-time Communist Party organizer. I'm not ashamed of that. You know what he said? He said, I know all that, Bill. I would have been one myself if I thought Communism was going to win."

She laughed.

"I hate it when you laugh that way," he said. He looked directly into Anne's face. The look brimmed with hatred and anger, but it was a relief to have been contacted—even with loathing.

"I'm sorry," she began, "but . . ."

He interrupted. He had shifted his loathing to the rickety washbasin against which he braced himself with a powerful, naked, hairy arm.

"Look at that crummy thing," he said. "He's right. This is no way to live. A six-foot man expected to use a thing this size." He struck it with his fist. It complained in a plumbing noise very like the sound of Bill grinding his teeth. He bent to the discolored metal of the disposal drain and confided in it. "I don't know what the hell I'm doing in this family," he whispered.

XIV

Bill Morris had an affair with another woman, as it was then referred to, and conducted it in such a dumb, sloppy fashion that the whole damn family knew he was carrying on with a waitress before Anne did. Bad enough to choose a waitress in a restaurant right down the street from Barry's New York office, but to set up the office as the lovers' letter drop and telephone center was idiocy elevated to genius. It had to be that Bill wanted to be caught out.

At that moment in family history, the New York office of Goddard Products contained Merv (in training for the Dallas office assignment), Josh (in sales), Saul (in charge of the mail room), and Saul's wife Lil (in the general office).

"My heart is breaking for you," Lil said. "To have to hear such news."

"You're not telling me anything I didn't know," Anne lies to Lil, who true to Barry's name for her was spouting tears. "Bill and I have no secrets from one another."

"He's making a fool of you," Shana said. "There's no reason for you to take that."

"Let's not talk about it," Anne said.

Not that easy. The family had their job to do. Anne was a rejected, abandoned, betrayed woman. They must rush in to pity and protect her.

"I'll never forgive Bill," Anne said to the only person she could talk to about it—her friend Edith. Edith maintained a breezy distance from emotional matters.

"Come on, Anne, what did he do? Nothing."

"Not the other woman," she said. "That doesn't bother me. But the mess he made of it. And right in the middle of the family."

To have been exposed to their whispering and plotting, to become the object of their labors—the gathering of the evidence and its distribution among all members with directives to sift, weigh, and come in with a verdict. Unanimous. Bill must be put out of the business. Not to be trusted.

All this in the five-room apartment in Washington Heights among the noisy children and the bikes and strollers, the shared meals, and the long silences while Anne put up with Shana's exaggerated all-day pity and Merv's morning and evening salacious inquisitiveness, which he apparently hoped she would mistake for compassion.

Late one night, everybody else asleep, Merv put his arms around her, kissed her on the forehead. "Bill's a damn fool, Anna. You're really very attractive."

She told her friend Edith, "I'd like to line them all up and knock them over with a machine gun."

"Do it," Edith said. "For their own good."

She punished Bill by not letting him know that she knew. Let him learn that from others, the way she had learned about him.

"It's you I love. It is," Bill said when he knew she knew. They were in the little bathroom, for privacy. Bill tried to press her to him, but the washbasin blocked him. He was in a state of fear that made him stupid, uncoordinated.

"Sit down," she said and pushed him to the toilet seat. His eyes had disappeared in the white mass of his face. She turned aside, not to look at him, and saw in the medicine-chest mirror that she too was a white-faced monster with blazing, mad eyes. "Why didn't you tell me? And if it was a secret why did you let *them* find out? How could you be so dumb?"

"I wanted to tell you, but I was afraid. I was afraid of what you would do. I didn't want to lose you. I don't want to lose her either. She's kind. I love her. She listens to me. But I'll give her up, I promise."

"You're maddening," Anne yelled. "Who asked you to give her up?"

"Sh, sh," Bill said. "They'll hear you."

He had misunderstood her anger and taken heart from it. "I needed something, Anne, after all those years away. I needed something more than you were willing to give. I needed you, the you you used to be. I was looking for you, for Anne in other women, I swear it. Maybe this will help us, make our love stronger. . . ."

"Oh Christ, shut up," she said. "I don't want to hear any more drivel. Drivel, drivel, drivel." Her anger split into an intense pain in one eye, and she stopped.

She had made Bill afraid of her. He waited like a misbehaving child for punishment.

"What are you going to do, Anne?" he whispered.

"I'm not your mother, I'm not your teacher," she said. "We're supposed to be lovers." His fear offended her. The state of things between them was an offense to love.

She had set him going again. "I do love you, Anne. It's you I love. I'll give her up, I promise. I couldn't help myself. I needed something. You were always interrupting me when I spoke to you, to attend to other things."

"What other things? Cooking, cleaning? Our children? It's garbage—what you're saying. It's all garbage."

"Sh," he said, "they'll hear."

And again, "What are you going to do, Anne?"

"Do? What can I do? I'm going to get a job. Tomorrow."

"I'm fired," he said.

"Wasn't that what you wanted?" she said. "Do you want out of this too? Is that what you want? Get out. You're free to go."

She would have liked to kick him out. Let vengeance be masked as generosity.

"No. No." He began to cry—a large man crouched on the toilet seat with his fists in his eyes, sobbing. "It's you I love. It is. And the children—Danny, Katie. Please let's keep trying. Please."

What a man he was for trying.

"I can be a good man. I know I can be a good father," he said, later, in bed, whispering, after the first time with her in months that he had managed to hold an erection. She stroked his head. There was no voice in her to fit the straining posture which was to be their stand-in for love.

Riding the local subway on the way to the job Edith had helped her find, she thought about their marriage, above the clatter of the train and an acrid stench and the distraction of two high-school boys playing chess on a tiny board with little discs that magically clung to the squares. Why do we persist, she thought, locked in these painful, absurd rigidities, like two awkward kids in a game of statues holding an unnatural pose?

XV

After two bloody marys," Anne said to her boss, Charles Dannenberg, across the luncheon table, "I'm prepared to believe anything."

"Such as?" Charles inquired.

"The innate goodness of man. That we only exist because we think we do. That life is a dream, a nightmare followed by a better afterlife."

"Material?" Charles asked. He worked at the antipasto before him with tender interest, delicately inching out a tiny hot green pepper that he placed on the tip of a tongue so thin in his enormous face that she wouldn't have been astonished to learn that it was forked. He swallowed, and the tears came into his bright little eyes and oozed out, slowly watering the surrounding pads of flesh, before flowing down the landscape of his cheeks. "Or spiritual?" he concluded, and lifted his martini glass to his lips with the floating lightness of movement of the obese; but when he shifted his bulk on the little bentwood chair, she could hear the seat groan. "Struggle now—for the happiness of future generations?" he continued between forays at his plate. "Or suffer on earth, find happiness in God's heaven?" and looked into her eyes with smiling inquiry, an attention that produced in Anne the pleasant sensation of being desired to her core, helped along as it was by the dim lights of the cellar restaurant, the second lunchtime drink, the dressed-up Mafia types at the bar, and the waiters calling out orders in jolly Italian, saving their deferential broken English for the diners.

194 *Helen Yglesias*

"I like it *here*," Anne said. "Why don't we settle in here for a few years?"

"Ah, sadly, sadly," Charles said, "because of deadlines and press time, and husbands and wives, and children and mortgages, and aging parents to be put away in homes, and life and death."

"No mortgages," Anne said. "I refuse to get embroiled in mortgages."

"Very unsound," Guy Rossiter said at Anne's side without warning. "May we join you?" and with executive assurance was rearranging chairs and indicating by gesture to Dom, the owner, to set two more places at Anne and Charles's table. Edward Hurley stood behind Guy Rossiter—small, dry, clever Ed Hurley who wrote most of the magazine's edits and sprightly, learned pieces about new scientific discoveries and outrages perpetrated by organized religion. Before Ed Hurley was seated, he ordered a double vodka Gibson. Guy Rossiter ordered iced tea.

"I don't drink," he said. The remark was aimed broadside, in no specific direction. "I'm an alcoholic."

The others had obviously heard it before. Anne heard it for the first time. A transfixing comment, resonating with drumbeats of incantation. What must it cost him to drop it so casually?

She was involved with questions of the correct response to this astonishing piece of information from the man she was already disproportionately interested in. Disproportionate to the actual contact made, she reminded herself. But her response was of no matter. Guy Rossiter wasn't looking for one. He was involved with questions of ordering lunch (chicken tetrazzini) and in inquiring after the health of Dom's son, who had apparently broken an arm playing football.

The new arrivals ruined her relaxed pleasure with Charles. They made her nervous. She was sorry to be wearing her gray silk Cossack blouse. It was tacky—artsy-craftsy. She became aware of her hair slipping free of its French twist, and raised her arms to restrain the loose strands in a classic gesture that drew Guy Rossiter's attention. She was suddenly in an extraordinary enclosure that held the pose and his pleasure in it in a space charged with the sense of something happening—the shock of accident—a train derailed, a car smashed. He looked away when the waiter arrived, and she was released, but into another space within herself where an internal alarm chimed slowly, softly, and insistently. The encounter brought her to a total silence, accepted by the three men as her happy condition among their eminences. She was a lowly editorial assistant, after all, and a pleasant listener.

"Watch out for him," Charles Dannenberg said, weeks later, out of the blue, as they bent together over cuts in the page proofs. "He's a big womanizer."

She had seen Guy Rossiter leaving the building a number of times with a tall, carefully groomed blonde, and at other times with an expensively dressed dark girl beautiful enough to be a model or an actress.

"I'm safe," she said. "Not his type."

"If it's female, it's his dish," Charles said. "To him, there is no such thing as an ugly woman."

"Thanks a lot," she said.

"Not at all," Charles said, patting the curve of her hip. "Not at all, love."

That was the moment Betty Provenzano arrived at the doorway of their office, and at a swift, false conclusion.

"Excuse my interrupting, Mr. Dannenberg," she said. Small simper for Charles, then on to a gruff, businesslike manner. "As shop steward I have to have a talk with Anne before she sees Mr. Rossiter about her job title."

"Who's seeing Mr. Rossiter?" Anne said.

"I forgot," Charles said. "You are, at four thirty in his office."

"You can't see Mr. Rossiter without me," Betty said. "I'm the union shop representative."

"How did you even know about it?" Anne said. "Before I did."

"It's my business to know . . ." Betty began.

"Out! Out!" Charles waved a winglike arm to menace Betty but managed at the same time to wink and leer reassuringly. There wasn't a woman in the office who didn't believe that Charles Dannenberg hid a raging passion for her in his fat heart. "No talk until these page proofs are done. And then go scratch one another's eyes out in the ladies'. I have a column to get out."

In the washroom, progress was delayed by the pale-eyed bookkeeper, Grace, locked in her ritual of handwashing before and after peeing. They chatted about soaps and hard water until Grace left. Betty Provenzano latched the door.

"What's going on?"

"We don't want our conversation to get all over the office," Betty said.

She was years older than Anne, attractive in a hard, girdled, sprayed, stiff style, her hair hennaed to a polished cherrywood, her eyes heavy with deep blue eye shadow. There is no such thing as an ugly woman. The gospel according to Guy Rossiter. Some involvement here?

"You can't go in to talk to Mr. Rossiter about anything to do with classification without me. That's the union rule. I have to be present at the negotiations."

"But I didn't make the appointment," Anne said.

"That's the rule. I'm the union representative."

"But I just heard about it," Anne said. A tremor of anger started in her chest and rose to her head in a drilling pain. Migraine. Migraine coming. "What are you so angry about?" Was it because she was the youngest in a big family that her expectations were always off the mark? "I asked the union first. I went to you first. You said no."

"Well, no is no," Betty yelled. "Can't you take no for an answer?"

She didn't answer that.

"You went to Mr. Dannenberg first. Then you came to me, to the union."

"If Charles said no, I wouldn't have had anything to ask you, would I? It was Charles who had to decide if I could be his assistant editor instead of an editorial assistant."

"Editorial assistant, assistant editor, what a fuss over nothing."

"It's not," Anne said. "They're totally different categories."

"You had no business moving ahead on this. Getting an appointment with Mr. Rossiter."

"I didn't ask for this appointment. I don't know anything about it."

"You threatened to quit," Betty said. "That's a maneuver. That's not taking no for an answer."

That was true. She *was* maneuvering. She wanted them to let her stay on her terms.

"And wheedling Mr. Dannenberg to let you do a book review. Anybody can see right through that."

"To what?" Anne said.

Betty P. didn't answer that.

"I don't understand," Anne said. "If I'm qualified to be an assistant editor, why shouldn't I be? What's wrong with that?"

"Who qualified you? Listen, girlie, you're technical staff, just like me, you're not editorial, you're technical, that's what it says on your s and jc card, and that's that."

She felt her limbs softening and tears at the ready, attacked by this outlandish scene and by too many bloody marys at lunch. She lowered her head—not to show the tears. There was no appeal to Betty P. Yet she did appeal.

"But not forever and ever, Betty. That would be a life sentence. And I'm innocent."

Betty P. didn't laugh.

Charles wasn't happy with her either. "Here you are turning into a pain in the ass just when I thought I had found the perfect secretary."

"You see," she said, "you see? You said secretary. That's what I am."

He lifted the staple gun to threaten her. "Put your lips here," he said. "I'll shut them for all time." He looked at her with mock sorrow. "Why don't you cultivate happiness? I was so happy with you. Don't you like to sit at the corner of my desk and record my elegant prose in those squiggly marks you do so well?"

"No," she said. "I hate it."

"For shame," Charles said. "Take pride in your work. That's a skill. Now you've ruined everything. I won't be able to lean back and dictate to you with pleasure. I'll have to return to that lousy typing pool and put up with a moron."

"Why don't you take me to a publishers' party? I'll record your witticisms for all time."

Squeezed between the pads of fat, his bright eyes opened a slit wider. "She's ambitious," he said. "She lusts for an editorial chair."

"Don't make fun of me," she said. "Don't make me feel ridiculous."

"You are ridiculous," he said, but reached out and pressed his hand against her forehead—a blessing.

His hand was like a great paw of a creature, there was so much of it. Was he a grotesque in bed, or a soft, supportive mountain?

"Why did you take this job if you hate the work?"

"I love it," she said. "I love you. I hate the typing and shorthand. Besides, you're the ones who cheated. I didn't read the fine print. *Tribune* always had an assistant editor on the back pages. Why did you change the rules on me?"

"To save money," he said. "And not six months on the job and
you're causing trouble."

"I don't care about the money."

"The hell you don't. First you'll grab the title, then you'll start
howling for money. Anyway the union won't let us upgrade you
without an increase. We have a tight little contract here.

"I don't care about the union. Why do I have to be in? You're
not."

"I'm management. I hire and fire. So keep a civil tongue in your
head. Curtsy. And run down the hall and fetch me a cup of water.
It's time to take a pill."

When he had given her a book to review, he had accompanied
the honor with a challenge.

"I'm not pulling any punches, doll. If you turn in a rotten review, you're going to be the first to know."

"Don't count on it being rotten, Charles," she said.

"With my luck," he said, "it'll probably get a Pulitzer."

She read the book on the subway going to and from work and
wrote the review in the quiet of the office after the others had left.
Her anxiety to turn in a good piece addled her brains. When she
finished she had no idea whether it was good or bad. She left the
office when Charles read it.

"It's okay," Charles said when she returned. "An acceptable,
workmanlike job."

"First-rate," Edward Hurley said, and screwed up his mouth in
distaste at his own extravagance. It was unpleasant for him to
praise others.

Later that day, Hurley called her a colleague. "Let Anne pay for
her own lunch," he scolded Charles. "Come now, no more of this
nonsense, paying for a colleague's lunch. I don't pay for your lunch
or you for mine."

She had never been so pleased to pick up her own check.

Charles asked her to go along to the next publishing event.
"They're a waste of time, but if you're dying to waste your time,
come along."

"Any way you waste your time, Charles, is good enough for me."
She followed in his flat-footed, waddling steps.

He halted at the doorway, leaning against it, breathing in a
pained, openmouthed concentration. His clothes came to a rum-
pled rest long after he had stopped moving, continuing to quiver

with the masses of flesh underneath. He smiled when he caught his breath.

"Smart, smart," he said. "New York Jewish smart. Get me some water."

"Confess," he said, after swallowing his pill. They waited for the lumbering elevator to arrive. "You took this job to be close to my enchanting person."

She said, "The fact is that when you hired me I was so happy I had diarrhea for a week. To work here with you and with Guy Rossiter and Edward Hurley in the very same building, in the same rooms where—you know, everything, the whole gorgeous *Tribune* tradition."

"Sickening," Charles said, closing his eyes. "Not surprising you came down with diarrhea. Keep up that stream of hogwash and you'll go far."

"Don't be disgusted with me," she said. "You'll see, you'll be glad about me. I'm going to work very hard for you. I've been trying out heads. I'm good at them. And I can take all the routine editing off your hands, the junk with the copy-editor and the printers. . . ."

"You're a monster," he said. "You want *my* chair. Display a little modesty and patience, girl. If you're good, I'll will it to you."

"He's dying," Guy Rossiter said.

She didn't want to hear it. She didn't want to be seated opposite this handsome man confronting the awful intelligence that Charles Dannenberg was dying and be aware that she was thinking: *I am uncontrollably attracted to Guy Rossiter*, and thinking: *If Charles Dannenberg dies, maybe I could become an editor.* She stood up, felt sick, sat down again.

"Are you all right?" Guy Rossiter asked.

She nodded. She thought, *Live, Charles, live. I swear I don't care if I ever become an editor.* And yet base professional hope glimmered. She felt that her agitation must be emitting a menacing yellow ray that a camera should be clever enough to record. Surely Guy Rossiter was reading her confusion for what it really was? Monstrous ambition, ugly and deforming. No, she thought, I vomit it up. I give it up. He was talking to her but she wasn't hearing.

Then she picked up on the sense that he was persuading her to stay on with Charles.

"Charles likes you. It would be another cruelty at this point for him to adjust to a new assistant. He tells me that you're extremely helpful. I'm certain that we can come to an agreement about your classification reque͟ in time. I told Betty not to be concerned, that we wouldn't be taking up any matters of union substance at the moment. That wasn't what I told Charles. Somebody must have left a switchboard key open. Office politics," he said and smiled. "I didn't want Charles to know that I would be telling you," he said.

"That's okay," Anne said. She needed to end this interview quickly, to get away from her own unbearable reaction, and from Guy Rossiter's coolness. He sat behind his large desk, leaning forward, balancing a pencil between the backs of his fingers. It bothered her to see that cool manipulation of the pencil between his fingers. "I'll stay."

"I'm glad," he said and dropped the pencil. He clasped his hands together. The hush in his office swelled the sound of her blood, whooshing in her ears like a windstorm. She stood up. He did too. "It will take some toughness," he said. "You won't want Charles to know you know."

"Does he know?" she forced herself to ask.

"Yes," he said.

"I can't believe it," she said. "How well he acts."

"He's a beautiful man," Guy Rossiter said. She saw feeling flood his face. "The best. I love him. I'll miss him terribly."

"I'm so sorry," Anne said, but she was glad because she had seen Guy Rossiter show his feelings.

The upper floor which holds the library and Guy Rossiter's office is unlike the rest of the small building in which the magazine is housed, an effect of rugs and soft lamps, of drapes and a show of sky through the high windows, of less dust and more distance from the racketing presses below. The street on which the buildings sits narrows to a point so that the small lobby opens out front on a broad busy avenue, and, by way of another lacy iron cage exactly like the passenger elevator but called "the freight," a back door opens out to a narrow alley of tenements, shoe repair shops, cellar laundries, and a luncheonette set down in a corner of Greenwich Village that has seen better days and will see them again with the renovation on the tenements already in progress. Anne prefers the alley entrance—more convenient to the subway. She rushes toward work in the morning as toward love, and leaves it with regret at night. It is a case of loving her work so much that she loves the building as its body. The bumbling, clanging elevator and old man Peter who drives it. The stairs, and to hear her high heels clack on the metal, to feel the panting physical exertion of running up and down with copy. The smell of the presses is hot, live, contentious. She loves fighting with the compositors, defeating their ideas of what cannot be done and winning their grudging admiration when what she suggests works. Her special compositor calls her "Mine Nemesis," and glares at her with Papa's outraged fury when she's "making trouble" and beams with Papa's bemused twinkle when things go quietly. Like Mama he worries that she's too skinny. "A mama, too. You know she's a mama?" he calls out over the noise to a linotypist. "Eat," he commands her. "And the main thing is to enjoy while you eat."

She eats lunch with her fellow editors—"the men"—in an excitement that burns up food before she's swallowed it. If Guy Rossiter joins them, she cannot eat at all, too preoccupied with drinking him in and carrying away with her not the details of his contributions to the bright conversations with Charles Dannenberg and Ed Hurley, but the sense of his beauty, of graceful feelings and a wild wit and beneath that, escaping his control, flashes of temperament—annoyance, ego, fear, anguish. She is so acutely conscious of his body she is always slightly nauseous in his presence.

She is at the heart of where she always wanted to be. She works charms and makes obeisances to her remarkable good luck. Before reaching Guy Rossiter's desk with whatever she carries in her hand, breathing hard from her run up the stairs, she slows down in a ceremonial tribute to the bound volumes of *National Tribune* lined up on the shelves of the library. One evening a week Bill takes the children to dinner at his mother's and she stays late at the office, carrying her sandwich and container of coffee to the library where she reads, in the volumes that go back to the 1860s, the old stately reviews and the old passionate arguments. Guy Rossiter's books are on the library shelves also. She picks up *New England Son*, published years before when Guy Rossiter was twenty, a book she had never read, partly because it had been

described by a "Marxist" critic as "an upper-class writer's celebra-
tion, unconscious perhaps, of the American expansionist, imperial-
ist dream in the guise of a boyhood memoir." In the opening pages
she encounters Guy Rossiter's immigrant ancestor arriving in Boston in the early 1700s,

Nathaniel Sawyer, a Jewish merchant from whom we inherit the dark
good looks displayed in the family every now and then, if Nathaniel
Sawyer's portrait in the south gallery of Hampshire House does not lie.
The portrait has a high gloss, as does the family treatment of the vivid old
boy. Let him hang there decently and bring no attention to our origins.

Guy Rossiter's dark good looks are displayed in the picture on
the back of the book jacket. It is a picture of a young, pretty Guy.
The older man in the flesh is more beautiful. In the flesh. She
brings out all his books, looking for the latest photograph, the one
most like him, and lifts it to her face, placing her cheek against his
paper cheek.

"Why did you warn me against him?" Anne asks Charles. "He's
a good friend to you."

"He's my best friend," Charles says. "I don't have to watch out
for him, *you* do."

"He doesn't know I exist," she says. "Do you know that the
beautiful blonde I thought was one of his women is his *mother?*"

"Certainly," Charles says. "She's the world's greatest pain in the
ass. You're nearsighted, and she's had more than one face-lift. As
my mother says, with wonderful unconcern for her faulty logic,
'The best thing that could have happened to poor Guy is that his
mother should never have been born, God forbid!' "

Guy Rossiter is forty-nine years old. He has never married. He's
an alcoholic. A womanizer. His mother is a pain in the ass. He has
a Jewish ancestor.

"Well, is he some kind of sex maniac?" A succession of beautiful
women lunching with Guy Rossiter has maddened Anne.

"Out of Krafft-Ebing. A psycho of the liberal pinko degener-
ate . . ."

"I hate people who refuse to gossip," Anne says.

"I don't gossip with virtuous, happily married women," Charles
says. "I venerate the happily married woman."

She will not burden Charles Dannenberg with complaints

against her marriage. At lunch, she makes the mistake of reporting difficulties in organizing her housework and obtaining sitters during a seige of chicken pox, measles and mumps hitting Danny and Katie in a round robin as bad as a medieval plague. Edward Hurley waves her to silence.

"Nobody knows the trouble you've seen—and nobody wants to," he says, and returns to savaging a piece on the function of the little magazine, written by a former *Tribune* editor who had moved on to *Time.*

"Don't you have an unpublished novel in a drawer at home?" Charles says. "I've taught you everything else I know. Maybe I could help you with it, make some suggestions, get it to the right editor."

"All I have at home are my children," she says.

"Children are a woman's true novels," Charles says.

She thinks he's kidding, and then sees that he isn't. Dislike his comment as she does, what had she meant by answering as she did? My children have stolen away my chances? My meaning is in my children? She is reminded of Katie's clear violet eyes and dips into them as into restorative waters.

She is often alone in the office now. Though she misses Charles, she likes being alone to do things her own way, make her own decisions. Charles stays at home to rest, to be doctored. When he comes in, he's draggy, gray. He breathes with heaving difficulty and has developed a weak little cough which, once started, cannot be stopped. She runs to the water cooler more and more often. He sips from the paper cup slowly and the cough is transformed into a steady hiccup. Now the hiccup won't stop.

Staring ahead out of tiny, wet eyes, sipping coffee from a paper container, late in the afternoon of a quiet day, he says, between jerking breaths, "If the truth be known, I'd rather live than not."

"Oh yes, you must, please, yes," she says in an idiotic jumble, and throws herself to her knees on the dirty floor at his feet, putting her head down to cover her shame at being young and well, hiding herself in the huge thigh overflowing the seat of the chair. The great mass of flesh slides from under her crying face. He is slipping backward and sideward. He has dropped the coffee container to the floor, where it leaks its dark remains on her skirt. His frightened eyes appeal to her.

"I don't think . . . I can . . . get up, Anne." Between the hiccups he holds his voice to a tone of tenderness and apology.

He was taken to the hospital from the chair. She couldn't watch the attendants struggle with his bulk. She went to the washroom and stayed until she heard the elevator descend. He never returned to his desk. It became her desk. She talked to him three times a day on his bedside phone, mostly banter, until the drugs overpowered him, and after a garbled talk with him she burst into unseemly, loud sobbing, first closing tight the door of her office, not to be overheard.

Betty P. reported the closed door and the sobs to Edward Hurley.

"Are you in the habit," Ed Hurley said, banging the door wide open against the wall files, "of going off into hysterical fits during working hours, and if so, would you be good enough to arrange to break down in the ladies' room so that the door to the literary offices may remain open at all times?"

"You want everybody around here to be as dried up as you are?" she yelled. "He's dying."

That fight made them better friends. After Charles died, it was to Ed Hurley that she carried her rage when Betty P. magnanimously invited her to a Dutch lunch and the information that Anne was being recommended for an increase of five dollars a week to recompense her for the additional responsibility she was carrying. "It's an interim arrangement," Betty P. said, "just until the new literary editor is hired."

Ed Hurley made one of his eloquent lip movements of distaste. "You need lessons in ignoring Betty's provocations," and added, "I should think, based on your performance, your future is not in jeopardy, but I'm not in a position to say, of course."

When she talked of her work at home during supper, Bill cut her off. "I'm so sick of Betty P., Ed Hurley, Guy Rossiter, and the rest of the *National Tribune* staff. Moratorium! Okay?"

Good enough. She was sick of him too, sick of his floundering. "What I think I'd like to become now," was an introductory phrase her heart sank to hear. After Goddard Products, in reaction perhaps, he became a worker in an electronics factory on an assembly belt line, but he couldn't stand it. Stultifying, exhausting, and rotten pay. He got some organizational work with a union, then some fund-raising work with a Y, then some one-shot community work with delinquent boys. Each new thing became *the* thing, the only thing, the whole answer. Then he decided to go back to school, finish his studies, take the bar exam. He was a lawyer now, in a big firm, daily swallowing his outrage that at almost thirty he was no more than an errand boy—Bill Morris, who had been State Educational Director of the Communist Party before he was twenty-five.

The FBI came after him, trying to get him to "cooperate."

"I'm not talking to you boys," he yelled, and slammed the door.

Two pleasant-faced FBI men followed Anne and Bill to the subway station one morning, suggesting that perhaps Mr. and Mrs. Morris would like to talk to them about their past relationship with the Communist Party? Bill put his arm around her, hurried her down the steps. The men followed. She could feel Bill's hand trembling on her arm, but when they were on the platform he amazed her by addressing the crowds on the station platform.

"See those two men, right over there, folks, they're FBI men bothering two law-abiding citizens on their way to work. Mr. and Mrs. Bill Morris, right here. Now why don't you two men tell all these people here what you want with us? Gather around everybody. These two want you to hear this."

The going-to-work crowd at the 168th Street station of the A train startled into attention. They stared at the respectable-looking young couple and at the two supposed FBI men, also very respectable-looking. The two FBI men started for the stairs, then one turned back and called out, "Is that the way you want it to be on your record, Mr. Morris? Is that the way you'd like us to report your attitude at McKuhn, Williams, Mr. Morris?"

"Exactly," Bill said in a loud, friendly voice. "Go right ahead and do that. Why don't you come along with me right now? That's where I'm going, to my place of work."

They knew he was out of the Party, no longer a member. They wanted him to name names. He could have named the whole New York State leadership. It was public information anyway, but they were looking for leads, for ways of using disaffected former members. It was a bad time for people who had been Party members. He had acted like the old Bill and Anne felt the old admiration for him, in spite of her fear. But the two men turned their backs, went up the stairs.

"Fucking bastards," Bill whispered to her in the subway car. People were still staring at them. Bill looked marvelous, elated, on fire. "Let those boys scare you and you're sunk."

"You were terrific," she said. It was a joy to be able to say so. She actually anticipated being with him that evening, but he tired her out by talking of a new project, wondering about going into legal aid to the poor. Fine. She had encouraged him in so many flights of fancying what he wanted to become that he was quite right to resent her lazy acceptance of whatever he chose as not caring at all. She didn't care.

Some of his early-morning elation was still with him when they went to bed, but the habits of their lovemaking were set, no shot of elation could much alter them. Love was a contest which he was determined to win, a match in which he pinned her down under him as if she were his worst, fierce enemy. Those were the bad nights. The good ones were a brisk, friendly Ping-Pong game, exhilarating and good for the body, to be followed by a cigarette and a shower. Either way he won. For her to have won would have meant stopping the contest, stopping the game. She didn't know how. The worst of it was that she knew she was harming him, unraveling his ego.

But daily he knit up the fabric that their bad loving had ripped the night before. He visits his mother twice a week, once with the children, once alone. He bounds up the steps of the old apartment on East 174th Street in the Bronx. He's proud of his working-class mother, still driving her sewing machine, paying her own way. She stands as straight as a peasant woman with a basket on her head, as tall as her beloved firstborn, her level eyes smiling gravely into his, putting God firmly back in his breast. When he leaves her, he stands straighter, he rises like a tower from the debris of the war, and the shocks of marriage and fatherhood.

But when he arrives home, he and Anne get into a fight. About anything.

"This city is going to the dogs," he says. "The IRT stalled for twenty minutes."

"Do you think so?" she says. "I thought it was getting better."

"Why can't you simply accept something when I say it? Why must you always set yourself in opposition to me?"

"I didn't mean . . ." she says.

"Let me finish," he says. "I haven't finished. You've been interrupting everything I say since I've been home. You don't know how to listen."

These stupid struggles are exhausting.

It is as if she has opened a window in a stifling room when she tells him she thinks they should separate. He becomes very animated—quite charming. He entertains the notion of separation the first time she mentions it. It has possibilities.

The following night, he's desperately against. "Think of the children, Anne. For God's sake, think of them." And, "You won't be able to manage without me. I'll have two burdens instead of one if I try to build another life for myself."

He becomes an attentive lover. He calls her at her office. He tells her "I love you" after he has pinned her down and wrung her out. He tells her that he knows she must have found out about the legal stenographer at his office, but that he doesn't care about the girl, he'll give her up, he promises. But Anne has hit a hard substance of determination. Nothing will shake her will to separate. He seesaws from one day to the next, from one scene to the next. Then one night they're working it out—who does what—how to tell the children. Specious explanations recommended by the finest child authorities on separation and divorce. Anne is assigned the dirty work, since it was her choice to live apart.

"It has nothing to do with our love for you. We both would love to be with you all the time, but there are times when it's best for people not to live together. So you'll live with Mommy, and Daddy will come to see you a lot."

Wrong reaction. Not according to the book.

"I don't care," Danny yells. "I want my daddy in my own house. You're lying. My daddy told me he wants to stay here. You both better stay here."

It is Katie who comforts Danny. She's too slim and small to take her brother in her arms. Awkwardly she places her head alongside his. His face is smothered in the couch. Hers points outward to the room. Only their ears touch. She whispers, "It's okay, Danny, don't cry. Lots of kids don't have daddies. Then their daddies come and take them to eat spareribs. It's okay." Her ear-to-ear resuscitation works. He stops crying. Katie smiles comfortingly at Anne, her eyes brimming with a sorrowing liquid for herself and Danny and her poor daddy that loyalty and love for her mommy halts unshed. The water discolors her vivid eyes to a pale, sickly blue. Remarkably, the tears stay without falling, a shimmering testimony to Katie's sense of moral justice, a more terrible reproach to Anne than any other.

Bill's mother joins in the attack.

"I know this poison isn't originating with you. You've always been a good girl, a good mother and a good wife. I know where it's coming from. Your family never liked him. I saw it clear from the beginning. They never liked it that he came from a poor background. And that he was such a big radical."

She tries another approach.

"Annie, I understand. I'm a woman like you. You haven't had it so easy with Morrie. There have been plenty of financial problems, plenty of problems in general. But that's life. Isn't that life? Morrie didn't make the world. The world was here before he was born. He's a wonderful boy, Annie. You're making a mistake. What's a little hardship when you're young? Don't think he's going to be a nobody forever. Not my Morrie.

"Please, don't give my Morrie such a terrible kick in the heart," she begs, and breaks into hoarse, manlike sobs.

Anne is appalled by guilt and shame at the disturbance she's creating. She serves Bill's mother hot tea in a glass, with a wedge of lemon and two squares of lump sugar on the saucer. She kisses her on the cheek of her big-featured, homely face, so much like Bill's.

"Don't try to understand, Mama", Anne says. "I can't help it. There's no explanation. I just have to."

Bill's mother wipes away the tears of her weakness. "I'm sorry, I don't accept that. No explanation? That's not logical. It's not such a big mystery. You were always a sensible girl. And now all of a sudden you don't know what you're doing? If a person can change so fast, maybe they can change back just as fast. Don't listen so much to your family. Morrie told me plenty what their attitude is. By them everything is money, money, money. With people like us, it's different, am I right? We have ideals. We live for more than money. Don't give up so easy. In the long run life will be better. Life isn't only pleasure."

Bill's mother drives the argument ahead energetically, between zoops of tea: She clamps a lump of sugar firmly between her large front teeth, one of which is a bright yellow gold, and she zoops the tea through the sugar. She looks at Anne with her honest, level eyes.

Only Anne and Bill know, though neither one has said it outright, that Bill is eager to take off. He has already found his own little place, and imagines it cozy and complete (with the new bookcases he will build himself) lined with his books and with the new hi-fi components which he must (and does) take with him, carefully packed in a carton under the Beethoven quartets. In the room, on the simple daybed covered with an India print, he pictures a new, soft, vague woman. She smiles, she listens, she opens her arms.

Bill also knows that Anne couldn't put him out herself, and that there is no force she would call in to do so, but while packing and arranging and renting his new room, he complains to any available ear that he has been pushed, and departs with the help of two friends in a disorganized hauling of cartons, suitcases, the kitchen table, and their only umbrella—because it's raining.

"Don't tell me that he took the kitchen table," Connie says. "I'll never believe it. From his own children?"

Her sisters are calling in from all points, and it was Danny in his innocence who told about the kitchen table, before Anne reached the phone.

"He definitely never came up to our high standards," Jenny says, "poor thing. What a pity it had to end this way. But he does come from a very coarse background."

"You'll be able to start a whole new life, Anna," Shana says at lunch. (Shana and Merv have served their term in Dallas. Merv is now in the New York office. Shana has a splendid modern house on the Island.) Shana is dazzled by visions of a lost adventureland of teen-age curiosity and arousal, and seems as tempted to follow Anne's lead out of marriage as Anne had been to follow Shana's lead into it.

The fact is, it is desolating to see Bill go out the door and to realize herself really alone with the children early in the evening of the Friday of a long weekend. She settles to the job of smoothing the mangled field on which she and Bill have battled, but it takes longer than expected. She hallucinates Bill sprawled in the armchair, disappearing down the hallway to the bathroom, she feels him beside her in the double bed, she hears his voice in the other room talking to the children. She is just beginning to feel free of him when he storms in with the decision that their breakup is a mistake. He must come back, and she must have him back. They struggle over the same ground again, a dreary retake, this time ending with the further spoils of the armchair to Bill.

Even thus equipped, he abandons his new place in a few weeks, gives up his job at McKuhn, Williams, and is off to Mexico to think things through, to decide what he wants to do with himself. He stops sending any money. He lets Anne know that since it was her choice to divorce, she'd better be the one to pay for it, and mails her the name of a lawyer friend who will put the action through for a "minimal fee," two hundred and fifty dollars that Anne doesn't have.

Weakened by a moment of renewed intimacy with her sister Shana, she is telling more about her life than she trusts Shana to understand, lured into hinting confidences by a soft, pregnant, glowing, irresistibly receptive Shana across the luncheon table at Longchamp's (Shana's treat). When Anne tells about the divorce money, Shana whips out of her large leather bag a checkbook and a pen, and quickly writes out a check for the amount.

"No, no, no," Shana insists, turning aside Anne's objections. "Bill Morris was never the right man for you. I'm glad to help."

As soon as Anne hears Barry's voice on the telephone, Anne assumes that he is calling because Shana has gotten to him. Anne freezes with apprehension. What maddening, garbled, family distortion of her difficult-enough situation is she going to be forced to confront in this unwanted conversation?

"How's everything with you, Anne?" Barry says.

"Fine, fine."

She is answering from her kitchen in a mess of half-washed clothes and undone supper dishes. The washing machine has broken down during the rinse cycle and flooded the downstairs neighbor's linen closet.

"I thought I'd check up on how my little sister is getting along."

"Fine, fine," she repeats.

"Shana tells me," he says, and she alerts herself to hear about the money, "that you've been doing some wonderful writing for that publication you work on."

"Has she?"

"Don't they pay you for your work?" he says and laughs in a quick bark.

She says nothing.

"Well," he says, "I'm sure they have their problems, too."

"Tell you why I'm calling, Anne," he says. "Your mother and father are worried about you. Your sister Shana is worried about you."

"In what way?" she says.

"Well, they say you're alone with two children, you don't have enough money, you don't have a husband, you don't have anybody with you, you have to take money from Shana. They're worried about you."

"Not to worry," Anne says briskly.

But he continues, "You know they're two old people. They've had a hard life. They deserve a little peace."

"How is Mama?" Anne says.

"She's failing," Barry says. "You ought to be in touch with them more often. That's another thing. They haven't heard from you in a long time.

"They're very concerned about you," Barry says. "They want me to do something for you. Do something for poor Anna, your mother said. 'Uhruma Hannahle.' What do you think I ought to do, Anne?"

"I can't think of a thing, Barry." She tries to keep her voice from shaking.

"Well, I'll tell you. You seem to be having some trouble supporting yourself and your children. So I have a proposition for you. I'll set you and your children up in an efficiency apartment in Miami near your mother and father. You can stay there as long as it takes you to find a new husband. You have two wonderful children there. They need you. Keep on this way and God knows where it will all end up. I'll be paying for institutions to take care of the lot of you."

"Keep on what way?" Anne says.

"We-ee-el." He drags the word to cover unspeakable depths. "Maybe we'd better not go into all that."

"All what?"

"We-ee-el," he says, and after a silence picks up again. "Shana painted a certain picture, shall we say?"

"Such as?" Anne says. "I'm fascinated."

She has angered him. "Listen, little sister, you can do whatever you choose with your life. It's *your* life. You want to wreck it, that's your privilege, it belongs to you. You married the wrong man, you're getting rid of him now, I don't quarrel with that. Smartest move you've made so far. But don't go charging into more trouble. Older man, another radical, not Jewish, some kind of a drunk—a man who isn't even interested in you—what is this? Do you know what you're doing? I certainly doubt your good judgment from what I heard."

Her anger is so fierce it frightens her, and Barry is such a formidable opponent, it frightens her further to attempt to silence him. She's afraid of him. She's always been afraid of him. ¶This is what a daughter must feel, she imagines, toward a powerful governing father—love, hate, fear, submission and defiance, an ambivalent violent passion capable of murder, at the moment. She holds herself in check.

"You know what I need, Barry?" she says. "I badly need to be left to myself by my family. Is that a deal?"

She has made him furious.

"What you badly need," he says, mimicking her, "is some good advice. You need some sense knocked into your head. You won't ask to be left alone when you come crawling for help, when your actions have put you in a helpless mess. The only reason I'm calling you is because your mother was in tears about you. She's a sick, old woman. Crying about you. 'Hannahle had to go to Shana for two hundred and fifty dollars. Uhruma Hannahle, help her, Baruch, please. She works so hard. She tries to do so much.' I made you an offer because of your mother. Take it or leave it. You can live like a princess down there, you can set your mother's mind at rest about you, you can meet the kind of people you should be meeting, or you can go on the road you're headed and when you're in the condition of a helpless drunk lying in the gutter with a broken leg, you can come back to me for help, and you undoubtedly will. And you know what? I'll help."

"Barry, would you excuse me," Anne says, controlling the sobs of rage threatening to split her throat, "my bell is ringing. I have to get off."

"Just one more thing, Anne," he says. "Next time you need two hundred and fifty dollars, don't bother with the middleman. Come directly to the source. Just ask me for it, will you? Just ask your brother Barry for what you need, will you, because that's where Merv and Shana's money comes from—me. You understand that?"

When she's through at the door assuring the irate downstairs neighbor that she will compensate them for the flooding, she calls Shana and sobs out her fury.

"Damn you, Shana," she screams, not even caring that Shana is pregnant and shouldn't be upset, "damn your dumb interfering helpfulness, blabbing to Mama and to Barry, don't you ever sic my brother Barry on me again, do you hear? Don't you dare put him in my life. The big boss. Never, never, never again. You hear?"

Shana is sobbing too. "You're a very sick person, Anna," she screams back. "I swear to God, I'll never try to help you again as long as I live. I don't care what happens to you. I don't give a damn what happens to you. Are you satisfied?" and she hangs up.

XVI

Thatmiserable washing ma-
chine is going to cost me twenty dollars before I even have it fixed,
and I don't know what that will cost. I have to send my neighbor's
entire linen closet to the laundry," Anne said to Edward Hurley.

The shrimp marinara on Edward Hurley's plate absorbed the
glance of comically severe distaste meant for her complaint. "How
am I ever going to convince Guy Rossiter you're fit to be a senior
editor with that kind of trivia preoccupying your mind?"

"*Senior?* I haven't made assistant yet."

"We can't very well appoint you assistant to nobody, can we?"

"I don't see why not," she said. "I've been an editorial assistant
to nobody for three months. That's even harder to do. Why do you
suppose he hasn't called me in to make the necessary adjustments,
as Betty P. would say?"

"It's the way of the New England Boston wealthy," Ed Hurley
said. "Guy Rossiter never parts with a buck until forced. It's his
way of reminding us that every cent of operating *Tribune* comes
out of his own pocket. Why don't you march in there and ask the
man? He's very generous once he gets past the first wrench. I'll
stand behind you."

Standing at Guy Rossiter's side with a galley marked by his
questions, waiting for him to end a telephone conversation that
has interrupted their work, Anne kneels and lowers her cheek into
the curved bowl of his hand lying open on the desk. The moment
hangs in suspended time. She has the sensation of having jumped

from a height without landing. He has put down the phone and is watching her, waiting, responding with the slightest pressure to the slow, sliding movement of her cheek against his palm. When she stops, he raises her face to his, to be kissed she thinks, but instead her eyeball is licked by a warm, slippery surgical wash of his tongue. He cannot possibly know that Mama would remove a dust speck from her eye in just that way. She is so enchanted with his response, she laughs. Her eye waters down her cheek, and he smiles and licks the tears too, before releasing her. They have both heard the elevator arrive and the shuffling of the copy editor's slippered feet.

She dreams that night that she's in a boat on a lake, its waters bright and dark with alternating brilliant sunshine and black shadows, the gunmetal heaving surface dancing with whitecaps. There is a gusting wind that takes her breath away. The man in command of the sailboat is a stranger. The boat is headed away from a vague shore into danger, into heavier wind and thick spray. The stranger plays the craft with great skill, a performance in her honor, for her admiration. The boat cuts, turns, leans, rides like a bird. She is cold and wet, then warm and dry, she is content, she is horribly thirsty, she is panting, her tongue hangs out of her mouth, and she is awakened by her own rasping breathing. "It was Papa," she decides. "No, Barry." No, it was neither.

She has never been in a sailboat. The scene of her dream conjures up wealth, the daring, beyond-the-Pale, goyish play of American vacation spots where Jews are not allowed to enter. She gets out of bed, puts on the light, pads through the hall to the living room, and comes back to bed with Guy Rossiter's latest book. She studies the full picture on the back of the jacket. His arms are folded across his chest in a casually formal pose. He is dressed up. *I know where I come from* is in his bearing; *I come from money* is what the expensive cloth of his business suit says, and so does his shirt and tie and the handkerchief in his pocket. On his long, finely modeled face, a slackening of the jowls has begun and on one cheek there is the shadow of an indentation that she had seen, magnified, before he licked her eye. Marks of age. She brings her face very close to the picture to see the indentation on his cheek. She tries to remember how he had smelled but it was too quick, she has forgotten, if she noticed. The eyes of the photograph look directly into hers—straightforward, intelligent, cool eyes. His lips are parted. Restlessness and insatiability in the lips, denying the control. A woman must have taken this picture. She checks the credit and sees that it is so.

"Why don't you just go right in and *ask* him for the title and the money?" Edith says to Anne. "It might be as simple as that."

"Ed Hurley said he would stand behind me," Anne says. She doesn't tell Edith what, the day before, she had done in Guy Rossiter's office, or how he had responded. It is as if she's still in the middle of that leap, still in motion, and the landing uncertain.

"He'll stand wa-aa-aa-ay behind you," Edith says, wise in the ways of men colleagues on magazines. "Chickenhearted Ed Hurley will stand so far behind you you'll need field glasses to find him."

They are seated in a large, drafty hall. On the brightly lit stage, Guy Rossiter and four other men are grouped around a table, a girl fussing about them, arranging mikes, a pitcher of water and glasses, pads and pencils. From this height, Guy Rossiter recedes from her. She had been poised above him since yesterday, in tentative motion, as if hovering over the keys of a piano she will play in a moment. She folds her hands in her lap now. Next to her, Edith has already begun doodling, drawing stick figures of herself and Anne shooting the speakers with long rifles—squiggly dramatic lines for the movement of the bullets, and funny positions for the falling, dying speakers. Edith hates meetings, lectures, symposiums. She has come because Anne asked her to. From his center chair as moderator, smooth-talking Professor Angel Andrade leans forward, addresses the men at the table in smiling banter. They all join in hearty laughter. Anne is swamped with anonymity. The auditorium is permeated with a familiar, damp, stale, depressing coolness. In the dim pit Columbia and Barnard students exude a shapeless excitement of expectation and dull worship Anne doesn't want to be identified with.

"I forgot how gorgeous he is," Edith says, doodling Guy Rossiter with very long, elegant stick legs. "I think he's getting more gorgeous as he gets older."

The glare of the lighting has washed out his skin color. The result is a silvery tone that puts him further away from her. He is like an actor on a silver screen up there. The white lights sculpt the deep eye sockets and the indentation on the cheek. When he speaks his voice is lower, richer than usual, its cadence measured in carefully structured sentences. She doesn't hear what he says. Nervousness grinds in her stomach, roars in her ears, as if he were indeed her lover, or a son, being put to a test she is afraid he might not pass.

But the audience responds gently. They savor, murmur, laugh, applaud. His elegance is an unusual adornment. The speaker who shares his anti-McCarthy point of view is a good-hearted, muddle-headed shouter. Guy Rossiter lowers his eyes when Donald McDevitt unwinds his set performance, but joins in the applause at the end of McDevitt's passionate burst. Angel Andrade smoothly moves the talk from speaker to speaker. In the opposition, Arthur Blau is formidable—radical turned anti-Communist, the quintessential Jew, a spitting, twitching, words-jumbling, brilliance—rocketing from a physique branded by a hook nose, kinky hair, and bowed shoulders. He thickens the air with innuendos of conspiracy and treason, dozens of marvelous quotes, too many obscure names and events. In the question-and-answer period, Guy Rossiter rebukes him by invoking a patrician aura of revolutionary democratic simplicity. The discussion sputters to no conclusion. On the platform, admirers gather. Funny-looking, spray-spitting Arthur Blau is surrounded by a crowd of pretty girls and earnest young men. So is Guy Rossiter, and Anne waits her turn, urged on by Edith, who is eager to save the evening by mingling intimately with the mighty. Face to face with Guy Rossiter, Anne fears a wild bursting chord from the tangled strings of her obsession with him, and doesn't trust herself to speak, but she stands before him and applauds softly until he stops her by seizing her hands.

"Why did you waste your time coming *here*?" He is embarrassed by her action. "It couldn't have been to hear Arthur. He's not worth listening to."

That was said for Arthur's enjoyment, and Arthur laughs genially. The savageries of the platform are put aside. The combatants pick up the gossip and the life they share and all go out together for coffee—Andrade, McDevitt, Blau, Rossiter, and Hughie Winter, who had hardly spoken at all at the round table but who is now bubbling with talk, aimed to amuse Anne and Edith on either side of him. Guy Rossiter is far from Anne, seated on Edith's other side, the two more or less intimately tied into a conversation. It occurs to Anne that there could be an inevitable listing of the two to Guy's or Edith's bed. Anne settles under the pall of that possibility and of Hughie Winter slumped stupidly on her left, having quickly talked himself out, and of Arthur Blau's moist rain of information steadily drifting in from her right in anecdotes about the old days with Franklin and Eleanor. But when they all rise to leave the table, Guy takes her arm, leads her somewhat away from the others.

"Are you really divorcing? Your friend told me you were. I don't understand. What was all that I was always hearing from Charles?"

"What?" she says.

"You were *the* happily married woman of the western world."

"I'm sorry I don't qualify," Anne says. "Maybe there aren't any."

"There are," he says. "There must be."

"It's people like you who don't marry who can afford to be romantic about it," she says.

"Would you believe," he says, "that more than anything else I want to be happily married?"

"I don't know," she says. "It's hard to believe. I think I'll never marry again. I don't think it works very well—marriage."

"Why don't we say good night to these people," he says, gripping her arm firmly, "and talk about it."

XVII

The geography of love is pornographic; its climate is much improved by money; when love comes it comes without effort, like perfect weather.

Naked, rising from his bed, where we arrived rather directly from the round-table discussion, Guy and I are about to get dressed, leaving this garden of delight, because I must get home to my children. He insists on accompanying me.

"I can take a cab," I say. "It's right across the park."

"No," he says, "I want to be with you as long as possible. And I want to see where you live."

I know what he means. It is primarily his body that has made him piercingly real to me, the thin picture on the book jacket pumped and swelled with real blood, but the background too has been filled in, the vague outlines solidly bedded in the comfortable luxury of his apartment. Won't everything fade if we step outside? I experience a damaging slippage in which I doubt the actuality of what's happening. Am I here with Guy Rossiter? He had said, propping himself on his palms above me and looking into my face, "I love you, I love you, I love you." Three times. An unlikely story. I feel the whole adventure will slip away as we enter the run-down lobby of my West Side apartment house. Cinderella—or worse. What if, when I arrive at his desk tomorrow, we have gone back to what we were before, whatever that was?

I shiver, and gather my plain white everyday underwear to put on, turning away from him, ashamed to be seen, suddenly. Does he feel the turmoil of pulling away in me? He is coming toward me. His bare feet make no sound on the thick rug. In the soft light of the bedroom, his deliberate naked advance seems staged. I expect a kiss, but he lifts me to his body and raises me clear of the carpeted floor, feeling my weight along the length of his body and on the extended leg with which he lifts and lowers me, swaying back and up, watching my face as he weighs. At first I hold myself stiffly, but gradually I yield my whole weight, my whole body, and more, more, I yield everything, my whole soul flows from me in a heavy stream down his chest and along his thigh from every opening in my body. Another miracle, because afterward, from having been heavy as water, I have become incredibly light.

At work the following day my nightmare comes true. I encounter him at the receptionist-switchboard operator's desk, and his "Good morning, Anne" is exactly in his usual manner. Good thing it's a quiet day for me, because I can't work. I stare out of a dirty window in my office to a roof opposite, where a man beats a flock of pigeons into the cloudy sky. Later I pass Guy again in the passageway between my office and Ed Hurley's. He has a young man with him. The young man wants to talk to me about some pieces for the back pages. There is nothing, nothing, nothing (three times) in this second encounter that secretly signals our new position to me. I have clearly fallen for Guy Rossiter's cheapest womanizing trick. In the effort it takes to control my rage I become hideously depressed. I feel myself a wounded, ugly animal —Guy Rossiter's latest *thing*. Whose fault? It was I who let it happen. I heap my stupid life on my head, a mass of mistakes, the garbage of my failure to be myself, to take myself as the center of my life. I am always leaning against the wind of a man's energy. I am indeed the helpless slob of my family's reckoning.

I'm not listening to the young aspiring journalist making a heartbreaking, stammering effort to break through my indifference and impress me somehow. My phone rings.

"Ed Hurley and I are lunching with Senator Dickey. We'll be talking about the poll-tax fight. Will you join us?"

Because I don't know how to punish him, I say, "Sorry, Guy, I'm busy."

He says, "I have to go uptown after lunch. I should be back about four thirty. Will you be here or are you leaving early?"

"I'm taking my kids to the zoo at three thirty," I say.

"I've always wanted to do that," Guy says. "And the carousel. Could we meet at the carousel at four thirty?"

"Do what?" I ask.

"Take kids to the zoo. And the carousel. Catch the ring for them. Buy them balloons and Good Humors." He sounds drunk with joy.

"Okay, then?" he says. "See you then."

The young journalist takes heart from my new liveliness. Ideas pour out of him. I'm still not listening, but my face is bright. He talks too fast to allow for swallowing and his lips show spit curling in the corners. I don't mind. Now I like everything about him, even his wet, brown eyes that had seemed far too doglike before.

Guy straddles an outside moving horse, straining toward the carousel ring, lifting a child as if in offering, first Danny and then Katie, so they can seize the ring in their own hands. I watch from a bench. Katie's T-shirt twists under Guy's grip. Guy's seersucker Brooks Brothers suit is wet under the arms from his exertion— details too homely to be anything but real, but I still can't believe that I may have gotten what I wanted. Is that really Guy Rossiter playing Daddy to Danny and Katie on the Central Park carousel? I am remote, enveloped in a haze. I have dreamed this dappled late-afternoon sunshine, these airborne sounds of children squealing, the blurred movements of strangers on the paths surrounding my enchanted island of happiness. It will fade or harden and freeze.

They come toward me from the carousel. Katie is ecstatic. She screams, runs in circles, flops around, yelps, "I'm drunk, I'm drunk," and flings herself on Guy's lap the second he's down on the bench.

"You'll be sorry," I say to him.

He hugs Katie, puts an arm around Danny, who is holding himself aloof, his face lowered shyly; but by the end of the afternoon, after Guy has bought him everything he asks for from the vending carts, Danny too is won over. Heady on this unexpected happiness among the inexplicable grown-ups, the children run zigzag on the winding park path, racing to see whose gas balloon is more powerful. Guy and I follow, and the people resting on benches lining the path view us with interest and some disapproval for our excessive attention to one another.

Ah money, money, how beautiful it is, how I love its power to make everything easy. For my trip to Miami to see Mama in her last illness, it is Guy who picks up all the tabs and takes the agony out of arranging it. He sends his housekeeper to care for Danny and Katie while I must be away. He pays my round-trip plane fare. Our night in an Atlanta Holiday Inn is a ridiculous enchantment. Earlier in the evening, he had introduced me as "my fiancée, Anne Goddard" to the hosts of the group before which he had lectured. We are in our hosts' home for drinks and coffee after the lecture. Guy had felt we must go. They are Guy's old friends from Boston, retired to the South to do good in the peace movement and in the crusade to repeal the poll tax. The man is a pink-faced, hearty sixty year old, who loves me because I'm young and kisses me on the lips and hugs me to his potbellied front. His wife is younger, in her fifties, short, dimpled, with the squashed button nose of a small dog and a head of cropped, grizzled curls.

"You must be one of Letty Goddard's daughters. Didn't you come out with our youngest, Caroline?"

I laugh out loud. "Oh no, Mrs. Chisholm. I'm a New Yorker and I never came out."

I try to explain to Guy how funny that was, but I can't convey the joke of it—Myrtle Avenue, my mother, the grocery store, the elevated outside the window. Come out, come out, wherever you are.

"Well, it *is* a WASP name, however you came by it. You have to accept the consequences of deception," Guy says.

"Blame it on British immigration," I say. "Not me."

I'm immensely pleased with the cover of my false, WASPish, distinguished name and that Betty Chisholm looked into my Jewish face and thought that it had come out in Boston with her daughter's. I enjoy a long, delicious laugh on the Holiday Inn bed. Guy puts his arm flat on me and kneads my hollow stomach. I twine around the heavy snake of his arm.

It was a stroke of genius that I knelt at his desk and put my cheek in the palm of his hand and that I laughed with pleasure when he tasted the liquid in my eye. He likes to taste. He likes to try his tongue against a tiny space between two of my teeth, created by a crooked incisor. He has a woman's feeling for lovemaking, of rendering it its full due, of descending into the heat and blaze of blackness with trust and yielding. He doesn't let me use the diaphragm that drives Jenny mad later. He insists that I'm not to do anything about protection. He becomes very strange about it. He's sterile? I do as he says, I let the matter rest, we don't discuss it.

I worry when I get back to New York, not only that perhaps I have conceived anyway, but that it will be all over by the time he returns from the rest of his lecture trip. Guy is in Austin, then Dallas, then back to New Orleans and to Asheville. I am free to check his itinerary on the bulletin board. The routine of the life that claims me puts him farther away from me. Its tone is all wrong. Imagine if Guy had overheard my fights with members of my family. His mannerly world must reject such sounds—screams, yells, accusations, threats, the whole cheap drama of comic anguish.

Shopping at the corner store on my way home from work, burdened by two heavy bags of groceries, while steering around my tired, hungry kids, who are worn to a thin edge of exasperation by their long, social day at a chaotic day-care center, I enter the scratched and scrawled elevator of my apartment building convinced that I'm doomed to hard labor for life. Among the junk mail I had taken from my box is a note from Guy. No love letter, but it encloses a thousand-dollar check. "It occured to me that you might be pressured for money. The tour goes well. I'm eager to be back. Love, Guy."

How gratifying to meet Shana for lunch (my treat) and insist on paying back the two hundred and fifty. (Spread the word that I paid it back, Shana.) Our luncheon scene is complete with tears, apologies, forgiveness (on both sides), and a grand finale of convulsive laughter in the ladies' room at the sight of Shana's underpinnings. Literally, because she's in the last days of pregnancy, and to support the huge bulge, she has trussed herself up in a towel, pinned like a sling around the swollen melon she proudly leads before her.

A part of the family meets Guy for the first time months after we have married. Word has filtered through that my new husband is not the lumpen of Jenny's imaginings or of Shana's bits of information. Merv and Shana have now met him a couple of times. But even with preparation, the others are not prepared for Guy. I read in Barry's eyes the new respect by association I have earned through marriage. Barry's wife, Pauline, is killing herself to impress Guy with her knowledge of Ionesco. Between Papa and Guy it is love at first meeting. The party is a dinner, hosted by Barry to welcome Papa and Jenny to New York, held at an Israeli night-club in the West Forties, and Guy is happy to be steeped in the rich, thick juice of the family accompanied by balalaikas, Jewish waiters, strolling accordionists, fruit soup, blintzes, and "Ruzhin-kas mit Mandlen" sung by an exotic, tiny Yemenite woman in diaphanous pants and wearing jewels on her forehead.

"It's a beautiful song, Guy," Papa says. "I only wish you could fully appreciate it. The raisins and the almonds, the thought of them, brings back all the memories of her home. That's the best I can translate, but in Yiddish it's beautiful."

"A sort of Yiddish madeleine," I explain, and intercept Barry's glance of disquiet. He suspects that I'm making fun of Jews to Guy. I sense that he would like to reprimand me, but is uneasy before Guy. Good. I enjoy that. I enjoy watching Jenny putting on her grandest manner with Guy as they move around the tiny dance floor. Guy is very correct. He dances once with each of the women. He is attentive to Papa's slightest comment. He is at ease with Barry and with Merv and makes no distinction between them. Men like Barry, with Barry's authority and money, are nothing special to him, he grew up among such men. In my new Claire McCardell dress, I dance with Guy with satisfaction in the fact that I have pleased my family, and in myself that at long last it doesn't matter to me or to my fortunes whether I pleased them or not.

While Guy is dancing with Pauline, Papa makes discreet inqui-ries. "There wasn't any trouble with his family, Hannah? I under-stand he comes from a very fine background. His family didn't object that he was marrying a Jew?"

"There's only his mother—and Guy's almost fifty. He doesn't ask his mother's permission to do anything."

Papa is taken aback. "Fifty?" He looks at Guy more specula-tively. "I'd never dream he was so old. I couldn't guess it in a million years." And, after a pause, "I'll tell you it's not such a bad thing to marry a man a little older. They're more settled down."

More settled down—or more rigid? Guy is set in his ways. He has come to me from a long past that he has charted in a code not always clear to me. Why must it be clear? I take him as he is. When he's away, as he frequently is, I can lose my bearings and think he'll never return to me. Why should he? He comes back re-freshed and eager. From what? If I were to list the things I absolutely know about him, what a little list it makes. He's secretive about money and jealous of his magazine. (I'm careful about messing around in those areas.) He is passionate about work. I understand that, but not that he's equally passionate about games and about winning, whether it's tennis, poker, or charades. He will stay up all night to conquer a difficult jigsaw puzzle. He takes play seriously. He swims, sails, skis, rides. He has opened his bosom and gathered in my children as if they were his own, and screams at them about the telephone bill exactly as if they were. I don't understand about him and his mother, perhaps because I can't understand her at all. When we marry, she's a grotesque woman in her eighties, with a face so shortened by uplifts, she looks like a Pekingese. I cannot meet his unspoken but clear request that I also love her. She becomes more and more ridiculous to me and lives on and on into her nineties. She arrives at our summer cottage for drinks one afternoon in a tennis dress that ends at her pitifully flattened buttocks, the muscles of her once fine legs stretched into stringy lengths discolored by raisin clusters of varicosity. Even Guy can bear no more.

"For God's sake, Tessa," he says, "isn't it time to stop dressing like a Radcliffe undergraduate?"

But the deafness she will not confess to has saved her from her son's displeasure. She thinks that she has heard him saying something about Clifford Rossiter, her brother-in-law, and she embarks on one of her favorite tirades against Eisenhower for having appointed "your Uncle Clifford ambassador to that South American republic. He was never suited to the life. Couldn't speak a *word* of proper Spanish. Just because he ran the family sugar business all those years. Never knew what he was doing *there* either. The man was nothing but a nincompoop, you know that, Ross."

Guy responds with irritation. "Caribbean. And I'd hardly characterize it as a republic, then or now."

She has misheard him again and laughs a helpless, misdirected, wheezing laugh that wobbles the badly fitted wig she has bought because she can't resist a bargain. It's from his mother that Guy learned to be tight about money, for all his generosity.

"That's exactly what *I* always say, Ross," she says when she catches her breath.

My children, whom she never addresses by name directly, but sings out to in a falsetto so false they flee her call ("Chil—dren, chi-il—dren") and indirectly refers to as "the offspring of my son's wife," avoid her as much as they can during summers at the cottage when we are all much thrown together. Our houses are on the same cove. The entire property is hers—though she has given Guy the cottage. When her sister Abigail Smith-Hendley comes up from Boston to stay with her, we see more of Guy's mother and more happily, because Aunt Abby makes visiting easier. Close up, Abby's skin hangs on her cheeks like a painter's drop cloth, gray and limp and splattered with odd discolorations, but from across a candlelit room she's a young, theatrical presence, floating a chiffon scarf from her ruined eighty-year-old throat, sending dramatic beams from eyes trained to sweep a house with intensity— even if they were only amateur houses kept going mostly by her own inherited money. She speaks passionately of Sacco and Vanzetti. For her they were executed yesterday.

"Ah, my dear," she touches my arm. "We didn't save those dear men. A great tragedy." Her heavily made-up eyes are dim but still arrestingly beautiful. "The dear, dear, innocent men. How terrible that we couldn't save them."

Danny loves to have Abby read a story aloud. Katie fears it. She knows that she will end in tears brought on by the thrilling, sorrowing voice that great Aunt Abby brings to any storytelling.

Guy loves his mother and certainly loves his Aunt Abby and even loves Thomas Jamieson, his oldest friend. Jamie is an old school friend and drinking companion. He's an editor at a Boston publishing house. He comes up to the cottage, he comes down to New York on visits. He spends his time with us drinking. His round, bland face, well tanned in all seasons, is soon vacated of all sense, and his sky-blue, vapid eyes become glazed and bloodshot. The staircase in our New York duplex curves in a tricky fashion, and when he's too sloshed to make it up the stairs, we put him to bed on the couch in Guy's downstairs study, where he sleeps with his feet awkwardly extended over the edge and wakes with his face deeply marred by the tufting in the leather.

"Guy used to be a lot more fun before he stopped drinking," he says wistfully. "I think perhaps Jews don't understand about drinking," he admonishes my stiffness toward him.

Is that an anti-Semitic remark? Whether or not, it's accurate in my case. Alcoholics are figures out of my childhood nightmares and childhood truths, the derelicts under the el, the dregs of goyish vomitous bloody wrecks being poked to the safety of the side-

walk or propped against a pillar of the elevated track by a disgusted Irish cop while a gang of kids stand nearby and jeer. Nothing to do with Guy Rossiter.

Early in our marriage Guy gets drunk—once—with Jamie, of
course. They have been out with a third old school friend. I go to
bed before they return to the apartment. I'm awakened by the
repeated ringing of the doorbell to an instant, automatic response
of paranoid fear. The knock on the door—the seizure in the night
—here it is. Before I reach it, the door is opening to a general
accompaniment of poundings, bellowings, laughing, coughing,
hawking, shushing noises, cello grunts, and Guy and Jamie are half
carried, half urged into the room by our short, square superintendent, Mr. Fernández, dressed in the dark suit, white shirt, and
dark tie he always wears (though it's three twenty in the morning)
and assisted by Al, the new night doorman, dressed neatly in his
uniform.

"Sorry to disturb you, Mrs. Rossiter," Mr. Fernández says. "Can
you manage them?" Fernández has a very faint accent, more an
intonation than anything else. He's not a Puerto Rican, though
there are tenants who insist he is. He's Cuban and as eager to join
in knocking a PR as any East Side, Republican-voting tenant.

Guy embraces Mr. Fernández with slobbering love. "Not a bit,
Fernana . . . Not disturb . . . Fernan . . ."

He will not allow Mr. Fernández to release him. He gazes at him
with a loose, loving, imbecilic smile, swaying above Mr. Fernández's short frame dangerously, holding him with both arms. Al
releases giggling, hawking Jamie, who slides to the floor, grabbing
at the wing chair as he goes down. It obligingly supports him,
though in a helplessly twisted position. Jamie works to maintain
the look of controlled astonishment which is his present concept
of sobriety, but breaks out again in giggles followed by a series of
great belches.

Mr. Fernández struggles loose from Guy. Free-standing, smiling
an imbecile smile, Guy throws out his arms in a wide, disjointed
gesture and attempts to walk toward me. He staggers and stumbles, and in Mr. Fernández's fumble to aid him, Guy is pushed to
his knees. Guy steadies himself with his hands. The intricate pattern of the rug engages him very closely, and he rests on his hands
and knees, his head hanging like a dog's, and like a dog he makes
wet breathing noises.

"It's nothing," I say to myself, but I want to run.

Now Guy carefully unbends his full length to the floor. His head
hits the tea table a shuddering little blow. He lifts his head, bewildered, and then very slowly lowers it again, face down to the floor.
The jacket of his suit twists around his middle. He lies perfectly
still and stiff. He is as terrifying to me as if he were a corpse.

"Please," I say to Mr. Fernández, "I can't manage."

They lift Jamie to the couch, where he immediately sleeps with
his face buried in the down cushion. I'm grateful not to have to
look at him. They can't lift Guy.

"Just turn him over," I direct them, and put a pillow under
Guy's head and cover him with a crocheted afghan.

Alone in the room with the two drunks, I discover that I'm
crying. I force myself to stop. On his back, Guy looks like himself,
but his breathing is miserably labored. I open the knot of his tie
and remove it. It's very hard for me to touch him. I unbutton his
shirt and push the afghan down to undo his belt and the catch on
his pants. He seems to breathe more easily. What else does one do
for drunks? I remove his shoes, and cover him again. Silly, childish
tears run down my face. I put my head on Guy's broad chest,
which rises and falls, rises and falls, an ocean upon which I float
as alien matter.

I never see Guy drunk again. One afternoon, walking through
a path we have had opened in the woods as a shortcut from our
cottage to his mother's, Guy takes a turn into another section of
the woods.

"I want to show you something," he says.

We follow an overgrown footpath. I've never explored this area
of tangled woods. I have a city person's fears of getting lost, of
snakes, poisonous bugs, quicksand.

"Quicksand!" Guy laughs at me, but he waits for me to reach
him and takes my hand to lead me through the mysteries of these
woods. Wherever the sun reaches in, bittersweet has taken over
to choke and smother what was once here.

"An apple orchard," Guy says. "It was all cleared land once.
There were blueberry fields beyond the orchard and beyond that
—pasture."

"Cows?"

"And sheep."

"Do you remember it?"

"Sure. I've been coming here since I was born. Here," he says
and halts. "It should be here."

We don't seem to be anywhere. A thick screen of brush surrounds us.

"Barge right through this stuff," Guy says.

Beyond the brush is an old stone wall and beyond that climb we are in an overgrown, open spot—a small, neglected, family cemetery.

"Here we are," Guy says.

I walk among the headstones and the dry, sweet-smelling grass. The headstones are knocked about, some covered with moss and yellow lichen, broken and worn smooth, but some can still be read. Carter seems to be the name of the family. The burial dates begin in the early 1800s, end in the 1860s. Some of the smaller stones obviously marked children's graves and these carry a roughly carved little lamb. The spot contains itself and its history under a shy, natural cover, like a tiny striped animal hiding among the leaves, touching in its molested survival.

"Is it your family from way back?"

"Oh no. The Rossiters bought after the Civil War from a Dedman. The Carters were a farming family, probably, that moved on, maybe even moved their house to another spot. There are many Carters around. I found this place one summer when I was about eleven. Then I always came here."

"It's a wonderful place, a wonderful hiding place."

Guy nods. He isn't looking at me, but I'm looking at him. Lucky man, to go so far back on a particular piece of ground.

"Later, I stashed my bottles here. That's when I knew I was an alcoholic. I wanted to show it to you."

He turns to start the walk back. I don't understand what he means to be explaining to me, and it's the only time he tries.

WHAT'S NEW
WITH THE FAMILY?

Barry on the telephone to Anne. His voice is dry, cold. It is a couple of months after Papa died. "My lawyer tells me yours is the only signature he's still waiting for."

Anne, busy with page proofs at her office, preoccupied, genuinely puzzled. "What's that? I don't understand."

Heavy silence at Barry's end. Short bark of a laugh. "Slipped your mind, has it? The release. Everybody else has signed but you."

"Oh," Anne says, recalling the paper releasing Papa's estate to his son, Baruch Goddard. Papa's sons and daughters foregoing any claims to his estate, according to the terms of Papa's will. A formality, merely, she had been assured. Then, why this anxiety on Barry's part? In the middle of his busy day, and in the middle of hers? "That paper I signed. Right. What's the trouble?"

"That's *my* question," Barry says. "What's the trouble? What's on your mind? Why are you holding it up?"

"I had no idea," Anne says, waving the copy editor in, motioning that she'll be through with the conversation in a minute. "I sent it off at least two weeks ago. My secretary mailed it. I'll check with her, but I'm sure she sent it, she's very efficient."

"I see," Barry says. His voice is being deflated of its tension. "There was some family talk. A mysterious letter from Papa. A mysterious legacy from Papa. I thought you might need some reminder that Papa didn't own anything except what I gave him."

230

Barry's anger, though it has no place to go, is too pent up not to spend itself. She can visualize the dull, lidded glance that accompanies his hard, deliberate speech. He thinks she was holding her brother up for Papa's promised thousand dollars?

"I thought you might have decided you had some reason not to sign that release," Barry says. "I thought there might be some problem in your mind."

"About what?" Anne says. "The only problem seems to be that the paper was lost somehow. If it's important send me a duplicate, and I'll sign again. I thought this was a formality?"

"As long as there isn't any problem," Barry says.

"Check with your lawyer again, and I'll check my desk."

"No problem," Barry says, more cordial now. "Probably misfiled somewhere. If my lawyer doesn't get in touch with you, you can assume everything's been straightened out."

"Okay," Anne says.

"Thanks, Anne," Barry says, easy now. "Everything fine with you and Guy and the children?"

"Fine, fine," Anne says. "Busy, busy."

"Good way to stay young," Barry says. "Give my best."

XVIII

Anne is writing an article. She turns her chair from the oak desk, where she's been scribbling on a long yellow pad, to her typewriter on its wheeled table. She types, copying from the longhand.

> Han Suyin's current work presents a problem to the reviewer whose mentality is trained in the direction of skepticism, aloofness, objectivity—a cold harbor for this vessel with its cargo of open-hearted, innocent, passionately partisan views.

Anne stops. She doesn't like the image—harbor, vessel, cargo—but she will leave it for now. The first paragraph is always the hardest. She can cut or change later.

> In *The Morning Deluge: Mao Tse-tung & the Chinese Revolution, 1893–1954*

Anne stops. She checks for the correct data. There is relief and security in handling the actual book—a physical object, matter made solid and authoritative between hard covers. What Anne writes is drawn from the air, but the book itself is real. She continues:

> 1893–1954 (Little, Brown, 571 pages, illus. $12.95

She pauses, checks again, closes the parenthesis,

) Dr. Han

She stops. She feels a rush of love for Han Suyin, for the woman she has never met but knows from her autobiographical writings. She feels close to her. She understands how Han Suyin worked and studied and fought to become the world-famous author. She admires her. She has read all her work except the early romantic novels, which Anne has prejudged as "junk." How does Anne know that? It gnaws at her that she is approaching this task incompletely equipped. And what about her ignorance of China? More to the point. What the hell does she know about China? She's taken courses. She's read books.

She begins to slide down a slope she endlessly climbs up. *Not good enough* is the conviction waiting to receive her at the bottom of the pit.

The review Anne is working on has been commissioned by a prestigious publication. Any writer would be pleased to appear in it, and Anne is particularly pleased because she's eager to be published outside the pages of *Tribune,* owned and operated by her husband, where she functions as editor of the "back of the book." But there's a catch in the assignment. It was some editor's bright idea to throw a bunch of women into the same arena. Han Suyin and Anne Goddard, who is a Simone de Beauvoir enthusiast and will undoubtedly measure Han Suyin's book against de Beauvoir's *The Long March.* Fight it out, girls. Another bright editor had the idea of working up an article about women writers known as "the wives of." "Among the country's fifty top intellectuals," the article said, "husband-and-wife combinations are prominent, though some, alas, are now ex-wives." Anne Goddard appears in a list among names: Diana Trilling, Elizabeth Hardwick, Midge Decter, Eleanor Clark, Gertrude Himmelfarb, Katherine White. Make a game of it, readers. A column of "wives" on one side of the page and husbands on the other, in scrambled order. Link the wife to her husband. Watch out for tricks, now. Mary McCarthy has two listings (Edmund Wilson *and* Philip Rahv). Even international waters are fished—Simone and Sartre, Pamela Hansford Johnson and Lord Snow, Q.D. and F.R. Leavis. Stupid, gossipy shlock, full of misinformation, yet it gnaws at her. Admit that without her marriage to Guy she would be no place, not even the slippery place she rides on Guy's coattails, scrabbling for a grip, struggling not to coast down the slope that always yawns for her below.

She brakes. None of that. Get on with this review.

She fingers the white paper markers she has placed in the book. A good place for the first quote?

> . . . but there is a need, a desire in man to harness his own strength and capabilities in a struggle worthwhile and enduring. All societies thrive only in the measure in which they have succeeded in inspiring individuals with worthwhile, stimulating aims; exacting sacrifice and abnegation; these aims exalt and transcend the self. . . .

Is Han Suyin talking about real societies? Ones that have actually existed, do exist? How can she write in such a vein and not instantly undercut the elegiac tone with skepticism? There is no note in the margin of the book, just the marked passage. What had Anne had in mind when she marked it? How to use it in the review? Anne sighs. She is inundated by laziness, washing over her like an attack of nausea. She doesn't want to write this piece. She doesn't want to critically examine Han Suyin's words. Hats off to you, Han Suyin, is all she wants to say. Read this book, reader, is all she wants to say, believe it or not as you choose, but read it because reading it can only do you good even if you read it as pure romance—a romance of good or evil, depending on your political views.

Anne knows that that won't do. A review must be clever to be noticed, and she wants her review to be noticed—whether or not the book is. That's what reviewing is all about. A different energy must take over, the energy that drives her own ambition. She leans to the desk and reads the notes she had scribbled on her pad:

China and the Soviet Union. Revolution by telegram. Stalin's inconsistency. The Comintern. Explain Borodin. Withdrawal of Soviet advisors. Compare to Czech situation & entrance of Soviet tanks. 100 Flowers Campaign. Naïveté, social faith, social submersion. Suffering. Real suffering of real people—that is history, not its rewriting by victors. Franco and Spain.

She contemplates her notes with leaden discontent. She doesn't really know anything about all that stuff. She reminds herself that she was much complimented on her review of Solzhenitsyn's *August 1914*. She didn't know anything about that subject, either, but what she had read of it. Only the direct evidence of one's senses is to be trusted? All the rest is fakery? She has studied fakery in her time. If she's an ignoramus and successful, it must be because ignorance is enshrined. How diligently she had studied works of literary criticism; yet did Isabel Archer need anyone's help to leap off the page alive? Vronski's soft, brown-dog eyes lure Anna to her terrible fate. Carrie enters Chicago, and looks for a job. Why don't we let books alone? she thinks.

She concentrates on her unfinished sentence. She types,

> has written what may be easily read as a romance—of good or evil, depending on the political views of the reader. And that is just the trouble with romance that masquerades as history

Her reluctance to criticize the woman she admires drags her to a stop. Her reluctance to examine a society she knows nothing about. She would rather say, *Good luck, Soviet China, good luck, millions of Chinese.*

She knows that won't do. She pushes on. She is working at the apartment, in a room that has been turned into a study for her now that Katie and Danny are no longer much at home. Anne is rich in studies—another at the summer cottage, and her own office at the magazine—she, who never had a corner for herself until she married Guy. With her luxurious work space she should be turning out books by the dozens.

"Will I see a book from you before I close my eyes for good?" Mama asked and died. But suppose Mama had lived long enough to see a book by Anne Goddard, and had actually held it in her hand, shaking her head in wonder and pride as Papa had, unable naturally to read it in English; but suppose she could have read English, suppose Mama could have read every word of Anne Goddard's books, would any one of them measure up to Mama's standard of a *book*? A book was a story that made Mama laugh and cry and speculate about between installments in the *Jewish Daily Forward*. A *roman*. A story. That was *a book*. Everybody in the family kidded Mama about her adored storyteller in the *Forward*.

Laughing indulgently, Anne listened to Mama's retelling of his tales. That laugh is definitely on me, Anne reminds herself. Isaac Bashevis Singer—twenty years later—hailed, honored, explicated by the academy and translated into English for the dummies who couldn't read him in Yiddish.

Anne Goddard's books piddle around in the ponds of other books. Collections of comments on a comment. The titles tell all. *Henry James: Modernism and Money. The City and the Novel: Dickens, Dreiser and Bellow. Shadows and Images: Women in American Fiction.* Not a sob in the lot. A grimace of wit at a rival critic's expense—a sort of Ed Hurley bitten-down humor—the quick feint and deft withdrawal. Live to stab another day. Guy has written every kind of book—essays, reportage, memoirs, criticism, short stories, novels, poems. Guy Rossiter, distinguished man of letters, her husband, her love and joy. A piece of luck that admiration, love, and passion have come together for her in one man. What, no anguish—competition, rage, oppression, frustration, jealousy, distortion? Of course, of course. She doesn't live on the last page of a romance, but in the real world. In the real world, take it all in all, Guy Rossiter chose her above all others to endow with all his gifts, good and bad, and generously accepts from her her marred but precious treasures. It happens, she assures her friend Edith, it can happen that love and admiration and passion come together—and stay. Nevertheless her friend Edith listens with great skepticism. Not to her has it happened. Edith believes in what she has experienced. Good enough.

Get on with your review, Anne commands herself. Go on coolly eyeing Han Suyin's passionate admiration for the Chinese revolution.

"Would you believe that Anne had the most terrific imagination when she was a kid?" Her brother Barry to Guy at a family gathering some years ago. "A terrific imagination!" Obliquely, Barry comments to Anne, at the same time, on the kinds of books she writes: "Very impressive. Hard reading, though. A little out of my line of reading. You ever read a book called *The Forty Days of Musa Dagh*? That's quite a book. That's my idea of *a book*." Not so obliquely?

A terrific imagination. The wrong tool, perhaps, for viewing the times? Or any time in recorded history? Hard enough to comprehend what is, what happens every day. Try, try to imagine the real sufferings of the real Chinese people, the real sufferings of the real Vietnamese people, the real sufferings of the real Jewish people who walked into the showers of gas under their own power. The real suffering of the real Armenian people worked up into the best-selling *Forty Days of Musa Dagh.*

Her brother Barry always said, "None of this will matter in a hundred years," meaning, perhaps, that man's purposes are small compared with God's, or history's. Or, more likely, more narrowly, that Baruch Goddard would be dead and gone in a hundred years so to hell with the future. She hated to hear him say it. It matters. It will matter.

Frederick Law Olmsted had trouble sleeping, kept awake by worries about the state of things a hundred years after he'd be dead and gone. Anne is working on a book about Olmsted. A couple of chapters have already been written. The book has already been titled—one of her dry, thoughtful titles. *Frederick Law Olmsted: The Landscape of the Democratic Ideal.* Awful title. The writing goes very slowly. She's dissatisfied with the effort so far. A marvelous man. He deserves better than Anne Goddard can bring to this job. A terrific imagination is what the Olmsted story needs. Run as a serial in the pages of the *Forward.* Olmsted, the hero of a *roman*, a story that Mama could read with pleasure. Bring them together into a single landscape—Mama, the immigrant who came from a Polish *shtetl*, and Frederick Law Olmsted of the pioneer family that settled Hartford, Connecticut, who grew up to design the parks of New York City, including Fort Greene Park where Mama *shlepped* picnics for her seven children and healed her eyes on the sight of a little greenery.

What if Olmsted had been her grandfather? Anne daydreams— again the child who lied about her royal parentage. That would make either Mama his daughter or Papa his son. Too comical a concept, Mama or Papa as proper New Englanders. But of course they would have been entirely different. The landscape of our life shapes our nature. Olmsted's law.

She sees Mama in the tiny kitchen of one of their many flats. It's the one that turned out to be on a street used as an open-air market. What had been misery for Anne at the time is now suffused with happiness in her remembrance. She is vivid with joy, running through the jammed, milling scene on her way to buy fresh horseradish, a pint of sauerkraut, and two half-sour pickles

for Friday-night supper. Mama sent her for them an hour ago but
she has wasted time wandering around the stalls, fascinated by the
varieties of things for sale. The market is closing down, because
the Sabbath is arriving. The pushcart merchandise is being packed
up and the vehicles being lugged off by horse or man, in a gypsy
operation. It is a mild winter evening, just before sunset. The air
of the appetizing store into which Anne runs is sharp with the
pungent smell of the salt herrings and dill pickles floating in open
barrels. Irving, the storekeeper, is just about to fix their wooden
lids. "You had to wait for the last minute?" he scolds her, but tosses
into the package a wedge of halvah, "for your Mama, tell her
Irving wants she should have a taste. It's a special quality." Breathing hard, with a stitch in her side, Anne bursts into a Sabbath
kitchen, the floor scrubbed, everything polished and shining, the
table covered by a carefully laundered white tablecloth on which
sits the freshly baked golden Sabbath bread, the challah, shaped
by Mama with a long elegant braid across its rounded stomach,
and covered with its Sabbath cloth, embroidered in cross-stitch;
and nearby the plain white candles, in the brass candlesticks
which Mama brought from England, stand ready to be lit as soon
as the sun goes down.

   And it is only now, sitting at her desk in her study, that Anne
understands that the gleaming eyes which Mama turned to Anne
then, and the holiday air of joy and peace emanating from Mama
(after the lighting of the candles and the ritual prayer and greeting, "Good Sabbath, my child," given not in English but in Yiddish,
of course, "Gut Shabbas, mein kind") were signals of victory over
the hard, ugly smotheration of daily life, a triumph of scrubbing
and shining, of cooking and baking, of hard labor against dirt and
chaos, and that the orderly beauty of Mama's Sabbath landscape
served up to her family as their due and as her gift was a weekly
act of heroism without reward and without record, but significant
and valuable, and that it had taught Anne something penetrating
and lasting.

   How extraordinary—the surprise harvest of strength and sweet-
ness she has discovered in this memory of Mama, after all the years
Anne had spent fiercely rejecting her example.

WHAT'S NEW
WITH THE FAMILY?

Have you been out to Barry's Connecticut place?"

Anne's oldest sister, Connie, in her too-loud voice, though the Fifth Avenue bus is so noisy she must yell if Anne is to hear her.

"It's fabulous. Fabulous. It makes the Westchester place look like nothing in comparison," Connie says. "Barry doesn't drive anymore. Himself, I mean. He goes only by chauffeured car. He has a full-time chauffeur. Or they come in by yacht."

"Really? That seems a trifle showy," Anne says. "And slow, I imagine."

Connie laughs. She's enjoying a good gossip with Anne. She's visiting New York by herself, staying with Anne.

"What do they care? They have all day. When they want to get into New York fast they use a helicopter. It lands on the Pan-Am Building and they're right where they want to be in the heart of the city. Of course they always keep the town apartment. Barry said I was welcome to stay there, but who wants to be in New York alone?"

An elderly couple sitting on the seat directly in front of Anne and Connie are listening in.

"Especially when I can stay in a Fifth Avenue duplex?"

"That whole Connecticut house is covered with fresh flowers every day," Connie says. "That alone costs a fortune. A big family could live on what Barry spends on gardeners and cut flowers alone. It's fantastic. It's the most gorgeous place you ever saw in your life.

"For Melissa's wedding," Connie says, "Pauline had everything in the downstairs section of the house moved out, moved right out of the house in big moving vans, honest. Honest, I never heard of anything like it. You can call it ridiculous or what you like, but there it is. Then a complete redecoration of the whole place—a chapel in one of the rooms for a ceremony, another room done up into a big dance floor, another with a string group playing in the corner, you know, just for listening and talking quietly and drinking, like for the older folks. I don't know what else to tell you, I can't begin to tell you what else they did to the inside of the house. And that was just the inside. Outside, the entire lawn covered by a huge tent. More bands. More food. The entire lawn covered by a carpet to protect it. It was fantastic. I wouldn't even hazard a guess what that affair set Barry back. I'm really sorry you and Guy missed it. You would have gotten a bang out of it, and who knows, maybe an article or two. It was something, I'm telling you. It made Jonathan's bar mitzvah at the old Westchester estate look like nothing in comparison.

"I don't know why you don't keep in touch with Barry, Anna," Connie says.

"No reason," Anne says. "He doesn't keep in touch with me either. For no reason, I'm sure."

The couple ahead turn their heads slightly to hear better when Anne speaks.

"Everybody was asking for you at the wedding, Anna."

"It would have been nice to see everybody, but Guy had to be in Geneva, and I wanted to go."

"Of course. Who doesn't want to go to Geneva?"

"Was Jenny there with her husband?"

"Certainly. He's an absolute doll. That is one lucky girl to have gotten such a doll. Everything she does is fine with him. Anything she says goes."

"How are Merv and Shana?" Anne says. "I hardly see them anymore."

"Fabulous. They've enlarged their house. And they bought the farm. You know about the farm? Now they have horses, too."

"What do they do with them—farm?"

Connie laughs heartily. "They ride, what do you think they do with them?"

The bus pulls up to the curb sharply. Anne braces herself and frowns against the pull.

"I know what that look was for," Connie says. "I know just what you're thinking. That with all her money she could be a little more generous. Look at this pin," she points to a cameo pinned to her coat. "Brought it back to me from the last trip she took. Limoges. From the Limoges five and ten. That's her style in gifts."

"Who?" Anne says.

"Shana."

"I thought you meant Pauline. What does Pauline look like these days?"

"Wigs," Connie says. "Nothing but wigs.

"I never thought Pauline was good-looking," Connie says. "Did you? Good looks have to be natural. If you don't look good in bed first thing in the morning you're not good-looking."

"Brenda still copying Pauline's style in everything?"

"To copy Pauline these days you need to have Pauline's money. I don't know what's the matter with Brenda. It's a tragedy. She got fat, she looks like a slob, the only thing she's interested in is her daughter. She treats Josh like I-don't-know-what, a piece of furniture or something. Her daughter's a doll. She looks just like Josh. She's a beauty. She's truly exquisite."

"Somebody told me Josh had taken up painting?"

"Please don't ask me about Josh's artistic gift. What he's doing is plain crazy. I can't even explain to you what it is, but you can get the idea when I tell you his studio is full of styrofoam."

Anne laughs.

"Did you see the article in the financial section of the *Times* about Barry?"

"Yes," Anne says.

"And the story about how he gave two million to Israel right away as soon as the trouble started?"

"I didn't realize that it was two million."

"Every penny of it."

"It's hard to think of Barry that rich."

"Are you kidding? That's not even the half of it. You know what he's giving to universities and hospitals and Jewish charities? He's rich, my little brother, he's rich. Did you read that the antitrust division is forcing him to divest?"

"Really?" Anne rings the bell to stop the bus at 91st Street.

The couple ahead studies them curiously when they get up.

"A bunch of lies, from beginning to end, if you ask me," Anne hears the elderly woman say to her husband as Anne passes them.

XVIX

hat if I were to do the story of Frederick Law Olmsted as a film? Fantasize. Return to my childhood and tell a made-up story, the legend of Frederick Law Olmsted. Ham up the story of Fred's life. Take him away from the scholars and give him to the people in an action-filled, heartthrobbing drama full of laughter and tears and a cast of thousands. And every detail true to his life. Like this:

February 1848. Europe in democratic revolutionary turmoil. (Background music, a Chopin Polonaise. Shots of street fighting, banners, kings toppling.) Retreat to the quiet of Staten Island. Night shot of the great harbor seen from a farmhouse window. Olmsted at the window. Six lights spaced about the harbor "presenting a cheerful, neighborhood effect . . . they have a very sociable look." Coming of light, sunrise over the water through a February mist. (What about the Statue of Liberty? In 1848? The audience *wants* it there. Okay. Float the lady in, subliminally or something. Your huddled masses effect. Promise of the future. I don't know. Try it, see if it works.) Back to 1848. Shot of the Staten Island Ferry. Researched, authentic. Arrival at the shore. Cut back to the farmhouse. Closeup of Olmsted in the light. (Young, open face, visionary eyes but not fanatic, dreamy, generous moustache, longish hair, not too long, not too wild. Very contemporary look. Robert Redford but not so pretty. Shorter.) Olmsted bursts from the room in a woolen cape coat made of a heavy pin-striped cloth, pulling a little peaked cap down on his hair, curling at the edges.

Straggly farm road, but signs of care, of repair. The road is being rerouted to curve gracefully up to the house entrance. Shots of new decorative shrubs, trees, protected new pear trees. Landscape is bleakly beautiful. Olmsted at the ferry slip, hearing some extraordinary news. He turns and runs. Shot of the road under his feet, patches of mist, fields, tall grasses, birds startled into flight, the camera falls and rises with the young man's loping run. Breathless, lopsided rushing excitement. Shot of his exalted face, of his cape billowing and settling, his feet on the dirt road, now the Russian effect of sun through overarching, great elms, the mist between the branches, the sun slant-striking the young man's flecked eyes. Over a stone wall, shot of a flock of sheep grazing on the far side, on the near side a wide, well-kept lawn fronting a handsome, white clapboard house. On the porch a white-haired gentleman and a tiny, enchanting young woman. (What's the name of the lovely girl who played the wife in *Walking Tall*? Something Hartman. She'd be perfect.)

Old gentleman: "Why, it's young Fred Olmsted. What brings him running here so early in the day?"

Close-up of the young woman eagerly watching the young man advance.

Close-up of the young man running. Radiant face. Calls out breathlessly before he has reached the couple on the porch. "Wonderful news! Wonderful news!"

The young people's eyes connect with ardent interest. Shift to the older man.

Olmsted: "I rushed at once to Holly Hill, sir, to share it with you. Louis Philippe has abdicated! All Europe shall become a democracy now. The people have won! Ah, how I revel in a *righteous* war!"

Cut.

Perhaps a TV series? The Olmsted story is complicated. Lots of detail, lots of *tsuris*, practically a soap. The young girl will become his wife, but only after plenty of *tsuris*, for example. And look at the history of Europe, if you can bear to.

A bit of background is needed here. Frederick Law Olmsted was born in Hartford, Connecticut, in April 1822, into a solid, secure Anglo-Saxon heritage. (No Jewish merchant in Olmsted's background.) His ancestors arrived in Massachusetts in 1632. One pioneered into the wilderness of the Connecticut Valley, killing his share of Indians, and founded a huge family which came to own a sizeable chunk of what became the thriving city of Hartford. Fred's father is a dry-goods merchant. Fred's mother dies when he is young. Fred is sickly, indulged, not given much formal schooling. Bits of learning are meted out to him by a succession of ministers. There's a halfhearted, doomed attempt to turn him into a dry-goods merchant, and then he's apprenticed to a farmer. (His true education is seeping in from underground sources; he is accumulating mysterious secret stores to be spent lavishly later.) The history of the country and the history of his family are naturally intertwined. He sits at his grandfather's knee and listens to his account of trekking through the Maine forests with Benedict Arnold's troops to capture Quebec. A disaster, as any American history book can tell you.

He follows in a sound family tradition when he signs on as a seaman at age eighteen to voyage to China. If the thought was pure romance, the actuality almost kills him. He's horribly seasick, squashed like a beast into an overcrowded forecastle, suffering the abuses and fatal illnesses common to sailors of the 1840s. He is never flogged himself but he witnesses the vicious punishments that are the rule. He is kept on watch so long in his weakened state that his body no longer deconfuses waking from sleep and he experiences a Castaneda-like loss, or gain, of consciousness that he writes out in detail for William James (naturally) almost fifty years later. The China voyage (perfect movie material, including a mini-mutiny) that was to teach him a lot about the great world, and return him to his agreeable father physically hardened and matured, returns him so frail, yellowed, and permanently weakened that his father has difficulty recognizing his son.

Home again, he casts about for a way to be

useful in the world, to make others happy, to help to advance the condition of Society, and hasten the preparation for the Millennium, as well as other things too numerous to mention . . . to foster in the popular mind generosity, charity, taste . . . independence of thought, of voting and of acting. The education of the ignoble vulgus ought to be much improved and extended.

He is, plainly, a man of his class. ("The ignoble vulgus" is a vile phrase.) Naturally he considered Anglo-Saxons the cream of humanity. Naturally he was anti-Semitic and racist in the casual manner of his class, just as he was well-mannered and clean, and became converted to the Congregational Church, caught up in a somewhat faddish religious fervor and lured on by the charming piety of a Miss Lizzie Baldwin, but he never made it all the way to steady churchgoing. (He met Miss Baldwin at the home of Thomas C. Perkins, whose wife was the sister of Harriet Beecher Stowe and Henry Ward Beecher.)

His agreeable father sets him up on the Staten Island farm. Fred has chosen model farming as his way to improve the world. He and his brother John have a deeply loving relationship. John too is sickly, and his studies are interrupted. John stays with Fred at the farm and meets the enchanting young woman of Holly Hill who stood on the porch and received Fred in his passionate radical enthusiasm. Fred believes in work, like any good Protestant. Trouble is, Fred's flighty. He's ambitious. He wants to leave a mark on the world, but he doesn't know where to begin. After a walking trip through England with his brother John and a friend, he writes a book, *Walks and Talks of an American Farmer in England*, and his enthusiasm for model farming wanes in favor of a literary career. (It's a lovely book and clearly shows the interests he will develop later.) How people live is what matters to him now. The power of surroundings to calm and to civilize, or to warp and make morbid, is what interests him now. "Degradation and supine misery" must be attacked head-on by "improvement, restoration, regeneration."

When *The New York Times* asks him to travel through the South and report on conditions in the slave states, he jumps at the chance. Farming is quite forgotten. He is a highly charged young man, permanently ill, permanently insomniac, permanently driven, perhaps because he is so ambivalent. He thinks of himself as fairminded, and he turns up on all sides of an argument. When he was twenty-four, he wrote to his father, "The tyranny of priests and churches is as great a curse to the country and the world as negro slavery." Perhaps he meant only Popish priests and churches. Perhaps it was only Miss Lizzie Baldwin who got to him, not God. In his middle years he has no use for any religious observance and spends his Sundays sinfully—reading, smoking, playing with his children.

He's ambivalent about slavery. He scolds Northern abolitionists:

"Who are we to condemn our brothers? No slave freezes to death for want of habitation and fuel, as have men in Boston. Remember that, Mrs. Stowe. Remember that, indignant sympathizers."

A man ahead of his time? Or at the head of his time? Not only slavery must be abolished but wage slavery as well? Not exactly. He also says this:

I do not consider slaveholding—the simple exercise of the authority of a master over the Negroes who have so wickedly been enslaved—in itself necessarily wrong, any more than all forcible constraint of a child or lunatic is wrong. . . .

His Anglo-Saxon prejudices are strong: He reports about Virginia getting mucked up by a "considerable population of foreign origin, generally of the least valuable class, very dirty German Jews . . ." whose shops "(with their characteristic smells, quite as bad as in Cologne) are thickly set in the narrowest and meanest streets . . . otherwise inhabited . . . by Negroes."

That comment starts up all sorts of reverberations in me, of which Olmsted's anti-Semitism is the least important. Everybody in Fred's crowd was a touch anti-Semitic, so we won't make a big thing of that. What worries me are those Jews sitting around in Cologne. Will they never learn? They've already been expelled once in the fifteenth century. Why don't they stay gone from Cologne instead of settling in again to be wiped out in the twentieth. And finally, and this is the last of it, how about those few smart Jews who did leave Cologne for Virginia—if Olmsted's sense of smell is to be trusted—how come they got to be so damn uppity by the time my parents arrived, putting on the airs of an aristocracy of American Jews, looking down on their poor brothers and sisters crowding into New York City tenements, if they were Olmsted's dirty German Jews—no better, in his eyes, than the rest of us?

Okay. Let's not become too exercised about this.

Olmsted works away at some other sticky problems:

It is difficult to handle simply as property, a creature possessing human passions and human feeling, however debased and torpid the condition of that creature may be, while on the other hand, the absolute necessity of dealing with property as a thing, greatly embarrassed a man in any attempt to treat it as a person. . . .

Fair-minded, levelheaded, racist, elitist, he puts the matter coolly. Slavery in the flesh, however, robs him of his cool. For his *New York Times* reports, he describes a tour of a large plantation in the company of a white overseer. Let him speak for himself. Think of the scene as part of the movie.

. . . We had twice crossed a deep gully, at the bottom of which was a thick covert of brushwood. We were crossing it a third time . . . when the overseer suddenly stopped his horse exclaiming, "What's that? Hallo! who are you, there?"

It was a girl lying at full length on the ground at the bottom of the gully, evidently intending to hide herself from us in the bushes.

"Who are you, there?"

"Sam's Sal, sir."

"What are you skulking there for?"

The girl half rose, but gave no answer.

"Have you been here all day?"

"No, sir."

"How did you get here?"

The girl made no reply.

"Where have you been all day?"

The answer was unintelligible.

After some further questioning, she said her father accidentally locked her in, when he went out in the morning.

"How did you manage to get out?"

"Pushed a plank off, sir, and crawled out."

The overseer was silent for a moment, looking at the girl, and then said, "That won't do; come out here." The girl arose at once, and walked towards him. She was about eighteen years of age. A bunch of keys hung at her waist, which the overseer espied, and he said, "Your father locked you in; but you have got the keys." After a little hesitation, she replied that these were the keys of some other locks; her father had the door-key.

Whether her story was true or false, could have been ascertained in two minutes by riding on to the gang with which her father was at work, but the overseer had made up his mind.

"That won't do," said he, "get down."

The girl knelt on the ground; he got off his horse, and holding him with his left hand struck her thirty or forty blows across the shoulders with his tough, flexible, "raw-hide" whip (a terrible instrument for the purpose). They were well laid on, at arm's length, but with no appearance of angry excitement on the part of the overseer. At every stroke the girl winced and exclaimed, "Yes, sir!" or "Ah, sir!" or "Please, sir!" not groaning or screaming. At length he stopped and said, "Now tell me the truth." The girl repeated the same story. "You have not got enough yet," said he; "pull up your clothes—lie down." The girl without any hesitation, without a word or look of remonstrance or entreaty, drew closely all her garments under her shoulders, and lay down upon the ground with her face toward the overseer, who continued to flog her with the raw-hide, across her naked loins and thighs, with as much strength as before. She now shrunk away from him, not rising, but writhing, grovelling, and screaming, "Oh, don't, sir! oh, please stop, master! please, sir! please, sir! oh, that's enough, master! oh, Lord! oh, master, master! oh, God, master, do stop! oh, God, master! oh, God, master!"

A young gentleman of fifteen was with us; he had ridden in front, and now, turning on his horse, looked back with an expression only of impatience at the delay. It was the first time I had ever seen a woman flogged. . . . I glanced again at the perfectly passionless but rather grim businesslike face of the overseer, and again at the young gentleman, who had turned away; if not indifferent he had evidently not the faintest sympathy with my emotion. Only my horse chafed. I gave him rein and spur and we plunged into the bushes and scrambled fiercely up the steep acclivity. The screaming yells and the whip strokes had ceased when I reached the top of the bank. Choking, sobbing, spasmodic groans only were heard. I rode on to where the road, coming diagonally up the ravine, ran out upon the cotton-field. My young companion met me there and immediately afterward the overseer. He laughed as he joined us, and said:

"She meant to cheat me out of a day's work, and she has done it, too." . . .

"Was it necessary to punish her so severely?"

"Oh yes, sir" (laughing again). "If I hadn't, she would have done the same thing again to-morrow, and half the people on the plantation would have followed her example. Oh, you've no idea how lazy these niggers are; you Northern people don't know anything about it. They'd never do any work at all if they were not afraid of being whipped."

. . . Accepting the position of the overseer, I knew that his method was right, but it was a red-hot experience to me, and has ever since been a fearful thing in my memory. Strangely so, I sometimes think, but I suppose the fact that the delicate and ingenuous lad who was with me, betrayed not even the slightest flush of shame, and that I constrained myself from the least expression of feeling of any kind, made the impression in my brain the more intense and lasting.

Yes, indeed.

But this movie must get on with his love life. He has switched interest from Miss Lizzie Baldwin to the daughter of the Perkins household, Emily. Their love is of the lofty variety. His brother

John makes fun of their exalted courtship, conducted mostly by letter, over a period of years. To Fred his beloved is "the noblest and most sensible woman . . . a union of Faith and Courage— Religion and Freedom." She ups and jilts him for a handsome young minister, Edward Everett Hale. (Swept off her feet? If so, about time.) He dashed to Hartford to ask Harriet Beecher Stowe, Emily's aunt, to help him plead his cause. (That's an unreported conversation I would have liked to overhear.) Brother John, meantime, has engaged himself to the enchanting young woman we met on the porch, Mary, an orphan, living with her grandparents (the white-haired gentleman at her side). She has a strong sense of herself, having been petted and indulged by people like Daniel Webster and William Cullen Bryant and other such close friends of her grandfather.

(These prominent connections thrill me, I admit. The real American thing. It lures; I follow, though the significance of the connections evades me. Guy laughs at me. I get tears in my eyes when I sing "Oh beautiful for spacious skies," etc., etc., especially "and crown thy good with brotherhood," etc. etc.)

So John and Mary marry. Fred loves them both. They both love Fred. John and Mary have their first child, but John is already tubercular. In the spirit of the medicine of the times (if the patient survived, the treatment must have been good for him), John accompanies Fred on a second reporting trip to Texas and a foray into Mexico, which improves neither John's health nor Fred's, but involves them in the fate of the German settlements of West Texas. We are back to the spirit of 1848. In these pleasant, prosperous, civilized communities of German immigrants, were a number of radicals who had fled the 1848 reaction—among them Adolf Douai, editor of the San Antonio *Zeitung*, and Edward Degener, dedicated to the cause of social and political freedom and to keeping Texas a nonslave state. The Olmsted brothers, back in New York, raise funds for Douai's newspaper and buy type for it, and become part of the secret gunrunning to the Free-Soilers in Kansas, shipping out a howitzer and its carriage, twenty-four shells, twenty-four cannister cartridges, five hand grenades, fifty rockets, and six swords.

(The fate of the Texas German radicals is instructive. As the Civil War approached, local support for Douai's paper was withdrawn. The Texas Free-Soil movement was crushed, and sur-

rounded by hostile native Southerners, the immigrant community
became fearful and self-interested. Douai lost the newspaper and
left Texas for good. Degener and other forty-eighters who stubbornly remained paid a price. Many were imprisoned when war
came. While Degener was in jail, his two young sons were am-
bushed and killed.)

Olmsted's reports on the South appeared in the newspaper and
were published in segments: *The Seaboard Slave States, A Journey
Through Texas,* and *A Journey in the Back Country,* and later *The
Cotton Kingdom.* (Historians still argue about Olmsted's views of
the South as it was. Make your own decision. He's worth reading,
as you can see from that long excerpt about the slave girl's punishment.) Olmsted believes himself a literary fellow now. He goes
into publishing with the help of his agreeable father's money, is
swindled, and fails. His beloved brother John is dying of tuberculosis. Fred has been jilted, remember, and between one thing and
another, he's in a low state of mind when the job of superintending
the building of a park in the center of New York City falls right
into his lap—an accident, one might say, yet perfectly inevitable.
"If a fairy had shaped it for me," Fred Olmsted writes to his
brother John, who is dying in Europe, "it could not have fitted me
better. It was normal, ordinary and naturally outgrowing from my
previous life . . . and it occupied my whole heart." He has been
given this post as superintendent of the park which will become
Central Park because he's safe, no threat to any of the warring
political groups seeking power in the city. His troubles begin immediately. When he reports to the chief engineer of the Park on
a purely ceremonial introductory visit, Fred is treated to a hazing.
A foreman in work pants and hip boots leads the formally dressed
Olmsted

through the midst . . . of vile sloughs, in the black and unctuous slime of
which I sometimes sank nearly half-leg deep. . . . The low grounds were
steeped in the overflow and mush of pig-sties, slaughter houses and bone-
boiling works, and the stench was sickening.

(The scene writes itself.)

Out of the stench, pigsties, vile sloughs, and unctuous slime of
some of the rottenest real estate in the city, Olmsted creates the
jewel of Central Park. His design is no accident. He knows what
he's about.

The Park is a single work of art, and as such subject to the primary law of every work of art, namely, that it shall be framed upon a single, noble motive, to which the design of all its parts, in some more or less subtle way, shall be confluent and helpful.

He is plunged into the cesspool of city politics. A million and a half European immigrants have poured into the slums as the Park is begun. There are gang wars between native-born and foreign-born, and prostitution, thievery, pickpockets, beggars, alcoholics. The police force is made up of thugs. The panic of 1857 creates a huge force of idle, penniless, hungry men. Work on the park is used as a political handout by the Democratic Party.

It was a general impression that the pretence of work was merely a form of distributing the public money to the poor and my office was for several days regularly surrounded by an organized mob carrying a banner inscribed "Bread and Blood." [*Sic*, Fred. Bread *or* Blood.] This mob sent in to me a list of 10,000 names of men alleged to have starving families, demanding that they should be immediately put at work. I had almost no assistance, but within a week I had a thousand men economically employed and rigidly discharged any man who failed to work industriously and to behave in a quiet orderly manner. Since the plan was adopted, from two to four thousand men have been at work. . . . But with a single exception, when a thousand workmen on an adjoining work struck for higher wages and two gangs on the park joined them and were immediately discharged, there has been the most perfect order, peace and good feeling preserved, notwithstanding the fact that the laborers are mainly from the poorest, and what is generally considered the most dangerous class of the great city's population. . . .

In a setting of patronage, rake-offs, and deals, dreamy Olmsted carries on and proves himself tough and practical. He builds the park that he and Calvert Vaux designed. By 1861, Fifth Avenue richies are driving their carriages over Central Park's curving roads. Traffic is heavy on the underpasses of the sunken transverse roads, an innovation of genius. Ice-skating on the pond, band and classical music concerts, horseback riding on the bridle paths. The land adjoining the park has jumped in value. The park is a success. Everybody loves the park.

Politicians naturally continue to mess around in the project. There's pressure to remove Olmsted. The Tweed Ring moves in. Olmsted writes to the board that controls Park projects in a man-

ner which he thinks will most impress them with his practical
abilities:

You could not . . . doubt my ability to organize and control efficiently and
economically . . . for I had . . . brought out of a mob of lazy, reckless,
turbulent and violent loafers a well organized, punctual, sober, industri-
ous and disciplined body of 1000 men. . . . I feel if you are now unwilling
to trust my judgment . . . it is time you were rid of me altogether. I feel
this . . . I feel it, and I have felt it in spite of my . . . real love for the park.

The first of a series of resignations, dismissals and further resignations. Olmsted will be attacked in other ways, investigated by
the legislature, kept under the "paw . . . wet with blood and sweat"
of a rigidly interfering comptroller, tossed about in a game involv-
ing millions spent on a major project in a powerfully growing city
of the new industrial age. Still he keeps his vision. No locked gates.
No iron railings.

We should undertake nothing in a park which involves the treating of the
public as prisoners or wild beasts. . . . All the art of a park is to influence
the mind of men through their imagination . . . and the influence of iron
. . . can never be good.

He expresses a vision of paradise on earth:

. . . A man of any class shall say to his wife, when he is going out in the
morning: "My dear, when the children come home from school, put some
bread and butter and salad in a basket, and go to the spring under the
chestnut-tree. I will join you there as soon as I can get away from the
office. We will walk to the dairy-man's cottage and get some tea, and some
fresh milk for the children, and take our supper by the brookside;" and
this shall be no joke, but the most refreshing earnest.

The "man of any class," please notice, in Olmsted's paradise is
middle-class, and he walks out of an office, not off a work gang.
   Once, the Goddards tried to have a family picnic in Central Park
—Jenny's classy idea, I think. I was little, seven or eight. It was just
after the Fort Greene Park days. We came by subway, and walked
and walked and walked forever it seemed through streets of familiar steaming heat and unfamiliar cleanliness and quiet grace.
Everybody carried something. Mama carried a bag of fruit and

shtrudel; Josh, two heavy shopping bags of sandwiches; Barry, iced tea in a milk can; Jenny carried me, and Shana carried herself. I remember the pleasure of being jogged and of being lucky enough to be carried. The tar in the gutters was sticky from the heat. I was old enough to know how to read. Signs in the Park, when we reached it, said, KEEP OFF. KEEP OFF. I remember Mama's flushed, bewildered face, and her astonishment at a park that was not for picnicking. "So what is it here for?" she demands to know. A pleasant Irish cop who will not allow us to settle under a tree near a bridle path warns us that we won't find a spot anywhere in the Park where picnicking is allowed. He advises us to go home. Barry is obstinate and pushes on. He and Josh discover a pond without KEEP OFF signs around it, but as soon as we begin to unload, again a cop appears to move us along. We don't move fast enough for him and he mutters "filthy kikes" under his breath before he turns away. I remember my brother Barry's black, black anger, and then I don't remember any more.

Olmsted more or less founded the profession of landscape architect. In addition to Central Park, he designed Morningside Park, Riverside Park, Prospect Park, and my Fort Greene Park, among dozens of other small city parks. He was a remarkable fellow, and I don't want to seem to be maligning him, with my story of our failed picnic, when I'm only attempting to understand.

But, the story. Frederick Law Olmsted married his brother John's widow after John died. Did he love Mary Cleveland Bryant Perkins Olmsted, John's widow? He had seen her first, remember. His brother John is dying far away in Europe and sends a heartbreaking last letter:

Dear dear Fred . . . It appears we are not to see one another any more—I have not many days, the Dr says. . . . I never have known a better friendship than ours has been & there can't be a greater happiness than to think of that—how dear we have been & how long we have held out such tenderness.

And lays a heavy burden on Fred with the letter's last line: "Don't let Mary suffer while you are alive."

How does Olmsted pick up this peculiar burden? With the cheerfulness he cultivated as a major virtue? He has no qualms? "Thou shalt not uncover the nakedness of thy brother's wife: it is

thy brother's nakedness." He is through with that old testament
stuff?

For the purposes of my movie, let's treat it as true love at long
last. He marries Mary and embraces his niece and two nephews
as his own, as Guy Rossiter embraced my children. Soon Mary is
pregnant with his child. Fred has his Central Park job; he's given
a house to live in; his agreeable Papa will always help. Olmsted is
troubled by insomnia, indigestion, headaches; his stepchildren
have all the common children's ailments plus eye trouble and
boils, Mary's servants are "she-devils," but Fred writes his father
". . . We have a good deal of happiness between the drops: that's
a fact." Flashes of happiness, flashes of tragedy—the ingredients
are to hand. A son is born to the couple. He is a couple of months
old when Olmsted, Mary, and the infant are dashed out of a carriage by a runaway horse that has been tormented by flies. Mary
and the infant are miraculously untouched. Olmsted is badly
smashed up and expected to die. Yet Olmsted stubbornly lives on
with a lifelong limp, and a week after the accident, the infant dies
of cholera. In 1861 they have a daughter, and in 1870 another son
named Henry Perkins, whom they call "Boy" and then rename
Frederick Law Olmsted, Jr., when he is four years old. He will
follow his father into landscape architecture and so will Olmsted's
stepson-nephew, John Charles. What of the others? Of his brother's two other children, Owen will die at the age of twenty-four
of tuberculosis like his father. Charlotte, volatile, handsome, and
unhappy, manages to marry well and to have two sons, and then
flips out, is institutionalized, and dies after a time. There isn't
much information about Fred's daughter, Marion.

It's clear that there's far too much material in the Olmsted story
for a single film. TV it must be. A series.

A Civil War episode: Olmsted, on leave from Central Park to
respond to a call from Washington to help form the Sanitary Commission. Cleanliness. He carries on about cleanliness. He works
himself into exhaustion and more illness. He initiates hospital
transport systems, rail and ship, but there are never enough facili-
ties for the masses of wounded, the dying, and the already dead,
packed into boxcars, suffocating in the stench of disease and death
on a scale never before dealt with. Scene: Olmsted in command
with his lieutenant, Katherine Prescott Wormeley, at his side. The
mess of war, the heartbreak of planning for the unpredictable.

Violent struggle for supremacy of his idea that *sanitation* is everything. Ardent partisanship for the Union, for Lincoln, for Grant.
As for Miss Wormeley, let's have a bit of additional love interest
here. She idolizes Olmsted. (Miss Wormeley was a homely, Eng-
lish-born daughter of a rear admiral, a clever, devoted, and levelheaded young woman, but for our purposes, we must have her
beautiful, warm, deeply understanding, and in love.)

The Sanitary Commission is another lasting Olmsted contribution, since it became the Red Cross in time.

He has kept his connection with Central Park during his Civil
War work. Under pressure, he and Vaux resign from Central Park
once again, and utterly sick, overworked, and overwhelmed,
Olmsted temporarily gives up and resigns from the Sanitary Commission as well. Almost immediately he's involved in an ambitious
plan to launch a weekly which will bind the nation together. In
time *The Nation* appears, dedicated by Godkin, its first editor, to
"equality . . . in all parts of the Union."

Ah, Olmsted, wonderful, visionary, active fellow—restless, im-
proving, hard-working Olmsted, never still while there's work to
be done.

And right here he makes one of his biggest mistakes, taking on
the duties of Superintendent of the Mariposa Mining Estates. He
is twelve thousand dollars in debt when the Mariposa offer comes
through. The pay is ten thousand dollars a year, and the extra
bonus of a house and five hundred shares of stock, worth fifty
thousand dollars at the time. Mariposa comprises seventy square
miles of territory in California, with half a dozen villages, half a
dozen working gold mines, and a floating population of seven
thousand. The town Olmsted settles in consists of a couple of bars,
two inns, a billiard parlor, a bath house, livery stables, a company
store, a Wells Fargo office, and so on. (The script writes itself.) A
rough place. Each layer of humanity stamps on the layer beneath
—Yankees, Southerners, Chinamen, Niggers, Mexicans—Digger
Indians are at the very bottom. Olmsted's sympathies are with the
victims, but, characteristically, with the violent and ignorant prej-
udiced as well. What is needed is a civilizing influence. He tells
himself that under his management the Mariposa Mining Estates
will be developed into a model community where industry will
flourish and diversify in harmony with a happy, prosperous population, raising crops and grazing cattle in the green spaces to be

created between the defacing mining operations, the whole bathed in the civilizing light of fellow feeling, culture, and education. (He is a Fidel Castro of enlightened capitalism, working with his vision in his little territory.) The money men back east are with him all the way as long as the profits keep rolling in. But by the time of the Mariposa's sale to the corporation Olmsted represents, the mines had been exhausted by ravaging exploitation. The books had been falsified by the seller so as to be grossly misleading. These facts are quickly discovered by Olmsted, but the more important fact—that Mariposa is at the wrong end of the mother lode—takes longer to be uncovered. Olmsted persists for two years. Then Mariposa fails and he leaves the desolate spot in a worse state than he found it.

And what of Olmsted? Profit, gold alone on his mind? Certainly not. The vicious, spiritless, and coarse life of the region astounds him. The endurance and decency of the humble and degraded give him pause. He is horrified by tortures and lynchings. The vilest acts are treated as jokes: distribution of gifts as peace offerings to the Digger Indians deliberately including the soiled handkerchiefs of smallpox victims. (Like most of the enlightened men of his generation Olmsted doesn't discuss the systematic destruction of the North American Indian.) But he believes in the essential goodness of man, even savage man, and in man's capacity for change and growth. He doesn't care for the view of Americans given out by Dickens and Mrs. Trollope. He means to disprove them and make a strong case for the glories of American democracy as an idea and an ideal, and to explain to the world the good, rough people who are the raw material for its making. It is the obligation of an elite to give these mute people a voice. He had already begun an extraordinary social experiment, for its time, during his Sanitary Commission days, gathering information on 7700 volunteers of the Union Army in the form of a questionnaire on their backgrounds and views, and he continues this experiment in California, the information to be gathered together in a book which he never writes. After his death, the material is destroyed. (What ignorant idiot did that?)

He and Mary and the children ride their horses to the valley of Yosemite and the Mariposa Big Tree Groves, where immense, ancient sequoia trees stand like "distinguished strangers . . . come down to us from another world." These great natural wonders must be secured for the public. Later he will do the same for Niagara.

It is the main duty of government . . . to provide means of protection for all its citizens in the pursuit of happiness against the obstacles, otherwise insurmountable, which the selfishness of individuals or combinations of individuals is liable to interpose to that pursuit.

Perhaps there is too much Olmsted material—even for a TV series?

We aren't even up to the Columbian Exposition, the Chicago World's Fair, at the close of the century. How charming the man was. He proceeds with touching concern that "incidents of vital human gaiety" be introduced on the grounds—"small groups of singers, strolling banjo players, lemonade peddlers in colorful costumes, bands of musicians on the boats . . ." The man is a positive Walt Disney.

He speaks and writes and exhorts men to make life lovelier.

The most brutal Pagans to whom we have sent our missionaries have never shown greater indifference to the sufferings of others, than is exhibited in the plans of some of our most promising cities, for which men now living in them are responsible.

In his seventies, Frederick Law Olmsted became dotty. Senility overtook him. I don't know what I would have done as his wife or child or grandchild, but I think he earned the indulgence of a bit of dottiness, after all those years of cheerfulness through insomnia, headaches, indigestion, and the tragedies and triumphs of his life and his work. His family hid him away on Deer Isle, off the coast of Maine, where they summered. They made some inane efforts to keep him busy and happy with landscape and gardening makework, but he wasn't that much of a fool, and took long, raging walks instead. He could become dangerously irritable, to the point of shaking the living daylights out of his wife's female companion and throwing things at his male guard. The precious genius of a man has retreated into an empty, noisy, meaningless hulk. His family are ashamed of his senility; they fear that he might "make an exposure of himself." Soon they give up on the Deer Isle arrangement and turn him over to McLean Hospital in Massachusetts. He becomes a prisoner in a cottage on the grounds he had himself designed. He's not so dotty, after all. He's quite aware that his original plans have been altered and spoiled, "confound them!" and he raves on about that and about loneliness and uselessness and pain and neglect in letters reportedly quite mad though with occasional flashes of lucidity. He carries on in this pitiable state, and after five years or so, he dies.

Within my legend of Olmsted there's another legend, concocted by an imaginative man who had more success in its being taken for true than he had bargained for. People wanted to believe in it. Every man has his secret knowledge that deep down a richie is a crook and a cheat. The tale even hit the newspapers and was circulated so widely that after his father's death Frederick, Jr., had to step in and write, print, and circulate a disclaimer declaring it just a made-up story.

The Olmsted legend told a tale of an ancestor, Cotton Mather Olmsted, inheriting Deer Isle from Chief Winnipesaukee of the Penobscot tribe, because in his fair and honorable dealings as an Indian fur trader, he had befriended and tended the wounds (from a fight with a bear) of the chief. In 1892 (so the story continued) Frederick Law Olmsted himself, walking about at low tide on his island, wandered into a cave, noticed a rude cross on the inner wall, and digging into the matter, uncovered markings of "rows of bolt heads . . . as if an iron box, heavily bolted at its joints, had been buried in the compact clay . . . long enough to have left a perfect impress. . . ." The clear indications of buried treasure were traced back to Captain Kidd and thence to Jacques Cartier, a French-Canadian trapper employed by John Jacob Astor. Since the box was bolted closed, rather than mess with it himself, the trapper had carried it down to his boss, John Jacob Astor, on one of his regular runs to New York City. The trapper became mysteriously richer by five thousand dollars immediately thereafter, and John Jacob Astor, who had been moving along in his fur-trading business at a modest pace, was suddenly buying valuable chunks of New York City real estate and building the Waldorf-Astoria. The story is decorated with nice touches of derring-do: fragments of burnt documents in the trapper's abandoned hut, still standing on the Olmsted land . . . John Jacob Astor's signature and a decipherable phrase—"absolute secrecy must be observed" . . . Captain Kidd himself, seconds before swinging by the neck, slipping his wife a scrap of writing . . . the numbers 44106818 . . . an almost perfect reading of the latitude and longitude of the cave's location; swollen Astor bank deposits at the time of the discovery of the treasure; proof of Astor having laundered his ill-gotten gains through London banks and lawyers; tracing the chest itself to a junk dealer with the wonderful name of Melechidescec Jacobs of Brooklyn, New York, who had bought it when the first Astor mansion was torn down to make way for the second, or perhaps it was the Waldorf-Astoria. (The old one, of course, that was torn down to make way for the Empire State Building.) His case as tight as an overhauled vessel, Olmsted presented his demands to the Astors: payment of the full amount of the original haul, plus interest, the whole amounting to five million, one hundred twelve thousand, two hundred thirty four dollars and thirty cents, with the offer to wipe out the thirty-four dollars and thirty cents for immediate cash payment. The story ends: "The case was not tried but settled out of court for $5,000,000."

End the Olmsted story with a Marxist fairy tale? A fable for our times. The democratic knight against the grubby business barons. And the knight wins! He wins! My legendary grandfather, my real American hero, Frederick Law Olmsted, I want you to win.

WHAT'S NEW
WITH THE FAMILY?

S am Schwartz on the telephone from Los Angeles. "We're suing. We're instituting suit. The lawyers are very optimistic. In their opinion we have a watertight case. Especially with your grievances."

"*My* grievances?" Anne says.

"Certainly. Papa promised you money in his last letter. You figure out what it would have come to after all these years—riding on the right investments."

"Is that part of your suit?"

"Definitely."

"How ridiculous. What kind of lawyers do you have? There's no case in that."

"We've got a case. Don't worry. It's a solid case. The lawyers know what they're doing. We're getting every penny he owes us."

"Barry doesn't owe me anything."

"He owes you plenty. That was your father, your father's promise, practically on his deathbed. Barry made you sign a paper, remember, remember? After Papa died? That wasn't an exercise in penmanship, Anna. Don't kid yourself. He needed your release. Yours. Mine and Connie's. Jenny's. Saul's. Everybody's. Josh's. Shana's and Merv's. Like fools we all marched in with our signatures. Me, too. I offered it. 'Community property' could create trouble. So what the hell, I offered my signature. I should have had my head examined. Who knows the shenanigans that were going on, what kind of financial arrangement he had with Papa? On the books, on the books," he yelled over Anne's exclamation of disbelief.

"Tax reasons, tax reasons, don't you understand? On the books, for all we know, Papa owned Goddard Enterprises outright. He could have been on the books as a leading executive, with a tremendous insurance policy on him. He could have owned God knows how much stock. On the books. For all we know Papa was a millionaire ten times over, on the books. Like a pack of nitwits we signed that all away. You had a definite commitment in writing. Okay, it was a drop in the bucket, what's a thousand dollars, it's nickels and dimes compared with what we're talking about, but it was a wedge. It gave you a wedge. Barry was plenty excited about getting your signature. I heard him with my own ears. 'What's holding up Anne's signature?' Baruch Goddard doesn't worry over nothing, believe me. The lawyers jumped at it when I told them. I told the lawyers everything from the early days too, all the stuff we have on him, you and I know plenty, we're the kingpins in this."

"Sam," Anne says, "I'm not having anything to do with it."

"The lawyers are friends of yours and of Guy's. They're big liberals."

"Is it political? They want to smear him?"

"What do I care if it's political? So it's political. He's a big man, your brother. He's got the Mayor of New York in one pocket and the Governor in another. They want to smear him a little, I have absolutely no objection. You know Harrison—he says he's a friend of yours."

"We know him," Anne says. "He's not one of my favorite people."

"He's not one of my favorite people either. You can smell anti-Semitism on him from across the room. But he's a smart lawyer. And Bernberger is a whiz, a genius. We've got the best. I'm flabbergasted by your reaction. I thought you would be the first to join in.

"With your views," he adds. "Your liberal views. We counted on you without any question."

"Well, don't count on me," Anne says.

"Talk it over with Guy. Ask Guy for another opinion."

"It doesn't have anything to do with Guy. And he wouldn't touch it anyway."

"What's the matter with you?" Sam Schwartz is shouting. "We need you. We need your know-how, to publicize, he's keeping it out of the newspapers."

"How does he do that?"

"It's very simple. They lose his advertising. That's something to lose. Two full pages, every week. Every *week*."

"Who's in on this?"

"Who's in on what?"

"In the family, I mean, who's in, who's participating?"

"Everybody, everybody. The process has been started. It's moving. I assure you that everybody will be in, in time."

"But Papa left a will. He left everything to Barry," Anne says.

"You talk as if nobody ever contested a will before. It's been done before and it'll be done again."

"But if what belonged to Papa was just a setup, just a way of Barry manipulating his money, then it's certainly all Barry's money. I don't understand."

"That's worse for him. Don't you see it's worse for him if he was letting his accountants fiddle around with his books? He doesn't want any of that to come out. He might settle the whole thing quietly out of court."

"Aren't any of you still working for Barry?"

"Everybody's out. We're all out. O-U-T. That man has no feeling, no loyalty, he's absolutely without a heart or soul. He understands one thing and one thing only—money—and we're going to hit him where it hurts, in his pocket. Twelve million dollars—two million apiece. Are you prepared to sneer at two million dollars?"

"Don't do it, Sam. He's a winner. You'll lose, and end up paying the lawyers a fortune."

"I didn't call for advice, Anna. I called to give you the information."

"I'm not having anything to do with this, Sam."

"Merv and Shana are your close, warm relatives, aren't they? Aren't they? You know what your brother did to Merv? After everything Merv did for him? There wasn't anything, there wasn't a single shitty thing that Barry asked Merv to do that Merv didn't run to do for him and no questions asked. Now he's dismissed like an office boy. The man is absolutely insidious, heartless, he doesn't know the meaning of the word brotherhood."

"Weren't you all vice-presidents? You must have had some security, some protection?"

"Vice-presidents! Window-dressing! We didn't have an ounce of power between the whole bunch of us. Your brother saw to that."

"Come on, Sam, you're not exactly babes in the wood."

"Of course we're not babes in the wood. We're supposed to be penalized because we're smart?"

"I wish I knew what you were talking about, Sam. I really don't understand anything you're telling me."

"He forced us to retire. Did he force Jake Weinstein to retire?"

"Who in the world is Jake Weinstein?"

"Jake Weinstein, his old friend from Brooklyn. He's been one of his top men from the very beginning. You know Jake. You met him at plenty of parties in the old Westchester place. Jake's ten years older than me, but you don't see Jake Weinstein retiring. No, because Jake Weinstein isn't in Baruch Goddard's family."

"Sam, I don't know Jake Weinstein and I don't want to talk about him." She has begun to laugh.

"What's so goddamn funny?" Sam Schwartz yells at her. "I can't seem to make you understand the simplest facts of business. We got a bad deal. A bad deal is a bad deal. We should have received two, three, four times what we received. What we got was a load of sanctimonious talk. He tells me that the times have moved beyond me. I don't have the contemporary know-how of the younger men. He can tell that bullshit to your brothers, he can tell that to Saul and Josh, but not to Sam Schwartz. The younger men. Younger minds. Who are these younger men with their young minds? Big surprise! His sons. His son-in-laws, his daughters' husbands. He has to make room for them so he shoves us out. Wait. His time will come too. They'll give him a kick in the pants when they get going and he'll be out on *his* ass. Mark my words."

Anne says nothing.

"Besides the humiliation. It's outrageous."

"Wasn't there severance, pension? How about those stock options—that started years ago, didn't it?"

"Anna, please, you think we're a bunch of babies? I know what's what. And I'll tell you something else about Goddard stock. We'll be papering the walls with Goddard stock. Take my word, if you have any, sell while the selling's good. That man's in trouble. He's in deep trouble. He's overextended himself. He's going to come crashing down. He's going to crumble."

"Then you're better off out—if he's crashing, if he'll be penniless."

"You've got a lot to learn about business, Anna. A lot of stockholders will go broke and Baruch Goddard will make another fortune. Penniless! He could live off his art holdings alone for the rest of his life—in style, in style."

"How about the foreign industrialist tie-in? What are those stories about?"

"Sure, sure. Iranians, Italians, Greeks, you name it, he's in there, he's in there."

"Well, which is it, is he crashing or is he soaring?"

"You know how he treated his brother Saul? Worse than a child, worse than a dog, like a menial slave. Saul doesn't want to come in. You're going to be another fool like Saul? Saul went all the way to New York. He gave me the most peculiar answer I ever heard in my entire business experience. I come to the man with a straight proposition. 'I want to look my brother in the face before I decide,' he tells me. Takes a plane all the way to New York at his own expense, grabs a cab at the airport direct to the Goddard Building, rides up to the forty-fifth floor to Baruch Goddard's penthouse office, looks into his brother's face, no conversation, no questions, nothing, Barry must have thought he was dealing with a certified lunatic, then he turns on his heel and back to the airport and home. His answer? 'Count me out.' No elaboration or explanation. 'Count me out,' and 'That's my unswerving, final decision.' "

"Forget it, Sam. Maybe it's just one of Barry's moods, his anti-family moods. For all you know he may be getting over it right this minute and tomorrow you'll all be back in again."

"It's too late. The die is cast. He knows we're suing. And if nobody comes in with me, I'll go the whole way alone."

"How is Connie?" Anne says.

"I'll do it alone," Sam yells. "I'm going to drag that man in the mud. I'm going to expose him to the world. I know plenty. I know him and his operations from cover to cover—including his personal shenanigans with the women on the side. That man is going to be pulled down and all his lying, cheating immorality and hypocrisy exposed. Suddenly after years of criticizing him, you're a big partisan of Baruch Goddard. You've forgotten the kickbacks? You know, we think we can prove Mafia entanglement? I've always been a friend to you. You act like I'm an enemy."

"Because I don't want to sue Barry? I don't have any claim on him. That suit is just harassment. He earned his money like any other businessman. It's his."

"I thought you were some kind of Marxist. You talk like a naïve ignoramus, totally ignorant of the financial and economic world. Men in Barry's position don't work for their money. Their money works for them. It never stops, around the clock. You know he could have fixed it so that your son didn't go to jail for contempt? He could have dropped a word, just a word, in the right person's ear. It would have been a whole new ball game. He gave the University millions. There's a Goddard chair established. And millions to the Building Fund. He could have put a little pressure where a little pressure would have done a little good. He's cold. He doesn't have any family feeling. He lets his nephew go to jail for a month. You owe him nothing."

"How about Danny's family feeling?" Anne says. "That was the Fay Goddard Hall he and his friends seized."

"You'd go to any lengths to weasel out," Sam says. "You know that your son had your full support in his activities."

"I know he didn't have yours," Anne says.

"I don't have any use for that war anymore. As far as I'm concerned it can't end fast enough."

"Sam, this call is costing you a lot of money."

"Don't worry about that. I still have my company credit card."

She laughs. "You mean Barry's paying for this call?"

"He's going to pay and pay and pay. It's big news, this suit. It's news. Talk it over with Guy. An exposure story in the magazine could be terrific. All around."

"I have to get off, Sam."

"If you had real integrity you'd be the first one to help. What's the matter, you're scared?"

"Help what?"

"Help clean up this whole mess."

"What mess? How? There's no social justice involved in moving money around from him to us. What have we done if we take twelve million from Barry and give it to ourselves? When you're ready to tear the whole works down, call me again."

"For God's sake, we're talking about a lousy twelve-million-dollar lawsuit—not a world revolution."

"I know," Anne says.

Shana on the telephone from the farm. "Did Sam Schwartz call you yet, about the conference?"

"Wait, wait a minute," Anne says. "How are you? How is everything? How's Merv and the children?"

"Terrific. Everything's terrific. We retired here. We're farmers. Merv's a gentleman farmer. I'm more of a sharecropper woman." She roars with laughter. "We raise pigs, chickens, lambs, goats. Two apiece. Watch out for goats. They'll eat *anything*. It ate a letter I was writing." She roars again. "We have a vegetable garden the size of a state park. Merv's been carried away."

"Sounds good," Anne says. "Do you grow your own tomatoes and corn? That's my idea of heaven."

"Of course. Everything. Strawberries, eggplant, rutabaga, asparagus. Sparagras, our hired man calls it. Don't you grow anything at your summer place?"

"We don't get up there long enough or early enough to plant. Our man tends the perennials, and puts in some greens and herbs. I have to have dill for the chicken soup. It makes the kitchen smell just like Mama's used to."

"Mama," Shana says. "It would kill her—what's going on now."

"The suit?"

"Did he call you? He's driving everybody crazy. In self-protection we demanded a telephone conference where we can all talk together. Each give our answer. Go in with him or stay out."

"I'm out," Anne says.

"Oh, thank God," Shana says, and calls out to Merv at the other end. "He was lying, Merv, he was lying. She's not going in," and back to Anne, "Sam Schwartz is telling everybody you're in with Guy's blessing and Guy's backing. Publicity. The works."

Anne sighs. "Sam Schwartz. Why isn't Connie stopping him?"

There is a quivering, sad silence at Shana's end. "I thought you knew that Connie isn't well."

"What's the matter with her?"

"You don't know?"

"No. Tell me. Is it bad? Is it cancer?"

"Oh, God forbid," Shana says.

"Well, what's the matter with Connie?"

"All we have is Sam Schwartz's word for it. And you know what I think of his word. I'm going out there next month to see for myself."

"But what does he say?"

"Depression."

Anne hears in Shana's voice the encroaching, contagious terror that the word holds for Shana.

"Isn't she being treated?"

"I'm going out there next month. See what's going on. I don't like Sam Schwartz's answers. I'm so relieved that he was lying about you, Anna, it's a tremendous relief."

"I had the impression from him that you and Merv were strongly in favor of the suit."

Shana is hollering again for Merv. "Merv, Merv, it's just the way we had it worked out. He told Anna that *we* were in." And back to Anne, "He's up to his old tricks. A real Sam Schwartz production. Saul figured it out right away. Telling each one the others were in. Saul suggested the conference, and Sam had to agree. He can't fool us if we're together. It's tonight at eleven o'clock, our time. You'll be home?"

"I'll be home."

"You're going to say no, no doubt about it?"

"Not the shadow of a doubt," Anne says.

"Sam insisted on having his lawyer on the line, so be careful. We want to keep things perfectly straight. There isn't much love lost between me and my brother Barry, but that doesn't mean I'd go out and crucify him."

"Sam Schwartz told me that Merv got a bad deal from Barry," Anne says.

"Sam Schwartz doesn't know what he's talking about," Shana shouts. "Sam Schwartz ought to keep his big mouth shut."

"Okay," Anne says. "Don't get upset."

"Please don't go around repeating anything Sam Schwartz tells you. That kind of talk can get us in a lot of trouble. Everything isn't finally settled between Merv and Barry. Barry could turn around and take everything away. He could, Merv, he could," she shouts without covering the mouthpiece. "You know damn well he could and then where would we be?" and then, back to Anne, in a voice tight with anxiety, "Listen, I have to get off. It's been great talking to you. Give my love to all your gang."

"And mine to everybody, to Merv, and the children. And from Guy and Danny too. He's right here. My son is honoring us with his presence for dinner."

Shana laughs. "You sound like Papa. Listen, hugs and kisses to

Danny. Talk to you later. Eleven o'clock. Don't forget. And thanks for everything."

"For what?" Anne says.

Shana laughs again. "I swear you're turning into Papa."

"Nail him," Danny says. "That's what I'd do in your place. What a chance to nail one of them. Why not? Get him. It's good for the movement to get one of those guys."

"I thought you were fond of your Uncle Barry." Guy puts on his teasing smile. "You always said so as a kid."

"I really liked him," Danny says. "Especially his collection of maps and historical documents. I always felt good with him. He never did me any harm. But you have to admit, he never did society any good."

"We protected you from harm," Anne says. "Free of family contamination. We avoided it like the plague."

"Not I," Guy says. "Best fun in my life, mingling with your family. Including your brother Barry. I enjoy him. Charming man, fantastic energy, wonderfully interesting type. Of course, he's a bastard in the social sense, but all businessmen are."

"I would have given a lot to know him, really know him, know him intimately," Danny says. "It's fascinating to get to know a guy like that from the inside."

"Like what?" Anne says. "What do you think he represents?"

"Come on, Mom, don't get naïve on me just because he's your brother. He's a man who moves things around, makes things happen, buys up Fifth Avenue, pockets the Mayor of New York City, doesn't give a shit about his responsibility to the people. He's a prototype. He's interesting. His name comes up all the time. I love to see the shock on their faces when I say at the end of one of those sessions, 'He's my uncle.' They fall off their chairs in surprise. I'd sue him in a minute. You should do it, Mom. What the hell? At least it would throw up a lot of dirt. That's good for the movement. Stir things up, throw confusion into the camp of the bourgeoisie. He's *got* to be into a lot of tricky, dirty stuff. He's *got* to. There's too much talk about him. There has to be some substance to it. A suit like this could uncover his whole operation and maybe more. Pin something on *him*, and maybe he'll talk about something bigger, to get *himself* off the hook. Do it, Mom."

"Danny," Anne says, "he's my brother."

"Well what does that mean?" Danny says. "You're as bad as one of the kids in my group who keeps insisting her father is a wonderful man even though he heads up CIA operations in the Far East. He never put *her* in a tiger cage, so what the hell?"

Anne is holding, waiting to be connected with her brothers and sisters strung out across the country. Now the operator signals. They're on.

"Hello, everybody, this is Sam Schwartz."

"Hello, everybody, this is Saul." Unmistakably Saul. Toneless, oddly rich voice.

"And Lil, Lil here, on our extension." Shrieking, giggling, choking.

"Hello, folks, this is Josh, greeting you from beautiful downtown . . ."

"Stop wasting money," Sam Schwartz interrupts.

"Hello, this is Shana, everybody."

"Jenny here." Jenny has perfected a high-pitched, formal tone for this event. "Jenny on this end, everybody. Isn't this exciting? Isn't this a marvel of our times?" And calls out to her husband, "Darling, get on our extension. Saul's wife, Lil, is on an extension. I told you it would be perfectly all right. Pick up, dear, pick up the extension."

"Are you on there, Anna?" Sam Schwartz asks.

"I'm here," Anne says. "Hi, everybody."

There is a general babble, then only Jenny, talking—about the weather. ". . . very cold up there, dear? How often I find myself thinking about you, dear, locked away in those snowy mountains." Addressed to Shana, apparently. "We saw on the television that you had a blizzard last week. In April! Imagine! It's eighty-four degrees down here in Sarasota right this minute. I'm looking directly at a thermometer. Absolutely glorious weather for a few weeks now. Not a drop of rain. You have your courage living in those freezing cold climates. You too, Anne, insisting on remaining in New York City. But you love it, don't you dear? And who can blame you? Most wonderful city in the world."

"We're wasting time, we're wasting time," Sam Schwartz interrupts.

"I'll be more than happy to send a check for indulging myself in a few extra minutes of civilized talk," Jenny says. "The amenities must be observed, whatever the cost, my dears, isn't that so?"

Josh hoots. "Anybody want to know the exact temperature in beautiful downtown, smoggy, foggy . . ."

"Where's Merv?" Sam Schwartz interrupts.

"I'm representing me and Merv," Shana says. "Merv's busy. I'll speak for me and for Merv."

"Okay, if that's the way you want it," Sam Schwartz says. He draws a deep audible breath and begins again. "We all know the business of this conference . . ." Stops short. "Mr. Harrison, are you there? Sorry, Mr. Harrison, are you there?"

"Right here. Harrison here." The voice is calmly professional, deep-toned, soothing. "Good to be with you all."

General babble of responses.

Sam Schwartz now. "Mr. Harrison is recording this conversation so that there won't be any question of . . ."

"Is that legal, my dear?" Jenny, of course.

"As long as we know that we're being taped, it's legal," Josh says. "But will it play in Peoria? Will it make the top forty?"

General babble of talk and laughter in which sounds of Lil, choking, are the loudest.

Sam Schwartz loses his temper. "You want to act like a bunch of fools, it's okay with me. Whenever you're ready to attend to business, let me know."

"We're ready," Saul says. Hollow, velvety voice.

"Our purpose is very simple. We're going to stand and be counted. Are you joining in this suit against Baruch Goddard? Yes or no. It's as simple as that. We all know the basic facts, no need to review them again. However Mr. Harrison as our attorney would like to say a few words of clarification. Mr. Harrison."

"Yes," Mr. Harrison says. "Before we begin I think we should have the mutual assurance that all questions have been dealt with adequately. If you have any questions, please don't hesitate to put them to me at this time. In general I should like to make it very clear that the case against Mr. Baruch Goddard is, in our carefully considered opinion, an entirely solid one—a very viable, sound compilation of claims adding up to a strong chance to win substantial sums for the plaintiffs. In the case of Mrs. Guy Rossiter . . . If you will allow me a moment, how are you, Mrs. Rossiter?"

Anne murmurs.

"And Mr. Rossiter? Last time I saw him he had suffered a slight ski accident, but that was a while ago."

"He's in excellent health," Anne assures him. "Won't you continue?"

"Yes," Mr. Harrison continues. "In the case of Mrs. Guy Rossiter there is the existence of a letter addressed to her and signed by the elder Mr. Goddard, your deceased father, in which a binding promise of a portion of the estate, his estate . . ."

"Mr. Harrison," Anne interrupts. "There's no point pursuing that angle because I have no intention of filing any claim . . ."

Shana says, "Why don't we start the voting? We don't need a lawyer's peptalk."

"Who was that?" Sam Schwartz says.

"That was me, Shana," Shana says. "That's who that was."

"No need to be rude to Mr. Harrison, everybody," Jenny says. "One can be absolutely sure of one's own mind and still act graciously to those holding different points of view."

"We're wasting time," Josh says. "Call the question. Call the question."

There is a pause. Then Harrison again. "If you are all in agreement that there should be no further discussion, and if there are no further questions, we can consider the discussion terminated and move to record your wishes on the matter of the litigation."

He pauses again. Sounds of fused breathing.

"Are there indeed no further questions?" Mr. Harrison asks.

Babble of response. Lil chokes on a giggle. Saul reprimands her, in a whisper. Jenny too speaks in a whisper, but it's to her husband. "Are you on the extension, dear? This is so fascinating, I want you to hear it." He replies, in a hoarse, startlingly loud voice. "I'm here, I'm here, Jenny. I'm listening."

Babble of greetings to Maxie Levine, Jenny's husband.

"Shall we begin, then?" Mr. Harrison says.

"Shoot," Josh says.

"I will call your names in order of birth," Mr. Harrison says. "Please confine your response to yes or no."

Babble of objection. "What is this, what is this, the third degree?" Josh says.

"Mr. Saul Goddard." Harrison raises his voice firmly above the others. "Mr. Saul Goddard. May I have your response?"

"No," Saul says. "My answer is no."

"Mr. Joshua Goddard." Harrison moves ahead, quickly.

"Undecided," Josh says.

Babble of comment. "Can he do that?" Sam Schwartz is asking in a loud, harassed voice.

"Yes," Harrison says. "Let's push on," he says. "Mr. Sam Schwartz and Connie Goddard Schwartz."

"Yes," Sam Schwartz says, strangely hesitant-sounding.

"Where's Connie?" Shana demands. "Shouldn't Connie vote for herself?"

"I'm speaking for me and for Connie," Sam Schwartz says. "Two can play at that game," he adds.

"Jenny Goddard Levine?" Harrison resumes.

"Undecided," Jenny says in her high-tone falsetto and clears her throat, "ahem, ahem," like an actress on stage.

Silence greets her vote. Harrison moves on. Shana says no in a clear, strong voice. Anne says no.

General babble. Sam Schwartz clearly above the others then, "Would any no votes care to reconsider?"

"No!" Saul, almost roughly for him.

"Disgraceful," Shana says. "Absolutely not."

"No, no possibility," Anne says.

Josh yells. "What did you do to me, Sam? You told me everybody was in agreement. I thought all I would hear was yes, yes, yes. Except for Saul. Instead what happens? Three outright noes. No, no, no, and here I am with egg all over my face with my dumb undecided. What is this, Sam?"

Jenny is shouting too. ". . . misuse of confidence" or "abuse of confidence" and her husband is muttering and threatening, vaguely.

Sam Schwartz says, "We have the signal that the conference must be terminated now, folks. Mr. Harrison, would you like to sign off first?"

"Good-bye," Mr. Harrison says, but there is no click.

"Listen," Josh says, "before you all hang up, as long as I have you all together, how about everybody coming out here for my show next month? I'm having a one-man show at the Community Center. We'll have a ball. Come on, how about it? Brenda would love it, I know she would. We can't put you up at the house, but there's a very comfortable motel nearby. After all, folks, this is one of the most beautiful spots on the West Coast. You can't go wrong. How about it? We'll have the time of our lives, a real family reunion."

"I'm sorry, Josh." Anne rushes in first with her regrets. "We just can't make it out to the Coast this year. Maybe next year."

"Think about it," Josh says. "Don't answer yet."

Shana says, "I'll be calling you, Josh. I want to speak to you anyway."

Jenny says, "Anna, darling, why don't you write? Why don't you ever pick up the phone? I don't hear from you for months on end. How are your wonderful children?"

"I will, I will," Anne says. "They're fine. Everybody's fine. Stay well, everybody. Do I hang up now?"

"Yes," Sam Schwartz says. "Hang up, everybody. Good-bye. Good-bye."

Shana says, "I'll call you tomorrow night, Jenny. I want to speak to you."

"Do that, darling," Jenny says. "We'll have a nice long chat. I'd call you, dear, but my phone bill last month was killing."

"Good-bye," Josh says. "Think it over, all of you. We'll have a ball."

"Good-bye," Mr. Harrison says, again, and clicks off this time.

"Good-bye, everybody," Sam Schwartz says. "No hard feelings and thanks for your cooperation."

"Good-bye, good luck, and God bless you, as Mama always said," Josh says.

"She wouldn't say it if she heard your vote," Shana says.

"None of that," Sam Schwartz says. "No undue pressure."

"You're someone to talk," Saul says.

"Who was that?" Sam Schwartz asks.

"That was me, Saul."

"Another county heard from," Sam Schwartz says.

"What's that supposed to mean?" Saul's wife, Lil, shouting from her extension.

"The conference is over," Sam Schwartz says. "Everybody say good-bye and hang up."

"Good-bye, good-bye, take care," Jenny says.

"Good-bye, good-bye, take ca . . ." Lil repeats on her extension, but before she finishes all the connections are broken.

XX

On a rare, clear, soft spring evening in New York City, Guy Rossiter, out for a trial run on a new bike he had bought for Anne's birthday, was killed on a path in Central Park. He was seventy-one years old, but so trim-bodied that until his identity was established his age was incorrectly estimated as middle fifties. He had left the apartment with nothing in the pockets of his Brooks Brothers chinos but a handkerchief and an opened package of Life Savers mints. He was wearing glasses and a wristwatch, but neither were touched. He had been hit on the head with a heavy object and was dead on arrival at the hospital. Nobody had seen the attack or the theft of the bicycle. A young couple, with a child who liked to dart underneath the bushes, had come upon his partially concealed body, perhaps an hour after he had been struck.

Guy and Anne had eaten dinner at home, shrimp in green sauce, white rice, a salad of bibb, rugola, and watercress, fresh strawberries and black coffee (they were watching their weight). They had had a dumb discussion:

"I'd like you to try that new bike while it's light. I want to try it myself first, to make sure everything's in order."

"I hate to leave things in a mess," Anne said.

"Amelia will do it in the morning," Guy said.

"You go ahead," she said. "I'll be through in fifteen minutes."

Guy was already on the move. "I'll run it up and down a path and meet you back in front of the house at"—he checked his watch—"ten to eight."

274

His impatience annoyed her and she turned away from him to begin the tidying. (She will obsessively relive this moment of turning her back on him.) She didn't see him leave the apartment with the bike. She heard him leave, but she didn't look. She has missed her last sight of him whole and alive, walking the bike out the door with his straight-backed, vigorous stride, his long arms stretched to steady it at either end. She has missed a chance to have been with him.

("You musn't think that," her daughter Katie says. "That if you had been with him you would have saved his life. That's sloppy." Katie and Danny have come to be with her, to stay with her in her apartment for a few days. Katie doesn't speak harshly. She means to console, to fortify. Anne sips at Katie's good intention, but the original thought persists.)

At ten to eight, finished tidying, she goes downstairs to meet Guy on the street. She and Guy are prompt. They never keep one another waiting. She comes through to the street; the heavy door is held open for her by Al, the uniformed doorman. Anne is dressed in a soft, expensive French work shirt and dungarees; her step is light on her cork-soled, Swiss-made canvas shoes; her casual hairdo is blown about by the warm, caressing breeze. She is one of the blessed of the earth, enjoying the sight of the streetlights of Fifth Avenue melting and blending in the early twilight in the wash of the moving traffic lights, backlighting a sidewalk dance of humanity and its pets—a performance, a complex work produced by a magic social process she finds endlessly pleasing to watch. She has no premonitions. She isn't uneasy, at least no more so than she ever is in New York. She stays on the house side of the street to wait, that is, instead of the park side. Better to be nearer the doorman keeping an eye on her from inside the lobby. She is happy and secure, passively watching the scene, waiting. When Guy is a half hour late, she begins to become uneasy. She goes back up to the apartment, leaving word with Al, the doorman, to tell Guy that she's waiting upstairs. Perhaps Guy may telephone. She checks with the desk a number of times. She waits. She paces. She thinks of Papa pulling on his knuckles. She sits on the velvet-cushioned window seat of an open window and listens to the city sounds. Across the lighted activity of Fifth Avenue, Central Park is becoming too dense with darkness to penetrate. Guy is forty-five minutes late. She calls her son, Danny, but there is no answer from the apartment he shares with other students. Katie lives too far

away. It would take Katie hours to get into the city. Time to call
Katie later. She leans her head against the window frame. The
unthinkable is assuming amorphous shape.

She calls her friend Edith and then Ed Hurley, working late at
the magazine. Edith is with her in ten minutes, but Ed Hurley
takes longer to arrive from the Village. It is Edith who calls the
police. The unthinkable is in the process of becoming a fact. Ed
Hurley brings along a bottle of Scotch. He pours a drink for her,
and for Edith and himself. Anne doesn't say, "Thank you, we don't
drink." She admits the unthinkable to the whole territory.

The death of Guy Rossiter becomes a public occasion. The obvious ironies excite newspaper columnists and call out editorials,
statements, TV panel discussions, meetings, general outrage at the
"perpetrators of a senseless crime."

The morning paper:

> Out of the labyrinth of social nightmare that Guy Rossiter devoted
> himself to healing, out of the victimized population that he cham-
> pioned with his exceptional writing and editing gifts and a rare
> social awareness, came the instrument of his death by violence, a
> senseless act for which an entire city must consider itself responsi-
> ble.

"Et cetera, et cetera, blah blah blah, blah blah," Danny ends his
reading aloud.

Danny and Katie are the only people whose presence is not
intolerably abrasive.

Edith consoles: "Anne, be thankful that Guy lived a full life, a
full, gratifying life. Think if it had happened to a young man."

Katie responds for her. "Edith, how would you like a punch in
the mouth?" she says, pleasantly.

Danny attends to Edith's suggestion that it might be helpful to
Anne to visit Edith's women's CR group.

"I've been toying around with an idea for a consciousness-lower-
ing service. Tell me what you think. Like, an advertisement in the
Village Voice. 'Is your consciousness uncomfortably high? Guaranteed instant amelioration through our unique method of lowering
levels of consciousness to your individually adjusted comfort zone.
Treatment absolutely painless.' "

There is no adequate form in which to pour grief. With her two children, she invents a substitute in which laughter is medicinal. And games. They play three-handed bridge. It's difficult to keep others away from the apartment, but Katie manages. Katie can appear forbidding, now that she has gained twelve pounds and no longer looks fifteen years old.

"I did it," she says, having successfully put off Jamie for another day, and offers her open palm to Danny to slap in congratulation.

Danny holds off the TV, newspaper, and radio reporters, a skill he learned in the days of the student actions. But they swarm at the funeral services. Anne leaves all the talking to the press in the hands of Ed Hurley and Thomas Jamieson.

It doesn't feel like a proper funeral without her family present. Illogically, Anne wants to bury Guy next to Mama and Papa. "Let me love entire and whole." Guy's will calls for cremation anyway. She refuses to accompany the body from the services to the crematorium. No thanks.

She wants her brother Barry. She wants him to come and beat up every kid on the block.

Barry is on a world cruise. Shall his secretary get in touch with him? No, don't bother. Shana and Merv are in Puerto Rico. Who's tending the crops? Calls come in from Jenny, Josh, Saul; and flowers and baskets of fruit and delicacies from the West Coast and from Oregon and from Balducci's.

Anne is locked into pain as in a traction device. It binds, but also holds her in suspension, keeps her from crashing apart.

She must rouse herself, she knows, to think about keeping the magazine going—talk to Ed Hurley—talk to the lawyer about the estate—let her daughter go home to her husband and children and let Danny go back to his friends and his complicated life.

"Will you be all right, Mom?" Katie, at the doorway, at the last moment, before leaving. Her eyes have turned navy-blue with concern, and a certain wariness. What, after all, could Katie do if Anne were to say, "Don't go. Stay with me. Don't leave me alone."

When she is left alone, it is in a space filled with black holes of anguish into which she is sucked as into dangerous downdrafts. Guy's papers exert a diseased pull. Why diseased? She feels that her longing to have him totally explained is a diseased need. The explanations are all to hand, written out by him in diaries and journals in the locked cases of his study. She has only to open the cases and read the journals, if she likes. A revolting act. He kept them locked from her. Let a stranger unlock him. She will make a bargain—the revelations of his mysteries for the return of his body, his self. The loss she cannot sustain is solid.

He would have died naturally, sooner or later. What does she want—immortality, bodily immortality for him and for her?

Danny remains attentive. He's with her at the apartment the day after the case has been broken and the announcement is made that five teen-aged Spanish Harlem youngsters have been arrested. The youngest isn't quite teen-aged—only twelve. Ed Hurley and Jamie are at the apartment also.

Jamie is very excited. "That's what pressure can accomplish. This quick action is definitely the result of having gotten on top of the situation and having stayed on top of it. That's the only way to accomplish anything these days. Just keep driving at it."

"You're glad?" Danny says. "You're pleased by these results?"

Jamie's prim little mouth opens into an astounded O. For a second, he seems unable to work his voice. His vapid eyes fill with tears and bug out, the little they can. "Danny," he says, "I don't want to hear a mitigating word out of your mouth. I promise you, Danny, I will not tolerate your defending any aspect of that vicious attack. I will not stand here and listen to it in the presence of your mother. I don't want to hear it, young man, I don't want to hear it."

Ed Hurley makes a grimace of pleading and a gesture toward Anne. *Spare her*, his look says, but all he says is, "Come, now. You two. Come now," and gets himself and Jamie out the door as soon as he can.

"Nobody gives a shit," Danny says. "If it was an important crime done by important people there would be investigations going on for weeks, months, years—and then everybody would be cleared because of insufficient evidence. They wound up this case in two days. Sure, all they had to do was find the fence. But will he be arrested? No. Stealing bikes is work for these kids. There's money in it. Even the cops are in on it. They're all over East Harlem, collecting a piece of whatever's going on. You can't tell me the cops aren't in on the bike-stealing racket. They're into junk, so what's a little theft? Instead of blowing the whole thing sky-high they'll arrest five kids."

"Lately," Anne says, "everybody seems to be talking to me as if I were a newborn, ignorant babe."

"Okay, okay," he says and becomes silent.

Is he remembering what it was like to be in a jail? The noise. Unbelievable noise. Instant, violent, sick headache guaranteed even for visitors. Communication shattered to smithereens by the shouting presences of a dozen other visitors and prisoners in the same space, herself shouting and trying to hear above the accumulated noise and to see through a separation, between Danny's body and hers, of a double-meshed steel screen, through which Danny's face is crisscrossed as on a bad television set. Easier to go to jail oneself than to visit? Stupid thought. But she had enjoyed her one day in a huge pen in the Centre Street jail, singing and jabbering with her fellow convicts arrested for a nonviolent antidraft demonstration. What was no fun at all was the lockup. She had been formally processed: fingerprinted, photographed with a pleasant arresting officer, then stripped and searched and locked up, alone, in a narrow, tall cell like an upright coffin. The incredible clang of the door closing on her, and then on the others down the line of six or eight cells, the hard, ringing voice and smashing steps of the matron, and the final brutal clang of the steel door closing down on the cell block. They were kept there only for fifteen minutes, but it was a true taste of the real thing.

Guy had been one of the leaders of that demonstration. They had both been released in time to catch close-up views of Guy sitting on the sidewalk surrounded by cops, in a fleeting report on the evening TV news, and she and Guy watched, side by side on their oversized bed, resting on pillows bought in Madeira, propped up against the carved headboard they had had shipped back from Spain.

She smiles at Danny. He looks back gravely. He is a powerful young man, built like his father, Bill Morris, though Danny plays basketball instead of handball, and swims and sails and skis, and hikes up and down mountains, like Guy.

"The Lawyers' Collective is going to defend them," Danny says.

His quick, darting, apprehensive look alerts her, but she doesn't know what the Lawyers' Collective is.

"Is that your friend Steve's group?"

"No," he says. "It's Bill's group."

"Your father?"

Danny nods. His eyes redden as if brushed by hot liquid. "You know I loved Guy. I don't mean to . . ."

She gestures that aside. "I know you did. But do you mean that

the lawyers think these aren't the kids? That they just picked up
some kids and are going to frame them?"

"No, they're the ones.

"They didn't mean to kill," he says.

"I don't know why not," Anne says.

He seems relieved. "The defense will be, you know, Barrio kids,
fucked over, exploited. Try to ease the sentence so that they're not
put away for good."

She nods. "Could we not talk about it, Danny? Not yet."

"Sure," he says. "I'm sorry." And after a while, into the silence
between them, he says "Mom?"

She looks at him, waiting.

"I'd like to take the name Rossiter. Add it to mine. Be Daniel
Morris Rossiter." He is speaking with difficulty, holding back tears.
"I mean Guy never had a son of his own. Just me."

She can't hold back her tears. "That's beautiful, Danny," she
says.

But he looks as if he is in misery.

"I'm afraid, though. I'm afraid it would hurt my father's feelings.
I mean I am *his* son. You know? I don't want him to think I
. . . because, you know, I'm not . . ." He pauses, breathes deeply,
subdues his shaking voice. "What do you think, Mom?"

She too breathes deeply, to control her voice. "I don't know
what to tell you, Danny. I really don't. Except—don't hurt yourself
with it. Don't torment yourself."

"There's no way without torment," he says. "Unless you forget
the whole thing. Throw it all away."

"What?" she says. "I don't understand."

"Fatherhood. Sons. Fathers and sons. Family."

She dreams about Mama that night, and waking, fights to re-
tain the happiness of the dream against reality. What had been
happy about it? The comfort of a presence—a loving, mischie-
vous, wise presence. She remembers nothing of the dream but
a few details. Mama was making fresh coffee, and she was
wearing the dusty pink dress in which she was buried. There
was a clump of damp, dark earth on the silky sleeve of the
dress. She irritated Mama by calling her attention to it. Mama
brushed the dirt away with a show of annoyance. "It's nothing," she said in the dream, but Anne felt badly because Mama

had put herself to great trouble, in making this visit.

Without planning it, the next afternoon Anne mounts a Fifth Avenue bus and rides to Washington Heights, looking for a small synagogue Mama and Papa attended the year after she and Bill were married. Anne had visited her parents then during services, paying her respects in the customary fashion. The synagogue is still here, she sees, locating the narrow door and the two steps down into the dreary little place. A very young rabbi greets her with greedy curiosity and expectation. A Jewish newcomer in the neighborhood, substantial and respectable-looking, in these days when the whole area is going to the dogs? He half accompanies her down the aisle to a seat among the men gathering for evening prayer. She has told the rabbi she's here for the prayers for the dead. He swallows his disappointment that she may be a transient, and rises to his compassionate duty.

"I am grieved for your suffering," in the voice he summons for consolation, "and I hope that God's peace will come into your heart."

She murmurs and nods.

"The dear departed is not a member of the congregation . . . ?"

Now another man is consoling her. She has become "the bereaved." And the rabbi would consider it "a privilege to include the name of the beloved departed in the services . . ."

"Guy Rossiter," she says.

He doesn't blink at that. But neither is he satisfied. "Guy Rossiter," he lends the name a strange, thick pronunciation, "is your dear, departed . . .?"

"Husband," she supplies, and realizes what is expected of her. "May I make a small contribution?"

He grimaces and nods in deep gratification.

"Husband of Hannah," she says.

Though the night is cool, the synagogue is very hot. The door is left open throughout the services, and in counterpoint to the intoning of the chants, she hears the grinding movements of traffic toward the bridge and the wailing cries of city disasters—ambulances, police sirens, fire trucks—and the screaming joy of kids in a wild street game. After a while the rabbi signals her to stand. Guy Rossiter, beloved husband of Hannah, mourned in a jumble of Hebrew.

What else is there to do?

She leaves for the cottage the next day and takes with her her accumulation of notes on Frederick Law Olmsted. Work. Work will save her.

She doesn't dare the big house alone. Now everything is hers. Tessa Rossiter is dead. Guy Rossiter is dead. It all belongs to Anne Goddard. She has had the little guest house on the waterfront prepared for her coming, to sleep in and work in, but she doesn't sleep except for snatches, and can't work at all. Uncontrollable, obsessive images sink their teeth and shake her awake, night and day, which merge indistinguishably, except for light and dark. In the night she is afraid of noises, in the light of silences. Sun, wind, leaves, and water play on her fears in a design to undermine and madden—on the side of the bathtub in which she soaks and stares at dancing messages, on the ceilings, reflected in a glass. On the refrigerator door opposite the pantry window seen obliquely from her seat at the kitchen table where she drinks coffee, a slender horse is hung on a noose, jerked to an agonizing death, in a continuous repetitive shadow play she cannot tear away from observing. When she closes her eyes and tries to sleep she sees Isadora Duncan, choked to death by her frivolous scarf. The long, diaphanous, coquettish prop winds around the heavy car wheel, pulls the beautiful face into hideous distortion, cracks the neck, bulges the eyes and swells the tongue.

"It's not even Isadora," she argues with herself reasonably. "It's Vanessa Redgrave, and it's a film trick." She puts on all the lights, walks about, talks aloud. "It's called going mad," she says conversationally to her quite-normal-looking self in the mirror.

When she tries to read, day or night, another image intrudes, created by the kindness of a neighbor. A wild, black duck, shot by the neighbor and cooked by his wife, is being carved for Anne's benefit. The smell of the bird is odious, as of a rotten thing, oily, spoiling, thrown up from a stale, polluted sea. Blood runs from the breast, rounded as an infant's, and under the knife, the meat slices surprisingly dark, red-black, and in the cavity from which its guts were torn, a quartered onion sits, lapped by blood. There are dark spots on the innocent breast—the marks of shot? Between herself and the page she tries to read, the image cannot be dispelled. The overpowering smell persists. The corpse must be lying on her kitchen table right now while she pretends it was never there, and concentrates on reading.

Why these insistent images? What do they mean?

There is one more, out of her travels with Guy, but she knows what that one means.

She and Guy are on a third-class train in the Middle East. They like to take buses and trains when they are traveling, for the interest of it. In the passageway of the overloaded train, a family group crouches, a woman in traditional black draperies and veil, holding a nursing infant, the father hunkering next to his wife. In the corner of the infant's eye, a green-black fly feeds as steadily as the infant does at the mother's breast. The infant's eye is wide open, untroubled and unblinking under the lazy, antenna-waving ministrations of the fly. The baby's eye is wonderfully black, liquid black. The mother's eyes are half closed; one is liquid black, like the infant's, the other is pale blue, unfocused and diseased. The father stares fixedly at nothing. His black, black pupils sit in the center of his eye, showing white below. He is filthy, smelly, barefoot but otherwise dressed in cast-off Western clothing. Anne is intensely agitated. She moves forward to wave the fly from the baby's tender eye. The baby looks at Anne trustingly. The father turns, not to look at Anne directly but at a point somewhere off to the side of her head. He shouts in Arabic to the woman, and in a sleepy, automatic response the woman encloses the child and the fly totally under her draperies. In her agitation, Anne calls out to a student sitting in the carriage who had earlier said "Pardon me" in English as he climbed across them. "Please tell them that they mustn't let the fly feed from the baby's eye," she says. "The child can be blinded." She has read that somewhere—and look at the mother. The student adjusts his surprise to polite assent. Guy looks up from his guide book. "What is she getting into now?" is his look. Before the student speaks, the father of the child turns his head (he has understood her?) and spits words in a fierce spill. The student lowers his head to his book without comment. Guy shakes his head, no, no.

Surely there was a way to keep one fly out of one infant's eye?

A crew of carpenters arrives early Monday morning. Guy had ordered the barn roof shingled and the beams repaired months ago, but the work has been waiting on dry, warm weather. She knows that if the men pass by the cottage, she will be seen through the kitchen window, dressed in a robe in the disarray of her sleepless nights, eating peanuts at seven forty-five, playing four-handed bridge by herself. She forces herself to wash and dress and to sit at her typewriter and at her desk, pretending to work. She is in a small, book-lined study from which she may step out onto an open deck that levels with the upper leaves of the pines and aspens which descend a steep slope to the beach of a protected cove. She walks out into the fragrant air of the spring morning. Its touch is vivid, restorative. Tide is out. Down on the beach, she steps between tidal pools and the handsome, forbidding boulders of this coast. Fat, golden seaweed lies about, exhausted. Sandpipers skim the wet, gleaming edges of the calm waters and at her approach rise to the clear, clear sky. Two stiff-necked cormorants share seating on a mooring log, as haughty and silent with one another as a quarreling old married couple. First one, then the other takes off in a black, laborious struggle to get off the ground and into the air. It's comical. She laughs, stops herself. The men will spread it all over town that she's gone queer. In this uncluttered air, sounds carry distinctly. The charming music of the men's Down East speech reaches her with perfect clarity.

"Hit it right there, dear," she hears. Tough-looking, hardened men addressing one another as tenderly as sweethearts.

Guy would laugh at her. "Don't romanticize our locals into your noble poor. Watch out. They bite."

She needed no prompting from Guy to fear Anglo-Saxons. A description of her as "a full-blooded Jew" had preceded her arrival when she first came as Guy Rossiter's bride. Tessa filled her in on what was being said. "A full-blooded Jewish woman with two full-blooded Jew children, as far as I've been told. But it's his life, now, isn't it? No point carrying on about what's said and done," was what was being said by the locals.

In the center of the silken bay, there is a round island of pines so green it appears black. On the near shore, gray boulders dominate the coast; on the shore beyond, the sharply defined blue hills of Acadia. In this light, assign Cézanne to paint the hard, solid forms of the landscape and Velázquez the luminous, silver surfaces. Okay.

"He's raising his prices every day," she hears the men talking. "He's just altogether given up thinking about the other fellow. He's turned into a regular Jew."

Anger and despair hit her violently. She'll confront them, that's what she'll do. *I come from poor people. I was poor. I still never*

*take hot water for granted. I grew up with a single cold-water
faucet in a flat under an elevated train. I can draw the pattern the
kerosene stove made on the ceiling.* Pulling at flowers roughly, she
gathers a handful of day lilies and daisies, holding them before her,
a protective banner of golden love between her and their ignorant
hatred. She mounts the sloping field to the barn.

The workmen respond to her presence with what she thinks of
as sly respect. A put-on? Wayne Forrest lowers his eyes to the
ground when he greets her. He's the foreman on this job and the
caretaker of the Rossiter estate. He calls her "Anne" at her insistence, but her name has a different sound in his Down East accent,
with the meandering, pleasant ramble he lends the vowels. Curiously, there is nothing servile in Wayne's lowering of his head. It
is a gesture of conserving himself, pulling himself back and into
himself, without offense to anyone else. She understands that reaction and responds to it. She feels at sea, hears soft applause and
giggling, feels dizzy. The silence hangs between her and the men.

Wayne Forrest is the only one she knows anything about. She
knows that he's thirty-five, father of four children, married to a
local woman who is housekeeper for another large estate on the
same cove; that he is one of eight brothers and sisters who are
notorious in the area for continuous trouble with one another and
with their cars and their shacks and their muddy roads and with
the army and the state police and the welfare and the town general store and the banks, but that Wayne himself is known to be
decent, hard-working and honest. He has the scrubbed look and
open beauty of his Swedish ancestors and the body of a dancer,
though it's hard physical labor that has shaped his grace and
planted his head on his columnar neck and settled his torso in
perfect balance on his strong, light legs. He looks like Pat, Miss
Patricia of her Miss Alma days, whom she had totally forgotten.
Nothing is lost then? She believes it was he who made the comment she heard.

The silence spreads. It occurs to her that she must be ludicrous
to them even apart from her Jewishness—a woman in her fifties,
dressed in slim dungarees and a body shirt, a long, red, knitted
coat hung like a cape over her shoulders, and her hair flying about
in a young girl's loose sloppiness. She slips sunglasses out of her
pocket and covers her naked, pleading eyes.

Two men sit astride the peak of the barn roof. Though she thinks

of them as shapelessly old, they may in fact be younger than she.
They age early. Their teeth are gone, the skin of their faces is
blotched and broken by too much beer, one body is bloated, the
other is worn thin as a string through similar misuse—the bad food
and hard work that began in childhood. She's ashamed before
them.

A faint flush rises on Wayne's fair skin. Is he reading her mind?
No, his blush is for Clifford Robbins, staggering into view from
around the corner of the barn. Can Cliff be drunk this early in the
morning? Taking a leak perhaps. Cliff halts at Wayne's side. Cliff
lists, like a comic playing drunk. His pale, rounded face is slack and
empty, and he smiles and nods in her direction with idiotic plea-
santry. Everybody knows he's an alcoholic, but he's the contrac-
tor's brother, and if Guy contracted Brig Robbins to mend the
barn, she must put up with Brig's brother Cliff, leaning on the
wind and doing nothing at forty dollars a day. The sharpness of her
annoyance surprises her. Well, why pay him for nothing? A day's
work for a day's pay. She knows she's right. Of course she's right.
Regular Jew.

Well, what now? Only silence and discomfort. She feels herself
frowning, notes that Wayne has glanced at her with concern, she
thinks, before he quickly casts down his eyes. She's keeping the
men from working. And paying them. *Regular Jew.*

She sees that they have partially moved a granite slab to a side
door of the barn, where she had told Guy she wanted it for a step.
She gestures with the flowers at the slab. "That's terrific," she says.
"That's exactly what I wanted. How did you know? And how in the
world did you ever move that heavy thing?" Her admiration and
pleasure are genuine. It makes her feel better and seems to clear
her head.

"It wasn't easy," Wayne says. Another quick, darting look before
he pulls back into himself. Is she mistaken? His expression seems
one of feeling for her. "We knew you wanted it that way, Anne.
That's what *he* told us." He has ringed the word "he" with special
meaning. "We were glad to do it for you."

"Where there's a will there's a way," one of the old men on the
barn roof says. The slim one. He smiles, and shows a shocking
absence of teeth. The effect is startling, because when he is grave
his long aristocratic, ascetic face in steel-rimmed spectacles is the
face of a professor, ready for retirement and honorary dawdlings,

until the toothless smile turns it into the face of a derelict. He singsongs the old saying and it emerges as fresh as if he had thought it up new that instant. "Where there's a will there's a way."

"Glad to do it, glad to do it the way you like it," Beefy calls out now from the barn roof. He too has a single tooth left in his mouth, but the sight is less unexpected on his face.

She takes off her sunglasses. Shakes out the flowers toward the men. "Aren't they pretty this year?"

"They really are pretty this June," Wayne says. He keeps his head lowered.

When she turns away, he follows her for a few steps. "You call us any time of day or night if you need us, me and my wife want you to know that. Don't be suffering here all by yourself now."

She tries to look into his face, but he keeps it down. "That's kind of you, Wayne. Thank you and thank Millie for me."

"We'd say that to any neighbor. And we say it to you. So don't forget now. You call out if you need to."

XXI

S he booked a flight out of Maine to New York with a change at Logan Airport, but during the first leg of the flight, terror—worse than terror—nothingness took over—nothing under the plane and nothing above—endless layers of nothingness. She abandoned flight and went into the heart of Boston. Downtown she gravitated to the stores Guy had preferred—through Bonwit's elegant entrance to join a parade of smart, middle-aged women, mirrors of herself, in a glut of expensive objects and the hushed commotion of luxury spending, an activity as intense as if it were necessary work. She left and automatically crossed the avenue to Brooks Brothers, as Guy would have. At the men's shirt counter, she found herself discussing the procedure for returning seven shirts Guy had bought a few days before he was killed. At eighteen dollars a shirt, it was no joke, though the nervous young clerk wasn't sure. He listened with round, frightened eyes, then slipped away to fetch the manager. She herself slid past a high counter of men's cashmere sweaters (how soft the colors were), ducking so as not to be seen, and sneaked out the front entrance. There might be penalties for being disconnected by grief.

She walked into the public gardens, wandering down a path aimlessly, but that wasn't a good move; walking through a park, expecting to meet Guy at the other end of the Common was bad, it was too bad to be bearable, and she turned to the bus station. She felt better there. The steamy, mean, smelly place, all noise and movement and disconnected talk, absorbed her hurt, drew it out of her, sucked it into the mass of surrounding life and healed by the mysterious exertion cities worked. She waited a long time on a long line, eventually bought a ticket, then helped a helpless girl in jeans lift a huge duffel bag and jam it into a too-small locker, gave an old man a dime to make a phone call, told a young couple that she didn't know a thing about the bus to Saratoga Springs, bought a newspaper and a bar of chocolate, and boarded the express bus to New York.

The ugly landscape passed in a dirty haze outside the bus window. She slept a minute, woke to spy on a black mother across the aisle whose proud, contained love for her enchanting little girl seemed an extraordinary event staged solely for Anne, full of meaning that she couldn't quite reach in her dozing state. She slept again and woke, this time alert and levelheaded, full of plans for the magazine. It was hers now. She thought of the old compositor who had fought all her suggestions and called her "Mine Nemesis." "Old compositor." He had probably been in his fifties then. Still alive somewhere, living on, perhaps. To her he's gone, and the whole press room gone with him, noise and flame and the smell of ink and the sense of the substance of a magazine being produced. Now there was a magic science-fiction room to transport copy thousands of miles and make it reappear almost instantly, in proof, by way of electronic machines too smart for her to comprehend. The building was the same. The sweet, small building that encompassed her loves—for work and for Guy. It was a long time, but the years had slipped by as magically and instantly as the machine transformed copy. There were new elevators in the old body, new air conditioners, lots of new gadgets around— soundless ones. No clanging addressograph racketing away in the mail room. A few stylistic changes in the design of *Tribune*, but very little, most of it the same as when she first arrived. The old staff—growing old alongside Ed Hurley and herself. Too much the same, too dull? Maybe Danny would like to come in with them, shake up the old pages? She can do what she likes. It's hers now. Why then does she feel like Papa asking herself, as he had, *Is this all there is to life, to my life?*

She slept again, and woke, slept and woke, slept and woke, waking each time as if from a blow. First a massive truck passed, then a massive structure loomed, its huge stacks billowing bright-orange smoke—a garish stage set for hell under the industrial revolution—and at last the city itself struck, entered by way of a massive walled approach filled with a fierce roaring noise. The bus rode streets she couldn't recognize, the sidewalks spilling with blacks, then Latins, emptied out into the warm air from their blocks of devastated brownstones and ruined apartment buildings. In an empty lot between two buildings, she was astonished by a great mountain of used tires. Wasn't that against the law? She felt like a stranger, or else it was the terrain that was strange and belonged in another country—one of the poverty-stricken places of South America or the Middle East; but in a few minutes the devastation had been left behind and the bus had moved on to the reassuring sights of the back of Lincoln Center and the new buildings of Lincoln Towers.

It would be good to have a sister waiting at home for her. She longed for Jenny or Shana or Connie. To console, to hug her, to laugh with. To drive her crazy. What was their power to console but a power she had herself invented? In their flesh-and-blood lives her sisters were infinitely less—and more—than she imagined them. They belonged to themselves, not to her idea of them.

She wanted to revisit the old places in Brooklyn. She asked Danny to come with her. He came to be good to her, and to make it look good he whipped up some interest in Brooklyn's impressive public buildings and the stunning views of Manhattan from the Esplanade. She dragged him around, checking out her memories. The Flatbush Extension really was the wide, dangerous street of her memories, but with the Myrtle Avenue El down, the dark, dreadful street she remembered was changed into a broad, sunny boulevard. Some of the old structures that had housed Papa's little hole of a store were still standing among a group of empty, destroyed storefronts, marked for demolition. The old tenement was gone. The street itself had been obliterated by a housing development and paved parking lots, the whole not too bad-looking, viewed dispassionately, which she couldn't manage, too disappointed in the loss. She circled, searched, hunted for other landmarks to match against her remembrances (whatever had happened to the Raymond Street Jail and the stone firehouse?), content, at least, to locate the Catholic church and its milky-white statue of the Virgin that had terrified her as a child, a mighty God of the kids who yelled "Christ-Killer!" and made the library across the street dangerous territory.

She led Danny, bored and dutiful son, around the edges of Fort Greene Park, searching among the indistinguishably ruined brownstones for the distinguished townhouse where she had attended her first children's party. The streets were almost empty of people. Now and then a single black man, loitering, and a group on one of the high stoops eyeing them, skeptical of the relationship between this woman and a much younger man walking by, arm in arm—and white. The park, which she remembered as a green country spot of trees and shrubs, rocks and hills, was now a blasted area of deserted fields and small plots enclosed by iron fencing; but open to what use or enclosed against what misuse? Still, the paved paths on which they walked retained some charm in the way that they rode the curves of the land underneath. The whole barren ground, open or enclosed, was covered with a brittle, glistening coat of gritty substance.

"What is this stuff underfoot?" she said.

"Broken glass," Danny said. "Broken bottles. It must be the local rumble area."

From beyond the rise ahead, she heard high-pitched, bantering voices and characteristic mocking laughter of blacks. Could the bright, empty, daylight park be dangerous? At the top she saw the group—a half dozen young men and two young girls, all astonishing in their getups and hairdos, a flock of gorgeous birds, wheeling and screeching, flapping their floating masquerade garments, collapsing into loon laughter and long-limbed slapping of palms and thighs, high-stepping in stilted, graceful, double-jointed movements on their incredibly tall platform shoes.

Anne said, "Let's go this way," and cut across an open, withered lawn.

"One minute," Danny said, and ran into their midst.

The comfort station was under repair and being cleaned of a mass of graffiti on its outer walls. Some white workmen stood around it, drinking out of cans.

"I thought I knew one of those guys," Danny said, caught up with her. "You know what that sign back there said? 'Restoration going on, on the most elegant comfort station in the world.' "

"Really?" she said.

"Did you hear any of that collective bargaining going on back there?" he said.

"No, what?"

"The two chicks. They were holding out for more money. It was heavy. They went right on with it while I was talking to that guy I thought I knew. Carnal acts being described and negotiated at the height of day, how do you like that?"

"See that?" Anne said. "And you expected to be bored."

He skittered ahead of her, leaping into the air, lifting his arm as if he were hooking a ball into a basket. He reached the farthest crest.

"This is great!" he called back. "Dyno. Fabuloso view."

It really was a grand place. Neglect hadn't altogether wiped it out, she saw. Indestructibly grand, as long as it stood at all. It was wonderful to see it again, to see that it really was as she had remembered it and to feel herself restored to one memory that held, even if her memory (because of her size then?) had recorded the view as less and the monument as more. She was unaccountably happy to be here, considering where she was and the impressive places of the world she had been. The view of Manhattan from such a height and distance was marvelous, and it was pure joy to stand on the broad, broken pavement of the plaza below the graffiti-covered monument to American seamen dead in the War of 1812, and look out over the view and down the imposing length of wide, descending stairs. The sensation of standing on a ruin was sharp—hot sun on old stones and the sweet smell of dried, weedy grasses—a feeling of Pompeii in Brooklyn.

"Once upon a time, we were cornered here by a street gang, me and Shana," Anne said. "We took the long way home from Papa's store with butter and bread and a bottle of heavy sweet cream that my mother needed for supper. They threw stones at us and the bottle of cream broke. Shana thought she had been cut. The cream ran down her legs and she began to scream, 'I'm bleeding, I'm bleeding.' "

"Just as I always suspected," Danny said. "If you stab a Jewish aunt, she'll bleed heavy sweet cream."

"Aha!" Anne said. "Anti-Semite."

It had been a terrible experience. Why couldn't she convey to him the tragedy of the spilled cream—the pure, white, heavy, sweet, sweet cream leaking from the bag? The innocent sweet cream.

An odd group appeared from around the monument, loaded with equipment, and took over the plaza. A photographer's crew, setting up for fashion shots of a male black model. Light brown really. The model had the square-faced, Caucasian good looks that would appear strong and virile in a blowup, but he was in fact a slight, pretty boy, sweating in the furred winter coat he was modeling under a June sun. She and Danny watched, sitting on the ledge of the plaza. A woman worked over the model, arranging his hair, renewing makeup, adjusting the coat. Then a director illustrated how to run up the last six stairs of the majestic flight. The model ran, again and again. The photographer shot him, again and again and again, against the splendid spread of the city beyond. Between takes, the woman made adjustments to the model's face and hair and to the coat. Then the model took the steps again, smiling this time.

"You think the photographer's Jewish?" Danny said.

He could have been, or any other non-Anglo-Saxon New Yorker.

"Why did I say that?" Danny said. "All that idiocy is catching, I think."

"What?" Anne said.

Danny looked out over her head, whistling between his teeth.

"I'm here looking for the place where I was born," Anne said.

"That's wrong," he said. He seemed angry. "You know that's not all of it. Otherwise you wouldn't have remembered that particular story. You were feeling sorry for yourself, feeling persecuted. So you and Aunt Shana were chased and a bottle of cream broke. So? That's pretty tame stuff when you think of what's happened in the world and what's happening right now."

She stood up. He did too. She had to tilt her head back to see into her tall son's face. It had tightened and flushed, as if he were fighting back tears.

"Let's go back to Manhattan," she said.

They started down the steps. Weeds and grasses grew between the cracked pavings.

"Olmsted's idea was for a large space to be put aside here for public meetings," she said. He turned to her with real interest. "Did you notice that the name of my childhood library is the Walt Whitman Branch of the Brooklyn Public Library? Walt Whitman didn't mean a thing to me then. I had never heard of him."

"I wonder if this spot was ever used," Danny said. "It would be great for a demo, even a rock concert. If you could get the people to come out here. That would be the problem."

"How about the people who are already here?" Anne said.

He didn't smile. She took his arm, and he hugged her hand to his side.

"Guy left us all a lot of money," she said. "Anyway it's a lot for me. It's mostly in property—real estate and stocks."

"Us?" Danny said.

"You, me, Katie. One half of one half of the estate is yours. I get one half, you and Katie the other. When I die it's all yours and Katie's."

"Come on, Mom," he said. "Don't talk like that. You've got a long . . ."

"You're a real Yankee," she interrupted, "now. You own Yankee property. See that?"

"What stocks?" Danny said. He was having trouble concealing his vivid interest.

"Mostly Anaconda and ITT. Some Long Island Light. Polaroid. Merck."

"Anaconda and ITT! They're the worst. I don't want them," he said. "Can't you sell them?"

"Selling them won't purify the money, Danny," she said, "But do what you like with your share."

"I could give the money away," he said.

"What's happening with the kids—the bicycle thieves?" she said. "Do you know?"

"Plea bargaining, Bill told me. He thinks he can get them off with eighteen-month sentences—something like that."

They had reached the bottom of the stairs, where the encroaching city streets lapped at the grand idea of this spot. She turned for a last look upward, but Danny stepped in the way, blocked her sight.

"Mom?" he asked in a man's voice, but with a child's questioning. "I didn't mean to hurt you by anything I said."

She took his face in her hands and kissed him. "That's okay. I know. I didn't mean to harm you either."

XXII

The city is a great bell. The city swings and rings, shuddering through the innocent air, announcing triumphs, disasters. It is a fact that skyscrapers are constructed so that they will sway with the wind. Look up. The thrusting glass-and-steel tower imperceptibly moves with the wind. See? It is not a trick, no illusion created by moving clouds. The strong, light, gorgeous suspension bridges that link the world to this little island also sway in the wind. It's dizzying, but it's true. The entirely unbelievable city of New York is real. The Goddard Building is real, thrusting steel and glass forty-five stories into endless space. An average skyscraper, nothing special, set back from the street, complete with plaza, decorative trees, and a fountain. My real fake name proclaims itself on this structure—my name rings out, announcing triumphs, and imperceptibly sways in the wind on the façade of the Goddard Building.

The elevator rises through the limbo of territory X. During this long, slow, uncharted journey there is time to think, to wonder, to listen to the outer-space nonmusic of the PA system—time, space, motion, sound, and I hang suspended. Ah, now the indicator panel declares us somewhere—31 lights up, 32, 33, 34, 35, 36 . . . Better. We are anchored.

The top is not the top, after all. On Floor 45, there is still another elevator to be boarded to reach Baruch Goddard. An obsequious receptionist escorts Mrs. Rossiter, Mr. Goddard's sister, to a small private elevator, and retires. In this elevator, there are only three buttons. 45. PH. PHR. I have become an imbecile to whom these symbols are total mysteries. But Baruch Goddard must be at the very top. Push PHR. Silently and smoothly the plush little elevator rises farther into space. It comes to a stop, the door slides open, and I have been delivered to a strange place. What is it? Step out, examine it. PHR is its name. It's the absolute top of the top of the building. It's a roof, that's what it is, a landing leading to a roof— a narrow, hardware level—neat, clean, and workmanlike. Pounding hysterical fear attacks me. I have been delivered to the heart of something awful, beyond even Barry, a place of pure power where curving, massive conduits conceal the mechanisms that run the whole show.

Mysteriously, with a minimum of noise, the elevator shuts its door and leaves me. Am I stranded—shipwrecked on PHR to be discovered months later, a starved and wasted skeleton? Two narrow steps rise to a heavy steel door whose direction can only be out—out where the Goddard Building sails in endless space on top of a world that spins and turns and spins again. I think I must open that door. Clinging to the structure that proclaims my name, I will unwind from my throat the frivolous Isadora Duncan scarf I'm wearing and spin with the world, waving my banner, crying out. Gingerly, one hand safely holding the side of the wall, I mount the steps, I try the knob. What a fabulous beast the wind must be up here.

The door is securely locked.

I hear the heart of the building flushing through its massive conduits, unconcerned with me, ignorant of everything but its own self-sustaining power.

Barry will notice that I have never arrived from the forty-fifth floor and send a rescue party.

The elevator is silent; its indicator remains dark. Come now, don't be an idiot. Go down the steps, press the button. This power works for you too.

Magically the indicator lights up, the elevator rises, opens its door, takes me back where I belong—to PH, to a carpeted reception room of soft lights, dark furniture, book-lined walls and a standing globe of the world. My brother Barry himself waits to greet me. He is more than ever a Persian prince, blacker than I remember, blue-black, with heavier, darker eyebrows and deeper furrows around his mouth, all the lines of his face deepened and blackened, the full smiling mouth and luxuriant black hair exaggerated, as in a charcoal drawing touched with caricature. Age, instead of fading and weakening, has made him more strikingly himself.

We kiss, though with a certain restraint. He escorts me to his handsomely furnished office and, settling me in a big, soft chair, seats himself behind his handsome desk. The late-afternoon sun streams across the golden room from a wall of windows overlooking the river, and illuminates my brother Barry in a wash of perfect light.

He is solicitous, kind. "You look tired," he says. "Are you taking care of yourself? Are you getting enough rest?"

("Terrible thing, terrible terrible thing," he had said on the telephone earlier in the day, offering condolences on Guy's death. "Why don't we get together sometime?" I said on the spur of the warm moment. "I'd like that very much, Anne. Why don't you drop by my office this evening?")

Now we are together. Here we are. What do I expect to gain from this contact?

I explain that today was my first day back at the magazine, and that it had been difficult. He nods, sympathetically, with a rabbi's gravity. I keep to myself my frightening adventure on his roof. "What a view!" I say. "What a setup you have here, all around."

He enjoys topping himself. "We've got a better view from the Board Room, a wonderful view of Central Park that I want to show you . . ." and halts, conscious that he may have rubbed a raw spot. He gets up, pats my shoulder, murmurs, "Terrible thing, terrible terrible thing," again.

"I'd like to see the Board Room and the view," I say.

"We'll do that before we leave here," he says, and then approaches me warily. "That is, if you don't have any dinner plans." He still is sensitive to refusals and rebuffs, I see.

"It would be nice to have dinner together," I say.

Now that he knows we have an unhurried visit before us, he expands. His energy flows in a more leisurely but still charged stream, gathering up ends, organizing me, my time, my visit. There's one more area to be checked out. He composes his face and studies his hands before he puts the crucial question.

"Anything I can do for you, Anne?" Quick, upward glance. "Was there anything special you had in mind to discuss with me?"

"Oh no," I say. Brotherly love was what I had in mind, I think. Really? Given our history, Barry's and mine? Am I serious? Has Guy's death made me softheaded?

"Don't hesitate now. If there's anything I can do for you, I'll be happy to . . ."

"No, no. I just wanted to see you."

"You're sure now? Guy left everything in order? No problems, no financial problems? You're sure?"

"Yes, sure. It's been a long time between visits, that's all."

"Hasn't it?" he says.

"Do you get lots of relatives trailing in here with requests?" I ask, and feel like a fink.

"I could a tale unfold," he says, and smiles his old smile. Not pleasant. "The sad truth is, Anne, that I don't usually get to see members of my family unless there's a problem."

"Well," I say, "we're scattered all over the country."

He blinks. Black lizard eyes.

"I heard about the suit," I say. "What's happening in that department?"

He leans forward. "Anne, I'd be happy to have you explain to me how your sister Connie lived with Sam Schwartz all her life. Can you explain that? Can you understand that?" He shakes his head. "Sam Schwartz. One of God's mysteries, one of God's little jokes, except I don't get it.

"Sam Schwartz," he says. "You know that that damn fool is going through with the suit? He's going to lose it. That's for sure." He laughs. "And if he doesn't lose it, he's going to lose his life. I told my lawyer, 'Martin,' I said, 'you lose this case to Sam Schwartz's team of lawyers' "—he interrupts himself—"incidentally, they happen to be the worst kind of phony liberals, 'you let Sam Schwartz win this case,' I said, 'and I put a bullet right through the middle of Sam Schwartz's forehead.' I really worried him, my lawyer. 'For God's sake, that's no way to talk,' he told me. 'Don't let anybody hear you talking that way.' What the hell do I care? It did me good to say that, and it would do me even more good to shoot him. I almost hope he wins the case so I can do it."

He laughs, openly, heartily.

"There's a biblical phrase I'm very fond of. 'Not one that pisseth against the wall shall be left standing.' When those righteous waves of God-fearing Israelites swept down on their enemies, that was their motto. 'Not one that pisseth against the wall shall be left standing.' That's my motto. If I have enemies, not one will be left standing, whether they're in the family or out of the family. He's going to lose, of course. He can't win.

"Did you know that he's in this so-called family suit all by himself? Nobody went into it with him. I heard some talk that Merv was going in—Merv and Shana. Merv and Shana, after what I did for them, turned those people's lives into a dream, a song. But Merv didn't go with him. He came by here offering to testify for me. It's a joke. The offers keep trailing in—Jenny and her husband, Josh and his wife, Saul and Lil, all ready to testify in my behalf. I just have to say the word. They're going to swear that I've been honest, I've been fair. Honest about what? Fair about what? Did any of them have a dime to their names that I didn't give them? I don't need anybody's testimony. The man doesn't have a case. The poor fool. The only reason that his wife is still behind him is that she doesn't know which end is up. Connie's off her rocker. The woman's nuts, absolutely nuts. Menopause went to her brain and stayed there. You know your sister Connie never leaves her house? They're rich, they've got a million bucks because of me, they ended up with a million apiece, and they talk about honest, fair. Would any of them take care of me if I was lying in a gutter with a broken leg?"

It's hard to get an opening to interrupt him. "That's awful about Connie. Is it getting worse?" Fragrant, comforting Connie. "I have to call her."

"I don't think she even talks on the phone anymore. She's nuts. Wouldn't you be if you were married to Sam Schwartz?

"We've got more than one nut in our family, you know that, don't you? Connie's not the only nut," he says.

"We have not," I say. "Connie's not a nut. She's too loyal, that's her trouble."

"We certainly do. We have one of everything in the family. Now we have an artist. Did you know that Josh is an artist?" He leans back and laughs. "Ah well, I don't have any kick against life. God has been very good to me. Very good to me. How are your children?"

My children are fine. How are his children? Fine, and his grandchildren are fine and my grandchildren are fine. Pauline is fine, away on a trip with some ladies' club.

"Don't ask me which one. She belongs to more clubs than I could ever keep track of. Needs a computer, that problem does." He looks down, closing in his face. "I'll tell you, Anne. We live our own lives—to a certain extent—me and Pauline. We're civilized." Another hearty laugh. "Sure, why not? She gets anything she needs from me. It pays her to be civilized." He closes down on his face again. "No, we really do have a good arrangement, me and Pauline, more or less.

"No objection to French food?" he says, looking up.

"Fine," I say.

A call comes in. He talks buying, selling.

"You think I know what I'm talking about?" he asks me, finished with his broker. "If it works I'm a genius. If it doesn't I blame it on the market, the falling dollar, Washington jitters, the weather, anything I can think of. Would you like a drink? Would you like to drop in at the house and rest before we go out? What do you say? Have you ever been to the townhouse?"

I shake my head. I no longer know what I want. I have forgotten what it's like to be with him—sucked into his circle of energy and whirled about helplessly—fascinated and repelled.

"I have to make a call," he says. "Will you excuse me?"

I excuse myself and wander out into his secretary's office. She smiles, studies me curiously when she thinks I'm not noticing. My brother's voice booms out and can be clearly heard. He's talking to a woman, telling her I have unexpectedly dropped in, that he'll be busy until much later. He'll call her then. He comes out to his secretary, asks her to arrange a morning flight to Montreal.

"Would you believe that one of the most important banks in the world is in Montreal?" he says to me, leading me back to my comfortable chair.

"I love Montreal," I say. "There's a great park in Montreal. If you have a moment, go to Mount Royal Park, if you like parks. It's one of Olmsted's, built on a height . . ."

"Who's Olmsted? Do I know him?"

"He designed Central Park."

He nods.

"And Fort Greene Park. Lots of others. I went back there, a couple of days ago. Have you been back, ever?"

"Not me. I don't have a nostalgic twinge in my body. Progress, that's my motto. Keep moving, that's my slogan. Never look back.

Why would I go back there?" He smiles. "I left my blood on those
streets. It's interesting, I bet, to go back."

"It's very changed. The el's gone."

"Would you like a drink?" he says.

"Sure. Bourbon and a little water."

He tells his secretary he'll have the same.

"What was that funny song Mama used to sing? 'Booze, booze,
booze, the firemen cried, someone set the house on fire.' Something like that."

"Mama probably made that up," I say. "It seems an unlikely
song."

He stretches out his legs and laughs with total enjoyment.

"You know who's ruining progress?" he says without transition.
"Your ecology people, that's who's ruining progress. Stupidest,
most shortsighted point of view. Save the birds and starve the
people. You can't stop progress and stay healthy, that's a basic rule
of growth. Pack of nonsense. Life is change, movement. All this
ignorant talk about using up the earth's resources. Nonsense. You
can't use up the earth's resources, not while the earth exists and
man's mind exists. Man will find new resources, new uses for old
resources. Use up the earth's resources! Nonsense. Life is energy
and energy is life. That's what energy is, the heart and soul of life.
Is life going to come to an end? Maybe in trillions of years.

"I looked old to you when you first saw me, didn't I? It was a
shock seeing me, wasn't it?" he says. "What do I care, I feel great.
You know what the theory is. If you reach sixty-five without con-
tracting heart trouble, cancer, diabetes, or high blood pressure,
then you're in the clear, you live to a ripe old age. So far so good.
I've got less than eight years to go." He laughs. "I have every
intention of living to a ripe old age. I get to feel riper as I get
older."

"It's a funny thing," he says. "Making money doesn't interest me
as much as it used to. What do I care? I could live off the artwork
on these walls if I had to.

"Would you like to look at the paintings?" he says.

"Soon," I say. I feel bewitched with laziness, floating on his
words. Does anything exist beyond this room?

"I'd like to write the story of my life," my brother Barry says,
"but I know I wouldn't tell the truth.

"Nobody tells the truth anymore," he says.

"I've become very interested in politics," he says. "They came to me with this talk about running for Mayor. Me. How would you like to see me Mayor of New York?"

"It's a pretty thankless job," I rouse myself to say.

"You bet," he says. "Nothing but a headache. They came to me with some other propositions too. They want me to back this particular fellow's candidacy. I can't mention his name, you understand. I told him, 'It costs two million dollars to become Mayor of New York. Do you have two million? Can you raise it?' You know that's a fact, Anne, it takes two million dollars to finance a campaign for Mayor. I guess that's why they came to me in the first place with the first proposition. Cut out the middleman." He laughs. "Okay, so here's this good man, best man for the job, liberal democrat but no kook—practical, smart. Only trouble is he doesn't have two million and he can't raise it. That's it. He's out."

Barry's secretary appears with drinks.

"I'm really keeping you here late, Peggy. I'm sorry about that. Did I introduce you to my famous sister, Mrs. Rossiter? I want you to know that my sister is considered one of the country's leading intellectuals, one of the country's fifty leading intellectuals. *Esquire* said so." He is beaming with pride. The secretary studies me curiously.

"That ridiculous article," I say. He has named the wrong publication and he seems to have missed the point of the gossipy piece, but I can't help being pleased that he saw it, and that what he's taken from it is the fact that his sister has importance in the world. *Admit me to equality at long last.* Perhaps he's making the same plea to me with his charm and talkativeness? *Admit I'm as good as you, sister, admit that I do the world some good.*

"The important thing is to get the notice," he says. "Who cares if the article was ridiculous?

"What do you hear from the family?" he says.

"Not much," I say.

"Sure, everybody's fine, that's what you hear," he says. "They sing a different song for me. Heartline, they're under the impression that I'm heartline. The *uhrumas.* Mama's *uhrumas.* I detest that word. The poor. Poor Saul. Poor Josh. Poor Jenny. Poor Connie and so on and so on. Now we've got them by the dozens— nieces, nephews, great-nieces and great-nephews. All I ever hear is everybody's troubles. I never hear about the good times, the good things. Did you know that even your first husband came to me for money?"

"What?" I am hurled out of my dreamy state.

"Forget it, forget I ever mentioned it. It has absolutely no importance, he's one of so many, it doesn't even matter. Who hasn't been to see me for money?"

"Did he pay it back?"

"Forget I said anything about it," he says, without answering the question. Perhaps he never gave Bill any money?

"The unfortunate of the world have to be helped," he says. "I always believed in that and I always will. I couldn't be my mother's son and think differently. You don't let people starve. The old, the infirm, the mentally incompetent, helpless children—they have to be taken care of."

I have lost the thread of his talk, too dismayed to follow, thrown back into the old fake shame by his reference to Bill.

"There's room for everybody in this world." I pick up again on his talk. "Plenty for everybody. Nobody needs to starve."

I make an impatient gesture.

"So how come they do starve, right? That's the question of the day, isn't it? The question of the day. We've got the best system in the world in this country—that's why nobody starves here. Anybody who starves in this country just hasn't availed himself of some very basic information—where to turn. For every hungry man, there are a dozen organizations to take care of him, not to mention his wife, his kids, his rent, and the payments on his television set. What a man wants is what a man needs. Nobody has the right to set any limitations on what a man wants. That's a man's need. His job is to go out and get it. In this country we have the freedom, any man has the freedom to go out and get anything he wants. That's precious. That's unique. Nothing like it exists anyplace else in the world. Where they have the will, they don't have the power, the resources. You have to have both, you understand me?

"Take this fellow Mao," he says. "He's working out an idea that really interests me. He's trying to run a huge country, hundreds of millions of people, like a family. He's got the kind of people and the numbers of people to do it with. Strong family people, the Chinese. Any operation I set up out there in the Far East immediately became a family operation. The way my local Chinese personnel would run those operations was a revelation. I arrive one morning at one of my plants out there, and hanging around inside the entrance are a couple of ancient characters who look as if they're one step out of their graves. 'Who are they?' I ask my manager, Mr. Chen, a Mr. Chen, marvelous man, wonderful worker, good as gold. He introduces me. One is his grandmother, the other's his grandfather. They're watchmen, he tells me. What the hell are they watching? All the workers in the plant are relatives—his father, his mother, aunts, uncles, sisters, brothers, nieces, nephews, sons of nephews, sons of nieces. It's incredible. If he were in charge of one of my operations back here at home, he'd be fired on the spot. Out there, in his terrain among his own people, he'd be a monster if he did any differently. Hard-working, close people, the Chinese, closely knit people. Mao knows his people. That's what he knows, that's what he's got to work with to bring out the untapped resources of that huge country. He's trying to use that feeling. Run the whole country like one big family, share and share alike. It's a beautiful idea, but it can't work. It'll never work. It'll go for a while and then grind to a halt. Has to. Then they'll come around to our way just the way Russia has."

He leans back. "Man wants to fulfill his needs, whatever they may be," he says. "You want to use your brains. I want to . . . who the hell knows what I may want to try next? Let me try, it may even do the country good."

"What about crooks?" I stick in quickly. "What about killers?"

He looks at me, looks away, shakes his head. "Terrible thing, terrible thing . . ."

"Not *them*," I say. "Not the little crooks or the little killers. The big ones, at the top."

"Sure, there are crooks up in the highest places," he says. "Sure, I agree with you. Men with Sam Schwartz minds. No vision. No conception of the public good. But they're brought down, always, always. Men ready to walk over their grandmothers for a buck are always brought down. I don't go for such thinking, I never did and I never will. Give as good as you get. Produce a good product, a superlative product, the best in the world for the price. The workingman is entitled to good wages, good working conditions, good living conditions; and the consumer is entitled to the best product his money can buy. That's the business I'm in whatever business I'm in. Shenanigans don't interest me. If I wanted to go into the rackets I would have gone into the rackets with Murder, Incorporated. But if you want to be in business, be a businessman, give value for value. No cheating. Respect the public."

He breaks up into laughter. "Respect the table!" he shouts, and slaps the desk top with the flat of his hand. I too break into laughter. "I never could figure out where Papa got that expression from. 'Respect the table!' " he repeats, slapping hard, just as Papa used to, and we smile, we smile, thinking of Papa, ruling our giggling and scrapping at holiday meals.

"I don't care what color a man is"—back to his monologue—"I don't care what combination of colors he is. I don't care what religion he practices or doesn't, I don't care how much money he has. When he goes out to buy something with his single dollar, that dollar is as good as mine. He's a man like me, he deserves as good as he can get for himself. When I first moved to the South the local bigwigs were the voices of doom. 'You can't come down here and mix up coloreds and whites'—only they called them niggers. The whites won't work alongside coloreds, Negroes, they said. I needed workers, not colors. I told them so. Anybody who works for me at a machine or anywhere else in my plant is going to work alongside the best man or woman for that job, and I don't care if she's purple and he's green. That's what I told them. I needed workers and I needed team workers. That was my system—a new concept in production, each production unit a team, with rewards for teamwork. The more produced, the more rewards, but only as a unit, a team. I didn't want to hear about colors. I needed to mix them all up. I didn't care about desegregation, I cared about profit, but I desegregated. It was the logic of the situation. I'm logical. I'm rational. That's my gift. To be logical, rational."

Tell the truth, I command him. *Tell the whole truth*, I want to understand you.

"The town I built around my first factory was a wonderful place. You ever visit there? You should have. A workingman had a wonderful life in that town. Good school, good hospital, public swimming pool—and the coloreds had their day, just like the whites, one day a week reserved for the coloreds—that town was a paradise for a workingman. If I called it socialism, you would have been rushing down to praise me. When the union came in, I wasn't upset. I figured it had to be, that's the motion of history. Right away they start in with the leaflets. I'm a bloodsucker squeezing

blood out of the workingman straight into my bank account. Big
drawings of me, depicting me as a fat slob with blood dripping
from my lips and my hands, and a little worker in my fist being
squeezed to death. I brought that town to a halt. I sold out. If the
union had approached me in the right way, there wouldn't have
been one bit of trouble. The damn fools knew as well as I did that
I was paying above union scale for the South.

"I'm talking a lot," he says. "I don't know why. Would you like
to look around, look at some of the paintings? I've got a Léger in
the Board Room that I'm very proud of."

"You're not supposed to like Léger!" I've said it before I can stop
myself.

"What do you mean—not supposed?"

He pauses for me to explain. He looks put out. Was there criticism of him in my exclamation? Am I turning him into a coarse
ignoramus? He feels he's being put down in some way, I can see.
He is, of course. My assumption is that he's bought Léger because
it was a good investment. I take it for granted that he knows
nothing of Léger's radical philosophy, and nothing about Guy's
extensive writings on Léger. Léger is almost a cult with us. Léger,
revolutionary artist. I wouldn't know where to begin to explain.
The primary colors. The happy workers, like children's-book illus-
trations. The liberation of technology. Making it human. But my
brother is impatient with this long pause and he plunges on.

"I love his paintings. There's happiness in his paintings—work,
achievement, machinery—there's peacefulness in his paintings."
He laughs. "I don't mean that I won't sell it at a good profit, if I
need to. I've been offered a lot for it. This thing about no deduc-
tions is going to knock the hell out of the art market, but not for
something like that painting. That's a true work of art.

"I'm talking a lot," he says again. His eyes harden and look
beyond me. "You know that nobody in my family cares for me?
The more I do for them, the less they like me."

He waits, but I say nothing.

"Connie's daughter calls me on the phone from Chicago. Will
I run out to Dallas to see Connie? I'm the only one who can help
Connie—pull her out of her depression. Do you get the picture?
Connie and her husband are suing me and their daughter is calling
me to go help Connie." He shakes his head, laughs. "Next phone
call, Saul's grandson, a pisher straight out of journalism school. Will

I use my influence to get him a job on a newspaper? How in hell can I get him a job on a newspaper? 'You have an aunt who's a journalist and publisher,' I told him. 'Why don't you go see your Aunt Anne?' "

"He did," I say.

"Did you help him?"

"I did what I could. Wrote a couple of letters and made a few phone calls, and he did get something on a small newspaper in Connecticut, but it's not much of a job and I'm sure he could have gotten it for himself."

He looks at me speculatively. "You're too modest," he says in a dry voice.

"You know what I always say," he says. "A hundred years from now none of this will matter to us, will it? Less, a lot less than a hundred years.

"These ecologists trying to turn life back, trying to turn away from the natural movement of history, stop progress—it can't be done. History only moves forward, that's its direction. You don't monkey with the direction of history if you're smart. You go with it, you don't fool around wasting time trying to stop it."

He says, "There's only one thing that scares me, one thing that I really fear. They've never left us Jews alone and they never will. One of these days our history will repeat itself, catch up with us. God has been too good to us. We're doing too well. That's when it hits, always has.

"You know, to them you're a Jew, whoever you married," he says.

"One of Guy's first American ancestors was a Jew," I tell him.

His interest is vivid. "Really? You never told me that. Are you kidding?"

I shake my head, raise my right hand. "God's truth," I say. "Though I don't know what there is to make of it."

"Did you know that more than half of the Goddard kids are marrying non-Jews?" he says.

"Is that good or bad?" I say.

He studies me. Lizard blink.

"Have you visited Jenny and her husband lately?" he says.

"We stopped over one night last year, me and Guy. Nice setup, if you like that kind of living."

"Sarasota's one of our best developments," he says. "My favorite is out on the West Coast. Handsome, handsome design. Brilliant young team of architects and planners. Terrific value. A paradise for people of limited means. Sure, I know what you're getting at. It's not for you and it's not for me. When I leave New York and Westchester for my ranch, I don't want to see anybody, I don't want people around. I want to be alone. I want to see space, sky. That's why I leave. But you have to be able to pay for privacy—not everybody can afford privacy, unless you go off like these kids in the woods with a kerosene stove. . . .

"Man doesn't want his life programmed," he says. "Man is an adventurer. He wants to go where his desires take him. Maybe freedom is doomed, a lot of thinkers say it is, maybe life as we've known it, the life we've lived, can't go on getting better, maybe it has to get worse. Who knows? Cities have toppled, empires have toppled before. Life is change. We could go under in time and the height of civilization move someplace else. That's the history of the world, isn't it? Everybody gets their turn on stage. We can't do anything about it but move along, move along, make room for what's coming and leave them something to work with—our children and our children's children . . ."

"I don't know how much more of this lofty thinking I can take before dinner," I say, smiling to remove the sting.

"Let me tell Peggy to order the car downstairs," he says. "Why don't I have her take you around for a look at the Board Room and the paintings? There are a few nice pieces of sculpture, too. While I make a couple of calls. Would you like to do that? Would you like another drink? I'll just be a few minutes."

I nod. I murmur. I dutifully go off with his secretary.

From the windows of the Board Room, Central Park is so far below that I see it whole, all of a piece, as from an airplane—a jewel in a fantastic setting. I tell the secretary to leave me there—I'll find my way back by myself—that I want to stay. While I stand at the window, darkness turns the air of the city deep, deep blue.

My brother Barry rises from behind his desk and comes toward me when I return to his office. The power of his presence exerts a remarkable pull. Is it a real property, the essence of his animal nature, an unpredictable, unanalyzed force? This is what is meant by magnetism. My brother Barry. Yield. In this hushed, luxurious room at the top, at the very top, what else is there to do? Be swept about in this vortex, and be ready to be flung out at any moment. No. I pull myself back to the positions I've won for myself, and we approach one another, smiling, from our separate corners of the ring that bounds us. There doesn't seem to be any way for us to embrace. And yet I long for it. *Embrace me, brother,* I will him, *in spite of everything.* I begin to laugh. In our way, we are repeating a family ritual. Barry is to play Papa. I play Aunt Sadie Jacoby. The note is one of trust. *Why should I embrace you first?* he will stubbornly insist. *You first, sister, you embrace me first, then I'll embrace you.*

He responds to my laugh. He thinks my delight is for the Arabian-Nights glitter of the lighted city below the wall of his windows.

"Isn't that a be-yu-tee-ful sight?" he says.

He has pronounced the word as he did when he was a boy. It touches me, it pierces me that he retains the childish pronunciation that links us to our beginnings. He waves his arm to encircle the scene.

"I call those lights my necklaces," he says.